FOUND

A HOUSE OF NIGHT
OTHER WORLD
NOVEL

FOUND

P. C. CAST + KRISTIN CAST

Printed in the United States of America

First edition: 2020
ISBN 978-1-982548-10-0
Young Adult Fiction / Romance / General

1 3 5 7 9 10 8 6 4 2

CIP data for this book is available
from the Library of Congress

Blackstone Publishing
31 Mistletoe Rd.
Ashland, OR 97520

www.BlackstonePublishing.com

To Kevin Cast, my little brother and the "real" Kevin—
faithful HoN fan and excellent brother.
Yes, of course that's a picture of you on the cover of Lost.

1

Other Neferet

It took a moment for Other Neferet's vision to clear. First, she felt solid ground under her feet, and then she was aware of Lynette's hand, still clutching her own as it had been when they left the highlands of Scotland and stepped into the portal between worlds. Neferet blinked several times. The blurriness that infected her sight made it seem as if she was trying to see underwater—were the water hazy and poorly lit.

Then her gaze suddenly cleared, and Neferet realized instantly where she was. She and Lynette had materialized in Woodward Park on its north side, near a cluster of azalea bushes and porous Oklahoma dolomite boulders. Though it seemed only seconds had passed from the moonlit moment Oak opened the portal between worlds and the moment they stepped into this mirror version of their own, the sky now blushed with dawn in the east, signaling that several hours had passed. Neferet reacted without hesitation. She went on the defensive.

"Come, we must conceal ourselves," she spoke quietly to Lynette.

She pulled her handmaid and friend with her as the human walked dazedly like she might topple over at any moment. Neferet

1

led her deeper into the azalea bushes where they sat on the boulders that created a small, cliff-like structure that elevated the bulk of the park, placing it atop a man-made hill that also held the top tier of the adjacent Tulsa Rose Gardens.

"Sit. Collect yourself while I reconnoiter," she told Lynette, and while the handmaid blinked and rubbed her arms as if trying to get rid of a chill, Neferet peeked through the bushes.

The well-tended, winter-brown lawn stretched before her to the sidewalk that framed Twenty-First Street. Neferet stared at the apartment complex and the modest brick homes that faced the park. They were so much like the ones in *her* world, though most of these houses still had Christmas lights decorating their facades—a human frivolity she hadn't allowed in her Tulsa.

She glanced to the right, where the rocky ridge curved gently to what should have been a shallow grotto—but which was instead drastically different than the Woodward Park Neferet knew.

A wall had been built with the same Oklahoma dolomite, completely concealing the grotto. It appeared to have a stone roof as well, which met the side of the ridge. Neferet's green eyes narrowed as what she at first mistook for shadows moved when several men came together under the wan, 1920s replica park lamp.

"Sons of Erebus Warriors," she spoke softly to herself while she observed them. There were half a dozen Warriors, dressed in full military regalia, complete with swords at their sides and bows slung over their broad backs. They emerged from the concealing bushes and oaks behind them in the main part of the park to meet above the entombing grotto.

"Stay here," Neferet whispered to Lynette. "I need to know what the Warriors are saying."

Lynette surprised her by grabbing her hand. "No! I won't be parted from you."

The woman's hand was cold, but her grip was strong and sure.

Neferet nodded slowly. "You are wise, dearest Lynette. We must

2

stay together. Follow me. Quietly. If the Warriors discover us I will have to order my children to kill them instantly, and that will alert the House of Night that something is amiss."

Lynette stood, looking a little more recovered from their miraculous journey. "I understand. I'll be quiet."

They crept closer, hugging the rock wall and staying between it and the concealing bushes, until they were close enough to hear the Warriors. It was then that Neferet recognized the Warrior who was acting as leader, though when he turned to face her, she was shocked to see his fully formed Mark proclaiming to the world he was a red vampyre.

"Are all the cameras set?" Stark asked one of the Warriors.

The muscular young vampyre nodded. "They are. The video's definitely not high resolution though—not until the better cameras arrive later this week, which we'll install right away. But these will work fine during the day, at least."

"That's when we need them to work. We'll be here watching at night. Did you or any of the other Warriors notice anything strange at all around the tomb tonight?"

"Quiet as the dead but for one weird incident," said the Warrior. "Earlier, like right around midnight, a group of young human women—probably early twenties—walked down the sidewalk. They started to approach the grotto, but when they saw us they must've changed their minds because they kept walking, though they stared a lot and looked pretty pissed."

Stark's voice was filled with frustration. "I don't understand those humans. It was just over a year ago that Neferet and her tendrils of Darkness ate an entire church full of people, and then held a couple hundred more hostage at the Mayo before slaughtering them too. *They were all humans.* What the hell do they think she'd do if they *could* break her out of here? Hold hands with them and sing campfire songs? She would eat them. She would enslave anyone left alive. How they could worship her? I'll never get it."

The Warrior shrugged. "Seems to me humans like to be told what to do by their gods."

Stark snorted. "Obviously." He glanced up, squinting at a sky that had gone from gray and pink to pastel oranges and blues. "Time for us to get back to the House of Night. Zoey will be glad that the cameras are up and rolling. She already has blue vamps ready to keep watch over the cameras in shifts during the day. Good job tonight." Stark smiled at the watching Warriors. "Good job, all of you."

They saluted before following him back into the park heading to the area that Neferet knew was a parking lot.

She also now knew either Warriors or cameras would always be watching the imprisoning grotto. But that didn't worry her. Neferet was more than prepared to deal with prying eyes.

She waited until the black House of Night SUV pulled out of the park and took a right as it headed back to the sleeping school. Then she turned to Lynette.

"I heard them," said her handmaid. "They left cameras. Do you want me to try to disconnect them?"

"No, dearest. But thank you for the lovely offer. If the cameras are tampered with, vampyres will surely be here within minutes. You know how close the school is to the park."

Lynette seemed herself again and was looking around, wide-eyed. "It's so weird. It looks like our park—our Tulsa—yet it isn't."

"Can you feel it, too?"

Lynette shifted the heavy travel satchel so that it rested more comfortably on her shoulder. "Feel it?"

"That this Tulsa is not ours. Even had there not been obvious differences, like the tacky lights on the houses and the wall around the grotto, I would know I am not home."

Lynette considered, her eyes sweeping the area. "It does feel different. I—I don't want to offend you."

"You could not. I value your honesty."

"Well, then the difference is that this Tulsa feels somehow *lighter*. If that makes sense."

Neferet nodded. "It does. It was exactly what I was thinking. They have not known war, my dear. Or at least not a human-vampyre war."

"Obviously," Lynette agreed. "Which means they will be weaker than vampyres from our world."

Neferet's smile was fierce. "Indeed. And oh, so surprised I am here. Though I am determined not to lose focus. I am not here for vengeance. I am here to attain immortality and return to our world."

Lynette nodded in agreement. "Of course. You're very wise not to get distracted. What now, my lady?"

"I want to get a closer look at the prison they've walled this world's version of me up in. But first I need a little help with concealment."

It was a simple spell that any mature vampyre—and many of the more adventurous fledglings—could easily cast. It was the first spell fledglings learned upon entry to the House of Night. One that kept them safe from human eyes should they get caught outside the walls of their school and surrounded by hostile humans. But Neferet was more than a century older than a newly Marked fledgling and even though she had renounced her position of High Priestess she still carried in her blood and in her spirit the magick granted to all vampyres—and she was well versed in how to use it. Neferet could cast a conceal spell that didn't just hide herself and Lynette from potential onlookers, Neferet could cast a conceal spell that covered all of Tulsa. She faced west, the direction from which water was conjured and also, coincidentally, the direction she would travel should she want to walk the few blocks to the Arkansas River. She drew in several deep breaths to center herself, and then spoke softly, coaxingly.

> *"Water, I call you.*
> *Come to me in the form of mist,*
> *conceal me from spying eyes,*
> *and make me one with thee."*

Neferet imagined thick, soup-like fog covering not just Lynette and her, but blanketing all of midtown and the heart of downtown Tulsa so that whomever was watching the cameras from the House of Night would be fooled into believing that there was nothing amiss—nothing at all to see but morning fog rolling in from the river.

From the west gray clouds billowed over midtown. They blanketed Woodward Park in a mist so thick that within minutes the grotto was completely obscured.

"Come, but stay close," she told Lynette. "We could easily get separated in this."

Neferet felt her way along the porous boulders until she reached the wall that jutted from the otherwise natural-looking ridge. The instant she touched it Neferet gasped and pulled her hand back.

"What is it?" Lynette whispered from beside her.

"It feels cold. And *wrong.*" The tiny hairs on Neferet's arms prickled as they lifted, and her stomach rolled. For a moment she thought she might actually be sick. Then she shook herself. *It is not me. I am not entombed there.* Then she pressed her hand firmly against the stone.

It was frigid. Neferet forced herself to keep her hand on the wall. She closed her eyes and concentrated, and through the rock she sensed several things at once: rage, restlessness, and hunger. An all-consuming hunger that was like a gnawing pain pouring into her palm and spreading throughout her body with each new beat of her heart.

With the rage and hunger an image began to form in Neferet's mind. She couldn't actually see within the tomb, but she could sense the trapped goddess. She was surrounded by darkness that seethed and moved restlessly like a nest of vipers.

Neferet pressed her palm harder against the icy stone, until she felt more—the thing that kept the goddess sealed within. It was incredibly powerful, and it was causing the cold. She sensed that the seal was round, and it covered the entire wall, extending to the top of the rock so that it pressed into the side of the ridge. It pulsed like it was alive and sent waves of ice into her body. She began to shiver.

Still Neferet kept her hand there—pressed against the wall of the tomb—until her children, the loyal tendrils of Darkness that had become so precious to her, began to move in agitation. They circled her legs, crawling up to her waist. They draped around her arms and neck like living jewels. They lent her their warmth as they clung to her and Neferet felt their worry as surely as she felt their protection.

"Oh!" Lynette gasped.

Neferet glanced at her handmaid and was shocked that her children had become visible and were also encircling Lynette's waist as well as hanging from her neck.

"My lady, they seem upset," Lynette said as she stroked the fat tendril that wrapped around her middle.

"Of course they are." Neferet gestured at the wall. "I assume they are agitated because they can sense that one like me is trapped within. I imagine they, too, know something very powerful has sealed her in there—something that is not friendly to them or to me." She caressed the tendrils decorating her neck and shoulders. "All is well, children, but Lynette and I do appreciate your concern. Do not fret. I shall break the seal and free the goddess within, who will, in return, provide us the knowledge I need to become immortal."

"And then we will go back to our world," Lynette said, still stroking the tendril.

"Indeed, we will—"

A girl's voice blasted across the fog. "Jesus Christ! I can't see a damn thing."

"Oh, Amber, stop bitching. At least those Sons of Erebus assholes are gone."

"Seriously," said a third girl, her voice moving closer than the other two. "I don't know why they get so butt hurt about us leaving

7

offerings. Neferet is a *goddess* and she's trapped in there. I mean, the *least* we can do is worship her."

Silently, Neferet moved away from the wall, motioning for Lynette to follow. Carefully ensuring the fog continued to cover the cameras mounted in the trees above the grotto, she concentrated on clearing a small portion of it directly before the tomb, just enough so that she could see who approached while remaining hidden herself.

Five people suddenly came into view. They were all women, young, though not as young as the fledglings at the House of Night. They were dressed in short, tight skirts, ridiculous boots with stiletto heels that kept sinking into the soft, winter grass, and fur coats. They approached the wall and stopped in front of it. Each young woman carried a large satchel from which they took velvet capes in the five colors that represented the elements: yellow for air, red for fire, blue for water, green for earth, and purple for spirit. They hastily donned the garments before they dug into their bags and brought out tea lights in colors corresponding to their capes, along with lighters and other trinkets—crystals, feathers, and even a small stone carved in the shape of a cat.

Then they dropped their purses on the ground and turned to face the wall, and Lynette gasped softly beside her. She didn't blame her handmaid. She'd never seen anything like it, either. Neferet looked more intently at the women's faces, trying to understand what she saw there.

The young women were obviously human. They had none of the signs that bespoke vampyre. Their eyes were the muted colors of human eyes and not the more brilliant orbs of vampyre eyes, which enabled them to see so well in the dark. They were attractive, but not otherworldly so. Their fingernails were well groomed but not particularly sharp and obviously not capable of slicing skin to allow them a sip of blood.

Still, Neferet sniffed the air. Yes, their scent was definitely human. But then, how had these women come to have Marks on their foreheads? Neferet peered closer. Each of them had painted on their foreheads an unusual Mark. In black, thick and dark as kohl, they had drawn the triple moon sign—a full moon in the middle flanked by two crescents. The Marks did not extend down their faces as would a true vampyre Mark. Instead, across their eyes they'd also painted a thick line of black that made them look like they were wearing masks.

The women lifted the hoods of their capes so that their faces were obscured just enough that they could be mistaken for ancient priestesses. Then they carried the tea lights and the small offerings to the wall, lighting them and tucking them into the small niches and dips in the stone. They bowed their heads and clasped their hands like they were at Saturday mass, lighting and leaving candles to the Virgin Mary.

"They worship Neferet," Lynette whispered.

"Which means they are our allies and exactly what we need until I can discover how to break that seal and free her." Neferet stroked a tendril fondly. "Darling children, cloak yourselves. Do not let these humans see you." The tendrils disappeared. "Lynette, stand behind me, there—in the mist—so that they see only me."

"Be careful," Lynette murmured while she did as her mistress commanded. "Remember there are cameras around the grotto."

Neferet nodded. She smoothed her form-fitting black sweater and stood straight and proud, shoulders back, head high. Then she flicked her long, elegant fingers at the grotto. "Cover the tomb, but part before me."

The fog swirled, wafting up and over the wall of the tomb in a thick wave of gray.

"This is super freaky weather," said one of the women as all five stepped back and the mist billowed in front of them.

Neferet cleared her throat and the five hooded figures turned their heads in unison. As one, their eyes widened in shock. Neferet wished she could see herself at that moment through their eyes. She must look magnificent, seeming to materialize from the fog before them.

9

The young woman wearing the purple cloak opened her mouth, but Neferet shook her head and pressed her finger to her lips before pointing up at the fog-shrouded cameras. Then she crooked her finger, motioning for the women to come closer. They did without hesitation.

The women stopped before Neferet. The vampyre flicked her fingers again, as she imagined the fog closing behind them to conceal them more completely, which it obediently did.

"Now, you may worship me," Neferet said.

The five women dropped to their knees as they stared in adoration up at her.

This world's Stark was right, Neferet thought. *All five of these humans are easy prey, and lucky that it is me they kneel before and not the ravenous goddess within the tomb.*

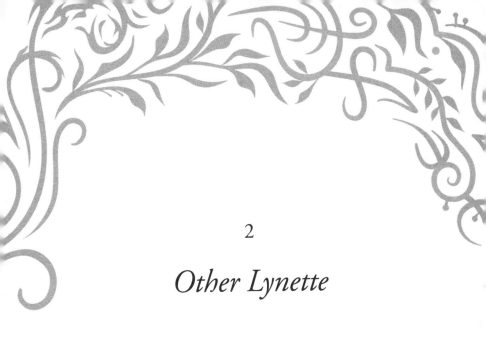

2

Other Lynette

"How quaint! You're cloaked *and* kneeling. What an unexpected, lovely welcome." Neferet spoke magnanimously to the five young women, though Lynette noted that she paused for several silent minutes before she continued. "You may rise. And remove your cowls. I wish to see those who worship me."

The five women stood and hastily swept back the hoods of their velvet cloaks. Lynette was behind and to the side of Neferet. None of them so much as glanced her way. Completely unnoticed, she studied the first humans she'd seen from this new world.

They were young—probably very early twenties at most—and pretty in the Oklahoma/Texas variety of beauty pageant attractive. They were all blond, though Lynette's keen observation told her that at most only two of the five had been born that way.

Before they'd cloaked themselves, Lynette had already noticed their clothes—expensive, and tiptoeing that fine line between overtly sexual and tasteful. Had she dressed them, the only thing she would've changed was their stiletto boots. Too inconvenient for walking in grass. Each of them wore their hair long and big,

11

bringing to mind the saying that must be the same in both worlds, *the bigger the hair—the closer to God*, and Okies definitely liked to be close to God. Or in this case God*dess*.

The one wearing the purple spirit cape spoke first. "Neferet, our Goddess of Tulsa, we—your Dark Sisters—are honored that you have appeared to us. Blessed be!" She fisted her hand over her heart, mimicking a vampyre saluting a High Priestess.

"What is your name?" Neferet asked.

"I am Vanessa, leader of the Dark Sisters," she said.

"Tell me, Vanessa, what is a Dark Sister?"

"Us!" Vanessa said with a smile that exposed perfect teeth that must have cost her father a fortune. "I started our coven a year ago. You know. After *what they did to you*." She ended the sentence in an affected whisper.

"Yes, well, that does not actually answer my question, but I shall set it aside for now. Introduce the rest of your sisters."

Vanessa gestured to each young woman in turn. "Jenna is air. Amber is fire. Kelsey is water. Jordan is earth. And I, of course, am spirit."

Neferet cocked her head to the side. "Do any of you truly have an affinity for your element?"

They looked confused, and then Amber, wearing the red cloak that signified fire, spoke up. "Well, uh, yeah. I mean, I've always felt, like, seriously *connected* to fire."

Vanessa nodded. "It's true. Each of us chose the element we're closest to. I've always been the leader. So, naturally, I am spirit."

"Oh," Neferet said. "Naturally."

Lynette had to press her lips together so that she didn't laugh. These girls had no clue what Neferet was really asking. Unlike the clueless girls, she'd spent enough time in the employ of vampyres to know the difference between a true affinity and *OMG I love fire*.

Completely missing the sarcasm in Neferet's voice, Vanessa continued. "The five of us have pledged ourselves to your service."

12

"Why?"

Neferet's one-word question seemed to suspend in the fog that surrounded them. The girls blinked in confusion, sharing glances. Lynette was sure she saw the earth girl and the water girl roll their eyes, but when Vanessa spoke it was with complete sincerity.

"Because vampyres are the most beautiful, talented, richest beings on earth. And out of all of the vampyres you are the only one who has ever wanted to be our goddess."

Amber, the fire girl, added, "Yeah, and even though we weren't Marked we want part of that."

Vanessa nodded and the other four mirrored her. "Seriously. We deserve part of that."

"Why?" Neferet repeated her question. This time she sounded truly curious.

"Because we're the same," Vanessa said.

In the green earth cloak, Jordan said, "Uh-huh, we're beautiful and talented and rich. Like you."

"That's right," Vanessa said. "And we're tired of people who clutter up our world and whine about everything."

"Right?" said the girl wearing water blue. "It's the twenty-first century. Stop whining about your issues. Racism is, like, *over*. If you can't get a clue, go back to where you came from and get a friggin' life."

Lynette did smile then, though she made no sound. She knew exactly what kind of women they were. Had they been from *her* Tulsa she probably would have recognized several of them. She would've definitely known their mothers—and/or their replacement younger-model stepmothers.

"Tell me, Vanessa, are there more of you?" Neferet asked.

"You mean Dark Sisters?" Vanessa said.

"Yes, of course that is what I mean."

Vanessa shook her head and looked smug. "Oh. No. We wanted our group to be *exclusive*."

Jenna in the yellow air cloak added, "But we have friends who would *love* to join our group. As soon as we tell them that you've escaped and—"

Neferet's lifted hand silenced her. "But you are incorrect. I am Neferet—sacred and powerful."

Lynette noted she didn't name herself goddess to them.

She continued. "But I am not the Neferet of your world. I crossed the veil between worlds to be here, before you."

"Oh, my *goddess!*" Vanessa gasped. "You're here to break *our* Neferet out of jail."

"I am, indeed. Will you help me?" As they sputtered to answer her, Neferet lifted her hand, silencing them again. "You should first know what I will ask of you before you agree, and if you cannot give it to me, then we shall simply part ways here."

Lynette readied herself. There was absolutely no way Neferet was going to allow those girls to walk away and spread rumors about her. The moment she told them that she was from another world and here to help their Neferet escape, their death warrants had been signed and sealed.

Lynette tried to tell herself it didn't matter. That the lives of five frivolous, entitled young women weren't worth risking their mission, but she couldn't help wishing that she and Neferet were back at Balmacara Mains, sitting before the fireplace, with the aroma of Mrs. Muir's freshly baked bread wafting around them.

The five women were watching Neferet with expressions so eager that Lynette almost began to relax. Almost.

Neferet continued. "I will need you to swear to absolute secrecy about my presence in your world. By speaking you could upset the very nature of the universe."

The five started to nod, but once again Neferet cut them off.

"My handmaid and I will need somewhere close to stay. I would prefer that the facility befit my status. I will need money and transportation as well as other things—elements for the spell I will cast to break the seal that entombs your goddess. I will need willing, attractive feeders who also must be sworn to secrecy, *or are disposable.*" Neferet's voice changed as she spoke the end of the sentence, leaving no doubt that *disposable* was synonymous with *killable.* "And, finally, I will need information. As I said, I am not from your world. In order to create the perfect spell to loose your goddess, I must learn everything I can about how she was able to be imprisoned."

"Vampyres did it—not us!" the air girl, Jenna blurted.

"Well, yes, of course," said Neferet. "But I need details."

"Details are easy to get," said Vanessa. "The House of Night's new High Priestess, Zoey Redbird, is super open about everything."

Amber nodded and her long, blond hair bounced around her shoulders. "Yeah, she even lets humans roam around on the House of Night campus. If we can't answer your questions, it'll be real easy for us to get the answers for you."

"Then, do you agree to my terms?" Neferet asked.

The five girls shared a look, then Vanessa turned back to Neferet. She cleared her throat and said, "Um, if we say yes, do you promise that you really are here to release our Neferet?"

Lynette didn't have to see the dark tendrils that were Neferet's children to feel them reflecting their mistress's irritation, but the vampyre appeared calm when she answered the girl.

"Vanessa, I give you my oath that I am here to release your Neferet from the vile prison that is trapping her."

"Ohmygod, yeah!" Vanessa almost squealed as she bounced up and down on the balls of her feet like an overgrown cheerleader. "Then, hell yes, we promise to help you! You're gonna love our house. We're all seniors at TU, but our place is closer to here than campus—like, within *walking distance* of here."

Jenna's face scrunched unattractively. "The neighborhood around TU isn't the greatest."

"Right, so my dad bought us a house in Maple Ridge," said Vanessa. "It's practically our own House of Night."

Neferet glanced at Lynette and, for the first time, the girls noticed her. "Maple Ridge—do you know it?"

"Of course. It's a historic neighborhood not far from here," she said.

"Wait. Who is that?" Vanessa asked, staring at Lynette.

"This is Lynette. She is my handmaid," Neferet said, gesturing gracefully to Lynette, who nodded slightly at the girls.

Vanessa was already looking away from Lynette dismissively as she spoke. "You mean maid, like servant?"

"Servant?" Neferet said. "No. A handmaid is …" the vampyre paused, searching for the correct analogy. "A high-level assistant." As she spoke she turned to Lynette and winked. Quickly.

"Yes, my lady. Exactly," Lynette said, curtsying low.

"Oh. I get it," Vanessa said without looking at Lynette.

"And the five of you live in this home alone?" Neferet asked.

Vanessa nodded. "Totally! Well, I mean, Juanita comes in to clean twice a week—or more often if we, like, have a party and need her."

"You will suspend her services for as long as I am staying with you," said Neferet.

Lynette could see that didn't go over well with Vanessa, but the girl didn't comment.

"Now I need two things—suitable rooms where my handmaid and I may rest and refresh, and a feeder." Neferet's emerald eyes scanned the small group of girls hungrily.

Lynette enjoyed watching them squirm.

"Well, um, there's a whole feeder registry," Vanessa said.

"Yes, but none of them will do, as they are *registered* and therefore not disposable. No matter." Neferet made a dismissive gesture with her long, elegant figures. "Show me to your house and I shall find a feeder myself while my fog still blankets the city."

Kelsey, the girl wearing the blue robe of water, stared at Neferet in starstruck wonder. "*You* brought this fog here?"

"Yes, child." Neferet waved her hand around the concealing mist that encircled the group, shrouding it from the cameras that watched the grotto. "This is but a parlor trick."

"Wow," Kelsey said.

"This is gonna be *awesome*," said Vanessa. "Come this way, please, um, Neferet."

"You five may call me 'my lady,'" Neferet corrected her.

"Uh, yeah. My lady. The house is just down the street off Norfolk and Twentieth."

"Lovely. You lead. My handmaid and I shall follow," said Neferet.

The young women headed for the sidewalk that ran along Twenty-First Street, heading west, toward the river and into the thickest part of the fog. Neferet followed with Lynette at her side.

"They're very naive and not particularly bright," Lynette said, keeping her voice pitched for Neferet's ears alone.

"Yes. They're absolutely perfect," agreed Neferet.

3

Other Stark

Other Kevin yawned enormously and stretched so hard that his hands brushed the top of the limo and his spine cracked. "You think Sgiach is actually gonna let us on the island?"

Other Stark looked up from the Dean Koontz book he was reading. "Oh, you're alive again."

"Dude, I don't actually die when the sun's up. You know that, right?"

"Of course I know that. Doesn't change the fact that you red vamps look dead while you sleep. You mind if I roll down the window now that the sun's set? Some fresh air would be good."

"No problem."

Stark hit the down button and the back of their limo filled with cold, wet air that smelled of earth.

Kevin stared out at the gray world as it sped by. "Wow. That's a lot of mountains. Where are we?"

"Only about thirty minutes from the bridge to Skye."

"So, do you think the queen's gonna let us on the island?" Kevin repeated as he stared out the half-open window.

Stark shrugged. "Anastasia seems to think she will. She said Sgiach was pleased we'd kicked Neferet out of power."

"Yeah, there's definitely no love lost between Neferet and Sgiach, which is why I was surprised she'd go to Skye."

Stark ran his hand through his shaggy hair. "Well, it's not like Neferet went to Skye for the queen's help. It's more like if she's here— or was here—she's sneaking around trying to use Old Magick."

Kevin grimaced. "Old Magick. That stuff is bad news. I am not looking forward to using it again."

Stark studied him. He understood the pain that crossed his face. Kevin had lost Aphrodite to Old Magick—just days before—and the kid was definitely not over it.

"Maybe we won't have to. She might still be here."

Kevin snorted. "Not likely. If Neferet had planned on hanging around, she wouldn't have taunted us in the elevator video after she killed Blake. And you heard what the London House of Night Warriors found out—that she'd ordered and eaten an entire dinner at a restaurant right down the street just minutes after she killed him. Let's hope that douchebag's last written words weren't meant to throw us off."

"I don't think he was smart enough for that. Plus, Neferet killed him. Pretty gruesomely too. That's fact. The video shows that the two of them were alone in that hotel room. They both went in. Only Neferet came out."

"While I was sleeping was there any word from Dragon about a Neferet sighting around Skye?" Kevin asked.

Stark shook his head. "No word on a sighting, but the pilot finally opened his mouth."

Kevin barked a laugh. "Did Dragon persuade him with his fists?"

"Actually, no. Anastasia got to him. Dragon said less than ten minutes alone with the guy and he told her everything. Neferet and Lynette Witherspoon, the human who was the flight coordinator at the private airport in Tulsa, had him fly them to London, where they deplaned. Neferet sent the jet on to Venice to await further instructions, which never came. He said he overheard the two of them talking about hiring a car to drive them to Skye. The human planned everything while Neferet slept for most of the flight. He heard her booking an entire B&B somewhere close to Skye, but she didn't say the name of the place—or at least not so that he could hear it."

"Yeah, Neferet was definitely lurking around Skye. She had to be messing with Old Magick."

"Dragon said the pilot told Anastasia that not only was Lynette obviously with Neferet willingly, but she called her 'goddess' several times."

Kevin's gaze went from the darkening scenery to Stark. "Shit. That's bad. The Neferet in Zo's world became immortal."

"Yeah, Anastasia's guess is that's Neferet's goal—to become immortal too, and then return to Tulsa when she's so powerful we won't be able to stop her. And there are plenty of assholes like Loren Blake—"

"And your buddy, Dallas," Kevin added.

"He's not my damn buddy. But, yeah, there are plenty of assholes like him who would flock to an immortal Neferet so they'd be back in power." Stark hesitated. The subject made him feel sick. When he supported Neferet and her war against humans he'd been doing what he thought was right—at first. But if he was honest with himself, he'd been questioning Neferet's methods for quite a while. "I shoulda spoken against her. I shoulda stood up to her."

"You did when it counted most. You were part of the reason all of the red vamps and fledglings got their humanity back. If you'd stood up to Neferet before then, I don't know how we woulda stopped her," Kevin said.

Stark picked at the jacket of the Koontz book. "I know that, but it still makes me feel like shit. Looking back, I don't know how I let it go on for so long."

"What could you have done?"

20

"Stood up to her," said Stark, his voice grim with self-loathing. "She would have killed you."

"I could've joined the Resistance like Dragon and the rest of you."

"Like I said, if you had, who woulda stopped Neferet from giving the order to the Red Army to kill the humans at the TU stadium?"

Stark moved restlessly in the cushy leather seat. "I hear ya, but I still hate that it took me so long to get it right."

"Dude, forgive yourself and move on."

One corner of Stark's mouth lifted in the ghost of his cocky smile. "Except for the dude part, you sound a lot like your grandma."

"I'll take that as a compliment."

The driver's voice interrupted their conversation as it came through the speaker system in the rear of the limo. "Gentlemen, we're approaching the bridge to the Isle of Skye. Remember that I will drop you off, but I will not wait there. I'll be at the Lochalsh Hotel for one full day before returning to Inverness. You have my card. Call if you're ready to return."

Stark tapped on the raised, tinted glass that separated the driver from the rear of the limo. Silently, the panel slid down so that Stark could see the driver, who had an adult Mark that looked like sapphire smoke.

"Hey, what's the problem with waiting by the bridge?" Stark asked.

The vamp gave him a dismissive glance in the rearview mirror before responding gruffly. "You'll see soon enough. Anything else?"

"No, I guess no—" The driver didn't wait for him to finish to put the partition up.

"Sheesh," Kevin said. "Have you noticed no one over here is very friendly?"

"Yeah, but I don't really blame them. It was our High Priestess who started a war with humans that is still not resolved. I heard one of the London Sons of Erebus call us 'colonists that can't sort their issues.'"

"And that's bad?"

Stark shrugged. "Apparently."

The limo took a hard left. Gravel crunched under the wheels as it crept forward toward a long, narrow suspension bridge that Stark got a glimpse of before his window automatically rolled itself up.

"You can get out here," the driver's gruff voice sounded once more through the speakers.

Stark and Kevin grabbed their backpacks and climbed out of the limo. They'd barely closed the door when the car pulled away so quickly that it threw gravel at them.

"Hey! Why be a dick?" Kevin called after him.

"I'm losing his damn card," said Stark.

"Good idea. And I'll give him a shit Yelp review," Kevin muttered as he stared at the long, narrow bridge that stretched between an outcropping of the Scottish mainland and the island. Live torches lighted it, but they did little to dispel the mist and cold that blanketed the island.

"All right. Well, this is the place." Stark started toward the bridge. "Anastasia described it perfectly, but it's not like there're a bunch of ways on and off the island." When Kevin didn't respond, Stark paused and glanced back. Kevin had taken a couple steps after him but was currently standing still. His gaze was completely focused on the bridge. He cracked his knuckles nervously and shook his head like a cat trying to dispel water. "Hey, you coming or what?"

Kevin blinked several times and finally turned his gaze to Stark. "You don't feel it?"

"The cold or the wet? It's nasty out here, but it is January in the Highlands. Not exactly tourist weather."

"Not that … Dread. Fear. And worse."

Stark opened his mouth to make a sarcastic response, but he could see that Kevin was completely serious. His face was so pale that his red Mark looked like fresh blood, and even though it was cold there was a film of sweat on his face.

"Hey, you feeling okay?" Stark asked him.

"Nope. Not at all. I don't want to do anything except run—and I mean *away* from the island. This isn't normal."

"Oh, shit. It's part of the spell that protects Skye," Stark realized.

"Then why the hell aren't you sweating and terrified?"

Stark shrugged and his lips lifted in a cocky smile. "Maybe I'm just a lot tougher than you."

Kevin frowned. "Riiiiight, no. I'm about one hundred percent sure that's not it."

"You wanna wait here? If Sgiach lets us in, I can text you."

"Screw that." Kevin drew a deep breath and shifted the weight of his backpack. "I'm coming with you."

Side by side, Stark and Kevin entered the bridge. Intrigued by the mist-shrouded isle, Stark gazed around him. Far below, the water was dark and choppy. Once in a while, a wave caught in the torchlight and looked out of place with its cheery white froth.

"Don't fucking look down!" Kevin told Stark.

"Dude, you sound panicked."

"You have no idea. And I'm not ashamed to admit it. With every step it gets worse. I *know* any second this bridge is gonna break and we'll fall down there." Kevin pointed at the water without looking down. "And be eaten by sea monsters."

"Sea monsters? Are you serious?"

"As a heart attack. A big, bad, painful, fatal heart attack with a side of Ebola and an extra helping of being choked, stabbed, drowned, and then eaten."

"Huh." They'd come to the end of the bridge where there sat an arch made of white stone with veins of silver running through it. It was mesmerizing, and not in a creepy way. The silver reflected the flickering torchlight with electric beauty, like a zillion lightning bolts had been trapped within the white marble. "Wow, that's incredible."

"Ah, shit, shit, shit, shit, shit." Kevin turned his face away from the arch.

"What the hell?"

23

Kevin sucked in long breaths and released them like he was in the middle of trying to bench too much weight. "I can hardly look at it."

Stark knew he wasn't playing. Kevin looked awful—like he might puke or bolt. Or both.

From the island side of the arch a deep, disembodied voice barked, "*Ha Gaelic akiv?*"

"We, uh, don't speak Scottish," said Stark.

Someone snorted. Loudly. "Are ye daft? It isnae *Scottish*. 'Tis the mother tongue—Gaelic."

"That either," said Stark.

"So, it'll be the English, then. What is it uze want?"

"To run screaming in the other direction," Kevin muttered.

"As this isle isnae fer wains—leave."

"Shh!" Stark shushed Kevin before facing where he thought the voice came from. "We're James Stark and Kevin Redbird from the Tulsa House of Night. Our High Priestess, Anastasia, contacted Queen Sgiach about our arrival." He squared his shoulders and added. "And we're not babies."

As the silence stretched between them and the misty island, Kevin shifted restlessly from foot to foot and whispered to Stark, "How'd you know what a wain is?"

Stark only answered him because he wanted to distract the kid. "My grandpa MacUallis called me that until the day he died. He didn't give a shit that I wasn't a kid anymore. Actually, Grandpa was a mean old dude who didn't give a shit about much of anything except my grandma and what he used to call a 'wee dram'—which was actually single malt scotch, and he drank way more than a little of it."

From the middle of the other side of the archway, a man materialized. He was muscular and built like an athlete, which more than showed because he wasn't wearing one of the kilts they'd glimpsed as they traveled through the Highlands on their way to Skye. This man was wrapped in a thick length of woolen plaid the color of the autumn leaves. Most of his chest was bare. He wore leather forearm guards carved with knots and swirls. The hilt of a knife gleamed at his waist and as Stark studied him, he noticed a gold chieftain's torque around his neck. His hair was shaven to his scalp except for a short Mohawk and his close-cropped beard was entirely white. Golden hoops decorated one of his earlobes. His face was deeply lined—he looked ancient—but the sapphire tattoos that framed his face in griffins' claws and extended onto his cheekbones were as crisp and as powerful as his Warrior body.

He glared at Stark. "What did ya say yer granda's name was?"

Stark blinked in surprise, but answered, "Robby MacUallis. He always said that we're from here. I mean the Highlands of Scotland. We came to the US in the mid-1700s after something called Culloden happened."

The Warrior snorted. "And that's all ye know of yer past? Culloden *happened*?"

Stark sighed. "You sound just like him. He talked like Culloden was yesterday and not April 16, 1746."

A woman's laugh sounded from the soupy darkness. It was a full, rich laugh, but there was something about the power it held that caused the fine hairs on Stark's forearms to lift.

"Seems this young vampyre isn't totally ignorant of his past—though obviously he knows nothing of his heritage."

Queen Sgiach stepped out from within the wall of mist. She was tall and moved with a lithe grace that made Stark think of a lioness. Her striking sapphire tattoo of swords with intricately carved hilts blazed against the fair skin of her face as if Nyx had just placed it there. There were lines at the corners of her eyes, which were an unusual shade of bright hazel mixed with green. Her hair was waist length and except for a single streak of copper, it was perfectly white. A silver coronet crowned her head. In the center of it was a fat piece of amber that reflected the torchlight with golden fire. To Stark she didn't look old or young; she looked like a warrior goddess.

Stark bowed deeply and respectfully to her, his hand fisted over his heart, and Kevin did the same.

"Merry meet, Queen Sgiach," Stark said.

When she spoke, her voice was surprisingly soft. She didn't sound pissed or welcoming—only curious. "Your High Priestess, Anastasia, contacted me saying two of her Warriors were going to request access to my island. Why should I allow you to enter?"

Anastasia had warned him that Sgiach hadn't let her explain why she was requesting entrance to Skye for them. The queen insisted the Warriors speak for themselves, so Stark had considered how he would answer that question all the way across the ocean. He and Kevin had talked about it and come up with an excellent answer that sounded important and mature, but as he faced Sgiach and felt the power radiating from her, his well-rehearsed words evaporated from his mind and left only the most basic truth.

"I'm trying to fix the mistake I made when I supported Neferet and her war. My mistake cost vampyre and human lives, and allowed an entire race of new vampyres," he paused and gestured at Kevin, who gritted his teeth and stepped up beside Stark. "Red vampyres like my friend Kevin, to be used—brutally, terribly. I have sworn to Nyx to stop Neferet before she hurts more of us."

Sgiach studied Kevin. "I have never before seen a red vampyre. Tell me, young Warrior Kevin, is it true that you sway human's minds and make them do your bidding?"

"Yes, Your Majesty, to some extent. Although, how well it works depends on the strength of will of the human. But that is just one of the differences between red and blue vampyres. We also must have an invitation to enter a private home, and full sunlight can kill us."

Seoras snorted. "And are all of you barely outta yur nappies?"

Kevin blinked in confusion and Stark whispered. "Nappies are diapers."

"Oh. Uh. Well, most of us are pretty young because our kind

hasn't been around long, but as far as I know, I am the youngest fully Changed red vampyre in this world."

"He also is the only vampyre, red or otherwise, in this world who has an affinity for all five elements," Stark added.

Sgiach's arched brows lifted. "Fascinating," she said. Her moss and amber eyes skewered Stark. "Tell me, young Warrior, why did you support a High Priestess who was so obviously not following Nyx's path?"

"That's something I've asked myself every day since I finally stood against her. I have no excuse. I didn't want to believe my High Priestess had turned to Darkness, so I did what she told me to do for way too long."

"May I ask something?" Kevin said, and then hastily added, "Please, Your Majesty."

Sgiach said nothing but nodded.

Kevin cleared his throat, cracked his knuckles and said, "Why didn't *you* do anything to stop her? You knew she'd turned from Nyx. You knew the human/vampyre war was wrong. You're a Warrior Queen. You could've fought her, but you didn't do anything. Why?" He repeated.

Seoras took a step forward, hand on the hilt of his dirk, but Sgiach touched his arm and he stood down.

"Your question is impertinent," she said.

"I apologize. I don't mean to be rude. But I'm one of the people who suffered because Neferet was allowed to use an entire race of vampyres to gain power over humans and her own kind. It's personal for me. So, I'd like to know why *you* didn't do anything to stop her."

Stark stifled a sigh and spoke up, even though he wished Kevin had kept his mouth shut. "Yeah, I don't want to insult you either. We're here asking for help, so that would be stupid. Neferet caused so much misery—so much death—I'm not blaming you. Hell, I was there. I was one of her generals and I watched it happen. That's something I'll regret for the rest of my life. I should've done something, but the truth is I couldn't have stopped her. I'll bet you could have, though. Why didn't you?" Stark held his breath and waited for the queen to let Seoras strike him dead—or maybe she'd just cut off his head herself.

She did neither, but she did speak to Seoras. "They remind me of you—especially the MacUallis boy."

"I was never that young," growled Seoras.

"But you were that impertinent," said the queen.

Seoras snorted. "*Were?*"

Sgiach faced Stark and Kevin, looking from one to the other as she spoke. "Do either of you know why I am queen of this island?"

"You control Old Magick," said Stark.

"No, young MacUallis. No one *controls* Old Magick. Not even those who wield it—perhaps *especially* not those who wield it."

"You guard the island," said Kevin.

"That is much closer to the truth," said Sgiach. "My affinity, granted to me centuries ago by Nyx, is to be Guardian and Queen of this isle where Old Magick retreated as humans spread across the world and the old ways were forgotten. If Old Magick was to be left unguarded and loosed on the modern world—a world that is predominately governed by men who believe money is power and view the earth as something to exploit—Old Magick, too, would have been exploited. The truth, Warriors from the Tulsa House of Night, is that I very much wanted to lift my claymore and lead my Warriors against Neferet and her foolish quest for power, but our world no longer respects the old ways, and if I had left my isle nothing would have dammed Old Magick. It would have flowed unchecked from Skye, and I believe the balance of Light and Darkness would have been tipped to the Dark, even though Neferet would have been defeated."

"So, you stood by and waited," Stark said.

Sgiach nodded, and the torchlight caught the amber jewel in her coronet so that it blazed with fire. "Yes. I waited. I believed those who still followed our Goddess would prevail, and I did what I could from here to encourage that."

"It was you! You were the reason the sprites suddenly came back to Oklahoma," said Kevin.

The queen's eyes narrowed. "Young Warrior, have you been trafficking with Old Magick?"

"Well, a little. I had to. But not on purpose—at first," said Kevin.

"Yer gonna need to explain that!" Seoras practically barked the words.

With a trembling hand, Kevin wiped the sweat that beaded his brow. "That'd be a lot easier if I didn't feel like I was gonna puke or pass out."

Sgiach raised one hand and spoke several words in Gaelic as she pointed at Kevin. Instantly Stark heard him sigh with relief.

"Wow. Thanks."

"Explain why you used Old Magick."

"Well, I had to protect the Resistance against, um, Stark and the rest of Neferet's soldiers who were going to slaughter a bunch of innocent vamps and humans who'd come to them for help."

Stark had to force himself not to hang his head in shame or apologize. Again.

"But how did you know to call the sprites?" asked Sgiach.

"Oh, well, because my sister, Zoey Redbird, told me."

The queen's brow furrowed. "Is that not the name of one of the first fledglings killed in the human/vampyre war?"

Kevin nodded. "Yeah."

"Does your affinity for spirit allow you to speak with the dead?"

"No. Well, maybe. Actually, I don't know. I've never tried. But the sister I was talking about isn't my sister from this world. She's from another world that's a lot like this one, only there they've defeated Neferet."

Sgiach's gaze sharpened on Kevin. "Another world?"

"Yeah. That's why we're here."

Seoras opened his mouth to speak, but his queen shook her head slightly, stilling him.

"The door between worlds has been discovered." Sgiach's voice was thick with dread.

"That's what we've been trying to tell you—why we need your help," Stark said. "This Neferet—*our* Neferet—found out about that other world and that her mirror image figured out a way to become immortal. We believe she's going there to help that Neferet escape and then learn from her how to become a goddess."

Kevin took up the telling of the tale. "When she's immortal she'll return here. If that happens, she will be almost unstoppable, and the war she started in Oklahoma will be nothing compared to what she'll do to our entire world."

"Not to mention," Stark added, "that releasing that Neferet, who is already immortal, would be very, *very* bad for that world. If our Neferet is already over there, they need to be warned. If she's still here, we need to stop her."

Sgiach stared from Stark to Kevin for so long that Stark began frantically thinking of something else, anything else, he could say to persuade her. At his side, Kevin cracked his knuckles restlessly.

And finally, he thought he might have it—one single reason he should enter the island. A reason tied to his grandpa—*the* reason the protective spell cast around the island didn't affect him. Stark drew a deep breath, dropped to his knees, and took a chance.

"Your Majesty, I am a Warrior who is of MacUallis blood—your blood. Your clan. And I am asking to enter your island so that you may help me, as well as Kevin, find out whether Neferet has already gone to the Other World or not, and if she has we need you—and Old Magick—to help us go there and warn them about our Neferet. To do that I will swear myself into your service."

"Warriors have stopped coming to me," Sgiach said in a completely emotionless voice.

"Warriors haven't stopped coming to you, Queen Sgiach, the

Great Taker of Heads. We're here, Kevin and me." Beside him, Kevin went to his knees as well.

"I would swear to your service as well, Queen Sgiach," Kevin said.

"Will you accept us? Will you teach us how to guard the rest of our world like you guard this island?"

Sgiach hesitated, but only long enough to share a look with Seoras. Then she lifted her hand, palm out, and spoke with such power it caused a great wind to whip around them.

"*Failte gu ant Eilean nan Sgiath.* Welcome to the Isle of Sgiach. You may enter."

Side by side, Stark and Kevin entered the Isle of Women.

4

Other Kevin

Even though he was a red vampyre and the sun would fry him like bacon, Kevin wished he could see Sgiach's island in the daylight. Seoras had very grumpily told them to get into the back seat of a Jeep Wrangler, and currently they were bouncing along an unpaved road toward a speck of light in the distance. Kevin suspected the old Scottish dude was hitting every rut and rock on purpose.

"Hey, where's Sgiach?" Kevin asked, suddenly realizing the queen was nowhere to be seen.

"Sgiach doesna need the motor tae be traveling her island," growled the Warrior.

"What does that mean?" Kevin whispered to Stark.

Clearly, the old dude's hearing was perfectly fine because he frowned at Kevin in the rearview mirror and said, "It means what the queen already told ye, wain. Sgiach's affinity is to her land. She commands it."

"Shit! You mean on Skye the queen is like a living transporter beam?" Kevin blurted, then realized there was no way Seoras could understand that, and he added. "Um, what I mean by that is that she can—"

"I know what ye mean. Like *Star Trek*. 'Tis a fine explanation."

"You know about *Star Trek*?" Stark asked.

Seoras snickered. "Aye, wain. And runnin' water too."

"I knew you had to be connected to the outside world," said Stark.

"Well, she's a queen. Not a fool."

They traveled on in silence as Kevin stared out the window. They'd come around a bend in the narrow road. Ahead and to their right, a castle sat a couple football-field lengths away. A stone bridge–like path that led to it was raised over a boggy stretch of land. Torches, like the ones that had been on the bridge from the mainland, lit it with a spectral light that flickered in the cold wind.

"What is that?" Stark pointed to their left, pulling Kevin's attention from the castle.

A strange-looking forest grew to the muddy road. Tree trunks were twisted and gnarled, but they held up a canopy of green that was thick, beautiful, and verdant. His eyesight, better at night than a blue vamp's, allowed him to peer into the forest, which was covered with a thick carpet of moss. Within, even in the darkness of full night, white boulders with the same silver veins as the arch they had so recently passed under, glinted and twinkled like jewels.

One tree in particular stood out. As Kevin stared, he realized that it was actually two trees that had grown together, their trunks and branches irrevocably entangled, and from the branches, long strips of fabric waved lazily, almost like they were welcoming him.

"'Tis the Craobh—the Sacred Grove. Sgiach's castle is just there, across from it." Seoras was saying. .

Kevin wanted to ask him about the twisted trees with the fabric, but Seoras had driven past it and had pulled off the road in front of the pathway to the castle. On foot they approached the raised stone walkway, and Kevin noticed that the castle was perched on the edge of a cliff that looked out across the sea.

"Impressive," Stark said. "Even without the protective spell it would be tough to breach."

"Tough?" Seoras snorted. "More like impossible, laddie."

The castle was beautiful. It was made of the same stone that filled the forest across the street. Kevin looked up and up as a cold gust caused a long flag to whip through the air. From the topmost turret of the castle it flew, illuminated by more torches. Painted on it was a massive black bull with the shimmering image of a goddess—or maybe a queen—within the body of the bull, stretched out across its back. When he pulled his gaze down to the pathway, Kevin felt a jolt of shock. Torches weren't all that lined the stone bridgeway to the castle. Between each pair of flaming torches were thick stakes that held decapitated heads.

Kevin couldn't stop staring at them. What skin remained looked like leather—the mouths gaped open—eyes were missing. He thought they were moving, maybe even grimacing at him, and then as he passed the first one he realized that it was just what was left of their long, stringy hair lifting with the breeze.

He spoke to Stark in a low voice. "That's some gross shit."

Stark had opened his mouth to agree, but Seoras, who walked before them, beat him to it. "Och, dinnae worry. They're just what's left of impertinent wains." The old Warrior glanced over his shoulder at them, his blue eyes sparkling with amusement. "Or maybe ye *should* worry." Chuckling to himself, Seoras picked up the pace so Kevin and Stark had to scramble to keep up with him.

Two Warriors, dressed like Seoras, stood silently before the huge, arched wooden doors. As the three of them approached, they nodded respectfully to Seoras before opening the doors to reveal a shockingly gorgeous interior. The floors were made of more of the silver white marble, and they gleamed from the blaze of chandeliers and candelabra that filled the enormous entry room. Kevin noted that the castle did have electricity, though there were still a lot of thick taper candles lit everywhere.

The stone walls were covered by incredible tapestries that depicted all sorts of different scenes—from peaceful landscapes with shaggy cows to amazingly realistic battles. They passed through the entryway, walked down a long hallway, and had come to an immense double stone stairway. Seoras halted and pointed up the stairs.

"If ye need to rest, or fix yer makeup, there leads to yer rooms."

"We don't have time for any of that," Stark said.

Seoras looked from Stark to Kevin, who shrugged nonchalantly and said, "I left my makeup at home."

To his surprise, Seoras barked a laugh before saying, "Aye, then, it's to the Queen and the Chamber of the Fianna Foil I'll be takin' ye." The old Warrior turned from the stairway and continued down the hall until he came to a huge set of arched double doors. Kevin thought they had to be at least twenty feet tall and a foot thick, and he watched eagerly, waiting for Seoras to use some of that old muscle to pry them open, but all the Warrior did was whisper, "Yur Guardian asks permission to enter, my Queen."

With the soft sound of a woman's sigh, the massive doors opened to a room so incredible Kevin had to remind his feet to move so that he didn't just stand there gawking.

Warriors, all fully armed and dressed in ancient kilts, stood around the perimeter of the large room, looking somber and ready to protect their queen. In front of a wall of windows there was a triple-tiered onyx dais that held a white marble throne on which Queen Sgiach sat. Seoras went to the dais, bowed low to his queen, and then took position standing beside the throne on her right.

Sgiach wore a long, formfitting dress made of golden velvet, belted low around her waist by the same plaid Seoras wore. A wicked-looking sword rested beside her, and the hilt of a dirk peeked from her plaid belt.

The throne on which she sat was like nothing he'd ever seen. Intricate knot carvings danced and swirled up it. Kevin thought he saw animals and people woven into the knots, but it was the floor-to-ceiling stained glass windows behind the queen that truly captured his attention. Though it was dark, the moon shining through the panels provided enough light for Kevin to make out the full-color scene that depicted Sgiach, hair streaming behind her, sword raised, holding a severed head in her hand as she stood on a cliff overlooking her island. Warriors kneeled to her and sprites hovered all around her as white-capped waves crashed in the background.

"So, young Warriors, I have considered your request. I agree. We must know if Neferet has used the sprites to open the portal between worlds, and I will ask them. But you must understand that if she has already passed through to that alternate world, I cannot condone the use of Old Magick to take you there."

At his side Kevin felt Stark stiffen, and before he could say something that might piss off the queen, Kevin spoke. "Okay, Your Majesty. Let's just take this one step at a time."

Stark sighed heavily but said, "Yes. We do appreciate your help."

The queen's raised brow said she believed Stark's frustrated sigh more than his appreciation, but she said nothing and stood. She walked to the edge of the top tier of the dais and took the dirk from her belt. Sgiach lifted her hand and with one swift motion, sliced through her palm.

The scent of her blood hit Kevin. It was rich and delicious—like Grandma's chocolate-chip lavender cookies and sunshine mixed together and sprinkled with honey. He wanted to rush to her, fall to his knees, and beg her to let him drink, just a drop. He glanced at Stark beside him. He, too, was staring wide-eyed at the queen's bleeding hand.

You cannot move, Kevin told himself. *Stay the hell right here. Don't slobber. Don't embarrass yourself and piss off this queen.*

Before Kevin lost the slipping grip he had on his self-control, Sgiach cupped her hand until the blood welled. She spoke words that Kevin didn't understand, but felt in every inch of his body, and finished by shifting to English and saying in a voice that was filled with command, "Come to me, oh mighty sprite of the earth!" Sgiach opened her hand and flicked her wrist. For a moment Kevin thought that her amazing blood was going to rain over Stark and him, but instead of spattering them or falling to the gleaming marble floor, the drops of scarlet hovered in a crescent moon around the queen.

There was a sound like the rustling of autumn leaves in a windstorm as something rushed into the chamber. It whirled like a minitornado, absorbing the droplets of sparkling blood before it came to a halt before Sgiach and materialized.

Kevin's eyes widened and his heart went cold as he recognized the earth sprite who had helped him before—and who had also led Aphrodite to her death. Without realizing it, Kevin started to move forward. He wasn't sure what he was going to do, only that his body was telling him he needed to fight—needed to make her pay for taking his love away from him.

Stark's strong hand closed on his wrist, holding him in place and giving Kevin time to get control of himself.

This isn't about me. This isn't about Aphrodite. This is about saving a world—maybe two, Kevin reminded himself.

His gaze met Stark's and Kevin nodded once, quickly. Stark released his wrist.

The humanoid sprite hovered several feet above the floor facing the dais with her back to Kevin and Stark. Her bark-colored skin was iridescent in the light of the chamber. She was naked, though vines twined around her nubile body, concealing much of it. Her hair was maidenhair fern and her voice was as compelling as Kevin remembered.

She nodded slightly. *"Queen Sgiach, you summon me and make blood sacrifice. What small task do you wish as payment for such a price?"*

The queen, too, dipped her head to the sprite before replying. "Oak, it has been some time since we have spoken, though I have felt your recent restlessness. Is all well with the fey folk?"

"Is that the question for which you spent your precious blood?"

Kevin gritted his teeth at her nonanswer, but kept his lips pressed firmly together.

"No. That was just an observation, and it seems you would rather not answer me, so I will dispense with small talk and get to the point. I want information. Has a High Priestess named Neferet called on your services, and if so, what did she want?"

Oak didn't answer. Instead she turned in a slow circle until she was facing Kevin and Stark. Her large dark eyes narrowed with recognition.

"Ah, Redbird Boy. I know you."

"And I know you too, Oak." Kevin managed to grind out the response through his anger.

She gestured at Stark. *"I see you have made friends with your enemy. Tell me, was that a difficult thing to do?"*

Before Kevin could say anything, the queen's voice cut through the chamber with an authority earned and owned by centuries of commanding Warriors.

"If you wish information from my guest, you will pay him a price—the same as you would demand from any vampyre who dared to question you."

Anger flashed across Oak's face, but she shrugged and continued her circle until she was, once again, facing the queen.

"I will leave your playthings alone. For now."

"Enough games, earth sprite! Answer me." As Sgiach spoke, the floor vibrated, as if the isle itself growled in anger with its queen.

Oak spoke quickly, her voice laced with contempt.

"High Priestess no more, Neferet did come to me—paid dearly, she did, to open a door no others can see."

Kevin's cheeks heated and his stomach clenched.

"Did this ex–High Priestess pass through the door?" Sgiach asked.

"I have answered you true—and now I shall leave as I have much, much to do."

The queen seemed to grow so that she filled the room. Her eyes blazed amber. There was movement behind her as Seoras drew his sword and stepped forward. Sgiach's voice echoed from the stone walls as wind filled the room, lifting the queen's long silver hair so that she looked eerily like the stained-glass battle scene behind her. "My blood is unique. It commands that you speak!"

Kevin and Stark staggered back a step as the power in Sgiach's voice battered them.

Oak cringed and also moved back, but when she spoke her voice was filled with spite. *"Of course she stepped through—what else would she do? Her payment was clear—the sacrifice dear. I could open the door for you, but Neferet's payment you must outdo."*

Sgiach said nothing for several breaths and Kevin realized she had locked her gaze onto the sprite. Finally, Oak's head turned to the side and she looked away, which is when the queen spoke.

"Remember that this isle obeys me—all that happens here, I see. Like autumn wind you bluster and blow. But I am queen. I command. Now leave my presence—go!"

And then, with a crack of thunder, the earth sprite disappeared.

Sgiach returned to her throne. As she reached Seoras, he took her bloodied hand and gently, intimately, drew it to his lips and licked the blood from it, closing the shallow wound instantly.

Stark swallowed hard, and Kevin understood completely. At that moment he would've given almost anything to take Seoras's place.

Sgiach didn't sit on her throne, instead Seoras returned to his place beside it as she paced back and forth across the dais in front of it.

"We're too late," Kevin said while the queen paced. "Neferet's in Zoey's world right now."

"It would appear so," said the agitated queen.

"But is that sprite telling you the truth?" Stark asked. "She, uh, seemed pretty—"

As Stark paused and searched for the right words, Seoras spoke sharply.

"Rude. Disrespectful. And unusually crabbit, even for that prickly fey."

"Your Majesty," Kevin said. "Is Oak always like that with you?"

Sgiach stopped pacing to meet his gaze. "She's the leader of the fey, and over the centuries has often been arrogant and difficult, but until today she has never shown such outright disrespect. She said she knew you. Was it Oak who granted you access to Old Magick?"

Kevin nodded. "It was. She was there every time I invoked Old Magick. And she was there when Zoey called on the sprites to restore the humanity to the red vampyres in this world."

"Ah, I see. The payment for something like that must have been immense."

Kevin forced himself to speak through the knot in his throat. "It was. It cost the life of Aphrodite, who was a Prophetess of Nyx and the vampyre I loved."

"I see. That must have been very exciting for Oak. No wonder she singled you out."

"Are all sprites so mean?" Stark asked.

"Not mean. Not usually. But they are bored, and they make their own rules. They do not choose Light or Darkness but walk somewhere in the middle—a place neither vampyres nor humans can tread safely."

"So, how do we get her to reopen the door to the Other World?" Stark asked. "Kevin and I have no choice now. We have to follow Neferet and warn Zoey and her House of Night."

"I have been on this isle more than five centuries," said Sgiach. "And I have never seen Oak like this. Before, I was reluctant to allow you to use Old Magick for the same reasons I have been guarding it and keeping it mostly confined to Skye all these many centuries." The queen ticked off the reasons on her fingers. "The sprites are capricious. Where they go, trouble often follows. The sprites always demand payment—a payment that gets higher and higher the more often you ask for their help. And, finally, Old Magick is addictive to anyone who does not have an affinity for it—and in the centuries of my long life, I have never known Nyx to gift any vampyre with such an affinity. As I said, the payment increases with each use, but ultimately, you pay with your sanity. Mortals were not meant to wield Old Magick. Respect it—yes. Appreciate it—yes. Even leave offerings to the sprites that embody it—yes. More than that and you are taking a chance with your mind and your spirit each time you make a request of it.

"But now, after what happened tonight, I can tell you that even if one of you had never called forth a sprite and made a request—"

"That would be me," Stark said, and then quickly added, "Your Majesty."

"Yes, not even you, Stark, could use Old Magick safely. Not for a request as big as being shuttled between worlds."

"But we have to!" Kevin said. "And not just for Zoey's world—for ours. Our Neferet will break that other Neferet out. She doesn't care if Old Magick is dangerous. She'll keep using it and upping the payment over and over without giving a shit. And when that Neferet is free she'll teach our Neferet how she became immortal, and then we'll pay—all of us. In *both* worlds."

"I understand that," said the queen. "Tell me, Kevin Redbird, which of the five elements are you most closely allied with?"

Kevin wanted to shout at her, *Why is that important right now!?* But one does not shout at a queen—especially not a queen who controls the entire island on which they stood. Instead, he answered quickly, hoping she would get to the point.

"All five, but especially spirit. Just like my sister."

"And you recently lost the love of your life."

It didn't sound like a question, but Kevin answered it anyway. "Yes. Aphrodite—Nyx's Prophetess."

"This question will seem too personal, rude even, but you must answer me honestly," said the queen.

Kevin glanced at Stark, who shrugged and looked just as confused as he felt. "Okay. I will. Promise," he said.

"You said Aphrodite was the love of your life. Did she love you equally in return or was it—and forgive me for being crass—more of a one-sided schoolboy crush."

41

Kevin's cheeks again flushed with heat. "She loved me! We Imprinted. I would've been her Oathbound Warrior."

Sgiach turned to Seoras. "It could work."

"Aye, it could."

Kevin and Stark spoke together. "What could work?"

"There is another way to move between worlds. It doesn't involve a door or the use of Old Magick. It involves the Land of the Dead—Nyx's Realm, which spans all worlds and all realms. If your connection to spirit and your dead love is strong enough, she could guide you there and back, though it will not be without a cost—and the cost is not cheap."

Excitement mixed with a healthy dose of nerves flooded Kevin, so much so that it took him a moment to gather the words to speak. When he did his voice was as raw as his heart.

"I don't know how strong my connection to spirit is, but I know one thing for sure. The love I have for Aphrodite is unbreakable, and I will pay *any* price to see her again."

5

Zoey

"I don't like it. There was something wrong about that fog." I shook my head and studied the screen that showed six different views of Neferet's grotto. None of them were clear. It was like looking into muddy water.

"Yeah, I don't like it either." Beside me, Stark leaned closer to the TV screen that displayed the camera feed at Woodward Park. It was the middle of the night, but we'd clicked from the live feed to the recording of earlier that day and were staring at nothing but fog. "That's why I called you guys here to review this with me. As soon as I saw all this fog, I realized it hadn't just been confined to the House of Night. I checked the weather, and when Travis Meyer did a whole segment on what he called 'the unusual fog phenomenon,' I knew something must be up. Something not good."

I sighed. Damien, Stevie Rae, and Aphrodite had joined me in the conference room, which we'd partially turned into a control center for the Woodward Park camera setup.

"Damien, can air tell you anything about the weird morning fog?" I asked.

Damien closed his eyes and whispered something to his element. His sandy brown hair lifted as air swirled around him. It didn't take long. He opened his eyes and shook his head. "No. Everything is normal with air. But that's not surprising. Fog is really a water thing. When did you say Shaylin is going to arrive?"

I sighed. "Not sure. There's tension between humans and vamps in San Francisco right now, and I agreed that she needs to stay at her House of Night until that's handled."

"Wait, what?" Aphrodite, who'd been lounging in a leather chair checking her Insta, looked up over the screen of her phone. "I thought the humans in San Francisco were cool."

"For the most part, they are," I said. "The problem is coming from a group of incels. They hate all vampyres."

"'Course they do. Incels hate all women, *especially* vamps because we're matriarchal," said Stevie Rae.

"Not to mention super attractive and *so* not interested in their pathetic asses." Aphrodite looked like she'd sucked a lemon. "Incels—ewww. Now I get it. You're right. Shaylin needs to stay there and handle that crap. And, again, ewww."

"I could call Shaylin. Maybe water would be able to tell her something, even if she is all the way on the west coast," I said.

"Why don't *you* try calling water?" Stark asked. "Maybe it will tell you something."

"Okay, I'll give it a shot." I closed my eyes and took several deep breaths, in and out, in and out. My affinity is for all five elements. That means I'm connected to air, fire, water, earth, and spirit. They'll answer my call, especially when I'm circling and doing spellwork or rituals, but I'm closest to spirit. As to the other four—I'm more attuned to them than a vamp with no affinity, but compared to, like, Damien and air, I'm definitely not as connected.

But I oriented myself quickly and turned to face west, the direction from which water was invoked. I thought about the ocean and whispered, "Water, please come to me." In a few breaths, I smelled the sea, which reminded me suddenly of the Isle of Skye and I made a mental note to email Sgiach, the queen of that isle and also my friend. Mentally, I shook myself, refocusing, and said, "Water, can you tell me anything about this morning's fog, please?"

The scent of salt and sand increased, so that when I closed my eyes I could easily imagine standing beside Sgiach on the cliff where her castle perched overlooking the ocean. I concentrated and got a vague feeling of unease, but nothing specific—no images and definitely no answers.

I opened my eyes. "Thank you, water. You may go now."

"Anything?" Stark asked.

"Nothing specific. The element felt uneasy, but that's all I got. I have zero clue why. I'm just not connected to it strongly enough."

"Z, I have an idea," said Stevie Rae. "I know she's inexperienced and all, but Kacie does have an affinity for water."

"As well as fire," added Damien.

"Speaking of fire, isn't Shaunee on her way here?" asked Aphrodite.

"She will be soon," I said. "She would've been here today, but she called and told me one of her fledglings just rejected the Change and she needed to be there for the rest of the students. She should get here tomorrow. I think."

"Back to what I was sayin'," said Stevie Rae. "Kacie's young and all, but her connection to water is strong. I'll bet it would tell her if something wonky is up."

"I vote for Ice Cream Shoes," said Aphrodite.

Stark and I shared a look. He shrugged, which is pretty much how I felt about it too. Technically, I was too young to be a High Priestess in charge of an entire House of Night, as well as being head of the new North American High Council, but that hadn't stopped me—or my friends—from standing up to Neferet's evil and taking on leadership positions.

"Good idea, Stevie Rae," I said. "Go get Ice Cream Shoes."

As Stevie Rae hurried from the conference room, Aphrodite muttered, "I knew that nickname would catch on."

I rolled my eyes at Aphrodite and returned my attention to the five foggy images. I pointed at one of the recordings. "Are those humans?"

"Shit! I didn't watch this far before I called you guys here. I can't tell whether they're fledglings or not."

"Damien," I said. "When we're done here, would you please pass the word to the professors to check in with their students to be sure no blue fledglings were out messing around just after dawn?"

Aphrodite straightened in her chair and stared at the screen with me. "Those aren't fledglings. I mean, kids can be stupid, but even teenagers know better than to hang out by Neferet's tomb."

Stark's lips curved up and his eyes glinted mischievously. "Aren't you a teenager?"

"Don't be stupid, Bow Boy. I'm twenty-one. Totally adult." She bumped him with her shoulder. "Move over. I wanta see."

Stark had slowed the feed so that we could study it more closely, and we watched the recording creep forward in time as five hooded figures approached the wall that surrounded the grotto. It was too foggy to see anything very well, but we could tell that they were carrying offerings.

Aphrodite snorted with disgust. "Oh, for shit's sake, are they actually bringing offerings to that crazy bitch's tomb?"

"Looks like it," I said, squinting at the screen.

"They're wearing cloaks that correspond to the elements," Damien observed.

"Hell!" I said. "We'll need to be sure they aren't fledglings."

Aphrodite's well-manicured finger pointed at the foggy group. "What are they looking at?"

As a group, the five had turned to their right after placing their candles and whatever else they'd been carrying in niches in the wall. They all froze, staring into the fog, before they began walking forward. Then it was like the fog swallowed them.

"What the hell?" Stark said.

"Can you rewind that?" Damien asked.

"Yeah, no problem." Stark picked up a remote and pressed the rewind button.

"Okay, stop there." Damien leaned forward studying the screen. "Now let it play, but slowly, and when I tell you to stop—pause it."

"Will do," said Stark.

We all watched the hooded figures walk forward as one and place their offerings on the wall. They waited a moment, and as they turned, in obvious response to something to their right, Damien said, "Stop!"

Stark hit pause, and I sucked in a breath. "What is that on that person's face?"

Aphrodite said, "*Her* face. They're women. Look at how the cloaks cling to their bodies as they turn. Those are definitely boobs—five sets of them."

I nodded. "Good catch, Aphrodite. But what's that on *her* face?"

One of cameras, the one farthest to the right and, like the others, situated in the limbs of the oaks that stood sentinel above the tomb, had just caught the face of the woman in the purple cloak. For a second I thought she was just one of those girls who liked to put on so much mascara and eyeliner that she looked raccoonish, but as I studied the grainy, indistinct picture I realized it was much more than that.

The tip of Damien's finger touched the screen. "She's painted a triple moon on her forehead. And this," he traced the girl's face, "is like a black mask, though I think it's also painted on. Is there any way to magnify this?"

Aphrodite scoffed. "Like we're the FBI?"

"Actually, I could get one of the computer fledglings on it," said Stark.

"Yeah, the new budget I approved at the end of last year had *a lot* of computer stuff on it."

"I'll take a screenshot and get it to them," said Stark.

Aphrodite plopped down in a chair and shook back her long blonde hair. "It's still hard for me to believe humans have such damn short memories. A year ago Neferet *ate* a couple hundred of them. What didn't they get about that? Do they think she's having a restful little vacay walled up in that grotto and will emerge to hold hands with them and have a fucking tea party?"

Kacie snorted as she entered the room. "Humans are morons."

We turned to see that Stevie Rae had returned with Kacie. I hadn't known the kid long—actually, I'd just been introduced to her a week before. That same day she'd rejected the Change and died in a pool full of blood, chlorine, and water during the first human-fledgling swim meet in House of Night history. But she'd kinda, sorta accidentally been granted a second chance by Aphrodite and resurrected as a fully Changed red vampyre with affinities for water and fire. Now, she was standing just inside the room with her hands on her curvy waist, and I was struck again by how pretty she was—and by the unique red tattoo that framed her face with waves that morphed into flames. Today she was wearing adorable overalls over a short little pullover made of the Tulsa House of Night's black, purple, and dark green plaid, which looked great against her brown skin.

Kacie took her hands from her waist and shrugged. "No offense. I know some of you have human friends. But, seriously, all the humans I know are total morons."

"Less commentary, Ice Cream Shoes, and more information," said Aphrodite. "Though I must say I tend to agree with you about the moronic nature of humans." She pointed at the still-shot of the face-painted human on the screen. "Let me present exhibit one."

"What's that in the fog?" Kacie asked, coming forward to stand between Aphrodite and me.

I shifted my weight and sighed. "Well, I'm afraid it's a moronic human. But that's not the point. Or at least not why Stevie Rae brought you here. See all that fog?"

"Yeah. Where is that?"

"Woodward Park—this mornin'," said Stevie Rae, moving up so that she stood near Kacie.

"Here? In Tulsa?"

"Yeah," I said.

"That's weird. I didn't think you guys got fog here like we did in Chicago. Plus, it's really the wrong time of year for it. Most Chicago fog is in the spring or fall."

"We get fog, but not a lot," Damien said as he peered over my shoulder at the screen. "Especially not in the middle of winter when the temperature has been the same for days and days."

"How long did it last?" Kacie kept staring at the picture. "And what's wrong with that woman's face?"

"Yeah," Stevie Rae asked. "What's goin' on with her makeup? She kinda looks like the Lone Ranger."

"The who?" Aphrodite uncrossed and crossed her legs.

"It's from an old TV show. He wore a mask. My mama and me used to watch reruns when I was little. I really only remember the mask and his horse."

"Which has nothing to do with the fog," said Damien. "Kacie, we don't know what's going on with those humans, but that really isn't important right now."

"Damien's right—as always." I grinned at him. I'll always love how studious Damien is—how he keeps learning and growing. "What's important is the weird fog and why it covered this city this morning. It could be a weather fluke, but we need to be sure. Could you ask water about it?"

Kacie's gaze went from the screen to me. Her big, dark eyes looked surprised and maybe even a little frightened.

"Hey," I said gently. "It's okay if you're not ready or if it's too hard. We get it, and no one will be mad at you."

"It's not that. I'll definitely try, but is water gonna actually *talk* to me?"

Aphrodite covered a laugh with a cough, and I talked over her, shooting her an exasperated look. "No, at least not with words."

Stevie Rae, whose affinity was earth, took over for me. "You'll get a feelin' from your element. You should be able to tell if it's upset, and especially if it's been messed with recently. It may even give you an image of somethin'. Like, remember when all those trees just outside the wall that surrounds the Chicago House of Night started dyin' and we couldn't figure out why?"

Kacie nodded.

"Well, I checked in with earth and knew right away someone was poisonin' 'em—shooting some crap into their roots that was killin' 'em. I couldn't see who it was, but I knew it was a human doin' it and not a disease that was makin' 'em die."

"Yeah, and then you had the Sons of Erebus keep watch and you caught that guy."

"Right! Earth didn't *say* anything to me, but it gave me an image of roots bein' flooded with poison and a feelin' that it was due to human intervention."

"Exactly," I said. "That's what you need to ask water to do. Just ground yourself, call water, and then ask it if the fog this morning was natural or unnatural. Then open yourself to the answer."

"Okie dokie. I'll try."

Before I could even point her to the west, Kacie closed her eyes tightly. Her forehead furrowed and she said, "Water, could ya please come here?"

Instantly, the room was awash with ocean scents—not just salt and sand, but the earthy twang of sea grass and coconut-scented suntan lotion.

Eyes still closed, Kacie said, "Cool! Grand Cayman! Okay, now, water, go back to this morning, especially around a park called Woodward—here in Tulsa, not on Cayman. There was lots of fog. What's up with that? Weird weather, or just plain weird?"

We all stared at Kacie as she gasped and staggered a little—and suddenly the water scents disappeared, leaving the newly Changed vampyre looking pale and sick.

"Here, sit down." I shooed Aphrodite out of the closest chair and guided Kacie into it.

"I'll get her some water," Damien said, heading to a refreshment counter in the corner of the room.

"Make it blood," I said, realizing just how bad Kacie looked.

"Got it!"

As Damien poured blood from the pitcher kept in the fridge and popped it in the microwave to heat, Stevie Rae and I crouched down beside Kacie. She trembled as she rested her head in her hands.

"Hey, it's okay. Close your eyes again and breathe with me— in to a count of four, and then out to four." She nodded, and we breathed together until Damien handed me a warm mug of blood and then pulled out a chair and sat beside Aphrodite. "Okay." I touched her arm and she opened her eyes. "Drink this. Slowly."

I helped guide the mug to her lips, but as soon as she began gulping the blood, her color returned and her hands stopped shaking. She drained the mug and handed it back to me.

"Thanks. That's better. It's really good too. I mean—gross that blood tastes so good, but it's true."

"Yeah, I remember feeling like that," I smiled at her. "Can you tell me what water revealed to you?"

"Sure, but it was weird, and it also made my stomach hurt. It was like I almost *became* water for a second."

"That means you already have an incredibly strong connection to that element," Damien said. "It took me almost a year to get that sensation."

"And that's good?" She glanced up at Damien, looking about twelve years old.

"Oh, honey, it's wonderful!" Damien assured her. "You'll learn to ground yourself better so you don't become disoriented and too immersed in your element—but it is truly a good thing."

"Okay, well, I'm glad. It was cool, but also scary."

"Kacie, what did water show you?" Stevie Rae prompted, touching her shoulder gently.

"Well, water gave me a super strong feeling about the fog. I can tell you for sure that what happened this morning was *not* natural. Water was told to create fog—actually, it wasn't just told. It's more like it was forced to make the city foggy, and especially Woodward Park. It felt like that first spell we all learn as new fledglings—the conceal spell. Only this one was on steroids."

"Kacie, do you have any idea about who or what cast this spell?" asked Stevie Rae.

"Yep. It was a vampyre. Absolutely zero doubt about it. I don't know who. I couldn't see anything. I could only feel, and then I started to get sick and I lost the connection. But I promise you it was a powerful vampyre and this morning she was in Woodward Park and totally did not want to be seen."

"She?" My stomach clenched. "And she was strong—like a priestess?"

Stark had just returned from taking the screenshot to our computer kids, so Kacie hesitated before responding and when she did, she sounded as frustrated as I felt. "No. I can't tell for sure. I'm really sorry. There were just too many sensations, and water filled everything, so concentrating was crazy. Also, I literally couldn't see whoever cast the spell. It was so strong that not even my element let me see."

I chewed the inside of my cheek. "That's okay. You don't have anything to apologize for. Because of you we know the fog was part of a spell cast by a powerful vampyre who doesn't want to be seen. That's important."

"Yeah, but now what do we do with that information?" asked Aphrodite.

"First, we stop worrying about humans who, for whatever bizarre reason, like to dress up like its Halloween and light candles for Neferet," I said. "As annoying as that is, it isn't dangerous."

"On the flip side, a powerful vampyre who could be in league with Neferet *is* dangerous," said Stark as he took a seat across the table from us.

"Let's not go there automatically," I said. "We need to remember that our new way of doing things—mixing fledglings with human students and opening our campuses to humans in general—has not been well received anywhere else in the world. The Vampyre High Council doesn't have power over us anymore. We know that's pissed them off."

Damien nodded in agreement. "So, it could just be one of the European High Council Members spying on us—and they started by checking out Neferet's prison."

"It makes sense that they would want to see for themselves that we have it handled," Stark agreed.

"Those fossils have always underestimated us because we're young. Except for Thanatos, that is." Aphrodite glanced up at the ceiling and waved her hand about as if Nyx's realm was above us somewhere (which, I suppose it might actually be), and said, "May she be having lots of fun frolicking in Nyx's Grove or whatever."

"So, really, what we need to be concerned about right now is keeping *vampyres* away from Neferet's tomb," I said.

Kacie started to raise her hand, then she frowned at it like it had somehow betrayed her, put it back in her lap, and cleared her throat.

"You don't have to raise your hand to speak," I said gently. "You're a fully Changed vampyre now and no longer a fledgling."

Kacie let out a relieved sigh. "Good. I have an idea."

"Let's hear it, Ice Cream Shoes," Aphrodite said.

"If the issue is a nosy vampyre, why don't you just put a spell around the grotto that keeps vamps out? That way if it is some busybody from the old High Council, she'll have to come here and check in with our High Priestess—like she's supposed to—if she wants answers. And if it's just a creeper vamp, someone stupid enough to think breaking Neferet out of there is a good idea, it'll keep that moron from doing anything annoying."

We all stared at Kacie. "How old are you?" I asked.

"Sixteen—and a half."

"I knew she was smart as well as a smart-ass," said Aphrodite.

"She was *my* fledgling," Stevie Rae reminded us smugly.

"That's a really good idea," I said. "A spell to ward off vampyres is way easier than a protective spell."

Stark met my gaze, looking worried. "And you don't have to tie yourself to it like Thanatos did to her protective spell?"

I shook my head. "Nope. Well, not if I have my circle to help me, with a special boost from earth." I elbowed my bestie.

Stevie Rae grinned. "Earth always has your back, Z."

"This sounds good," said Aphrodite. "But I'm getting a very strong feeling that we can't wait for Shaylin and Shaunee to meander here to set the spell in place. On the outside chance it's something more dangerous—like *you know who* from *you know where*, we need that vamp repellent up and working. Now."

Stevie Rae spoke right up. "Kacie can help. Can't ya?"

"Well, sure. If you tell me what I need to do," said the newly Changed red vampyre.

Aphrodite fluttered her fingers at Kacie. "Ice Cream Shoes, do you think you can call water into a circle and boost me if I stand in for Shaunee as fire?"

The girl tucked her long, thick hair behind her ears and shrugged. "I think so, but I've never actually done it."

Stevie Rae squeezed Kacie's shoulder. "We'll all be there with you. We'll help you."

"The spell isn't difficult," I said. "It's really more about spirit and earth than anything, but I do need a circle to cast it."

"I'll try."

I sat beside her and spoke earnestly. "How are you feeling? Do you think you're up to calling in water and fire to a circle tonight?"

"Well, yeah. But it'd help if I could have another big glass of blood." She grimaced, and I had to squelch the urge to laugh. I totally remembered what it was like to be squeed out by blood, even as I was craving it.

"Okay, then. Stevie Rae, would you take Kacie to the teachers' dining hall and fill her up with fresh blood. I don't think we should waste any more time. Let's do this. Tonight."

"Totally, Z. Where do you want to meet?"

I looked to my Warrior. "What do you think?"

"That I'm going with you," Stark said. "Darius and Rephaim will want to come as well, even though there are six Sons of Erebus Warriors already on guard at the park."

"Sounds good to me. We don't know for sure what we're dealing with, and the more Warriors the better," I said. "So, let's meet in the parking lot in thirty minutes. Be sure you each bring your element's candle. I'll grab spirit and some matches."

"Sounds good," said Steve Rae. "Let's go fill you up with blood, Miss Ice Cream Shoes."

As Kacie followed Stevie Rae from the room, I heard her say, "Am I really stuck with that nickname?"

Stevie Rae's answer floated back through the closing door. "Yepper, but it's better than being called Hag from Hell. Ask Aphrodite if you don't believe me."

Aphrodite surprised me by laughing softly and saying, "Aww, Hag from Hell! That brings back so many memories. Good times!"

I rolled my eyes at her and then turned to Damien. "Do you want to call Jack and have him there too?"

Without hesitation Damien shook his head emphatically. "Absolutely not. And now that the kid's gone we need to acknowledge that this could truly be Other Neferet—and be prepared for it."

Stark stood and brushed a hand through his hair. "Well, I'm not worried about defeating Other Neferet. At least *she's* mortal."

Damien nodded. "True, but I am worried about what seeing

her would do to Jack. I'm going to text him and tell him that I'm taking care of some business for you and ask him to stay at the depot and choose the flower arrangements for opening night."

"Good idea," I said.

"Something else we need to consider," said Aphrodite. "It sounds bad. Really bad, but my last vision was fucking awful. So, before you cast a spell keeping vampyres from Neferet's tomb, I think you need to check to be sure Neferet's still in there."

My stomach clenched, and at the same time Damien and I said, "Ah, hell."

6

Other Kevin

"Wait, what?" Stark looked pale as he stared at Queen Sgiach.

Kevin didn't say anything. Not because he wasn't shocked, but because, since he'd realized he was going to see his Aphrodite again, he couldn't seem to make words come out of his mouth.

"Are ye deaf?" Seoras scoffed. "Or just *glaikit*?"

Stark shook his head. "You know damn well I'm not deaf, and *glaikit* is one word I never heard my grandpa say, but my guess is it isn't flattering. So, no. I'm neither. I'm just making sure I understand exactly what this trip is going to cost us."

"I don't mind the boys questioning me," the queen told her Warrior. "They are the ones paying the price. They should fully understand what they're agreeing to." She turned from Seoras to face Stark and Kevin. "Hear me clearly, young vampyres. Kevin, as you have an affinity for spirit it will be your responsibility to call to your newly dead love, but spirit cannot enter Nyx's Realm easily unless it is freed by death, so you will need to mimic death through blood sacrifice. To call spirit and have it guide you to Nyx's Otherworld will be difficult and take extreme focus, and if you also are giving a blood sacrifice, you will be weak and distracted."

"That's where I come in," Stark said grimly.

"Indeed, it is. While Kevin is focusing on spirit, you will provide the sacrifice, and because you're mimicking death, it must be more than a simple bloodletting. It must be permanent."

Kevin finally found his voice. "You mean he's going to be hurt permanently? Like he has to cut off an arm or a leg?"

"Shit!" Stark said under his breath.

"That would work, but it wouldn't be a good idea for a Warrior to lose a limb, especially if he is heading into battle with a vampyre High Priestess gone rogue," said Sgiach. "Something that would permanently scar him should suffice."

"Yeah, that's what I thought I heard the first time," muttered Stark.

Kevin turned to him. "I'll go alone. It's okay. I've been over there before. I'll do what I need to do and get back."

"But you will still need a blood sacrifice," said the queen.

Kevin nodded. "I know. I think I can do both—guide spirit and make the sacrifice. Plus, I believe once Aphrodite hears me she'll come and help me."

"No," Stark said. "I'll do it."

"Guilt willnae help you, laddie," said Seoras. "It'll only get in yer way."

"It's not about my guilt," Stark protested. "It's about taking responsibility for my mistake and doing whatever I can to fix it. I said I'll do it and I will."

"But there's more to it, isn't there?" Kevin asked. "You said moving through the Otherworld to another realm isn't like using Old Magick, but there's still a cost. I have a feeling that's more than just scarring Stark and taking some of his blood."

"You are correct," said the queen. "Only the dead move freely through the Goddess's realm. When the living enter, the cost is linked to death. Every day you spend in that alternative version of our world will take a day from your life."

A chill rushed through Kevin's body with the quickened beating of his heart, and he heard Stark suck in a breath.

"Buck up, laddies," said Seoras. "Yer young. Vampyres are long-lived. What is a day or two from hundreds o' years?"

"Do *you* want to give away days from *your* life?" Stark said.

Seoras's gaze found Sgiach and he smiled. Kevin was shocked at how it softened his lined face. "That depends on what I'd be givin' it for. Be it my queen—there isnae anything I wouldnae give for her."

Sgiach reached up and rested her hand on his cheek. "Nor I you, *mo ghaol*."

"You don't have to go," Kevin repeated to Stark. "I seriously think I can do it by myself."

"No, damnit, I'm going too!" Stark growled the words. Kevin had to hide a smile because, for a moment, the Warrior sounded way too much like Seoras.

"Well, I'm definitely in. So, let's do this thing. No telling what kinda shit-pot Neferet has already stirred over there." Kevin paused as a thought came to him. "Your Majesty, may I ask you a question?"

She nodded benevolently.

"My sister told me that she was able to imprison her Neferet through the sacrifice of an immortal—a strange creature called a Vessel. He willingly gave his life to seal Neferet into a grotto. I really don't know the details, but I was wondering, do you have any idea how, or even if, a seal like that could be broken?"

As Sgiach considered her answer, her fingers restlessly stroked the hilt of the sword that rested against her throne. Her fingernails were long and rounded but completely bare of polish. Her hands were strong and graceful—a perfect reflection of the queen—and he felt a rush to serve her and realized that feeling, that desire to stand for and defend a vampyre High Priestess, or in this case a queen, must have been what kept Stark from acting against Neferet for so long.

Sgiach's voice interrupted his inner musings. "It would be difficult to break such a seal, but not impossible. I could be wrong, especially as I do not know the details, but it seems to me that the key to the seal is not the immortality of the creature who made the sacrifice, but his willingness to make it. Thus, to break it there would need to be an equally willing sacrifice made."

"You mean by another immortal?" Stark asked.

"Not necessarily. You're not trying to kill an immortal. That life was already willingly given. I doubt if one person's sacrifice could break a seal like that, but should several people give themselves willingly—be they vampyres or even humans—and there were enough power behind that sacrifice, well, the seal could break."

"Thank you. I'll let Zoey know." He looked at Stark. "Are you ready?"

"As I'll ever be."

"Okay, tell us what we need to do."

"Very well, then. Let your journey begin." Sgiach lifted her hand and commanded, "Raise the Seol ne Gigh."

There was a sound like wind rushing through trees accompanied by strange, mechanical clicking. The floor directly in front of the dais, just a couple feet away from where Kevin and Stark stood, slid open, and a rust-colored hunk of stone, big enough that a person could lay on it, rose from beneath the floor. The boulder was covered with knotwork that was beautiful, though somehow disturbing. The more Kevin stared at it, the more restless he felt— like someone was staring back at him, and that someone was within the rock. Or maybe it was the rock itself doing the staring.

On either side of the floor surrounding the huge stone were curved grooves. Their hornlike shape instantly brought to mind the massive black bull that decorated the flag over the castle. As Kevin continued to study the rock he realized that it wasn't rust colored at all. It was more of the island's silver-veined white marble, but it had been permanently stained by—

"Blood," Stark said.

"Yes," said the queen, rising to stand before the ancient stone. "This is the Seol ne Gigh, or Seat of the Soul. For longer than I have reigned it has been a place of sacrifice and worship—and a conduit to pure Light and Darkness. Through it you can call the bulls, the embodiment of good and evil."

"Which is which, and how do we call them?" asked Kevin.

"Well, ye dinnae want to be callin' the White Bull unless yer willin' to traffic with Darkness," said Seoras.

"And that would require an entirely different type of sacrifice," added Sgiach. "You will call the Black Bull—the embodiment of Light. Should your spirit and your love be strong enough," she nodded to Kevin. "And your sacrifice accepted," she turned her gaze to Stark. "Well, then he will take you to the Realm of the Goddess where your guide will meet you and show you through the grove to the Other World you seek—if she answers your call."

"My spirit will be strong enough because I know my love is, and Aphrodite will answer my call," Kevin said firmly.

"And I'll bleed," said Stark. Then he quickly added, "Willingly. My sacrifice will be strong because I have a lot to make up for."

"Uh, hang on," Kevin said. "How do we get back?"

"If the Black Bull accepts your sacrifice and your spirit is strong enough to enter the Goddess's Realm, it will earn you a return trip," said Sgiach. "When your business in your sister's world is complete, Stark will need to cut himself and allow his blood to flow freely on the ground. Then Kevin will summon spirit and ask it to call your lost love. She will return both of you to Nyx's Grove and, once again, guide you through. Then you simply remember your tie to your own world and follow it home."

"What if we get stuck? Either over in Z's world or in Nyx's Realm?" Kevin asked.

Sgiach explained. "If you remain in your sister's world your days will eventually run out. Your life will be half lived. You will die. And as the living do not belong in Nyx's Realm, if you remain there, you will be unable to eat or drink and you will waste away until you die."

"Okay, so, we need to get over there, warn Zoey, and then return here," said Stark.

Kevin said nothing.

Sgiach's brows rose expectantly as she studied him, but when he remained silent she sighed and gestured to the Seol ne Gigh. "All right then, come to the stone."

Kevin began to walk forward and then hesitated. "Can we take our backpacks?"

"You could take a car with you, should you drive it into this room and your sacrifice be accepted," said Sgiach.

Stark and Kevin exchanged looks, hefted their backpacks, and approached the stone.

"Stark must lie on yon stone. Young Warrior Kevin, sit beside him," Seoras instructed as he walked to the head of the huge rock.

Kevin cracked his knuckles and did as he was told, perching on the side of the stone as Stark laid down across it.

"Now, two things need to happen at once," said Sgiach. "Kevin, you must call spirit to you as Seoras cuts Stark. Concentrate on your love—that is of the utmost importance. Do not let any negative thoughts enter your mind. You are calling the Black Bull, the embodiment of Light and love and all that is good—and goodness does not flourish where there are dark thoughts."

Kevin nodded. "I understand. I can do that."

"Excellent. Then, if spirit comes and Stark's sacrifice is great enough, the bull will accept it and grant you passage to Nyx's Realm."

"How will we know if we've done everything right?" Stark asked.

"It willnae be hard to know. A great bull, black as the deepest depths of yon ocean, will rise," said Seoras as he unsheathed the dirk at his waist. "Roll up yer sleeve, laddie."

Stark rolled up the sleeve of his shirt and then pressed his hands so tightly against the stone that his knuckles went white.

"Now, I'll cut yer arm—here, just below the shoulder." Seoras touched the tip of the razor-edged knife to Stark's right shoulder.

"Okay. Got it. Um, is it normal that this rock is warm and … *pulsing?*"

There was a smile in the queen's voice when she told Seoras, "So, my love, if you had any doubt left that certainly clears it up."

"What does that mean?" Kevin asked.

"It means he's definitely a MacUallis. Only one of that blood can feel the living Seat of the Soul."

Stark's lips quirked up in a crooked grin that looked pretty damn cocky for a guy who was ready to be carved up by an ancient vampyre Warrior. "I like that I'm part of your clan, my queen."

Seoras smacked Stark's shoulder with the flat edge of the dirk. "Naw wain, yer not of the queen's clan. I'm the MacUallis Chieftain. You belong to me."

Stark swallowed. "Oh. Shit."

"Aye," agreed Seoras. "Now stop yer blathering and let me concentrate. I have to be carvin' into yer flesh—and need to see what I'm doin'."

And then the old Warrior pressed the tip of the dirk to the top of Stark's bicep, just below his shoulder, and closed his eyes.

"Hey, uh, Chieftain. I thought you said you needed to see to cut me," Stark whispered.

Seoras seemed not to hear, but the queen answered for him. "He's looking with his third eye, Stark. Ready yourself. When it begins my Warrior will cut you fast and deep. You must not move. Your blood will fill the grooves, and that will call the bull." She looked at Kevin. "When he makes his first cut, you must begin to summon spirit."

"Do you have a purple candle I can light?"

"You sit on the Seat of the Soul. You need no candle to call spirit," she told him. "Ready yourself. It begins."

With his eyes closed, Seoras cut into Stark's arm. Stark grunted at the first slash but didn't move and didn't make another sound. Except for his ragged breathing, he might have been napping.

Kevin only watched for an instant, but that instant was astounding. Seoras's hand moved so quickly it blurred. It seemed to Kevin that the Warrior was creating a pattern of blood and flesh, but he couldn't tell what it was, and he realized he had no time to decipher it. He, too, closed his eyes.

Kevin breathed deeply, centering himself as he called aloud. "Spirit, I ask that you come to me. I need you today like I've never needed you before."

The element to which he was most firmly connected responded immediately. Kevin felt it swirl around him, rustling his hair and playing against his skin. He smiled as it filled him with a sense of rightness that was better than power—it filled him with joy. Kevin followed that joy to his heart, which opened, allowing memories of Aphrodite to rush unhindered through his veins and into his mind.

He remembered Aphrodite's laugh and how it changed as she fell in love with him and became more open—more real. He thought about her eyes and how they were much more than beautiful—they reflected her soul and the wondrous wealth of love that had waited there, dormant, until she'd allowed him to release it.

Kevin thought about how it had felt to hold her in his arms. She had been gorgeous and sexy—more beautiful than any woman he'd ever known—but the sensation that he remembered most wasn't about lust or need. What he remembered was that holding Aphrodite had felt like coming home.

The scent of Stark's blood hit him then—thick and warm. Kevin ignored it and imagined that he was holding out his hand, and that Aphrodite was taking it, one last time, and twining her fingers with his and smiling up at him with that expression on her beautiful face that told him she trusted him, she believed in him, *she loved him.*

A roar filled the room and Kevin's eyes opened—only he wasn't in the queen's throne room anymore. He and Stark, who was sitting beside him, his right arm completely scarlet with blood that poured down the side of his body with every beat of his heart, were in total darkness. There was no stone—they sat on nothing. They were nowhere.

Panic pecked at Kevin's mind, but Stark met his gaze and said, "Don't lose it. Hold onto spirit. Whatever you're doing is working!"

Kevin nodded shakily and concentrated. "Spirit, stay with me. Help me find her again. Help me call Aphrodite."

The moment he said her name the world changed. From beneath them something enormous and dark surged up, lifting them with it. It was warm and solid, and the instant it touched him, Kevin's panic disappeared.

"It's him." Stark's voice was filled with the same wonder Kevin felt. "We're riding the Black Bull."

And they were. From the inky darkness a shape formed before them—twin horns, impossibly big and sharp, framed a massive head. Kevin could see one of the beast's eyes, and as he gazed into it joy crested over him, filling him so fully that he had to shout with happiness.

Kevin's jubilant cry echoed Stark's victory shout as the beast carried them up and up and up until finally Kevin began to see a wall of green. There was an explosion of light, and then he and Stark were tumbling from the bull's back, landing on a hard-packed patch of ground. As soon as Kevin got to his feet, he whirled around, hoping to get a glimpse of the incredible creature that had granted them passage. All he saw was the bull's velvet hip, wide as the back of a whale. Within his mind a deep, compassionate voice said, *Remember to hold on to love, young Kevin. Love, always love …* And then he was gone, and Kevin was staring at nothing.

Stark nudged his back. "Um, Kev …"

Kevin turned and his breath rushed from his body. Before them was an unending grove. It reminded Kevin of the forest across from Sgiach's castle. In the very front of the wall of trees there was a special tree, like the one he'd glimpsed on Skye, two trees irrevocably entwined. From their verdant branches dangled hundreds, maybe thousands of strips of cloth that shimmered magickally in the soft, silver moonlight.

And then Kevin could think no more of bulls or trees or the magick of the Goddess's realm because walking toward him, weaving her way through the grove, was Aphrodite.

7

Zoey

I pressed my hands against the cold stone wall of the grotto and felt it—a terrible sense of rage and restlessness. I quickly pulled my palms away and turned to Stevie Rae, who stood beside me. Wiping my hand on my jeans to rid myself of the awful sensation, I said, "She's still in there. No doubt about it."

"Is it real gross?" Stevie Rae whispered.

"Yeah, and she's pissed," I said. "Time has definitely not mellowed her."

"At least one positive is that she's still in there," said Stark. He joined my circle and me after he positioned the Sons of Erebus Warriors so that half of them were standing above Neferet's grotto, and the others—along with Darius and Rephaim—were spaced in a crescent moon shape on the wide lawn in front of the wall.

Aphrodite hurried up from the parking lot with Kacie following close behind her like a very cute little puppy—if puppies could invoke water and fire. "All right, partial Nerd Herd, let's get this spell cast. Now."

"What's up?" I asked, not liking the nervous way she kept glancing at the road.

"I don't know, but I have a finger-down-my-spine crawly feeling and Ice Cream Shoes has been in my pocket since we got here."

Kacie peered around nervously. "It feels wrong here. Like when you're downtown late and have to park in a really empty, really dark underground garage."

Aphrodite brushed back her hair and nodded. "That's a pretty accurate description. It could be because of batshit crazy over there." She pointed at the wall entombing Neferet behind me. "Or it could be because another creepy vamp is lurking around, but either way, I don't like it."

Damien joined us, carrying the bag that held our candles and spellwork implements. "And either way, what we're doing will help. Humans can hang around here all day and pretend like Neferet is their next messiah. What we really don't need is what Zoey described happening in that other world—hate-filled vampyres looking to support Neferet because they crave power."

My ponytail dusted my back as I hiked my shoulders. "Well, in this case I think it's more like old vampyres who are being super nosy, but I hear ya," I said. "And once this spell is cast, if the European High Council wants information about Neferet, or about our House of Night, they'll have to come to me to get it."

Stevie Rae asked, "Z, have you thought about givin' 'em a call? I mean, it's not like we're hidin' anything. We're just including humans 'cause, you know, when you actually get to know someone who's different than you, that's when you realize we're all a lot more alike than not."

"That's a good idea, Stevie Rae. I doubt that they'll admit if they did send someone over here to spy, but I'll call and issue an invite for them to come for Imbolc next month. If the weather cooperates, I thought we'd hold a community gathering on campus and invite humans too."

Damien spoke as he began pulling prayer candles in the five elemental colors from his bag. "You should give Sister Angela a call."

"I'll bet Street Cats would come—and bring kitties too," said Stevie Rae.

Kacie sighed so loudly we all looked at her.

"Sorry. I just wish a cat would choose me."

"Hey, give it time. Z and I still share Nala. I'll bet Nal wouldn't mind it if you gave her some lovins."

I grinned at Stevie Rae. "Better warn Ice Cream Shoes about that face-sneezing thing she does."

My bestie gave me an exaggerated wink and said, "Let's not tell her."

"Here," Damien handed me a purple candle. "I don't mean to be bossy, but less talk and more spell casting is in order."

"Right," I said. "Okay, let's take our places."

Stark kissed me quickly. "I'll be just outside the circle with Darius and Rephaim."

"Thanks." He started to turn away and I said, "Hey!" He looked over his shoulder at me. "I love you."

He grinned that cocky, one-sided smile I adored. "I know."

"Bow Boy's ego is even bigger than his—" Aphrodite began, but I quickly talked over her.

"Kacie, do you have any questions before we start?"

She was holding her blue candle and looking a lot younger than she had when she'd invoked the aid of water earlier. "Um, I don't think so. Stevie Rae told me that I need to listen to what you say, especially about setting our intention. Then I just hold that intention in my mind and also think of fire and water."

I nodded and smiled encouragingly. "That's right. And remember, you're not alone. We're all here holding the same intention and calling in our elements. You'll probably see visible proof when the circle is set, which is something unique to our circles because I have an affinity for all five elements—and that's a good thing."

"It's real cool," added Stevie Rae.

"Yeah, don't let it intimidate you," said Damien. "I'll be right across the circle from you. If you get distracted by anything that happens, just look at me. I'll breathe with you and that will help you ground and focus."

"Okay. Thanks. I think I'll be okay."

"Ice Cream Shoes, I *know* you will. How could you not be? You're wearing this season's glittery Jimmy Choo sneakers and making me super jelly," said Aphrodite.

"They're *last* season's. I got 'em on sale at the Nordstrom in Chicago before I transferred." Kacie's step seemed lighter in those sparkly sneakers as she moved to the westernmost side of our circle where water would be called.

Aphrodite let out a long-suffering sigh. "Why the hell can't Tulsa get a Nordstrom? It's inhumane. Seriously."

"Let's set our intention," I said.

"Getting Nordstrom to T-Town *is* my intention, but I'll put it on the back burner for a sec." Aphrodite took the red fire candle from Damien and went to the southernmost part of the circle.

I'd started to move to the center—the position of spirit—but stopped and mentally smacked my forehead. "Crap! I forgot to tell you to bring salt."

"Z, that's Spellwork 101," said Damien a little smugly. "Repel and protect spells need salt. I've got your back."

"You're the best," I told him as he tossed me a big velvet bag filled with salt. Then I moved to the center of our circle and pulled from my pocket a long strand of sweetgrass that Grandma Redbird had collected from the Tallgrass Prairie and dried and braided herself. I tied it around my wrist before I looked to the north, in the direction of Twenty-First Street, and asked Stevie Rae, "Do you have the smudge stick?"

"Easy peasy light and breezy," she said as she held up a tightly tied clump of dried white sage.

"Okay, good. We're ready." I glanced outside our circle and Stark nodded. Knowing he was there, watching and guarding, allowed me to focus on the spell. It was almost three in the morning, so there shouldn't be any human gawkers around, but over the past year Neferet's grotto had become a weird human tourist destination—and some of those humans liked to scare themselves with middle-of-the-night visits to her tomb.

I *really* wished they'd stick to checking out the Philbrook Museum and a nice dinner at the nearby Wild Fork.

I shook my head. *Forget all of that. Stark will handle it. Concentrate on setting your circle's intention.*

"Tonight, we come here with one clear intention—to set a repel spell to keep any vampyre from getting too close to this tomb that holds a being who chose to embrace Darkness." As I spoke I turned slowly, making eye contact with each of the other four members of my circle. "As I open the circle and begin the spell, I want you to concentrate on the fact that what we do here is in the name of love and Light. None of us have ulterior motives. We only wish to keep our world safe and the balance of good and evil intact. Circle! Set your intention!"

I strode to the east, where Damien was holding a yellow prayer candle and a box of extra-long wooden matches. I stopped before him, took the match he offered me, and struck it against the box, saying, "Air is the first element we call tonight. It surrounds us and fills us. Sustains us and is with us from the moment we're born, until the moment we return to the Goddess. It is the element of thought and communication and storytelling. Come to me, air!" I touched the lighted match to the candle and, as the flame lit, it flickered in a breeze that surrounded only Damien. We shared a smile before I turned to my right and walked deosil to the south where Aphrodite held a red candle representing fire. She was positioned directly in front of the wall that enclosed Neferet's grotto.

She, too, had a match and box ready. I lit the match while I invoked, "Fire is our second element. It warms our homes and from it we draw light and strength. It is the element of courage and willpower, as well as energy and confidence. Come to me, fire!" I barely had to touch the match to the red candle's wick and it burst into flame. Aphrodite flinched and shook back her hair to protect it from the intense blaze.

Our eyes met, and Aphrodite murmured, "Ice Cream Shoes is doing her thing."

"She sure is," I whispered in return.

From the south I walked to the west, where Kacie held out her blue water candle in one hand and balanced a long match and the striking box in her other. "You're doing great," I told her as I took the match and called water to our circle. "Water is our third element. It is present in our body as blood, tears, and milk. It cleanses and revives. It is the element of emotions, healing, and fertility. Come to me, water!" Even before the candle lit, Kacie and I were surrounded by the scents and sounds of the ocean. And then, just before I turned to head north, I heard her gasp.

"Oh, it's beautiful!"

I followed her gaze to a thin silver ribbon of light that stretched around the perimeter of our circle, connecting air, fire, and now, water.

"Yes, it is. And you helped make it so."

I traced the circle around and halted before Stevie Rae and her green earth candle.

"Hey there, Z." She handed me a long match.

"Hey there." I lit the match and invoked, "Earth is the fourth element of our circle. It is present all around us as well as in our bodies. It sustains us and supports us. It is our home. It is the element of our basic needs—our shelter and our stability. Come to me, earth!" Stevie Rae's green candle lit and for an instant I was transported to the Tallgrass Prairie in summer. I smelled the fertile ground and heard birds singing and insects buzzing.

When I headed back to the center of the circle to invoke spirit, I was filled with purpose at the sight of the silver thread that tied the four elements together.

My match was still lit, and I held it to my purple candle. "Spirit is the fifth and final element of our circle. It is what unites us and binds the other four elements to us. Without spirit we would be empty shells. It is the element of transformation. Come to me, spirit!"

All across my skin I felt the familiar prickle of spirit as it surged into the circle and turned the silver binding thread of light to a soft violet. I put my candle on the ground at my feet and picked up the velvet bag of salt as I unwound the sweetgrass from around my wrist.

"Earth, please smudge our circle and then join me in the center." My voice had changed. I no longer sounded like a young woman who was barely eighteen. I spoke with the power and confidence of a High Priestess, blessed by Nyx. My words carried across the park, filled with the power of the five elements.

Stevie Rae placed her candle on the ground and, careful to remain within the confines of the sparkling purple thread, she lit the fat smudge stick and walked clockwise around the inside of the circle as she wafted the sage around us. White smoke rolled in waves creating the shapes of flowers and trees above her, and as she passed Damien, then Aphrodite and Kacie, the smoke changed form. At Damien it became playful little cyclones, skipping around him. When she reached Aphrodite the funnels became flames, and at Kacie the flames changed to waves. Finally, Stevie Rae joined me, and all the shapes came together to form a beautiful set of wings.

Stevie Rae placed the stick on the ground, and the earth instantly extinguished it. I held out the rope of braided sweetgrass and said, "Let's go to fire."

Together, earth and spirit walked to where Aphrodite stood before the wall of Neferet's grotto. I used the red fire candle to light the strand of sweetgrass, then I lifted it and began tracing the pattern of a five-pointed star—representing each of the elements—as I said, "Just as sage cleanses, sweetgrass calls to the spirit realm. Tonight, I beseech the protective spirits of this earth to come to this place. I call not only with the power of this circle and our Goddess of Night,

Nyx, but I also beckon with the rich heritage of my Cherokee blood. My ancestors lived with the land—not on it. They cherished it and were its protectors. But even though I am the only vampyre here who carries the Tsalagi blood, we five acknowledge that the earth is not ours to own and pillage. It is instead our responsibility to care for it and keep it for generations to come."

Though I still traced the pentagram, I called to each of the elements saying, "Air, what is your role in protecting the earth?"

"I love it!" Damien said.

"Fire, what is your role in protecting the earth?"

"I cleanse it!" Aphrodite said.

"Water, what is your role in protecting the earth?"

"I nurture it!" Kacie said.

Stevie Rae didn't hesitate. "I am earth—strengthened by the other four elements!"

"And spirit indwells it!" I said.

I dropped what was left of the sweetgrass at my feet and loosened the drawstring of the velvet bag. With her left hand, Stevie Rae held the open bag for me. Her right hand gripped my left as I dipped my free hand into the tiny white crystals sparkling like diamond chips in the light of Aphrodite's candle. I inhaled deeply and said:

> *"Come, spirits of the earth.*
> *I call on you this hour.*
> *Repel those made vampyre through rebirth;*
> *Henceforth they cannot cross this white line of power!"*

As I spoke the spell, I threw handfuls of salt all around the tomb in front of me while I envisioned a barrier of white that encircled the grotto, much like the glistening purple light that bound our circle.

It worked perfectly—incredibly—magickally. The salt didn't simply fly through the air to scatter by the tomb. Directed by spirit and called by earth, the salt formed a thick white circle around the grotto. Within the barrier of that circle, the spirits of huge beasts lifted from the earth. I grinned as I recognized them and greeted them as my grandma would.

"Osiyo, yanasi!"

"Ohmygood*ness!* Bison!" Stevie Rae said.

I couldn't stop smiling. The giant beasts, iridescent and magnificent, materialized all around the tomb.

"May I look?" asked Aphrodite, sounding like a little girl asking for candy.

"Sure," I said.

Careful not to step outside our glowing thread, Aphrodite turned. "They're incredible! Will everyone be able to see them?"

"No, after we close the circle they'll be invisible unless a vampyre doesn't heed the repel spell. They they'll probably be visible to that vamp as they push him or her away."

"That's something I'd like to see," she said.

"See, maybe," I said. "Experience—no way. Bison are nothing to mess around with."

Like they heard me, several of the spirit beasts snorted and translucent smoke billowed from their wide nostrils.

"They're not playing," said Stevie Rae. "I can feel their power radiatin' from the earth. The Sons of Erebus Warriors are gonna have to stay way back from the tomb when they guard it."

"Why do we need them to guard it at all now?" Aphrodite asked as she stared at the creatures.

"You have a point," I said. "I'll talk to Stark about it, but I don't see why we'd need more than one Warrior posted here at night. That's enough to keep an eye on the humans who leave stuff for Neferet."

"Good," Aphrodite said as she turned back to face me. "I'm all for having more Warrior time—if that Warrior is Darius."

"Ah oh, speaking of humans who leave stuff for Neferet." Stevie Rae squeezed my hand and jerked her chin toward the street behind us.

I looked over my shoulder to see Stark striding toward a lone woman who was walking down the sidewalk that framed Twenty-First Street. I watched the Sons of Erebus Warriors close ranks so that she had a hard time seeing around them to where we were, but I wasn't worried about gawkers—not really. Stark and I had already decided he would say the House of Night High Priestess and her circle were simply strengthening the protective spell around Neferet's tomb—which was definitely a version of the truth.

"Nosy humans." Aphrodite shook her head as she squinted through the lingering sage and sweetgrass smoke at the woman who had already turned around to head back in the direction she'd come. "Hey, Neferet is not your friend!"

Aphrodite hadn't exactly shouted it, but the woman must have heard something because she looked back at our circle.

"Can you believe it? She's a grown woman," Aphrodite muttered. "You'd think she'd know better."

"We have to keep it positive," I reminded her.

Aphrodite's brows pinched together. "Right. Sorry. *I* should know better."

"No problem," I told her. "I totally get the frustration. Let's close the circle and head back to school. I can already taste the spaghetti waiting for us."

Closing the circle was simple. I began where I'd left off, with spirit, thanking it and then gratefully releasing it as I blew out my purple candle. Then I moved counterclockwise around the circle, thanking and releasing each of the other four elements until the glowing thread that bound us dissipated and the spectral bison disappeared.

"What was up with that human?" I asked Stark as the Warriors joined us.

He shrugged. "She said she lives near here and works the grave-yard shift at St. Johns Hospital. When she gets off she likes to walk around the park at night because the Warriors make her feel safe."

"Aww," I said. "That's kinda sweet. It makes me feel good that the humans who live near the House of Night have begun trusting us."

"Makes me feel good too. I told her she could come back tomorrow night and that the Sons of Erebus Warriors would be sure to look after her."

"You're a nice guy, James Stark." I tiptoed to kiss him.

He put his arm around me as we followed the others back to the parking lot. "Just nice? Not sexy or courageous or even cute?"

"I'll take nice over all those other things, but okay. You're all of them." I stuck my hand in his back pocket, appreciating his firm butt. "Hey, you wanta test the vamp repel spell?"

He snorted. "Hell no! My Warriors and I could feel it all the way outside your circle. Didn't you see the guys I'd stationed above the tomb backing off when those giant buffalo appeared?"

"No, I was busy watching the *bison*," I corrected.

"Well, it works. No need to rile up those beasts," he said. "Ready for some spaghetti?"

"I'm always ready for psaghetti." And, feeling safe, protected, and a lot better about everything in general, I sang my anticipatory psaghetti song all the way back to the House of Night—much to the amusement of Stark and the irritation of Aphrodite.

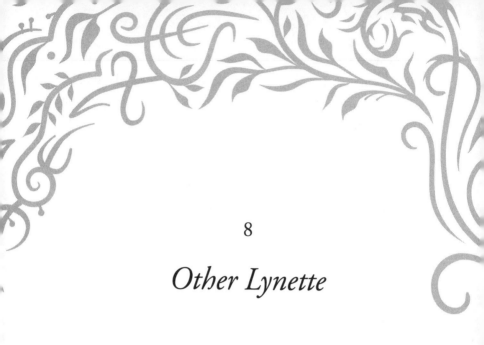

8

Other Lynette

Earlier that day

The mansion Vanessa and the other four college girls led Lynette and Neferet to was in the historic Midtown district of Maple Ridge, and as Vanessa had said, within easy walking distance of Woodward Park. It was a huge brown-brick Georgian villa with columns and what had to be more than eight thousand square feet of space over two stories.

"Oh, yes," Neferet had said as they'd approached, noting the wide brick walkway and the tastefully ornate facade. But the instant they entered the majestic home, Neferet had met Lynette's gaze and quietly corrected to, "Oh, *no*."

The bones of the villa were exquisite, but the inside had been utterly ruined by a horrible interior decorator. As Lynette stared around them, taking in the magnificent woodwork, beveled windows, gleaming wood floors, twenty-foot ceilings, and exquisitely detailed and original crown molding, she decided that the theme within was a mixture of self-aggrandizement, immaturity, and bad taste. Each room was painted a different color—the entryway being blue, which wouldn't have been terrible had they used moderation and understood that pastels work best with that type of color palette. Clearly, whoever was in charge of design didn't understand that. The elegant structure was no match for poor judgment—midnight blue changed to emerald green, which then became a fierce mustard yellow.

The horridly colored walls *should have* held museum-quality masterpieces. Instead, they were filled with huge prints of the five young women ranging from over-the-top baby pictures to posed portraits of each wearing what they obviously thought was couture. The majority of the ornately framed photos were of Vanessa, but each of the five women was represented—over and over and over again.

In the middle of the glaringly green sitting room Vanessa threw out her arms and spun around. "Well, what do you think, my lady?"

Neferet paused only a moment before saying, "I think this is a lovely villa and it is clear you have a deep connection to it."

"May I ask who did your interior design?" Lynette said.

Vanessa smiled smugly. "That would be me. I actually would *love* to have a career in interior design, but Daddy says it's part of the service industry, and so, totally not for me."

"Well," Lynette struggled for a moment with how to respond, then followed Neferet's lead and prevaricated, "you have a very distinctive eye."

"Yes, I know," Vanessa said dismissively.

"Show us to our rooms now. I must freshen and then find a feeder before the fog dissipates."

Vanessa made a sweeping gesture toward the wide wooden staircase that curved to the second floor and was carpeted in plush ivory. "Please, come this way."

"Yeah, it's super gorgeous upstairs too!" gushed Amber as the other girls nodded and smiled and followed them up the stairs.

Neferet paused every few steps to study the enormous black-and-white photos that hung against the red wall. "These nudes are quite—unusual."

Each photo was of one of the girls, naked and bareback on a horse. They all had extensions so that their blonde hair reached their waists and were in various positions from reclining to straddling.

"There's a story to those," said Vanessa.

"Yeah," Jordan, the girl who had represented earth, spoke up. "It was during our Epona phase. That's why we took the pics on the horses."

"Please, Jordan. Get real." Vanessa shot the other girl a narrowed-eye look. Lynette found it interesting that Jordan not only stopped speaking, but also faded into the background. *Vanessa controls the other four*, Lynette realized.

The young woman explained to Neferet as they slowly climbed the staircase. "I realized super fast that Epona wasn't a *real* goddess, especially when Neferet, well, *our* Neferet revealed herself as an immortal. So, we just keep these pictures for fun because they're, you know, gorgeous. Our photos honoring Neferet are in our bedrooms." She lowered her voice conspiratorially and in a mock whisper said, "We keep them up there because some people don't get why we worship her."

Neferet clicked her pointed nails against the banister. "Of course they don't. The general public is ignorant. That is a well-established fact," she said smoothly. "Now, Vanessa, tell me about how Neferet revealed herself as immortal to this world."

Lynette took mental notes as Vanessa, with occasional input from the other four women, outlined a bizarre sequence of events beginning with the death of Tulsa's mayor—which they blamed on Zoey Redbird—to the slaughter of humans at the Boston Avenue Church—culminating with this world's Neferet basically barricading herself within the Mayo Hotel while she was besieged by the Tulsa Police Department and House of Night vampyres. They also described a being who sounded a lot like Erebus who they claimed had been Neferet's Consort, but who was killed in the Mayo battle. Eventually, after literally hundreds of human deaths, which the five young women blamed on the House of Night, Neferet broke free from the Mayo siege but was ambushed at Woodward Park and sealed into the grotto through magick and the sacrifice of an immortal.

Lynette thought the story sounded about one-quarter truth and three-quarters the fabrication of rich girls who have little else to do.

Lynette cleared her throat as they paused in the upstairs landing outside five bedrooms and a dayroom that was Easter-egg purple. "Vanessa, does the rest of Tulsa, excluding the House of Night vampyres of course, feel as you five do about what happened to the Goddess Neferet?"

Vanessa barely glanced at her and made a dismissive motion with her long, squared-off fingernails. "Oh, the politicians and media and such don't, but whatever. They're all controlled by men. Of course they're going to say what the House of Night tells them to. We know better and so do a lot of other people. Just go look at our Neferet's tomb. It's practically *covered* with offerings." Vanessa turned her back on Lynette as she curtsied awkwardly to Neferet. "And now, my lady, I thought you might like Kelsey's room. It faces north and gets the least sunshine." She pointed to a modest-sized room painted a jarring shade of coral. "Oh, and there's a room downstairs off the kitchen Juanita stays in sometimes when the weather's bad or whatever and she can't get home. Your maid can have that one."

Instead of answering, Neferet strolled around the upper floor, looking in all of the bedrooms. Lynette followed her, intrigued by the photos that decorated the rooms. Each girl had filled her walls with framed naked photos of herself. In them, they'd had their faces painted with the strange black makeup they still wore that made them appear as if they wore Mardi Gras masks. They posed with their arms aloft, light illuminating them as if they were standing— or lying or straddling chairs—in the middle of a spotlight. Lynette decided that they were pretending to be divine, and she had to stifle the urge to laugh. She'd witnessed the power Neferet possessed, had watched her summon Old Magick, naked except for the tendrils she called her children. Compared to her, these women—these *girls*—looked like they were playing dress-up in their mothers' closets.

"Do you like them?" Vanessa asked breathlessly.

"Them? You mean the rooms?" Neferet answered.

"Oh, well, that too. But I meant our photos. They're a tribute to Neferet. If you like them then *our* goddess must too."

"I can only speak for myself, but I have never seen humans create such a tribute to a vampyre goddess before, and it says much about how you worship. I'm sure your Neferet will find it as fascinating as I."

"Oh, good! Yea!"

Neferet had stopped before a bedroom that was considerably larger than the others with an enormous marble bathroom attached and a closet bigger than Lynette's first condo. The suite's theme was gold. The walls were gold leafed. The ceiling was gold. The plush carpet was gold. The enormous bed had gold and ivory linens as well as a canopy in what looked like an impossible amount of gold lace. On the walls was photo after photo of Vanessa—naked, of course, and posing over and over in what she obviously considered to be proper goddess form.

"I shall take this suite, and Lynette shall take the one in coral that is beside mine."

Vanessa's cheeks blazed pink. "But, that's *my* room."

Neferet smiled. "Yes, I am aware of that as all of the photos on the walls are of you. Your room is the most luxurious. Would you expect a goddess to sleep in a second-best suite?"

"Well, no."

"Excellent. And I need my handmaid beside me, so she will take Kelsey's room. I must go out now and feed before the fog burns away. Please be sure that my dear Lynette has nourishment. Also, she will need access to a computer. You'll see to that, won't you, Vanessa? I count on you as I can tell from the décor of this villa how capable you are." Neferet paused a moment, but as Vanessa began to respond she spoke over her, saying, "Good. Lynette, while I'm out please draw my bath. You know how I like it." She went to Vanessa and took the girl's hands in her own, smiling at her so beatifically that even Lynette's breath caught at her beauty. "You have done very well today, Vanessa. When I release your goddess, which will be very, *very* soon, I give you my word that I will carefully relay to her all that you have done for me. She will be well pleased, and I am quite sure will afford you special attention."

Vanessa's expression had been getting more and more petulant, but Neferet's words transformed her face. She smiled smugly, giving I-told-you-so looks to the other four women, who watched raptly.

Then Neferet gracefully descended the staircase and disappeared out the tall front door.

Lynette also smiled at Vanessa as she walked past her and into what used to be the girl's excessively opulent suite. "That's *hand*maid—not maid. Big difference, my dear." Before Lynette closed the door in her face she said, "What's the password to that computer?"

Vanessa looked into her ex-room at a gold trimmed reproduction of a Louis XIV style desk on which sat a gold laptop. Her expression twisted like she'd sucked a lemon as she said, "Goddess123—capital G, no spaces."

"How clever. Have my dinner brought up on a tray. You can knock and leave it out here. I'll get it when I'm done preparing the Goddess's toilette. Thank you." Then Lynette firmly closed the door.

She could hear the excited and more-than-a-little-pissed-off chatter of the women from the hallway, but Lynette didn't trouble herself to listen. She knew their type. She'd grown up dealing with their mean, entitled attitudes. In high school those girls would have made her life miserable because she'd been what they called "trailer trash."

"Never again," she said to herself as she drew Neferet's bath and then quickly found her mistress suitable nightclothes. "Now I am the best friend of a vampyre who will soon be a goddess."

Humming to herself, Lynette opened Vanessa's laptop, typed in her silly password, and began searching for the real story of what happened to this world's Neferet.

(

The day passed quickly, and while Neferet slept in the golden-canopied bed, Lynette got little rest. She was far too busy researching this Tulsa's news—especially after she'd read multiple articles, as well as press releases from the House of Night—about their fallen High Priestess, the immortal Neferet. Though Lynette noted the House of Night was very careful to downplay her immortality. They talked around the issue—focusing on her descent into insanity and the fact that they were certain she could not break free of her prison and would not be a threat to humans again.

Lynette doubted everything she read, but there was one undeniable thread that ran through all of the stories. This world's Neferet was insane.

There were also several intriguing stories about a winged being named Kalona. Apparently, that was one of the many details Vanessa had gotten wrong. He wasn't Erebus, nor was he Neferet's Consort. Zoey Redbird had given a lengthy interview about Kalona, making it clear that he'd been firmly on the side of the House of Night and had been killed by Neferet right before she broke out of the besieged Mayo. Zoey had explained, briefly, that even though Kalona should have been immortal, he was vulnerable to Neferet's dark magick because he'd willingly given away a sliver of his immortality to save Stark. Without saying much, Zoey had made the winged being seem like a hero. The Tulsa Police Department was definitely enamored with him, so much so that over the past year they had erected a statue in his honor in front of their headquarters.

Vanessa and the other four girls left for classes at TU, but first Vanessa reluctantly gave Lynette the keys to her BMW as well as a platinum credit card, which Lynette used at several stores. Then, as dusk neared, she returned to prepare the vampyre's breakfast, doing her best to re-create the dishes Mrs. Muir had been so good at. As Lynette cooked, she was surprised by the sense of longing she felt for Balmacara Mains, Mrs. Muir, Noreen, and even poor wee Denise. She hoped with all of her being that they would soon return to their world. This version of Tulsa, with its intermingling of vampyres and humans, was unsettling.

Lynette's instincts told her that it was all a facade and that the peaceful appearance of this Tulsa was really a smokescreen covering a fire-keg ready to explode.

Neferet surprised Lynette by waking much later than usual—several hours past sunset, but when she called Lynette into Vanessa's suite the vampyre seemed completely refreshed and herself. As she helped Neferet dress, Lynette quickly recounted everything she'd found out about this strange world, as well as what their Neferet had *really* done to become entombed.

"I believe she is insane, my lady," Lynette said in conclusion.

Neferet waved away her concern while she broke her fast with Lynette in the sitting room adjunct to the bedroom. "Of course she is. She was immortal—a goddess—and she only aspired to be a Tulsa deity. I knew then that there must be something severely flawed within her. And if she wasn't completely mad before they entombed her, after a year of starvation, it is quite certain that she must now be so."

"Then what are we going to do?" Lynette asked.

"Well, first, I want you to make a copy of all of the news stories about this world's Neferet and tuck them safely within your travel bag. Should she try to cause me problems after I rescue her, I will need to know everything about her—and about how she was defeated. Knowledge is power. We must never forget that, no matter how powerful I become. Then we are going to do exactly what we set out to do—free her and convince her to tell me how to attain immortality. After that we will return immediately to our world and leave this one to either defeat their Neferet again or feel her vengeance for what they did to her."

Lynette said nothing. She didn't know how to share her concerns with Neferet. If her mistress could not see that this world's version of her was a monster, then she had a lot more to worry about than what would happen when the creature was let loose. Lynette had to worry about what immortality would do to *her* Neferet.

As if reading her mind, Neferet reached forward across the little table that held their food and drinks and rested her hand on Lynette's. "My dearest friend, I am not agreeing with the methods this world's version of me used. She was crass. She had no army to protect her. She killed indiscriminately. I have learned from my mistakes, and from hers as well. Loren made it clear to me that I have an army of Warriors awaiting my return, and you have shown me how blind I have been to the value of humans. My goal is to make our world safe for those of us who will not be controlled by the archaic leadership of the House of Night, as well as the ignorance of the human patriarchy. Trust me. I shall not fail you."

Relief washed through Lynette as she clung to Neferet's hand. "I trust you completely! And I absolutely believe that you will not fail. Do you know how you will break the seal of the tomb?"

"I believe so. I wish I could simply bring the sprites a sacrifice they find worthy and have them do it, but they have that annoying rule about not taking sides unless it is to correct an abomination— and while I could make the case that entombing an immortal is an abomination, after hearing your report of all that Neferet did before she was stopped, I do not think I can make the case that it is an abomination to entomb her, even though she's an immortal."

"That is a shame," agreed Lynette.

"But a seal is not an immortal. It is only the residue of one's power. It seems everyone at this House of Night believes that it cannot be broken unless another immortal makes a similar sacrifice, but what they are forgetting is that there *is* another immortal present. From what you told me, Neferet was gravely injured before they trapped her—and since she has been entombed, she has had no way of healing herself and regaining her powers. All I need do is to find a way to empower her and she will break the seal herself."

"That is brilliant, my lady!"

"Of course it is." Neferet smiled serenely and sipped her wine and blood mixture. "Now, I need the help of those ridiculous young women. I want them to disguise me so that you and I may pretend to be humans who have come to leave offerings at Neferet's tomb. I will have my children attempt to commune with hers and prepare her for freedom."

"Do you know how you're going to get power to that Neferet?"

"Sadly, I believe I will have to send it to her myself. I have the power of generations of High Priestesses flowing through my veins. I will simply cast a circle—perhaps using the ladies whose atrociously bad taste ruined this lovely villa—and call down the might of the full moon. Lynette, dearest, would you check and see how long before the next full moon?"

Much to Vanessa's obvious irritation, Lynette had completely commandeered her laptop. She opened it and hastily searched for the next full moon. Lynette looked over the screen at Neferet. "Well, not for a while. The moon phase calendar says that it'll be a new moon tomorrow night, so that means the full moon won't be for another couple weeks." Lynette's stomach soured at the thought of being in this world for two more weeks.

"How wonderful! A new moon is actually even more powerful for what I intend! All that dark energy is perfect. So, we need to move quickly. Are those girls returned from school yet?"

Lynette's smile disappeared. "Yes. Wait 'til you see what they're wearing. They think they're honoring you. It's the silliest thing I've seen in a long time. It's like their lives are a series of one dress-up event after another."

"Ah, but their foolishness has allowed us to use them, though my children could simply kill them if they give us any problems."

"I don't like them. At all."

Neferet tilted her head and studied Lynette. "I would sacrifice them for you should you desire it. It could be done easily before we return to our world. Actually, unless I become a goddess instantly and discover how to open the portal for us, I will have to call on the aid of the sprites again. I am quite sure that Oak would enjoy the novelty of drinking dry five vapid humans."

Goosebumps crested across Lynette's arms at the power she could wield with one word. "I don't really want their deaths on my conscience, but if we need to sacrifice them to return to our world, I'm sure my conscience would understand."

"If it happens, do not give it a second thought. I am your goddess. Their deaths shall be on my conscience. Now, tell them I have summoned them. I need to go to that tomb and no one must recognize me, which means I shall *temporarily* transform into a rather vapid, though attractive, human."

9

Other Lynette

With what Vanessa called her *expertise*, Neferet was transformed into a tall, slender human with long blond hair who looked about the same age as the five TU seniors. She was wearing skinny jeans and a plain, dark sweater. She wore no jewelry except for a silver heart pendant and something called a Fitbit. After much discussion the five young women had decided she should wear her knee-high black boots, but they insisted that she needed a knee-length navy peacoat that was two sizes too large so that her curvaceous and distinctly perfect body was covered.

Lynette would not leave the travel bag they'd arrived with in the villa for Vanessa and her minions to paw through, so she carried it with them, adding to it a couple tea lights and a pretty, thimble-sized quartz crystal they would leave as "offerings" at the wall of the tomb.

"But we really, *really* want to come with you!" Vanessa whined as Lynette and Neferet headed out the door to walk to Woodward Park.

"And you shall, but not this night. You, my little angels, would draw far too much attention," Neferet told Vanessa and the others for the third time. "Lynette and I will reconnoiter and if all goes well, tomorrow, using the dark power of the new moon, your Neferet will emerge from her tomb to embrace you."

Vanessa frowned and played with the sheer chiffon cape attached to the absurd gown she had changed into when they'd finished their classes that day. Her dress was purple because, as she explained to Neferet, she liked to be clothed in her element. The other girls had similarly ridiculous outfits, each in the color of the element they pretended to be attuned to. Lynette and Neferet had watched them literally flit about the villa, catching the wind of several fans they'd set up in each of the main rooms so that the diaphanous dresses billowed after them.

"Oh, Vanessa. Do not frown so," said Neferet. "It will cause you to wrinkle. You will already age far too fast."

Vanessa startled as if Neferet had just described a tragedy of horrid proportions. She fixed her face into a more neutral expression and acquiesced. "Well, okay. I suppose we do understand. And, of course, *Lynette* will go with you. She's old and plain. No one will pay any attention to her."

"See, you *can* understand if you try," said Neferet as Vanessa looked vaguely confused. "We shall return. Please clean my room and make my bed before we do." Then she breezed out the door into the cold winter night.

Lynette hesitated only long enough to say, "Honey, you know what else causes premature aging? Too much of that." She pointed to the glass of rosé Vanessa constantly carried around with her. Then she followed Neferet into the night.

"Did you say something terribly mean to her?" Neferet asked.

"No. Something true that will give her nightmares. I basically told her wine causes wrinkles."

"And does it?"

"Yes, if you drink lots and lots of it—and she does. Of course, it won't happen for another decade, but still."

"I do not like that they disrespect you. I'll have you know that I only tolerate it because keeping them alive and doing my bidding makes things easier for us."

"I understand that, my lady."

"Good, because my children have been whispering that they would like to rip their throats out—most especially Vanessa's. They have become very fond of you, dearest Lynette."

"That's sweet of them."

They walked on in silence. Lynette thought it best to approach the park from the west, walking along Peoria Street. Neferet had agreed, and also decided that they should circle around so that they would not be seen coming from the direction of the villa.

The night was dark and cold, and it was late enough that there were almost no cars traveling the midtown streets. As they crossed Peoria near the entrance to the Rose Gardens, Neferet spoke, though to Lynette it seemed more like she was reasoning aloud than actually conversing.

"They are decidedly irritating, but those frivolous children have taught me something."

When she said nothing more, Lynette prompted, "I do not understand how those entitled, vapid girls could teach *you* anything."

Neferet's full lips quirked up. "It was those horrid photos of theirs."

Lynette rolled her eyes. "Which ones? The ones on the first floor of the villa—the naked ones on the horses lining the stairway—or the naked *pretending-to-be-goddesses* ones in their rooms?"

"Well, all of them, but in particular the ones in their rooms. You never visited my office at the House of Night, did you?"

"No, my lady."

"I decorated the walls there much as those children decorated their bedrooms."

Lynette startled. "But, my lady, you cannot compare your beauty—your power—to those girls and their silliness."

"I can, because the photos of me were also an egotistical pretense. I was not a goddess. I was only a High Priestess looking for another path because I cannot bear to subjugate myself—not even to a goddess. In a way, I looked as foolish as those children—though more attractive."

"*Much* more," Lynette agreed.

Neferet laughed softly. "Those gowns they were fluttering about in—I've never seen anything like it."

"That's what happens when young women have too much money and too little concern for anyone except themselves. I could go into a whole diatribe on entitlement and such, but it wouldn't change things."

Neferet was silent for several minutes, and then she said, "I will change things when I return to our world."

Lynette flushed with pleasure. "You really could make such a difference, my lady."

Softly, in a voice that sounded nothing like the broken but arrogant and heartless vampyre who strode into the private airport in Tulsa, Neferet said, "I will be a goddess worthy of worship."

Lynette stopped and turned to face Neferet. "I believe you already are."

Neferet's lips turned up. "Thank you, my de—" Suddenly her words broke off. They'd passed the Tulsa Rose Gardens and the west entrance to Woodward Park that climbed up to the wooded area above Neferet's grotto.

Lynette started to speak, but Neferet pressed her finger to her lips and whispered. "A circle has been cast within the park. I can feel its power. Come, quietly. Follow me."

Neferet led Lynette off the sidewalk and through the manicured lawn that met the little ridge made of stone and mature azalea hedges. From there they crept forward, working their way toward the area of the grotto that held the immortal Neferet as they carefully hugged the ridge and stayed within the azaleas. The ridge curved to their right, allowing them a view of a group of people surrounding the grotto.

"They're circling," whispered Neferet. "I recognize the High Priestess in the center. That's Zoey Redbird. And there, among those Warriors standing guard, is this world's Stark. See the red tattoo on his forehead?" Neferet sucked in a shocked breath and continued, "That priestess closest to the grotto who stands in the position of fire—*that* is this world's Aphrodite. The little traitor who betrayed me along with Stark." She took Lynette's shoulders between her hands and spoke quickly and earnestly. "You must get closer. You must try to overhear what spell they are casting. Can you do that for me, my precious handmaid?"

Lynette's mind raced until it caught a plan. "Of course. I won't fail you. Should you wait here? Will you be safe? Maybe you should call more fog to hide yourself."

"I cannot do that without making them suspicious. Every vampyre in this park knows about concealment spells, and I'm afraid they would recognize it, especially after I so recently called fog for that purpose. No matter, I will remain here and await your return."

"Okay, I'll be as fast as I can."

Before she hurried back to the sidewalk, Neferet took Lynette's hand in both of her own. "Do not put yourself in danger. Do not let them take you from me, my dearest."

"Never. Don't worry. I'm good at this kind of thing."

Lynette went back to the sidewalk, moving briskly alongside Peoria Street until she came to the Twenty-first Street intersection, where she turned right and headed directly for the group of vampyres and their lit candles. She thought it would be difficult to overhear what the priestess in the circle was saying, but her voice was filled with such power that it carried across the lawn. As the words drifted over her Lynette halted, pretending that she had a pebble in her shoe. She bent to take it off while she listened and observed, memorizing the words of the spell as well as the faces of each of the vampyres.

> *"Come, spirits of the earth.*
> *I call on you this hour.*
> *Repel those made vampyre through rebirth;*
> *Henceforth they cannot cross this white line of power!"*

Lynette realized it was some kind of spell focused on keeping vampyres away from the grotto. A chill skittered down her spine.

Do they know Neferet is here?

Determined to glean more information, Lynette straightened and inched forward. She sucked in a breath and froze. From a white, glittering circle that surrounded the grotto and the wall concealing it, enormous spectral beasts rose. They stood shoulder to shoulder, shimmering with power and blowing iridescent smoke from their nostrils.

Lynette recognized them instantly. She'd visited the untamed expanse of Oklahoma's Tallgrass Prairie to view the free-grazing bison and their golden calves. It had always thrilled her and made her wonder at what it must have been like before the Native Peoples and their way of life had been strangled by European immigrants.

Lynette stared so long that she didn't realize the circle had closed until the bison dissolved into the earth—though even she could feel that they remained, vigilant and protective.

"Excuse me, ma'am."

Lynette startled and instantly recognized James Stark, who in her world wasn't a smiling red vampyre, but a blue vampyre general who had betrayed her mistress.

She clutched her throat and laughed nervously. "Oh, my! You frightened me."

He stopped several feet from her. "I'm sorry. I didn't mean to. I just wanted to let you know the park is closed right now."

"Oh, I didn't intend to go into the park. I work a late shift at

St. John's and taking a walk afterward always relaxes me." Then she added with gushing gratitude, "Since you Warriors have taken to being in the park at night, I feel safe walking. It's really quite nice."

"Thank you. It's our job to protect," said Stark.

"I do appreciate that so much. Will you be here again tomorrow night?"

He nodded. "Absolutely. Though there won't be as many of us tomorrow—but how about I tell the Sons of Erebus to keep an eye out for you?"

"Why, that's very sweet. And now I'll just head back the way I came so I don't interrupt you further. Thank you, young man, and blessed be."

"Blessed be, ma'am."

Lynette turned and briskly retraced her path back to Neferet, who joined her on the sidewalk. Silently, they hurried across Peoria Street to disappear into the winding, opulent midtown neighborhood of Maple Ridge. Only when they were several blocks away did Neferet speak.

"I could feel her words, but I could not hear them. Could you make them out?"

"Yes! Every one of them—and I saw everything! Here's what she said." Lynette repeated the spell, word for word.

Neferet blew out a long, frustrated breath. "That meddling child! She's cast a spell that will repel all vampyres from the tomb. I do not understand why this version of me didn't do away with that troublesome girl before she Changed and became a powerful High Priestess."

"She's definitely powerful. I even saw them."

"Them?"

"Bison! Or at least their spirits. They materialized all around the tomb—as well as above it. And you should've seen the response of the Warriors who were standing on top of the ridge overlooking the tomb. As soon as the bison appeared, they all jumped back—fast."

95

"Zoey Redbird knows something is happening." Neferet shook her head. "I was afraid of this when I used fog to conceal us yesterday. I should have considered the time of year and used a rainstorm, or even the concealment of shadows. So much fog was suspicious."

"That, or someone from our world knows we're here and they, too, have crossed the portal to warn Zoey and this House of Night," said Lynette.

"Lynette, dearest, you would know better than I, as you, too, are human, but do you think Mrs. Muir or her daughter could have betrayed us?"

"No, my lady," she said firmly. "At first, they were frightened of you, which made them keep your presence a secret, but you watched what happened. They changed as they got to know you and as they witnessed your glory and your power night after night. I also believe wee Denise's sacrifice moved them greatly. Humans are not as gifted or as powerful as vampyres, but we have an almost unlimited capacity for love and loyalty. My intuition says that they worship you and are faithful."

Neferet shook back her blond wig and looked relieved before her eyes narrowed. "Loren—that weak fool. I should've gone to him—surprised him—gotten the information I needed and *then* ended his pathetic life. If someone betrayed me, it was Loren."

"My lady, I didn't see anyone from our world with the group at the park, and I definitely would have recognized our Stark or any of the other higher-ranking vampyres."

"Did you see a Warrior who looked Native American? He would have had a red tattoo of a fully Changed vampyre that is highly ornate."

Lynette reviewed in her mind the Warriors before answering. "No. None of the vampyres looked Native American except for Zoey, and there was only one Son of Erebus Warrior who had a red tattoo, and that was Stark."

"Had Kevin crossed through the portal he definitely would have been at his sister's side. It could simply be that this world's Aphrodite is also a prophetess, and Nyx has warned her of my presence."

"Oh, that reminds me—this Aphrodite's Mark is highly unusual."

"What do you mean?"

"It's red *and* blue. I couldn't make out the pattern, but she was closest to the bison spirits and they were glowing, which allowed me to see her Mark," said Lynette.

"And you're quite positive it is red and blue?"

"Yes, absolutely."

"Then this world's Aphrodite is definitely a powerful prophetess. We must assume Nyx has warned her with a vision."

Stress pressed down on Lynette, making her shoulders burn and her stomach churn. "Neferet, my lady, are you sure we shouldn't just call the sprites and have them return us to our world?"

Neferet stopped on the dark sidewalk in the sleepy midtown neighborhood and faced Lynette. "I understand your fear. I, too, feel the trap of this world—this Tulsa I do not know. But I need the secret their Neferet holds. More than that, what if it were I trapped there? Would you leave me thus, starving and consumed with anger?"

Lynette's shoulders slumped. "No, never. I would do anything to help you escape. I'm just worried."

"As am I, though I do have a plan. I believe I know how to break the seal and loose Neferet."

"But you can't get close to the tomb," said Lynette.

"My new plan does not call for me to approach the tomb—only my children. And they are not vampyres."

Hope fluttered in Lynette's chest. "So, nothing will stop them from getting to the tomb."

"Exactly. I must warn you, though, my dearest. My plan is bloody. It requires sacrifice and death."

"Well, I have lived most of my life following the old adage, *nothing good comes easily*."

Neferet smiled. "We are very alike."

"That is a wonderful compliment," said Lynette, returning her mistress's smile.

Lynette felt considerably lighter. "My lady, my intuition says those five young women will play a key role in your plan."

"As you have said many times—your intuition is rarely wrong."

Neferet looped her arm through Lynette's and they began walking again, this time more briskly as they turned toward Twentieth Street and the villa filled with easily manipulated young women.

"Now, my dearest, I must feed, and I would save you the discomfort of watching me do so on an unwilling human."

"That is kind of you, my lady."

"Not at all. I agree with your distaste. I abhor the messiness that goes along with feeding in the wild." She sighed. "No matter. What I truly need you to do is to go ahead of me to the villa and do several preparatory things."

"Of course, my lady."

But instead of beginning a lengthy list of tasks, Neferet stopped and grinned, *grinned* at Lynette—as if they were girlfriends sharing a secret—and said, "I do miss that little computer device you tap-tap-tapped on so very much back in our world."

Lynette returned the grin, feeling better than she had since they'd arrived in this strange world. "I do too. But my mind is sharp, and I will remember everything you require."

"Oh, I do not doubt it for a moment. So," Neferet began walking again, her arm still looped with Lynette's, "the spellwork Zoey did today changes things, but not drastically. The first thing I must do has not altered at all. We will need concealment tomorrow night. When you reach the villa, you must ready four ornate bowls of offerings. Honey and wine in two, of course, and then use your imagination. You've witnessed my offerings over the past week. I trust you to know what is appropriate."

"You're going to summon the sprites?"

"Yes. I could, of course, go through the trouble of casting a circle and coaxing the weather I wish from the clouds, but why should I when I can simply call on assistance from the sprites?"

"You'll need a payment."

Neferet nodded absently. "Yes, yes, I know. That's why when you take the filled bowls and place them around that lovely fountain in the backyard of the villa I want you to also put my sgian dubh there as well—with a basin of warm water, a towel, and soap to wash off this horrid makeup that is concealing my Mark."

Lynette squeezed Neferet's arm. "Please be careful, my lady."

"You need not worry yourself, dearest. I ask a small thing from the sprites. My blood sacrifice should suffice."

"You will call the sprites to the villa grounds?"

"Yes. The wretched taste of those girls has not extended to the grounds. It is modest in size, but rather lovely."

"My lady, I have an idea that may help us with the girls tomorrow night."

"Yes?"

Lynette reasoned aloud. "I will always remember how it changed the attitudes of Mrs. Muir and her staff to witness your glorious power as you called to the sprites on the loch. With your permission I will enlist the aid of the five girls in filling the sacrificial bowls, and then I will instruct them to watch as you summon the sprites."

"That is an excellent idea! But do be sure they watch from a window of the house. I do not believe their reactions will be as sophisticated as were the Scottish women."

"Good point," Lynette said. "What else would you have me do?"

"You will need to begin readying those five for tomorrow. Remind them of the importance of their willingness to sacrifice for their goddess."

Stress began to build between Lynette's shoulder blades again. "My lady, I'm not sure how to spin their deaths into something palatable."

Neferet laughed. "Oh, no, no, no. You need not mention their deaths. Tell them that except for their cloaks, they must be naked. Their sacrifice is that they cast a circle around the grotto tomorrow even though they might be caught—naked, in the cold, showing their support for a vampyre goddess."

"Well, that makes it much easier. I'm pretty sure they're fine with nudity. And their daddies' money will have bought them out of much more difficult circumstances than circling naked at Woodward Park."

Neferet said, "So true."

"Watching you summon sprites and use Old Magick tonight will enthrall them."

"Of course it will. Oh, do be sure you warn them that the weather is going to be challenging, but remind them that it's as it must be. I need to blind the House of Night."

"More fog?"

"Oh, no! I do not make the same mistake twice. Two instances of blanketing fog in January would be enough to cause even the most obtuse High Priestess to be suspicious. And I need much more than momentary concealment. I need to make a show of casting a circle using humans, sacrifice them, and open the tomb. I will use weather to gain the privacy I need, but I must work with the type of weather the elements easily produce in winter in Tulsa."

Lynette smiled. "Ice storm?"

"Let's just call it freezing rain, shall we?"

10

Other Lynette

Lynette had never been a violent person—not even when her mother was sharing her with the loathsome men who used to visit their trailer when she was a preteen, but dealing with the five Tulsa debutantes had her rethinking her personal stance on nonviolence.

The young women were horrible. As far as Lynette could tell, they had no redeeming qualities and their only talent was the ability to grow long, thick hair. Then she overheard Kelsey and Jenna talking about needing to go to Ihloff Salon at Utica Square to get their extensions redone, and she realized they couldn't even do that on their own.

Vanessa was definitely the ringleader. She was closest to Amber, the girl who pretended her affinity was for fire, but the only way Lynette knew they were supposed to be best friends was because the two called each other "bestie," and not because they seemed to actually be friends. There was a definite pecking order between them, with Vanessa reigning at the top. Amber was second, with the earth girl, Jordan, and the air girl, Jenna, pretty much on the same level, followed at the bottom by the water girl, Kelsey.

Through listening and observing, two things Vanessa and her crew would never think to do, Lynette decided the reason Kelsey was so low in the pecking order was simple—her family had money, but they didn't allow Kelsey unrestricted access to it. Apparently, Kelsey was the only one of the five who had to turn in her grades to her parents and not just pass every class but maintain a B average. And that's why the other four belittled her.

Lynette would've felt sorry for Kelsey had it not been so obvious that the girl wanted nothing from life more than to win the approval of Vanessa and the others.

"And she's not bright enough to realize she will *never* win their approval—not unless they allow someone they think even less of than Kelsey into their group," Lynette mumbled as she sipped the cup of coffee she'd brewed and read another House of Night interview on the laptop.

Vanessa looked up from the copy of *Vanity Fair* she was thumbing through as she and the other four women drank wine in the green sitting room. "What was it you said, Nettie?"

Lynette swallowed the response she wanted to give and turned on the overly stuffed settee to smile at Vanessa. In the short time Neferet had been gone, Vanessa had decided to give Lynette a nickname. It was obvious she wanted Lynette to ask her about the name but, unlike the poisonous young woman, Lynette wasn't stupid enough to fall into her trap.

"I was just telling myself that the Goddess will approve of the offering you and the rest of the girls decided upon."

"Nettie," Vanessa said from her wingback chair that was angled in front of the sitting room's fireplace. "Please stop calling us *girls*. We are empowered *women*. Every one of us is well over twenty-one."

Lynette forced herself not to laugh. "I apologize. I didn't realize you were so *old*. You all are still in college, aren't you?"

Amber was sitting on a chair that was a twin to Vanessa's. She lifted the hand that wasn't holding a glass of wine and counted off. "One, we aren't old. You are. Two, yes, we're still in college. Our parents wanted us to have the *full* experience and not rush through."

"Oh, my mistake. Sorry. Exactly how long have you five been at TU?" Lynette pitched her voice to sound authentically interested, which was easy. She'd been catering to the rich and powerful for most of her adult life, and one thing was consistently true about them—most were entitled assholes who believed their money made them special and oh, so interesting.

"This will be our seventh and final year ruling the TU women's studies program," said Amber as four heads nodded in agreement.

"Well, except for poor Kelsey," said Jordan. "She's two years younger. Her parents forced her to graduate in five years."

On a plainer chair farther from the fireplace, Kelsey laughed nervously. "Yeah, they can be unreasonable."

Vanessa scoffed. "Unreasonable? They're *ridiculous*."

Thankfully, the front door opened then, and the girls stood and hurried to the foyer as Neferet breezed past them. She paused only long enough to wipe a scarlet trail of blood from her cheek with a finger and ask, "Lynette, is everything prepared?"

Lynette curtsied low, making a special show of respect in front of the vapid girls. "Yes, my goddess. All awaits you in the courtyard by the fountain as you instructed."

Neferet licked the blood from her finger. "Good." Then she continued through the house.

"You didn't tell her that *we* filled two of those four bowls," pouted Vanessa.

"She's a goddess. I don't have to tell her. She will know. Now, where will we have the best view of the courtyard fountain?" said Lynette.

"From the courtyard, of course," said Vanessa, rolling her eyes.

Lynette skewered her with her gaze—well and truly sick of the spoiled child. "I have watched the goddess summon the sprites. They require a payment. Their last was the life of one of the watching humans. If you are prepared to make that sacrifice, then go ahead, join the goddess in the courtyard."

Vanessa sighed. "Fine. We can watch from the dayroom upstairs. There's a balcony we can go out on, but it's really cold tonight."

"That's perfect, and should you go out on the balcony to observe, Neferet will know you are there and also know that you are prepared for what you must do tomorrow night," said Lynette.

Amber spoke up. "Bestie, I think we should go out on the balcony. I mean, Nettie already told us that we have to be nakey tomorrow in the middle of the night at Woodward Park. It really is good practice. Plus, it'll show Neferet how tough we are."

Vanessa nodded slowly. "You're right. Okay, let's go." She glared at Lynette as she led her posse up the wide stairwell. "But," she said, "there better be something good to see."

"You can watch and then decide how *good* it is," said Lynette. *And while you watch, I'll work hard at not throwing you from the balcony.*

"Oh. My. God. She's naked!" Jenna pointed as the five of them stood at the edge of the balcony, shivering and staring below.

Neferet stood a few yards away from the long, rectangular koi pond, the center of which was decorated by a bronze statue of a graceful woman pouring water from an urn—or she would be pouring water had the little pond not been frozen. Over the water feature was a pergola, draped with miniature lanterns, which Lynette had made sure were lit so that the five young women would be able to clearly observe Neferet's power.

Neferet had stopped at the stone bench where Lynette had left the soap, towel, and basin of water, as well as the tray holding the four offering bowls. Jenna had been right, Neferet had already stepped out of the disguise clothes she abhorred and was drying her face. She dropped the towel to the ground and pulled off the blonde wig, allowing her mass of auburn hair to cascade down her back. As she turned to lift the tray, they got a perfect view of Neferet, and the girls gasped.

Lynette didn't blame them. She had seen Neferet naked many times and her lady's perfection still shocked her.

"If in the Louvre, she would outshine Venus de Milo," murmured Lynette.

Vanessa scoffed. "Well, of course she would. That statue is super old, and has, like, no arms. But *of course* you'd compare her to that. The truth is she's even more gorgeous than *any* of the Kardashians."

That pronouncement had the other four gasping again. Lynette wasn't sure if she wanted to throw up or laugh in their faces. Instead, she reminded herself that tomorrow night would come soon enough, and simply said, "Keep watching. It's about to get interesting."

Lynette could tell that Vanessa wanted to say something sarcastic, but Kelsey was pointing below. "What is she doing?"

From the edge of the balcony, Lynette saw Neferet standing in front of the koi pond, facing the villa. She bent, placing the offering tray on the dark, frozen surface—and it was then that Lynette realized that the tendrils had swarmed over the ice. Looking like ink, they held the tray and guided it to the center of the little pond.

"The goddess is sending out the offerings to the four elements," Lynette said. "Watch and you'll see them be accepted."

As if Lynette had called the sprites, the pond came alive. One blue, webbed arm lifted through the ice and pulled the tray and its contents under. Lynette wondered briefly what the hibernating koi might be thinking, but then the night around Neferet exploded with fey, and Lynette could only answer the questions being fired at her by the five awestruck girls.

"OMG, what *are* they?" Amber whispered.

Lynette realized she needn't have worried about lighting the courtyard. It was ablaze with sprites. They flitted around Neferet, bathing her naked skin in their shimmering light. There weren't as many as had come to her in Scotland, and Lynette didn't see Oak among them, but that made their show no less magickal—no less impressive.

"The sprites have many different names—elements, fey ..." Lynette explained. "But what they are is pure magick that manifests in the form of creatures who embody each of the four elements."

"What about spirit?" Vanessa asked.

"I've never seen a spirit sprite. I think it's because it's around us all the time and doesn't need to manifest physically. And also, Neferet embodies that element."

"I wish I could hear what she was saying," said Kelsey.

Neferet was speaking, and though her voice didn't lift to the balcony, the power of it did. It brushed over Lynette's skin and had the five girls rubbing their arms and shivering.

"She's telling the sprites that she wants to make a deal," Lynette said. "This is the part where they barter."

"Barter? Can't she just command them to do whatever she wants them to do?" Amber said.

Vanessa added, "Or isn't she *that* powerful."

Lynette couldn't keep the disdain from her voice as she answered the clueless young woman. "Those sprites are part of the magick that made this world. They are not beholden to any goddess. They are dangerous and extremely powerful and should be treated with respect. For every service they perform they require a payment. That's just the way it is."

"Huh. I'll have to ask *our* Neferet about that," said Vanessa.

"Please do," Lynette said. And added silently, *though I doubt you'll get a chance. I almost wish I were staying here long enough to witness her answer.*

"Hey, she just picked up that little knife," said Kelsey.

"It's a sgian dubh," corrected Lynette. "The goddess brought it from our Highlands. Watch closely. This will be the payment part."

The sprites had formed a circle around Neferet, illuminating her incredible beauty. She lifted the sgian dubh and pressed it against

106

the meaty part of the palm of her hand, just below her thumb. With one swift motion, she sliced into her skin.

Five gasps echoed across the balcony.

"She actually cut herself!" Jordan said.

"Of course she did," said Vanessa—as if she hadn't gasped in shock with the rest of them. "She's a goddess. Her blood has to be super special."

That's the first correct thing you've said all day, Lynette thought, but she didn't bother speaking to Vanessa. She didn't want to be educated. Vanessa wanted to be coddled.

Neferet had closed her bleeding hand, capturing the pool of scarlet that was welling there. Then, with a grace that was mesmerizing, Neferet spun in a circle and as she did, she opened her hand and flicked her wrist so that blood rained around her.

The sprites went mad. They didn't allow one drop to touch the ground, but instead darted about, catching them in their greedy, open mouths.

Amber jolted half a step back. "Do you see those fangs?"

"Oh," Lynette said nonchalantly, "Didn't I tell you how they killed the human in Scotland?" She didn't wait for a response but continued. "They ate her."

Vanessa shivered. "Now *that* is cool."

The instant the last drop of blood was gobbled up, the dark sky above them opened and cold rain began to fall.

"Oh, shit! My hair!" Vanessa said.

"We can go inside now," Lynette said. "The goddess has done what she needed to do."

Amber frowned. "You mean she did all that to make it rain?"

"Honey, how cold has it been lately?" Lynette asked with exaggerated patience.

"Real cold," Amber said, rolling her eyes.

"And what happens when it's been 'real cold,'" Lynette air quoted and allowed her voice to sound as petulant as Amber's, "and then it warms up a little—just enough for it to rain before getting 'real cold' again?"

"OMG, she made an ice storm!" Vanessa said. Then she added, "That's gonna suck for us tomorrow night."

"It's also going to keep everyone away from Woodward Park and, hopefully, even knock out the electricity so those cameras don't report anything to the House of Night," said Lynette.

"Oh, well. Then I guess we'll just have to deal," said Vanessa.

Lynette nodded. "Nothing good comes easily."

Amber snorted. "Cliché much?"

"Do you know how sayings become clichés?" Lynette said as she walked from the balcony with the girls following her like annoying hens.

"Yeah, because it's repeated over and over," said Amber.

"Yes. And it's repeated over and over because it's true. I suggest you all get a good night's rest. Tomorrow is going to be exciting."

"Yeah, well, since we're not *old* we can stay up past bedtime," said Kelsey, which made first Vanessa, and then the others laugh.

"Good one, Kelsey!" Vanessa said.

Lynette paid them no mind and headed toward the bathroom to warm Neferet's bath and pour her a glass of her favorite wine.

"Hey, where are you going, Nettie? There's a serious mess to clean up in the kitchen," Vanessa shouted after her.

Lynette turned then and met Vanessa's mean, blue-eyed gaze. "I am in the service of my goddess. She will want a bath and wine—immediately. Do you want to explain to her why those things aren't ready?"

Vanessa shifted her weight restlessly from foot to foot. "I could do that. I could do the bath thing and get her some wine."

"No, child, you could not." Neferet's voice rang up the stairwell as she ascended, still completely naked, her long hair her only covering. She smelled of wilderness and blood, and her eyes still glinted with power. "You are not my handmaid. I have been patient with you because I understand you have never before been in the presence of a goddess, but you will not disrespect my handmaid again because if you do, *I will drink you dry.*"

"B-but, you'd have to answer to *our* goddess for that," stammered Vanessa.

"Actually, I would not. Goddesses answer to no one. Now, either clean the kitchen or rest, as my handmaid advised."

Vanessa closed her mouth. Her lips formed a tight little line, but she nodded and, with the other girls, headed toward the bedrooms.

"Oh, and Vanessa?" Neferet called.

Vanessa stopped and turned.

"Her name is Lynette, not Nettie. I find nicknames offensive. Do not call her that again."

Vanessa's head jerked up and down as she nodded.

Neferet's face transformed from ferocious vampyre to beatific goddess with her smile. "That's better, isn't it? Thank you for being so understanding and such excellent hostesses. I give you my word you will be repaid in kind tomorrow night."

11

Other Kevin

As Aphrodite left the boundary of the grove, her smile lit Kevin's heart. "Hello, handsome. It's really good to see you."

"Aphrodite!" He closed the distance between them in seconds and reached out to take her into his arms, but even though she looked solid and beautiful and really, truly there, he was met with nothing but air.

Kevin stepped back, looking around frantically. "Aphrodite?"

"Oh, shit. Sorry," she said from beside him, still looking like he could reach out and touch her. "I should've warned you. I look like me, but since I'm actually, well, *dead*, I'm really just spirit and spirit doesn't have a physical body—at least not here it doesn't."

Kevin ran his hand through his hair. "I guess that makes sense." Then he stood there helplessly, not sure of what he should do next.

"Hey," she spoke softly and moved closer to him. "It's okay. I know this is weird for you, but I'm still me—and I still love you."

Automatically, Kevin started to reach for her again, but he caught himself and instead fisted his hands at his sides. "I love you too. Goddess, I've missed you so damn much."

110

Her expression was so filled with love that Kevin's heart squeezed. "I love you too, and I know you've been in pain. I wish I could help. I tried, but I don't know if it did any good."

"You mean when the champagne bottle popped!"

"Yeah," she nodded, calling his attention to her thick mane of haphazardly curly hair that framed her face and swept down her back.

"I thought it was you! Grandma Redbird told me to expect a sign and you actually gave me one. Did—did you hear me talking to you too?"

"I did that night. I do hear you sometimes, but I think it depends on where I am in Nyx's Realm. It's a big place."

Kevin was studying her, trying to memorize every inch, and as he did he realized that many of those inches looked different than when she was alive. Her hair was the first difference. It was way more relaxed than he'd ever seen it. Actually, it looked kind of wild and messy and even a little frizzy. As far as he could tell she wasn't wearing any makeup—at all. Her clothes were *super* different. She had on a long skirt made of layers of pastel fabric mixed with what he was pretty sure his g-ma would call vintage lace. Her shirt was a simple aqua-blue tee that was just a shade lighter than her eyes and she had it tied up so that he caught a glimpse of skin. She wasn't wearing any jewelry or—he realized with a start—shoes.

"Hey, just because I don't always hear you doesn't mean I don't listen for you. I want you to know you can talk to me for as long as you need to. And I'll try to send you little signs."

"Okay, uh, thanks." He wiped a hand across his face and started over. "Sorry, it's just ... you look different. Good, but different," he added quickly.

She glanced down at herself and shrugged. "I don't pay attention to the things I used to obsess over." When she looked up at him, she grinned impishly with more cheeky joy than he'd ever seen before. "This no-shoes thing is obviously new to me. It makes you even taller." Then she peered around him. "Is that why Stark is back there gawking at me with his mouth flopped open?"

Kevin looked over his shoulder at Stark, who hastily closed his mouth. "Dude, are you staring like a tourist?"

Stark scowled and walked to them. "To not be a tourist here means something very permanent. Uh, hi," he said to Aphrodite, nodding awkwardly. "You look good. Different, but still good."

"Thanks. That's what Kev just said. You don't look so great. You're bleeding."

He grimaced at his bloody mess of an arm. "Yeah. It's the cost we paid to get here. At least it doesn't hurt right now."

She lifted one of her shoulders. "Well, Bow Boy, every choice you make in life has a payment and a consequence. The difference here is that you knew the payment first. Wonder what the consequence will be?"

"Hopefully, that we stop the Neferets from ruining our worlds," Stark muttered.

"You're no less grumpy than I remembered. That's a shame." Then she refocused on Kevin. "So, you being here has something to do with Neferet?"

"You don't know why we're here?"

"No! I just felt your call. I thought you were dead. Here's something you won't hear me say often—I'm glad I was wrong."

"But would that be such a bad thing? We could be together then."

"Hey, I want you to listen to me closely—*I do not want you to die young*. I want you to live a full, long, happy life. I want you to love passionately and often—to form your own kind of family—to experience the world and to fulfill your destiny. Do you hear me?"

Kevin stared down at his feet. "I hear you. It's just—don't you miss me at all?"

"Kev, look at me."

His gaze lifted.

"I don't know how this is possible, but here's the truth. We take love with us when we die, but it's like our souls get washed of all the bad stuff and when that happens, we no longer feel sadness or longing. We love without all that other crap. So, my feelings for you haven't changed—actually, if anything they're deeper than they were when I was alive—but I don't *miss* you. It's just love here—always love."

"It's hard because it's not like that for the people you leave behind."

"I know. And I'm really sorry. But you know what makes the missing easier to bear?" She didn't wait for him to answer. Instead, Aphrodite smiled and continued, "Loving again. Living a life full of adventures. Putting yourself out there. Promise me you'll try."

"I promise," he said softly.

Stark cleared his throat. "Even though a ghost will probably label me grumpy. Again. I gotta remind you that the clock is ticking and Neferet is ahead of us. Can we please get going?"

Aphrodite flipped back her hair. "I am *not* a ghost. And you *are* grumpy. Dying would definitely help your attitude."

Stark blanched chalk white.

Aphrodite rolled her eyes. "Oh, for shit's sake—I'm just kidding. I'm good, but I can't cause your death. And I wouldn't even if I could. Relax and take that stick out of your ass."

Stark frowned at her. "I thought you said that there was only love here."

"I said it with love." She returned his frown with a grin. "Okay, so, Neferet didn't die when she fell from the stadium, right?"

"Right," said Kevin. "She escaped to the Scottish highlands. Loren Blake somehow got into contact with her and told her about the Other World."

"Great—and probably also told her that the Neferet over there is immortal and entombed."

Stark nodded. "Yeah, we think so. She killed Loren, so we have no way of knowing how much he told her."

"Though he didn't know all that much," continued Kevin.

113

"He did manage to leave us a clue about Skye before he died. We followed the clue and met with Queen Sgiach."

"Seriously? What's she like?"

"Intimidating and really smart," said Kevin.

"Scary and beautiful," added Stark.

"She sounds awesome."

Kevin nodded. "She is. It's because of her that we're here. She called the sprites and Oak told her that Neferet used Old Magick to go through the portal to Zoey's world."

At the mention of Oak, Aphrodite looked away.

"Crap," Kevin said. "I'm sorry. I shouldn't have said anything about Oak."

"No, it's okay. It's just *weird* thinking about how I died. Like, I remember being in your arms and getting sleepier and sleepier, and then I woke up in the presence of the Goddess—which was amazing. I just don't remember the part about what Oak did to me to make me die."

Stark spoke solemnly. "You gave her your humanity for the red vampyres and fledglings. It was the bravest thing I've ever seen."

Aphrodite met his gaze and smiled. "Thanks. That was a nice thing to say, Bow Boy." Then she shook herself and the aura of joy resettled over her. "So, Neferet is over there. Why are you two here?"

Kevin said, "We need to get to that other world to warn Z. I was going to figure out a payment and call the sprites so I could use Old Magick again, but—"

"No!" Aphrodite interrupted. "Don't call the sprites. Do *not* keep using Old Magick." Her gaze went from Kevin to Stark. "Either of you. Old Magick *isn't normal*. It's leftover magick from when all of the worlds were created, and it's too powerful for mortals. Eventually, it'll turn you into the Old Magick equivalent of a human crackhead—or worse."

"That's why we're here," said Kevin. "Sgiach told us that Nyx's Realm connects all the versions of our world, and that if our blood sacrifice was accepted," he pointed at Stark's bloody arm, "and my connection to spirit and to you was strong enough—you'd be able to guide us to the portal that opens to Zoey's world."

Aphrodite blinked several times. "Huh. Who knew?"

"Wait, you don't know how to get us to the portal?" Stark asked.

Aphrodite shrugged. "No, but I also don't know how I materialized these clothes or the beach I spent some time on when I was first here that looked a lot like the one on Grand Cayman's Rum Point."

Stark looked completely confused. "What does that mean? Can you help us or not?"

"Of course I can help you. I just won't be able to explain how, that's all." She turned and began walking into the grove. Without looking behind her she said, "Are you coming, or what?"

"Coming!" Kevin said, hurrying after her.

Stark grunted and grumbled something, but also followed.

(

The beauty of Nyx's Grove dazzled Kevin. He'd thought the Craobh, the sacred grove on the Isle of Skye, was amazing, but compared to what surrounded them now it was like a poor copy of a masterpiece. The grove they walked through was every color of green Kevin could have imagined and, along with the glistening white and silver boulders and the thick carpet of moss, there were flowers everywhere. Their colors were incredible—the most brilliant blues, yellows, reds, and purples he'd ever seen. And their perfume was intoxicating. It changed every few feet from jasmine to honeysuckle, then to wisteria and moonflower—and those were just the scents Kevin could identify.

"I want to say that this place is beautiful, but that doesn't begin to describe it."

Aphrodite sighed happily. "Yeah, you never lose the wonder you feel when you first see it either. And this is just a tiny piece of Nyx's

Realm. I honestly think it stretches on infinitely. It changes too, and becomes what you need when you need it. It's really hard to explain."

Kevin nodded. "I think I get that. It's like me trying to find words to say how incredible this is. I can feel it, but I can't say it."

"Exactly!"

Aphrodite smiled up at him, and Kevin felt such a surge of joy that he reached out to put his arm around her, which passed through her body like there was nothing there.

"Sorry," he said quickly.

"Don't apologize. It doesn't hurt me—it only hurts you. Kev, I can feel you, but it's in here." She pressed her hand against her chest. "Not out here. And feeling you in my heart is so, so much *more*."

Kevin nodded but couldn't speak because along with love for her within his heart were pain and loss and grief.

Stark was peering around, looking through the magnificent flowers, flourishing trees, and shimmering boulders that had opened to reveal the moss path on which they had been walking. "Do you think we'll see any other ghosts—er—I mean, spirits?"

Aphrodite shrugged. "No telling. I'd kinda doubt it though. Well, unless you need to see someone who's here. The grove always knows what you need and sends it to you. But who knows if it works the same way for you guys because you're not dead. Plus, you're on a pretty specific mission and I'm not thinking that includes much sightseeing."

Stark went silent, and Kevin wondered what dead person he wished he could see.

"Do you have a house here?" Kevin asked Aphrodite.

Her laughter made little flashes of light happen around her that reminded Kevin of the fireflies that used to fill Haikey Creek Park in Broken Arrow on summer nights.

"No, I don't. Or at least I don't right now. Weird that I haven't even thought about it."

Stark found his voice again. "Where do you sleep?"

"I'm dead. I don't sleep. And time passes differently here than when you're alive," she said. "Oh, there are *a lot* of dogs here. I'm surprised there are none around right now. I never had a dog. My dad didn't care about them and my mother said that they were disgusting and dirty, but let me tell you—I like them. There's this one giant German shepherd that looks like a grizzly. He and I hang out a lot." Her grin widened. "Hey, how's Nala?"

Kevin smiled down at her. "She's great! She misses you."

Aphrodite snorted. "No, she doesn't. Cats know better. They're here too, but I expected that. It's the dogs that surprised me." She looked at Stark. "Hey, you need a dog. Seriously."

Stark frowned at her. "I'm a vampyre. If a cat chooses me that'd be okay, but a dog?" He moved his shoulders. "I've never heard of a dog at a House of Night."

Kevin laughed. "I guess I should've told you. Your counterpart in the world we're heading to has a dog. A big yellow lab named Duchess. She's cool."

"At the House of Night?"

"Definitely," Kevin said.

"Poor dog. I'll bet the cats are pissed about that," said Aphrodite.

Kevin shrugged. "I think Duchess has a lot of patience. Every time I saw her she seemed like a very happy girl." He gave Stark a wry look. "And I think Aphrodite's right. Having a dog would be good for you."

"Of course I'm right," Aphrodite said. "Being dead definitely doesn't change that. Oh, speaking of dead—I've spent some time with your sister."

"Zoey? Really? How is she?"

"She's good. She likes to hang out with the horses."

Stark said, "There are horses here too?"

"Yep. Try to keep up. There are *lots* of animals here. Anyway, yeah, I like her."

"In the world I'm heading to, you and Z are really good friends," Kevin said.

Aphrodite shot Stark a quick look before saying, "And in that world Zoey and Stark are a thing, right? Like an Oathbound Warrior *thing*?"

"Yeah, that's right," Kevin said, also giving Stark a look.

"What?" Stark said. "It's not like I didn't already know that. Plus, I never met our Zoey, the one that's dead and over here. The only one I know is the one from the Other World, and it's not like I'm in love with her or anything."

"Then why did you have to come with me?" Kevin asked—sick of how out of touch with his feelings he'd begun to realize this Stark truly was.

Stark blurted, "To make up for helping Neferet! Shit, man, how many times do I have to say that?"

His angry words echoed around them. Kevin could actually see them. They were dark, inky, and they lifted until they came to the verdant canopy where they were absorbed.

"That's what happens to lies," Aphrodite said. "They don't last here."

"They're not ..." Stark sighed. "Never mind."

Aphrodite paused and turned to Stark. "You and I definitely weren't friends, but I don't care about that anymore. I can see what's wrong with you, and because I know you can't, I'm going to tell you about it—once. What you do with it afterward is up to you."

Stark sighed again. "Okay. What?"

"You'll never be happy if you can't accept your feelings—and that means the good ones along with the bad. You are seriously the poster boy for toxic young male bullshit. And I say that with love because you can change it. Here's the truth—it is *not* good for men to deny their feelings. Crying isn't weakness—it's healing. Asking for help doesn't make you a pussy—it makes you mature. Until you deal with all that negativity inside you—all that anger and regret and jealousy—you're going to be like this. A guy who has potential but is kinda douchey." She flipped back her hair. "It's your choice. You need to fix yourself. No one can do that for you.

And, giant newsflash—it's no woman's responsibility to make you a better man. Do that on your own. Period. The end."

Aphrodite began walking again, and this time she moved more quickly. Kevin and Stark scrambled to keep up with her.

"Hey, I don't mean to rush you guys, but like I said, time passes differently here, and I just got a major feeling that you two need to be in Tulsa sooner rather than later."

"Can you tell what's going on there?" Kevin asked.

"No. I have zero clue. But I know you need to be there. I also know I need to have you promise me something—both of you. Especially you, Kevin."

"Okay, yeah, we're listening," said Kevin.

"I said this before, but it won't leave my mind, which means I need to say more about it. Do *not* use Old Magick. I know it's tempting, especially for you," she smiled at Kevin. "You're unusually powerful. It'd be easy for you to give the sprites a call, make a quick deal with them, and then go on about your business. But Old Magick will change you if you keep using it."

Stark lifted his hands and let them fall to his sides. "Yeah, you already said that. I think we need to go and—"

"James Stark, there is more going on here than you can understand. There is a reason Old Magick has mostly been confined to Skye and is under the watchful eye of a queen who isn't fully vampyre or immortal. It doesn't belong out in the world. Do you understand?"

Kevin spoke first. "Not entirely, but I think that's part of the issue with Old Magick. I won't use it though. I swear. I lost you because of it. I want nothing to do with those sprites."

Aphrodite looked at Stark with one brow arched. "Well?"

"Yeah, whatever. I get it. Old Magick is dangerous. I won't use it. Promise."

"Not a particularly moving promise, but you have pledged your word in Nyx's Grove. And that pledge is binding." Around

Aphrodite the air swirled and sizzled. "Now, come on. Let's go. You need to be in Tulsa."

As they walked on, Kevin focused on enjoying the sliver of time he'd been granted with Aphrodite. He wished he could hold her hand, but instead he walked beside her, talking about nothing and everything and memorizing each detail of her face, her eyes, and the way she looked at him and smiled.

There was no way to judge how long they'd been moving through Nyx's Grove when Aphrodite stopped abruptly and Stark almost walked through her. "There—that's the door to the world you need to enter."

The grove hadn't thinned. It had opened to reveal a large, oval-shaped portal that looked like a whirlpool of stars and moons and galaxies had been stirred together and poured onto the surface of a glistening mirror. The longer Kevin stared at it, the dizzier he felt.

He swallowed past the sudden dryness in his throat. "What do we do now?"

"Walk into it. Oh, and think about where you want to be. It'd suck for you if you were dropped, like, into the middle of the ocean or the Mojave or whatever. No way your cell service extends to alternative worlds—well, unless something major has changed with the different carriers."

Kevin said to Stark, "We need to go to the Tulsa House of Night."

"Definitely," Stark said. "How about the statue of Nyx in the courtyard across from her temple."

Kevin nodded. "Sounds good to me." Then he turned to Aphrodite and drew a deep breath. "I'll see you again on the way back—that's what Sgiach said." Her face softened, and Kevin thought she'd never looked so lovely.

"I'll be listening for your call. Hey, it's going to be hard, but you have to remember *she's* not *me*. She has her own world and life … and love." Aphrodite said the last word softly. "Don't let it break your heart."

Kevin wiped at the tears tracking down his face. "I know. And I'll try not to let it get to me."

"If she comforts you—accept it for what it is."

"And what is it?" Kevin said.

"You'll have to ask her, but when she answers you, remember what she says and know that she's telling you the truth—*her* truth. Just as it is my truth that I loved you when I was alive, and I love you still. I always will."

Kevin couldn't speak. He could only nod.

Aphrodite went to Stark. "Boy Bow, this trip is going to be difficult for you too, but for different reasons. It's up to you to learn from it ... or don't," she shrugged. "But if you don't, it'll make you even douchier."

"I'll keep that in mind. You know, you didn't call me Bow Boy much when you were alive."

Aphrodite laughed. "Oh, poor Bow Boy! Yes, I did—in my mind. *Constantly*, in my mind." Then she began backing into the grove. "Go now," she said. "You're needed there."

Kevin watched her smile one more time and blow him a kiss, then it was like the grove absorbed her, and Aphrodite disappeared. Reluctantly, he joined Stark at the portal.

Kevin cracked his knuckles. "Please take us to Nyx's statue in the courtyard of the Tulsa House of Night."

Stark ran his fingers through his hair, sighed, and said, "To the statue of Nyx at the Tulsa House of Night."

Together, they entered the portal.

12

Other Lynette

As usual, Lynette woke before Neferet. In the kitchen that someone—Lynette guessed bottom-of-the-pecking-order Kelsey—had cleaned, she hurriedly prepared Neferet's meal, then boiled an egg for herself and made toast with jam and a pot of coffee, which she took upstairs to her room to eat in peace as she waited for dusk and for Neferet to wake.

She went to the upstairs sitting room that bordered the balcony from which they'd observed Neferet the night before. Lynette pulled one of the overly ornate little tables over to the wall of windows and gazed out at a world covered with diamonds as she sipped her coffee and opened her borrowed laptop.

Ice blanketed everything, turning the lovely courtyard and rear grounds of the villa into something magickal enough for the sprites to call home.

"We have electricity. But let's see how bad it is," Lynette mused as her fingers danced across the keys. "Hum, Tulsa is a mess, but they aren't calling it an icepocalypse—or at least not yet they aren't." She glanced out the windows again. The sky still spit ice, but not like it had the night before. Lynette guessed that a drive to Woodward Park would be almost impossible. "But a *walk*, that should be just fine."

She was nervous about what the night would bring, but Lynette trusted Neferet. She knew her mistress would handle whatever situation arose. The truth was, she was hoping Neferet would fail—that the sacrifice of five vapid mortals would not be enough to siphon power to this world's totally crazy version of her friend. A fail tonight would be all it would take for Lynette to convince Neferet that they really must return to their world, if only to regroup and come up with plan B.

Lynette tapped her chin contemplatively. *I'd like to live in Scotland. I'll bet Neferet would too. We were happy at Balmacara Mains. I could wait there while Neferet goes to Skye and gains her immortality.* That was their original plan, and it was a good one.

She gazed out the window as she thought about this world— about how similar yet utterly unlike it was to hers. Lynette never imagined she'd miss Tulsa, but she would happily return there if it meant leaving this place.

And then a thought struck her, and after it did she was amazed that it had taken her so long to consider it.

"I wonder who *my* mirror image is in this world?" she murmured at the computer screen.

For a moment her fingers froze over the keys. What if she'd never gotten out of Camino Villa trailer park in Broken Arrow? Lynette shuddered. Could she leave a version of herself here to rot in poverty and ignorance?

"She's a version of you, Lynette," she told herself. "I'll bet she got out too. And in this world, there was no war. She's probably running a whole corporation and has a permanent table at the Summit Club reserved—by the west windows that look out over the river—just for her."

She typed "Lynette Witherspoon" into the search bar and began reading as her coffee grew cold and her stomach grew hot with bile.

She'd been correct. This world's Lynette Witherspoon had been a successful businesswoman. She'd lived in a mansion in midtown and thrived as the head of her own business.

And then last year, she'd been murdered—by Neferet.

(

Zoey

"Please tell me we're not having another icepocalypse. We already had one. Last year. We are not due for another for five years or so." I spoke into Stark's chest as he cradled me against him while we stared into our fireplace. "At least Grandma's been in town for the past couple days. I can almost smell her lavender chocolate chip cookies baking already—makes me almost wish for a week of ice."

The storm had pretty much isolated the school, and I'd suspended classes for the night (at least) because the buses that ferried the red fledglings from the tunnels beneath the depot to campus were currently stuck on the ice rink that was our parking lot. So even though the sun had set, Stark and I hadn't budged from our room and, the truth was, I was beginning to enjoy every minute of our unexpected laziness.

"Well, I'm no weatherman, but Trav Meyer is, and he says that this stuff seems stuck here for now, but he's expecting it to clear in a day or so. It's already kinda sorta stopped."

"Kinda sorta? Does that mean—"

CLUNK!

And everything electric went black.

"Ah oh," I said, though without much enthusiasm. Candles and gaslights lit the school, and we had a backup generator for things like the media center and our refrigerators, but there was something homey and romantic about the power being off and a snow day being called. The truth was, we could all use the break the isolation would bring.

Stark sighed. "I better go be sure the kitchen flips the refrigerators and freezers over to the generators."

I mirrored his sigh. "And I better call Stevie Rae and be sure everything's okay at the depot."

"She's not there, remember?"

"Oh, that's right." I grinned. After we'd cast the protective spell around the grotto last night, Stevie Rae and Aphrodite and I—as well as our guys, which included Damien and Jack—had hung out so long in the dining hall, laughing and eating and basically just destressing, that dawn had crept up on us and Stevie Rae and Rephaim had decided to stay on campus for the day. "Stevie Rae and Rephaim went to our old dorm room—well, more Stevie Rae than Rephaim. He was out there flying around in the ice somewhere while she snoozed the day away. I'm sure they're curled up together right now, though." I sighed and felt nostalgic. "I miss that room sometimes."

Stark made a show of looking around our large and awesome living quarters that included a sitting room that faced a wide stone fireplace, a kitchenette, a giant bedroom, and a really nice bathroom, *with* a claw-foot bathtub. "You seriously miss one tiny room you shared with Stevie Rae and Kenny Chesney?"

I giggled. "Well, memory might have made it a little more luxurious than it was."

"A little?"

"Okay, a lot." I wrapped myself more tightly around him. "Don't go yet. The chef is über-responsible. No way is she gonna let our food spoil. She'll switch over to the generators, and Stevie Rae has those tunnel fledglings so organized that there's nothing for me to worry about at the depot."

"And if there is, Stevie Rae will handle it," added Stark, squeezing me so tightly I made a little squeak.

"Hey, what about Woodward Park? The cameras won't be recording if the electricity is out."

"I think it'll be fine. Darius stationed a Warrior there for the night shift. I'm sure he's miserable, but I don't think we need to send backup. Not in this icy mess."

"Maybe you should call Darius and have him check in with the Warrior," I said. "And we really need to think about adding a structure on top of that ridge for our vamps. I know they're pretty much impervious to weather, but that doesn't mean they don't need some kind of shelter. I hate to think about the poor guy out there turning into a Son of Erebus–sicle."

"I promise you Darius has that handled. Want me to call him and tell him to have the Warrior stand down and come back to campus, at least for the night?"

I thought about it and felt the itch of intuition that said I needed to stick with our original plan, even if it meant a miserable night for one Warrior.

"Sadly, no. We need to keep an eye on that grotto. Plus, if Darius thought we needed to call the Warrior back to campus, I'd have already heard from him."

"I agree," Stark settled back into the cushy couch with me.

"Do you actually think we can get one night to just relax and—" I kissed his neck. "Do—" I followed the kiss with a teasing little nip. "Nothing but this." He met my lips and I sank into his kiss.

"Damn, I hope so," Stark said as he pulled off the oversized T-shirt I was wearing, which was only right. It was his …

13

Other Neferet

Neferet wrapped herself in the cashmere robe Lynette had purchased for her the day before and joined her handmaid in the second-floor sitting room. Lynette was already there, of course, with her breakfast expertly prepared and waiting on a tray with a carafe of blood and wine on ice.

"Good day, dearest one," she said as she swept past Lynette, who was, as usual, hard at work on her borrowed computer. Neferet poured herself a goblet of bloody wine and a took piece of toast slathered in butter and strawberry jam—organic, of course—with her to nibble and sip as she gazed out the window at the rear lawn of the villa where, just hours before, she had conjured sprites who had created the gorgeous and convenient icy wonderland before her. "Oh, this is exactly what I asked for. Of course, it would be better if the electricity went out, but there is still time for that."

Lynette said nothing.

"I hope those young women were duly impressed last night. So much so that they will not cause too many problems for us today, though I can imagine that they will whine and complain about the weather."

When Lynette still said nothing, Neferet turned from the wall of beveled glass. She realized she had been mistaken earlier. Lynette's fingers were not flying across the keys as usual. She was staring at the computer screen, hands clasped in her lap, looking exceedingly pale.

Neferet left the windows and hurried to sit across from Lynette. "Dearest, are you unwell?"

Lynette's gaze lifted to meet hers, and the depth of misery and fear within her eyes shocked Neferet to her core. She dropped the toast and put down her unfinished goblet, covering Lynette's hand with her own. "What has happened?"

"I googled myself. I don't know why I didn't think about it earlier. Of course a version of me would exist here. I—I was just busy, preoccupied. But I had everything prepared for the day, and those girls are, thankfully, still sleeping, so I had some time. I found her—me."

"Oh, no! Is she in trouble too? We shall rescue her. Just tell me where she is, and I will be certain it is done."

"She's in Oaklawn Cemetery off Eleventh."

"She's dead?"

Lynette nodded.

"How did she die? Shall we avenger her?"

Lynette opened her mouth to answer, but then shook her head slightly and turned the laptop around so that Neferet could see the story she'd been staring at.

As she read, Neferet began feeling something utterly alien to her—or at least alien to her for more than the hundred years since her mother had died trying to birth her brother. Neferet felt grief—a great sadness coupled with outrage and a healthy dose of fear for the woman sitting across the table from her—the woman who had become so very dear to her.

Neferet's mouth went dry. "She killed her. This world's Neferet killed her," she almost couldn't speak the terrible words.

Lynette nodded woodenly. "Keep reading. It gets worse."

"Worse than death?" Neferet mused. "I do not see how—" She gasped, clutching her throat. "Oh! It is worse."

"She could've escaped. But she willingly stayed with Neferet." Lynette stood abruptly and went to the wall of windows to stare out as she rubbed her arms as if she was freezing.

Horrified, Neferet kept reading. Lynette was correct. The version of her who had lived in this strange world had been found with her blood drained, slumped on Neferet's throne in the Mayo—dead, along with every human who had had the misfortune of being trapped in that building with the self-proclaimed Goddess of Tulsa. Police accounts, bystanders, and the House of Night all agreed that Lynette had remained with Neferet of her own free will, choosing to be the first human to worship her in goddess form. She had even gotten away from Neferet, yet she faithfully returned to her side only to be killed, drained of blood, and arranged on that monster's throne in the Mayo.

Neferet felt sick. She finished the article and downed the glass of bloody wine. Then she went to the ornate liquor cabinet in the corner of the room, chose an expensive brandy, and filled the bottom of a snifter with it. She took the glass with her as she joined Lynette at the windows.

"Here, dearest. Drink this very quickly."

Mechanically, Lynette took the glass and downed the brandy and then dropped it. It made a muffled sound as it bounced against the carpeted floor.

"Lynette, look at me." Her handmaid turned to face her and Neferet gently took both of Lynette's hands in her own. "This changes things."

"Are we going to go home now?"

"Almost. I will still break the monster from her tomb. I cannot leave her there, just as you could not bear to leave this world's version of you in danger."

"I'm too late. She's already dead."

Neferet squeezed her hands. "I know, dearest. Were that not so, I would do everything in my power to help her—to be sure she was safe and happy."

"If you release her from that tomb, she will try to kill me."

Neferet swelled with anger. "I would *never* allow that!"

Lynette began to sob. "But she's immortal. How will you stop her?"

"I am not without power—you know that. The sprites heed my call and Old Magick wields more power than an insane, starving goddess. I will protect you—always." Neferet drew a deep breath before she continued. "Lynette, my dearest friend, there is one way I can protect you more fully than any other. Do you know what it is to Imprint with a vampyre?"

Lynette sniffled and said, "I know the basics of it. It usually happens between mated pairs, and most easily between a human and a vampyre."

Neferet wiped the tears from Lynette's face. "Yes, dearest. When it happens between a human and a vampyre, it creates an attachment like none other. The Imprinted pair may be able to communicate without words—may know each other's location—and are always, always brought closer by the bond.

"Another very important side effect is that the blood of the Imprinted human changes. Its scent is repulsive to other vampyres, as they can smell and taste that it will never be freely given to them because it, and the human, completely belong to another vampyre. Dearest, if we were to Imprint, you would be safe from that monster's bloodlust. You would also be clearly marked as belonging to me, and *all* other vampyres would know, should they wish to harm you, they must first vanquish me."

Lynette stared at her. The human's eyes were unblinking and looked huge and liquid as they filled with more tears.

"Oh, please do not cry, dearest!" Neferet pulled her into an embrace. "I will not let you be harmed. I give you my oath." She held her out at arm's length so that she could look into her handmaid's eyes again. "I have never Imprinted with anyone. Not once in my long life. I have always avoided it and never, ever considered Imprinting with a human. But now I offer this bond to you as I do my oath."

"I'm afraid," Lynette said.

"Of me?"

Lynette shook her head. "No. I'm afraid to die."

"But, dearest, you will not die. You will simply be bonded to me."

"I have a horrible feeling that if that monster is released, she will be the death of me."

Neferet's grip on her shoulders tightened. "I will never allow that. You trusted me enough to come with me to another world. Will you trust me enough now to believe that I will protect you?"

"I—I will," whispered Lynette.

"And will you allow yourself to Imprint with me?"

Lynette's voice sounded stronger, more like her own when she answered. "Yes, my lady. I will."

The two women hugged, clinging to one another until it was Lynette who stepped back, wiping her face. "How do I do it?"

Neferet smiled. "*We* do it, and it is quite easy when both parties want the same thing. Often it is sexual, so do not be shocked at the feelings of pleasure." Lynette looked surprised, but not upset or repulsed, so Neferet continued. "I cannot say for sure what it will do to us or how it will make us feel, except that it will bring us even closer."

Lynette nodded. "How do *we* do this?"

"Come to the settee here." Neferet pointed at the gold velvet love seat positioned at the end of the wall of windows.

Lynette smoothed the cardigan she wore over her silk knit tank top and sat as Neferet returned to the liquor cabinet and poured brandy into another snifter—this time, considerably more than a taste. She sat beside Lynette and offered her the glass.

"Drink all of it—quickly. If you're a little tipsy the beginning will go easier. As I drink your blood, it will become pleasurable for you, but I would not have you experience any discomfort."

Lynette downed the expensive brandy in three gulps. "That's why you always had me get your feeders a little drunk before showing them to your suite?"

"It is. I used to enjoy the taste of fear on a feeder, but at Balmacara Mains I knew the panic and screams would upset Mrs. Muir and bring unwanted attention. That is, at first, why I asked you to get them drunk. Then, as I experienced the sweetness of their pleasure, my tastes changed." Neferet paused and touched Lynette's cheek gently. "Or perhaps I changed."

"We both have," said Lynette.

"I believe our friendship will change our world," said Neferet. "Now, I usually feed from the neck or the inner thigh—or even somewhere more intimate."

Lynette's eyes widened, and she hiccuped. "Oh, my! I—I didn't know about … that."

"Yes, well, I think it would be best if I fed from your arm. It will be simple to staunch the flow of blood there and won't be uncomfortably intimate for you."

"I am ready." Lynette shrugged off her cardigan, folded it neatly, and placed it across the back of the love seat.

Neferet wet her lips and slid closer.

(

Other Lynette

Lynette shivered, lifted her arm, and offered it to Neferet. She took it and gently rested it across her lap.

"Have I told you how much I appreciate your fastidiousness? And I do not mean only in regard to the work you do for me. You are always so perfectly coiffed, and you dress with impeccable taste."

Neferet's compliment and the brandy worked together to warm

Lynette, and she stopped shivering. "Thank you. That means a lot to me. All my life I've tried to be put together."

"I know. And I understand. It's because of your childhood. You never want to go back there," Neferet said.

"Neither do you," Lynette said.

"And neither of us ever shall. Now, my dearest, lean back and relax. This will not hurt. You will feel a slight tug as my fingernail opens your skin, but the moment I begin drinking, my pheromones pass to you. When Nyx created vampyres she made it so that feeding can be a very pleasurable sensation."

"Will I bleed a lot?"

"No. I will only drink from you until I feel the Imprint. Then I will close your wound. You saw no blood when my feeders left Balmacara, remember?"

Lynette leaned back and closed her eyes. "That's right. I remember. Go ahead. I'm not afraid anymore."

Neferet lifted her arm. At her wrist, where the skin is thin and the veins close to the surface, Neferet kissed her softly. Then Lynette felt a sharp tug. It made her inhale and tense with the anticipation of pain, but before it hit her system Neferet's soft, warm lips pressed against her skin and she began licking and sucking.

The pleasure shocked Lynette. At first it was indeed sexual— *very* sexual. She moaned, and the thought flickered through her mind: *We could be doing so much more than this right now!* Then Neferet drank deeper and the pleasure shifted to incredible warmth that suffused her body, spreading joy with each beat of her heart. The joy grew and grew. It poured from Neferet, and as it did the loneliness that had shadowed Lynette's entire life was chased away.

Lynette opened her eyes and cradled Neferet closer to her and stroked her hair as the vampyre continued to drink. As she took in her blood, Lynette began to sense Neferet's feelings. She could tell that the drinking of her blood brought pleasure to Neferet. She could also feel the worry within Neferet—the concern about

Lynette's safety and the vampyre's determination to protect her. And then she listened deeper, and Lynette found that secret place deep inside Neferet where she hid that which she never allowed anyone to see—that which had informed so many of her decisions.

"Let me give you that gift in return," Lynette said as she continued to stroke her hair. "Let me relieve the loneliness I sense within you." Lynette concentrated on sending everything she said—everything she felt—to Neferet with her blood. "As long as I live, you will always have a true and faithful friend. I will never betray you. I will never leave you. I will never, ever hurt you."

Neferet shuddered and then stopped drinking from Lynette. With one gentle lick of her tongue, she closed the slender wound, leaving only a pink line. Then she lifted her head. Her face was awash with tears.

"We have Imprinted, dearest, and the beautiful vow you just made to me, I swear to you as well. We are sisters now, and we always shall be."

Lynette embraced Neferet and they held one another gently as their new connection solidified and strengthened.

Lynette was the first to pull away. She wiped Neferet's beautiful face of her tears.

"Now I feel like I can conquer anything—even the monster that is this world's Neferet," said Lynette.

"Oh, dearest, no! You will not go to the park with me. I would that you remain here—safe—and await my return."

Lynette touched Neferet's cheek. "But don't you understand? I can't do that now. I have to be with you."

A staged cough came from behind them and then Vanessa's flippant voice said, "Oh, oopsie. Don't mean to interrupt, but at least now I understand why you two are so close. You should've just said you're gay. We're cool with that. Leaves more men for us."

Neferet's response was instantaneous. She stood and whirled to face the young woman. She bared her teeth fiercely and lifted her hands as if they were claws. The vampyre seemed to fill the room. When she spoke, her voice battered Vanessa so that she stumbled back and almost fell to the floor.

"*Your insolence will no longer be tolerated!*"

Vanessa cringed. "Sorry! I—I didn't mean anything."

Lynette stood quickly and touched Neferet on the shoulder. "My lady, I think it is time for the girls to put on their Dark Sisters makeup and prepare for tonight's ritual."

When Neferet looked at her, Lynette watched her eyes change from feral red back to emerald. The vampyre shook herself and when she spoke her voice was normal once more.

"Ah, dearest, you are absolutely right—as always. Vanessa, child, I do apologize. You startled me. Now, it would be best if you did as Lynette instructed. It is almost time for you to greet your goddess."

"Okay. Yeah. That sounds awesome." Vanessa bobbed an awkward curtsy and scrambled to leave the drawing room.

"Thank you," Lynette said.

"I should have done that the night we arrived."

"Oh, I wasn't thanking you for that. Vanessa is insignificant. Thank you for Imprinting with me—for keeping me safe."

"Always," Neferet said.

"And I will join you tonight. It would be too painful otherwise."

Neferet sighed but nodded. "Yes, I feel that too. Help me prepare. The sooner we get this over with, the sooner we can return to our world."

"Anything for you, my lady."

"You know you don't have to call me that," said Neferet.

"I like calling you that—and someday soon I will like calling you my goddess."

14

Other Neferet

With Lynette at her side, Neferet led the five vapid young women through the dark, empty streets of the opulent Midtown neighborhood that bordered Woodward Park. Her plan had been to wait until just before dawn, which would assure that the House of Night would be sleepy, and the Warriors stationed at the park would be heading back to campus, but Lynette—industrious as ever—had discovered that classes had been canceled. From her lengthy experience as High Priestess of her own House of Night, Neferet knew that meant that, like the rest of Tulsa and the surrounding area, the staff, students, *and* Warriors would be nestled inside enjoying the time off.

So, she'd moved up the timetable on that night's very important events.

It was almost midnight. Ice was still falling, but lazily—just enough to keep the roads closed and the electric lines down and unreachable for repair. As their small group approached the park, Neferet was filled with a surprising sense of nostalgia. The large, well-tended homes that surrounded Woodward Park glowed from within—not with the garish light of electricity, but instead with the warmth of candles. Add gaslit streetlights and it was easy to imagine that they had been transported one hundred or more years into the past.

What would I do differently if I had it to do all over again? Neferet mused to herself.

"Is this what it looked like a century ago?" Lynette asked softly as she gazed around.

Neferet smiled. Lynette couldn't read her mind, but their Imprint allowed them to share feelings. "Ah, you sense my nostalgia?"

"I do, my lady," said Lynette. "I know ice storms are destructive and, quite frankly, a pain in the ass if they last very long, but I've always been drawn to them. There is no denying that they touch everything with beauty."

"I agree. Perhaps when we return home, I will conjure another storm for us, and we can be stranded in Balmacara Mains with Mrs. Muir's fresh-baked bread and an excellent selection of red wine."

"That sounds divine."

"It does indeed. And, yes, you were correct. I was just thinking that Midtown looks like it has been transported back a century or so." Neferet took Lynette's hand. "I wish you had been with me then. I believe my life would've taken a different path had I known your friendship when I was young."

"Oh, my lady. You are still young."

"Um, excuse me?" Vanessa interrupted them.

"Yes, what is it?" said Neferet as she let loose Lynette's hand and shared a mutually annoyed look with her friend.

"We're almost at the park and we want to be sure we know exactly what we're supposed to do."

"How many times did you go over this with them?" Neferet asked Lynette.

"Five. But one more makes it a good, round number." She grinned at Neferet. "Remember, my lady, very soon these lovely young women will not be our charges anymore. We will hand them over to *their* goddess. I don't mind taking extra time to reiterate the parts they must play tonight to accomplish that."

"Very well, let us cross Peoria and then we will go up through the Rose Gardens and approach the park from the south, atop the ridge. The Garden Center will be deserted. If I remember correctly, the rear of the mansion will provide some protection from the elements. You girls can leave your clothes there while Lynette reminds you of your roles. Then we will enter the park and prepare to release your goddess."

"Ok-k-kay, y-y-yeah, that s-sounds good." Vanessa's teeth chattered, and she shivered violently before stepping back to huddle with the other young women as they continued to follow Lynette and Neferet. They wore their velvet cloaks that corresponded to the element they each pretended to represent. Beneath the cloaks they wore nothing but bathrobes. On their feet were thick Ugg boots that Neferet had always thought were terribly unattractive, but they did allow them to traverse the icy streets and sidewalks without slipping too much.

As Neferet had explained in private to Lynette—the girls were not to bring anything with their clothes that could identify their bodies. No purses, no credit cards, nothing personal at all. The fact that they were each wearing extremely expensive bathrobes they'd ordered specially through the Blue Dolphin, a posh linen shop in Utica Square, was annoying enough, but dearest Lynette had thought of a way to get rid of those as well. All Neferet had to do was to be sure their bodies couldn't be identified, and for that she had her ravenous children and the power of the new moon.

The driveway that stretched up to the historic Snedden Mansion that housed the Tulsa Garden Center was so ice covered that they were forced to walk up the expansive front lawn.

"Hurry, we are far too easy to see out here in the open!" Neferet commanded, forcing the girls to slip and slide behind her as she increased the pace.

Finally, they got to the mansion and rushed around back. In the distinctive style of the Italian Renaissance, majestic white columns held up arched stone that, more than a century before, had shielded gaily dressed party-goers from the harsh Oklahoma weather.

The five young women huddled beneath the protective stone, shivering and shifting from foot to foot in an attempt to keep warm.

Lynette faced them. "Why, I wish you could see how perfectly wild and dramatic you look! Your face paint is exquisite, and the ice has turned your cloaks to jewels."

Amber's voice was sharp with irritation. "If you'd let us bring our phones, you could take our picture."

"Would that picture be worth keeping your goddess trapped?" Neferet snapped. "Dearest Lynette already explained to you that what I am about to do is to conjure ancient spirits, and technology offends them. If they are offended, they will not be as powerful, and it will take a powerful spell to break loose Neferet!" Of course, nothing she said was true. The only spirits that would be used that night would be the power from their five deaths—and the only things conjured would be her children, who were already there surrounding them, though invisible to everything except Lynette and the strength of the new moon.

"We understand," Vanessa said. "We're ready to get this over with and go back to the house with our goddess." The girl's blue eyes narrowed. "Did you say you and your handmaid would be returning with our Neferet?"

"We didn't say," Neferet answered, carefully holding her irritation at the young woman's offensive question in check. "But there tends to be room for only one goddess per home, and Lynette and I shall be on our way back to our own shortly."

Vanessa and the others looked relieved, and Neferet was again amazed at their naivete. She'd read the news reports of what this world's Neferet had done a year ago, and how they could imagine she would be a gracious guest, holding court over ridiculous girls, was beyond her comprehension.

"Lynette, dearest, while you remind the Dark Sisters of the roles they must willingly play tonight, I shall scout ahead and be sure the park is empty. When I return we will be ready to begin."

"Yes, my lady."

"Oh, and one other thing," Neferet added. "Be sure each of the Dark Sisters takes several drinks of the excellent single malt scotch I tucked away in your satchel. It will help warm them." *And make their minds foggy and their reflexes slow.*

"Thank you for reminding me, my lady." Lynette faced the shivering women who had perked up the moment Neferet had mentioned booze. "Okay, ladies, after I remind you of your roles, it will be time for you to take off your robes and give them to me. I will fold and place them in this bag so that they remain dry and ready for you when the ritual is over."

Neferet smiled to herself. The women would never return, though the robes would remain dry. Well, more accurately, they would be tossed into a nearby dumpster and set ablaze by the fire starters Lynette carried inside the chic bag she'd borrowed from Vanessa.

"You know, *Lynette*," Vanessa had taken to pronouncing her name carefully since Neferet had put an end to her overt insolence. "You really were born to serve."

Neferet wanted to spin around and fly at the impertinent, spoiled child's throat, but Lynette's response drifted through the falling ice to make her smile.

"Yes, I was. Just as you were born to be a willing participant in the freeing of your goddess."

Still grinning, Neferet walked quickly to the uppermost tier of the Tulsa Rose Gardens. She wished she had time to enjoy the night. The ice had turned everything from bleak to magickal. The only light came from the greenhouse that sat to the rear of the Snedden Mansion. A generator must have powered it, because light poured from within. The peaked windows fogged from the inside heat and water rained down them, unable to freeze. The greenhouse lent a pool of light to the roses and a small portion of Woodward Park. There, ice coated everything, and the illumination transformed the park's dormant brown grass into jeweled spikes.

Moving stealthily, Neferet crossed the park, heading for the only other light in the area—a large metal brazier beside which stood a single Son of Erebus Warrior who was currently warming his hands over the open flame. He was several yards away from the top of the tomb, and as Neferet circled silently around, trying to see if he was truly alone, she understood why. The nearer she got to the tomb, the more uneasy she felt. Neferet knew should she get too close, the spirits of the bison would emerge, ready to repel her. But that would warn the Warrior, and that would not do.

Neferet took longer than she planned to observe the area, searching for more Warriors, and when she found none she almost scoffed aloud. This world's Zoey Redbird might be a powerful High Priestess who commanded all five elements, but she was still an inexperienced child.

I would never leave the guarding of something so precious to a lone Warrior.

Neferet moved closer to the brazier and the Warrior. From the concealment of a thick, winter-bare oak, she murmured to the tendrils that shadowed her everywhere. "Children, kill that Warrior—silently. Feed freely from him but be sure you drag his body far enough away that the girls will not discover it. I have tolerated enough from them and cannot abide silly hysteria. Go, now! And then rejoin me after you have disposed of him, but be certain you remain invisible."

Like eager kittens the tendrils of Darkness rushed across the frozen grass. Neferet only watched long enough to see one of the thickest of her children rise up, cobra-like, behind the Warrior, so tall that when the tendril hissed, causing the vampyre to whirl around, its ravenous mouth was even with his face. Before the Son of Erebus could make a sound, the tendril entered his mouth and slid down his throat. Without uttering a word, the Warrior crumpled. Satisfied, Neferet took a more direct path across the park, returning quickly to the Garden Center, but before she rejoined the group she detoured to the greenhouse. Silently, she used her preternatural strength to force open the door. No alarm sounded, and Neferet shook her head in disgust. In *her* Tulsa, security was much better. Lock broken, she gently closed the door and returned to the waiting cluster of women, who were still passing around the bottle of scotch. They did seem in much better spirits and they had stopped their annoying shivering.

As soon as Lynette caught sight of Neferet, she motioned for them to begin disrobing, which they did with only a minimum of complaints.

"Are they not taking off their boots?" Neferet asked.

"My lady, I believe were they barefoot they would be distracted from their circle-casting and would not concentrate on their intent."

"Ah, I see. Very well, you may keep your unattractive boots on. Now, Dark Sisters, follow me. Be silent. Go immediately to your places and lift your candles as you await spirit to light them and summon your elements."

"My, uh, lady," Vanessa hiccuped and giggled. "Um, don't you want to inspect us to be sure we are pleasing?"

"There is no need, sister spirit," Neferet said. "I am not your goddess. She who will be freed tonight will inspect you. Do you feel worthy of her?"

"Yes!" The five chorused together.

"Excellent," said Neferet. "And tell me again, do you come here to be the conduits through which my power will flow willingly?"

"Yes!" they said, even more eagerly.

"I have a question," said Vanessa.

Neferet stifled her sigh. "Yes?"

"This power you're going to fill us with—will we feel it?"

"Oh, absolutely," Neferet assured her truthfully.

Amber took a large swig from the bottle, burped, and added, "Can we keep any of the power?"

"One never knows," Neferet prevaricated as Amber and Vanessa shared an excited look. "Now, what is your intent that you will focus on all during your ritual?"

"That's easy." Vanessa answered with no hesitation. "We think about the fact that we're here willingly and that we're the conduits for the power that will free our goddess."

"Will—will it hurt?" asked Kelsey.

Lynette responded before Neferet could. "Only for a moment. Then you will be free of pain and filled with power."

"She already told us that!" Jordan snapped at Kelsey.

Kelsey should have chosen her friends better, thought Neferet. Then she said, "We go now to do a great thing, to right a terrible wrong—to free a goddess. The moment we enter the park, begin focusing on your intent. Once the five of you are in position, Vanessa, your spirit sister, will begin casting the circle. I will not be able to be close to the tomb, but you will be able to see me, and be assured that the power I use tonight will not be hindered by a vampyre repel spell. While Lynette is hiding the bag that holds your robes, follow me to your destiny!"

Lynette disappeared around the side of the mansion to where Neferet had noted the presence of a large metal dumpster in which she could burn the robes while Neferet led the women into the Rose Gardens.

They strode through the gardens, the five tipsy girls whispering to each other. Neferet did not feel the need to silence them, however, when she overheard that they were repeating their intentions aloud, over and over. Lynette returned quickly to her side smelling vaguely of smoke as the five willing sacrifices followed behind.

"The robes caught easily?" Neferet kept her voice low, for Lynette's ears alone.

"Very easily. The dumpster was filled with paper. Everything within will soon be ash," Lynette whispered. "Were the Warriors difficult to overcome?"

"Not at all, and there was only one."

"That was a grave error on Zoey Redbird's part."

"Just one of many, dearest."

The brazier was still ablaze, but there was no sign of the Warrior. Neferet's invisible children rejoined her, thick and warm with fresh blood. She pushed through the shielding azalea bushes. Neferet wanted to get nearer to the tomb, and she could have ignored the unpleasantness that radiated from a glistening circle of ice-covered salt that surrounded the tomb, but she could already feel the presence of the guardian spirits. The last thing she wanted was to waste energy on battling the spectral bison.

Neferet turned to face the women for one last time. "Dark Sisters, now is your hour to shine. What you do tonight will be remembered for centuries and repeated over and over. You will please your stricken goddess, and she will never forget the sacrifice you make. I will be below. Take your places!"

She and Lynette remained there long enough to be sure the women were in position around the tomb, though neither of them paid any attention to which girl stood where. They weren't truly casting a circle. They had no power in their blood to compel the elements to come to them, and Neferet did not need to cast a circle. All she needed was the power of the invisible moon above her, and that which writhed around her, eager for what was to come.

Lynette and Neferet circled around the tomb to carefully follow one of the slick stone paths down to the lawn that stretched to Twenty-First Street. The park was shadow upon shadow. No electricity fueled the streetlights. The only light came from the brazier above the grotto. The flames licked high, casting strange, tongue-like shapes against the stone roof of the wall that encased the grotto and the goddess trapped within.

Standing on that roof was Vanessa, dressed only in a purple

velvet cloak. In a circle around her—some above the tomb, some below, were the four women who represented the elements.

"I must admit, they make a spectacular sight," said Lynette. "They're young and beautiful. The cloaks glisten with ice, and the silly face makeup they're wearing works from a distance."

"Those boots do not though."

"I agree," said Lynette. "But Uggs are easy to buy, which makes them difficult to trace, and allowing them to wear boots makes the five more comfortable. I honestly am not sure they would have walked across the park barefoot."

"They are weak willed and spoiled," said Neferet. "But they are here willingly. You are right about the boots. It only offends my sense of spectacle, and that is all."

Vanessa turned to look around, squinting against the dark and trying to see Neferet.

"I forgot they would not be able to see me," Neferet said, annoyed with herself.

Lynette reached into the pocket of the down ski jacket she'd "borrowed" from Kelsey's closet and pulled out a small flashlight. "I didn't forget."

"You are a treasure."

Lynette flicked the on button and focused the beam on Neferet, who lifted her spread arms and then dropped them with a flourish, signaling that Vanessa should begin casting the circle. Then she turned to Lynette while Vanessa walked to Jenna and pretended to invoke air.

"I want you to remain close to me but stay out of sight there in the shadows of the azalea hedge. I am going to cloak you with a very simple conceal spell. It will be strongest if you are close to me. Dearest, what happens next will be decidedly unpleasant. You know how the children can be when I loose them. Please do not feel as though you need to watch."

"I don't think I should," Lynette said.

"I agree. When Neferet is freed you must remain still and silent. Should she be as volatile and mad as we suspect, I will not allow her to see you. Instead you must wait here, cloaked in shadow, until I have left the park with the goddess, then go back to the Rose Gardens. I noticed the greenhouse was alight and I broke the lock. Within, you will have warmth and safety until I rejoin you."

"I hope she isn't insane and is able to appreciate what you have done for her and reciprocate by giving you the information you need."

"As do I, my dearest friend, but we must prepare for the worst. She killed one version of you. I will not allow her the opportunity to harm another."

They embraced, and then Lynette backed to the azalea hedge. One of Neferet's fat tendrils unwrapped from around her and slithered across the icy grass to Lynette, where it wound up her leg and draped around her waist.

Lynette smiled and stroked the tendril.

"Ah, my child, thank you for volunteering to stay with dearest Lynette. Trust me that your loyalty shall be rewarded tenfold, and you will feast and feast and feast." Neferet raised her arms, pointing her palms toward the thickest of the shadows behind Lynette. "Blanketing night, I call you with the power that courses through my veins—conceal this one dearest to me—friend and partner—her blood is Imprinted throughout my body. Shadows come! Protect my Lynette!"

Night seemed to turn to tar, sliding from the deepest of the blackness above and below, to fill the space around Lynette as if a thick curtain of black velvet had closed around her. Satisfied her friend was safe, Neferet focused on the young women who called themselves Dark Sisters.

Vanessa had lit all four element candles and was returning to stand in the middle of the roof that covered the grotto. She turned to the north and lit her purple candle. It illuminated her face and Neferet thought that she had to agree with Lynette. The young woman certainly was a striking sight. She'd flung back her cape to reveal a body that had been expertly sculpted. As she'd been instructed to do, Vanessa lifted her purple candle. Still holding it, she spread her arms wide and threw back her head. The other four women mimicked her, and they began to chant.

"Neferet—Neferet—Neferet—Neferet ... "

Neferet raised her arms, palms up, hands cupped to accept the power of the dark moon.

> *"Come to me, power of blackened moon.*
> *My vampyre blood to you attuned.*
> *Add strength to my spell this icy night,*
> *As a wrong I do mean to set aright.*
> *Willing sacrifice feeds the bound goddess within,*
> *Now in this world a new dark reign shall begin!"*

Centuries before, the Goddess of Night, Nyx, irrevocably linked the power of the moon to vampyres and that night it readily answered Neferet's call. Energy flowed into her cupped palms. She trembled at its touch and had to concentrate to fight the desire to absorb the delicious strength and keep it for herself.

"Now, my children, it is your turn. Kill each of them. Drain them of blood and muscle. Shatter their teeth. Eat everything—suck dry their marrow. Strip them to their empty bones. And then take the feast you hold within you and the power I give to you from the moon, and penetrate that puny, mundane wall to gift the feast of blood and bone and power to the goddess trapped within. Go now!"

The tendrils unwound from around her and glided swiftly across the diamond grass as Neferet threw the power of the dark moon at them. They absorbed it instantly, and she smiled while they swelled in size, radiating the often-overlooked energy of a new moon. Together they descended upon the five Dark Sisters.

Neferet was surprised at how quickly it was over, and how

silently her children worked. Filled with energy gifted to them from the moon they entered each woman's body through their mouths with such force that their jaws were broken and their teeth flew in bloody arcs around them before the tendrils dived down their throats, slicing and tearing from within.

Neferet watched, glad their deaths were quick. Yes, the five had been spoiled, entitled, obnoxious children, but she took no pleasure in their deaths, and certainly felt no need for them to suffer. They were simply performing a service for her and, ultimately, the immortal they considered their goddess.

"Is it done?" Lynette whispered from the concealing shadows.

"The Dark Sisters are no more," said Neferet. "The children are still feeding."

Neferet couldn't see Lynette but she felt her relief. "It was quick?"

"Yes, dearest. The foolish girls did not suffer."

"I'm glad. I'm really, *really* glad."

"As am I."

Neferet watched her children rip and tear until there was nothing left but bones, dry as chalk. Then she raised her arms again and her children, thick and glowing with power, turned their heads toward her.

"*Into the tomb!*" she commanded.

The tendrils of darkness lifted, hovering off the gore-splattered rocks and then they hurled themselves down. They struck the roof of the tomb and appeared to liquefy, dissolving between the tiny cracks of the rock until the wall began to glow with the same inky power that had pooled in Neferet's palms.

Neferet steadied herself to wait. She had no idea how long it would take for the immortal within to absorb enough power to break the seal that entombed her, but she did not have to wait long. The rocks stopped glowing. At the same moment, the earth beneath her feet began to tremble and then the tomb exploded in a flash of ebony.

15

Other Neferet

Neferet only had an instant. "Duck! Quickly!" she shouted to Lynette as she slid across the icy grass to huddle under a stone bench not far away while broken bits of dolomite rained around her like shrapnel.

When the battery of stone stopped, Neferet stood. With the sleeve of her sweater, she wiped blood from a deep cut on her forehead and called to Lynette. "Dearest, are you well?"

"Y-yes. I twisted my ankle and I can't walk very well, but I think I'm okay."

"Remain in the shadows. Do not speak or move. I will protect you." Fearlessly, Neferet strode through what looked like thick, black smoke but smelled of decay, to the mouth of the opened tomb.

The smoke dissipated, and the first thing Neferet noticed was the spectral bison. They'd been awakened. The beasts pawed around the tomb, blowing through their noses, shaking their massive heads and looking for something to gore. Neferet staggered back as their repelling power pushed against her.

A voice boomed from the tomb. "*Begone!*"

Instantly, the protective spirits began to dissolve, though they were still roaring and snorting, until they were absorbed into the earth from which they'd been conjured. Free from the power of their repel spell, Neferet was able to hurry forward to the tomb.

As she approached, her children rushed to her. They were emaciated and terribly weakened. They wound around her, and Neferet could feel the cold and fear within them as they clung to her.

She would never forget her first glimpse of the thing that had been her mirror version in this world. Other Neferet did not frighten easily—if at all—but the creature before her filled her with terror.

It—she—was perched atop the remnant of the broken ceiling of the tomb. Upon first glance it seemed that she was clothed—then Neferet looked closer and realized that her body was actually covered by what must be her version of the tendrils. There were hundreds, maybe thousands of them. They writhed and pulsed over her elongated body, reminding Neferet of pictures she'd seen of beekeepers being covered with a swarm—only this swarm was serpentine and black as the moonless night.

The creature that had once been this world's Neferet was tall—easily over six feet—and skeletally thin. Her limbs seemed stretched to twice their normal length. Her dirt-smeared face was carved from bone, and her cheekbones protruded like an insect's mandible. Her eyes were enormous and disarmingly beautiful. They were emerald jewels in the bleak, horrible canvas of her face. Her hair was long and matted and the same auburn as Neferet's, but it was streaked with white.

Neferet could not even think of her as familiar. This creature was a bizarre monster—not vampyre. Not High Priestess. She was a dark goddess, terrible to behold, and Neferet knew she must show no weakness, no fear, or she would not survive even this initial encounter.

The Monstress turned her face to Neferet and her expression changed. Insectile, she cocked her head with jerky, odd movements and studied her counterpart.

"You freed me."

Neferet was surprised by the Monstress's voice. It sounded eerily like her own, only it had a strange resonance, like the vocal cords that produced it were humanoid, but no longer fully human.

Neferet drew herself up, lifting her chin and meeting the immortal's gaze. "I did." She brushed debris of rock and dirt and ice from her sweater as she continued, "Though had I realized it would be so messy I would not have worn cashmere."

The Monstress laughed, a sound that was more hyena than human. Then she lifted her hands and commanded, "*Reveal!*"

Neferet felt the power of the spell sweep across her body. Had she only been masquerading to appear like Neferet, that pretense would have been wiped away that moment. Instead, her visage remained normal and she forced herself to relax and smile.

"It is no spell. I am you. Well, more accurately, I am a version of you from an alternate world."

"How fascinating. You do look exactly like me."

Neferet bit back a horrified retort and instead said, "Because in my world I *am* you—Neferet—ex–High Priestess of the Tulsa House of Night."

"*Ex*–High Priestess." The Other's eyes flashed with anger. "Did they usurp you as they did me?"

"I was betrayed, as I believe you were—though I do not know the story that brought you to this wretched tomb."

"Take my advice. Keep a close eye on any creature of your own creation—even one you believe could never be disloyal." The Monstress shivered and the tendrils that writhed over her pale skin pulsed. She stroked them. "Yes, darlings, you will feed again very soon. Patience. We have learned the value of patience." She returned her gaze to Neferet. "What shall I call you?"

"Neferet is, of course, my name."

"Ah, of course. I shall call you that, Neferet, ex–High Priestess of another world's Tulsa House of Night. You may call me 'Goddess.'"

"I'd rather not," said Neferet, meeting and holding her gaze.

The Monstress laughed again. "Ah, we are alike." Then her expression shifted, and she snapped, "Why are you here?"

"To free you."

"Why would you come from another world to do that? What is in it for you?"

Neferet stared into the immortal's eyes, and in their soulless emerald depths she saw nothing recognizable or human. And that was the instant Neferet realized that she had made a terrible mistake. This perverted version of herself would never willingly give her what she sought.

Neferet kept a tight rein on her terror and her disappointment. She was acting on pure instinct, and it told her that if she showed any weakness at all, this dark creature would not let her survive.

She swept back her hair and answered in a voice that sounded rather bored. "I hoped we could be allies, you and I."

The immortal's look darkened and as it did, Neferet felt her children cringing and trembling. She did not glance down at them, but instead stroked them soothingly, willing them not to show their fear.

"Allies? If we are in different worlds, why would that benefit either of us?"

Neferet could have said, *Well, if they entomb me in my world, I'd hope you would break me out as I did you,* but she knew this creature would never come to anyone's rescue but her own. So, instead she shrugged and said, "While you have been *otherwise engaged* there," she gestured dismissively at the rubble that had been a tomb, "the vampyres from your world have been meddling in mine. I decided to free you, hoping that you might have the power to keep them in check—and in their own world."

"You were *hoping* my power would be great enough to keep them in check? It seems you know little of me, no matter your physical appearance. It also seems you are keeping something from me. I wonder what that could be?"

Neferet did not flinch from the Monstress's penetrating gaze, but simply said, "I am sure we each have our own secrets."

Suddenly, the Monstress levitated, hovering above the rubble and drawing a little closer to Neferet. As she did so, she sniffed the wind, as if scenting something.

"I do not smell immortality on you, my dear."

Neferet laughed cruelly. "Oh, *my dear*, in my world we do not tastelessly wear our power for everyone to see—or smell. That is so very banal. But perhaps your sense of smell is off after being in there," Neferet lifted a lip at the tomb, "for so long. It has certainly affected your sense of style, or did you clothe yourself in leeches before you were entombed?"

The floating immortal jerked back in shock. "Leeches! These are my *children*!"

"Oh, indeed? They are so much smaller than mine that I could not be certain what they were—how *interesting*." Neferet continued to speak even though the Monstress stared at her incredulously. "I have freed you. It is disappointing that you feel no need to ally with me, but no matter. I have done what I came to this odd world to do. If you cannot keep control of your subjects, I will continue to thwart them in my world. Now, I have prepared a suitable living space for you. It is within walking distance of here." She shook her head as her gaze swept over her counterpart's insectile body. "There you will find proper clothing and a rather excellent wine cellar. The décor leaves much to be desired—though it is a definite improvement over your most recent accommodations. Follow me, and I shall show you to it." Holding her breath, Neferet turned her back on the immortal. She stared into the shadows, trying to see Lynette, hoping that her dearest one would be feeling everything with her—the terror, the danger, and beyond all else, the understanding that they must flee this world and the creature they'd loosed upon it.

"Wait, *Neferet*."

The Monstress's strange voice came from closer than before.

Neferet turned quickly to see that the creature had drifted down to stand before the destroyed grotto. Her body was undulating back and forth in an odd perversion of a graceful dance, moving to the music that was the madness in her twisted mind.

"I do not scent immortality on you, but I smell something—someone I recognize—someone who belongs to me. Though you hide her from me, I know she is here." The immortal continued to sniff the air, and as she did, she skittered forward, angling directly at the shadowy spot in which Lynette was hidden.

Anger stirred within Neferet, mixing with her terror. "This world belongs to you. I do not. Nor do any of my subjects." She spoke firmly, preparing herself for what she must do if the Monstress attacked, fisting one hand and pressing a sharp nail against the meat of her palm—ready to draw blood in an instant.

The immortal's head swiveled to look at her. She stared at the cut on Neferet's forehead and scented the air more deeply than before. Her smile was a baring of teeth. "You have Imprinted with her." She moved closer. "I can smell her blood mixed with yours. Oh, Lynette—dear one—where *are* you? I am ever so hungry, ravenous really. I know how you hate the children. So as before, I will not let them drink you. I save you for me—always, only for *me*."

Neferet pierced her palm, drawing a rush of blood. As she did so, she sprinted into the shadows that concealed Lynette.

The Monstress shrieked and surged forward in a bizarre rippling movement that was part insectile, part reptilian. The loyal tendril that had remained with Lynette flew from the shadows at the immortal. It opened its fanged mouth and razor teeth ripped at her face.

The Monstress screamed and clawed at the tendril. Her long, skeletal fingers closed around its neck and she wrenched her hands until the tendril's head came off with a spray of blood.

But that was all the time Neferet needed. She threw the blood that had pooled in her palm on the ground as she stepped into the shadows with Lynette, who limped to her on the injured ankle—white-faced and sobbing—but alive. Neferet put her arms around her friend and commanded, "Oak! Appear! Take us from here!"

The sprite materialized from the ground, licking Neferet's blood from her fingers. She looked from Neferet and Lynette through the shadows at the crazed immortal, who shrieked as she sniffed the air and skittered closer and closer to them. The sprite froze, staring at the creature who had once been a High Priestess of Nyx. Neferet almost reached for the annoying sprite to shake her and tell her *let's go* when Oak finally spoke.

"*I accept this payment from thee; therefore, as you command, so mote it be!*"

Neferet and Lynette clung to one another as the world around them disappeared.

(

Neferet

Neferet knew the instant her vampyre duplicate and the human, whose blood reeked of her Lynette, were gone. The heat of their scent evaporated, and the shadows that had been obscuring Lynette from view lifted. Neferet went to the place the women had been, crouching to press her hand against the frozen ground. Her nostrils flared as she smelled her palm and brushed the tip of her tongue against it.

"Yes, that is you, my dear Lynette. It is so lovely to find out there is a version of you in another world and that even there you were drawn to us. Oh, how we shall enjoy draining you—again." Neferet had spent so much time entombed with her tendrils of Darkness that she was forever linked with them and felt their hunger, their need, as if it were her own.

Neferet stood and glared around her. "*Another* ice storm. Well, I suppose we should not let it upset us. Were the weather not atrocious, we would have been seen by now, my dear ones." Her hand caressed her waist and thigh, taking comfort from the familiar feel of the tendrils pressed against her bare skin. "And we need time to regain our strength, don't we?" She sighed in irritation. "That smaller, weaker version of us chose an inconvenient time to flee. Could she not have stayed to lead us to our sanctuary? What would it be like to drink myself dry?" Neferet licked her lips in anticipation. "She would have been our appetizer before dear Lynette. Though we might have spared Lynette—at least for a while. We do remember that she was terribly good at planning amusements." Her gaze went back to the destroyed tomb and the bones scattered around it. "We have the distinct feeling that she had a hand in planning the spectacle that freed us. I am sorry that our view of that amusement was hindered." She stared fiercely at the wreckage that had been her jail. "No one will ever entrap us again—not as long as I draw breath."

As she stared at the bones, Neferet began to salivate. "Enough of this! We must feed, and then we shall plan our future." She clapped her long, spiderlike hands together. "I know! She said the sanctuary is within walking distance, so she and our Lynette must have walked here. Darlings, it cannot be far. Could you track them for us?"

Clumps of writhing black worms dropped from her body and slithered through the icy grass, flicking out their tongues to taste the scent of Neferet and Lynette. Then, excitedly, they began to circle around the tomb and crawl up stone stairs to the upper level of the park.

"Yes, that is it, my darlings. That is it!" Under the cover of a night without illumination from the moon or from mankind's electricity, Neferet followed a mass of crawling Darkness through the Tulsa Rose Gardens, across Peoria Street, and through the silent, affluent neighborhood to the villa just a few blocks away on Twentieth Street.

She entered the mansion and explored it, halting in the bedroom suite so recently inhabited by the smaller, weaker Neferet. There was still a carafe of bloody wine waiting on the dressing table, which she helped herself to before she commanded her children.

"Go out into the neighborhood. Feed, but not from the houses closest to this one. Go to those distasteful apartment buildings that are eyesores on Twenty-First Street. Kill as many of the humans who infest them as you wish. Sate your hunger. We shall expect the homeowners to thank us later." The tendrils of Darkness fell from her body to glide toward the door. "Darlings! Bring us home something to eat too. Two humans. Try to find ones who are not too terribly old or unattractive. Oh, and be sure they are still alive. We dislike it when our food gets cold. And hurry. You know we cannot abide being alone."

She watched the stream of living Darkness disappear, then Neferet drew a bath as she gulped the wine and blood. In the well-appointed—though tastelessly decorated—bathroom, she lit candles and then stood naked before a full-length mirror.

She was thin and uncommonly pale. Her bones were plainly visible beneath her porcelain skin so that she seemed almost a living skeleton, but what struck her most about her altered appearance was the sheer length of her body and the power she exuded.

"We are no longer mortal," she told her reflection as her hands stroked her naked figure. "We are truly the Goddess of Tulsa who has emerged from her cocoon to become goddess of two worlds." She poured another goblet of bloody wine and drank deeply. "Yes, we shall go to that other world and claim what was ours, and what should be ours. Though I will need to do away with that weaker version of me so that our dear Lynette's blood is not tainted when we drain her." Neferet grimaced, which made her look even more alien. "She *Imprinted* with a human! How obscene. When Lynette was mine, I didn't Imprint with her." Neferet added bath salts to the steaming, claw-footed tub before sliding into the water. "We Imprinted once, though *never* with a human. What was that Warrior's name?" She shrugged her skeletal shoulders. "No matter. He was insignificant. We do remember he took his own life because he was too weak to be with us." Her laughter echoed manically from the marble walls, which Neferet decided she rather liked.

"But now a lesser version of us has Imprinted with *our* Lynette. Oh, no. That will not do."

Neferet sank to her chin in the fragrant water as she plotted a future that included ruling two worlds.

"It isn't usurping. It is the survival of the fittest," she said. "Which means we shall survive. That Neferet is not us, though she did us a favor. We shall thank her by making her end swift and relatively painless. And should she resist, well, perhaps she shall be brought here and gifted to Zoey Redbird and the boring children who follow her. *That* should keep them busy for some time."

She sat up in the tub, sloshing water over the sides. "That is it! That is how we get to the Other World! Oh, and he will be *so pleased* to see us. But not yet. Not until we have regained our strength. Then we shall call him—then it shall begin."

Neferet's laughter echoed from the walls as she drank and plotted and waited expectantly for dinner to be delivered.

16

Zoey

After midnight Stark and I had finally crawled out of the cocoon we'd made in front of the fireplace—only because we were starving, and I'd remembered the dining hall was serving tacos. "I'm really glad Grandma got stuck here. I know she's super healthy and all, but I worry about her out there on that farm all by herself."

"But I think she likes it out there." Stark pulled on a sweatshirt with the Andolini's Pizza logo on it, which didn't help my hunger level.

"Yeah, I know she does, and it's important for her to be independent, but I've been thinking about it and what if we start busing fledglings, with vamp supervision of course, to her farm? It could be part of an herbology class that I'll bet Grandma would really get into teaching."

"Which would mean she wouldn't be so alone. I think it's a great idea." Stark kissed my forehead. "I love how close you two are."

"It's the way it should be," I said as I sat in front of the mirror and gathered my hair into a high ponytail. "There's no reason for kids to lose their families when they're Marked—not if their families want to stay connected."

"No way was Grandma Redbird going to let a little thing like you turning into a vampyre stop her from being part of your life."

I leaned toward the mirror and ran mascara along my lashes as I answered. "Yeah, I was lucky like that, but lots of kids have families who are too intimidated or too filled with lies about what a House of Night is and what happens here to feel the same way. It's those families I'd like to reach. I think it will only make our adult vampyres happier and healthier if they know the students still have the support of their people back home—along with their new House of Night families."

"You're doing a really good job of opening the door to humans. And don't worry about that blip at the swim meet with Kacie. If humans want all of the cool things that go along with being close to us—like our artists, storytellers, actors, singers, historians; the list goes on and on—then they're going to have to accept that some of us die. It's something fledglings live with every day until their Mark is filled in. It's past time humans took their heads out of the sand."

"Or their butts," I said.

He laughed. "Exactly. Come on! You look fantastic, as always. Let's eat. Damien texted me earlier. They've brewed a new batch of blood beer we need to try."

"You know how nasty that sounds, right?"

"But, it's oh, so good!"

Holding hands, we left the section of the big stone building that housed the professors' quarters. Even though changes in weather, particularly the cold, didn't bother me like before I'd been Marked, I braced myself against what I knew would be a wet, icy Oklahoma winter's night, and stepped through the arched door Stark held open for me—and instantly started laughing.

The rear of the House of Night campus held an expansive grassy area that was home to huge, ancient oaks, stone benches, and a large marble statue of Nyx that was positioned across from her temple. In front of Nyx's Temple there was a circular cobblestone drive.

Someone—and I noticed right away that Stevie Rae seemed to be the orchestrator of what was going on—had pulled out a fat green hose and flooded the cobblestone area. The water was now frozen, and fledglings were sorta ice-skating. And by sorta I mean they were slipping and sliding across the frozen, homemade rink, but they weren't wearing ice skates. They were wearing—

"Are those slippers on their feet?" Stark said.

Stevie Rae rushed up to us. "Ohmygood*ness*, we're havin' so much fun! Do you know Rephaim has never ice-skated? Not once. Ever." She waved at Rephaim, who was tentatively sliding on the ice between Damien and Jack—obviously on standby to grab him whenever he started to fall. He waved back at her, and then they did have to steady him as he windmilled his arms and almost fell on his butt.

Stevie Rae giggled. Her cheeks were roses and she had ice in her curls, and she looked happier and more relaxed than she had in weeks. With Damien's help Rephaim righted himself and then the three of them plowed into the middle of a bunch of fledglings as they zoomed across the ice chasing something that looked vaguely puck-like.

"What kind of puck is that?" Stark asked.

"The kind your grandma makes you from the lid of a mason jar." Grandma Redbird grinned like a girl as she joined us. She was carrying one of the puck things, which she'd created with lots of duct tape and weighted with Goddess only knew what.

Stark looked appalled. "Grandma Redbird, do not tell me you've been out there with those kids."

"Okay, rooster, I will not tell you." Grandma winked at me.

"*I'll* tell him," said Stevie Rae. "Don't be a fun-sucker. Grandma Redbird is like some kinda genius on the ice."

"That is sweet of you, Stevie Rae. But I've forgotten more about skating than I remember."

I hugged my favorite human tightly. "Grandma, you always

amaze me." I mentally filed away the fact that I needed to get her to a real rink so that she could give me a pointer or twelve. It'd been way too long since she and I had gone ice-skating.

"Ah oh." Stevie Rae jerked her chin at someone behind me. "Talk about a fun-sucker. Z, please don't let her shut this down."

I turned to see Aphrodite, with a decidedly fun-sucking expression on her face, doing her best to hurry toward us—though her choice of thigh-high suede stiletto boots was not working for her. Between the ice and the wet she looked like a cat trying to cross a stream on slick rocks.

When she finally reached us, I intercepted her before she could say anything. "Hey, they're just having fun. I don't think we need to cut off anyone's head or whatever. We can just let them skate around while we—"

"Oh, for shit's sake, I do not care one tiny bit if any of those idiots break their necks." She glanced at Grandma Redbird and added, "Excluding you, of course. But I watched you earlier. You have some moves."

"Thank you," Grandma said.

"*This* is way more important than the low-rent Holiday on Ice going on out there." She waved her cell phone in front of Stark. "Is this the human woman you talked to at the park yesterday?"

"If you would hold it still I could tell you," Stark said.

"Here! Jesus! Take it." Aphrodite handed it to him.

"What's this about?" I asked.

"I'll tell you, if Bow Boy—"

"Yeah, that's her. So?" said Stark.

"Shit. I need to sit down." Aphrodite made her way carefully to the ice-covered stone bench near Nyx's statue and sat heavily. Then she shivered and rolled her eyes. "Goddess, I hate ice."

Damien slid up to us on icy slippers. "What's going on? I can feel your stress all the way from the rink."

"It has something to do with her." Stevie Rae took the phone

162

from Stark and held it so that she, Damien, and I could check it out together.

"It's Lynette Witherspoon. Remember her?" Aphrodite said.

"Ohmygood*ness*, I remember her!" Stevie Rae said as she sat beside Aphrodite.

"Ah, hell. I do too," I said.

"Who is she, u-we-tsi-a-ge-ya?" Grandma asked as she studied the photo.

"*Was*, not is," Damien looked as ill as I felt.

When Grandma and Stark both looked confused, I explained. "Remember the woman who escaped the Mayo? Kalona brought her here and then she snuck off campus and returned to Neferet."

Stark nodded. "Yeah, I remember. Neferet killed her. But I'm sure that's who I saw in the park yesterday."

"You're not wrong," said Aphrodite. "I saw her there too. Only I was a lot farther away from her than you were, but even that glimpse of her jogged my memory and I couldn't quit thinking about her. So, I went to the damn kitchen and charged my cell, then I did a quick search of news stories from last year."

"The internet is working?" Stevie Rae said.

"Yes, bumpkin, but it was cutting out, though I managed to download this to my phone."

"Ah, hell!" I said as the puzzle pieces fell into place. "This is the woman in your vision, isn't it?"

Aphrodite nodded.

"I do not understand," said Grandma Redbird. "Was this woman not truly dead?"

"Yes. She's dead," I spoke slowly, feeling a soul-deep chill that the weather could never cause. "But only in this world. There's a whole other world where she's had a different life and is, obviously, alive."

"And also allied with Neferet. Again," said Damien.

"Your last vision," I spoke urgently. "When you saw Neferet shifting back and forth between looking normal and looking like

163

she'd just broken out of that tomb—you weren't seeing one Neferet, were you?"

Aphrodite shook her head. "No. I realize now that I was seeing two Neferets—one who had just escaped from the grotto, and a second one who had just helped her escape."

Stevie Rae gasped. "Other Neferet! From Kevin's world."

"Oh, Great Earth Mother, no." Grandma Redbird paled.

"Sadly, yes," I said. "If Other Lynette is here, that means Other Neferet must be too."

At that moment, there was a *whoosh* like a giant had just inhaled, and a swirling sphere of dark glitter appeared before us, floating directly in front of the statue of Nyx. The kids who were skating started to yell and point.

Stark cupped his hands around his mouth and shouted, "Sons of Erebus! To me!" As Stark positioned himself between the swirling orb and me, Warriors flooded the rear courtyard. "Protect the fledglings!" Stark commanded as Darius and Rephaim rushed to Aphrodite and Stevie Rae, with Jack between them. He looked terrified and flew into Damien's arms.

The floating disc-like thing looked like galaxy soup. I had zero doubt about what it was. The only question was who, or what, would step through. A figure became visible, with a second close behind, and as they emerged I breathed a long, gasping breath of relief and rushed around Stark to throw myself into my brother's arms.

"Kevin!"

"Zo!" He caught me and lifted me off my feet and we hugged and laughed for a moment. Then I glanced over his shoulder and realized who was with him as he put me down.

"Stark. Hi," I said only semiawkwardly. "Welcome to my world."

"Thanks." He nodded at me and then I watched his eyes widen as my Stark reached my side. "I guess we don't need introductions." Other Stark held out his hand.

I felt the jolt of shock go through my Stark, but he took Other

Stark's hand, grasping his forearm in a traditional Warrior greeting. "You're bleeding," he said.

Other Stark glanced at his mangled bicep. "Yeah. It's a long story."

"We're here to tell you—" Kevin spoke quickly, but Aphrodite was quicker.

"That your Neferet is in our world." She'd moved up to stand beside me with Darius close behind her.

Kevin's gaze shot to her. He swallowed, cracked his knuckles, and nodded. "Yeah, that's why we're here. We had to come warn you."

"And help you," Other Stark added.

"We just figured it out, but thanks for coming to confirm," said Aphrodite. "And, hi. It's good to see you again."

"Um, hi," Kevin said.

I felt bad for him. I could see his hesitancy and I'm pretty sure he didn't know whether he should hug her or keep his distance.

Darius surprised me by approaching Kevin and taking his forearm in a warm, respectful greeting. "It is good to see that you are well."

"Thanks," Kevin said, clearly as surprised as I was.

Darius spoke solemnly. "I, more than anyone, understand and am sorry for your loss."

Kevin's jaw clenched and he nodded. He tried to say something, but Darius shook his head.

"There is no need to speak of it. Your pain is too fresh. I will ask Nyx to help you through it." Then Darius dropped Kevin's arm and returned to Aphrodite's side.

Aphrodite surreptitiously wiped at tears that had escaped onto her cheeks, but she said nothing.

My Stark called to the Warriors, who had surrounded the frightened-looking fledglings in the pretend skating rink. "Escort the fledglings to their dorms. The House of Night is currently on high and immediate threat alert."

I added, "Then stand by for more instructions. We will be leaving for Woodward Park immediately—and with this weather

we'll be going on foot. How many Warriors should come with us?"
I asked Stark.

"Besides Darius, Rephaim, and me—a dozen."

I nodded to Darius. "Get a dozen of our toughest Warriors.
Arm them. Meet in the foyer ASAP. Do you know which Warrior is
on duty at the park tonight?"

"Yes, that would be Max. He's young but dependable and
talented with the sword."

"Call him while you're gathering the Warriors." As Darius saluted
me and hurried away, I turned back to my brother from another
world. "Come inside. We'll wait in the foyer for the Warriors. We
have a bunch to tell you."

"Yeah, we have a lot to tell you too," Kevin said. He hugged
me again quickly. "It's really good to see you. I just wish it wasn't
because your world's in danger."

"Yeah, well, sadly, that's nothing new," I said. "And it's really
good to see you too."

Then Grandma pushed past me and was hugging Kevin, leaving
me to stare at Other Stark.

"You should go to the infirmary and get that cleaned up," I said.

"It's okay." Other Stark's gaze kept going from my Stark to me.
I didn't blame him for being shell-shocked. It was super weird to see
the two of them together.

"Don't be stupid," my Stark said gruffly. "That gets infected and
you won't be able to shoot a bow. You, uh, do have the same affinity
I have, don't you?"

"That I can't miss? Yeah," he said, sounding like a weird recording of my Stark.

"If you can't pull the damn bow, you can't loose an arrow. And I
have a feeling we'll need all the Warriors we can get—in this world
and yours—so you're gonna get it looked at before we leave for the
park. Come on." Stark turned to me. "We'll meet you in the foyer.
We won't be long."

Before I could say anything, they headed toward the door to the infirmary.

"Z, I'm going to take Jack to our room," Damien said. Jack was sobbing in his arms, and I realized how difficult it must be for him to see Other Stark, who had been in charge of the Red Army he'd been slated to join—and kill with—in that terrible Other World.

"Okay, no problem. If you need to stay with Jack, I totally understand," I said.

"No!" Jack wiped the tears from his face as he bravely choked back tears. "You'll need Damien's brains. And you'll need air if it comes to a fight with two Neferets. I'll—I'll be okay."

With Jack tucked safely under Damien's arm they headed back to the professors' quarters where they shared a room when they weren't staying at the depot.

"I'm going to change these boots," said Aphrodite.

"Are you sure you want to come?" I asked.

"Are you fucking kidding me? I need to see if it looks like it did in my vision. Plus, I'm a Prophetess of Nyx. I belong at my High Priestess's side during trouble."

"Thanks," I said. "I'll be glad to have you there."

"I will go arm myself," said Rephaim.

"And while he does that, I'll be puttin' on some real shoes," said Stevie Rae.

"Find Lenobia. Tell her what's going on. She's High Priestess in my absence. Also, get Kacie. I need a full circle, and since this weather has grounded Shaunee and Shaylin, she's my fire and water. Do you think she's ready?" *Not that anyone could ever really be ready to take on two Neferets*, I added silently.

"She's smart and tough. I think she's as ready as you were when you first faced off against Neferet," said Stevie Rae.

"I had my friends to back me up," I said.

"And so does she, Z. She has us." Stevie Rae saluted me formally and said, "BRB, High Priestess." Then she took off, sliding down the sidewalk toward the stables.

That left Kevin, Grandma, and me alone.

"Let's get inside," said Grandma. "I'll pour cups of hot tea before you have to leave."

"Grandma," I said as we walked into the main part of the big stone buildings that made up the House of Night, "I don't want you to be scared. You'll be safe here."

"Oh, u-we-tsi-a-ge-ya, when danger comes there is no place I'd rather be than at the House of Night."

17

Other Stark

Meeting the alternative version of himself was the weirdest thing to happen to Other Stark in a young life that hadn't been lacking in weirdness. In the infirmary Stark left him alone with the nurse while he went to his room to get a shirt that wasn't all bloody. In Nyx's Realm the arm hadn't hurt—or at least it hadn't much—but here, in this world, it felt like it was on fire, especially when the nurse flushed and then cleaned it.

"You need stitches," said the nurse as Stark hurried back into the room, carrying a black House of Night sweatshirt over his shoulder.

"Will butterfly stitches do?" Other Stark asked her.

"They will, but regular stitches will allow it to heal easier."

He shook his head. "Yeah, but they'll take more time. I need to go to Woodward Park with the Warriors. Just use the butterflies and wrap it up. I'll drink a bunch of blood and heal just fine."

Stark tossed the sweatshirt to him and he caught it, laying it across his lap as he tried to ignore the pain in his arm. The guy who looked exactly like him, every detail a perfect copy save for the color of his tattoo, studied the knife wounds as the nurse got together a tray of disinfectants and bandages.

"I recognize this work. You didn't happen to pass through Skye to get here, did you?"

Other Stark snorted in surprise. "I did. Do you know Seoras?"

"I did. He was killed last year."

"Damn, that's too bad. He was kind of an asshole, but also sorta a distant relative," said Other Stark.

"Yeah, that's him. Check this out. It looks like you have my scar." Stark lifted up his sweatshirt to expose his chest, which was covered with scars that were eerily like the new broken arrow slashes on his bicep.

"Huh. Well, I guess it's only right that I have your scars. Apparently, you have my girl."

From the other side of the room the nurse gasped, and then, very slowly, Stark met his gaze and said, "Yeah, you're me all right—but me from a while ago. So, let me help you out and maybe you won't have to go through all the shit I did to understand this. Zoey isn't *mine*. She isn't *yours*, either. Zoey belongs to herself. Am I her Oathbound Warrior? Yes. Actually, I'm more than that, but we'd need Seoras and a lot more time than I have right now to explain that part to you. And anyway, the most important thing for you to get is that Z is her own person. She makes her own decisions. I've sworn to protect her, and I will do that as long as I'm alive—no matter what. So, if she decides she wants to be with you while you're in this world, that is completely her decision to make and doesn't have shit to do with me."

"And you'd be okay with it if she hooked up with me?"

"*Hooked up* with you?" Stark laughed and, behind them, the nurse snorted. "Damn, you're definitely old me. Okay, look, whether I'm okay with anything that goes on between you and Zoey isn't the point. The point is that there's nothing you could do that would mess up the bond Z and I have."

"I'm not sure what you're telling me."

"Yeah, I can see that, and that's too bad. But if you're around very long, Z will set you straight."

"Hey, I don't want there to be problems between us," he told this strange version of himself that seemed wiser and calmer and somehow older too.

"That's part of what I'm trying to explain to you. There isn't any problem with me—nor will there be. Well, unless you try to be an asshole to Z. She can handle douchebags, but know if you piss her off, I'll be standing right beside her—and I'll be doubly pissed."

"I hear you—loud and clear."

"Awesome. I'll grab my extra bow for you and a quiver of arrows, then I'll meet you in the foyer in a few. Think you can find your way there?"

He nodded. "Yeah, I think you'll be surprised at how resourceful I can be."

"Yep. Arrogant and clueless. You're me all over again." Chuckling, he left the examination room.

"I'd listen to him," said the nurse as she returned to Other Stark's side.

Other Stark didn't say anything. He'd been surprised at the gut punch he'd felt seeing Zoey again, though he really didn't know her. But he'd wanted to know her. Ghost Aphrodite had been right. He had told a lie in Nyx's Grove. Sure, he'd traveled here with Kevin to make amends for not standing against Neferet sooner, but that had only been part of his reason for coming.

The rest of the reason was Zoey Redbird. Stark wanted to know if she could fill that empty place in his heart, and he wasn't going to allow anything to stop him from finding out—even another version of himself.

(

Other Kevin

Other Kevin handed Aphrodite's cell phone to Other Stark as he joined the expanding group that was waiting in the foyer of the school. "Is this the human woman who was helping Neferet?" he asked, pointing to the photo illuminated on the screen.

"Yeah, that's definitely Lynette Witherspoon. She was the concierge at our private airport. At first, we thought she was kidnapped by Neferet, but between what the pilot said about the two of them and the video footage from inside the Covent Garden Hotel where Loren Blake was killed, it's looking more and more like they're allies."

"Weird how things in this world echo your world," Zoey said. "Our world's Lynette was loyal to Neferet and then was killed by her."

"Our Neferet also killed Loren Blake in this world," added Aphrodite.

Kevin nodded and tried not to stare at Aphrodite.

Grandma Redbird entered the group carrying a mountain of rain slickers. "I know you don't get cold like humans do, but you do get wet and wet doesn't help you think *or* fight. And they'll keep your weapons dry. So, wear these. Please, children."

No one argued with Grandma's logic—not even the wide-shouldered, somber-faced Sons of Erebus Warriors who followed Darius to join them.

Even though she wasn't his world's Aphrodite, Kevin had to force himself not to help her with the slicker she frowned at. A joke about it being this season's couture wear for ice storms almost escaped his lips, but as Darius grinned at her and expertly slid it over her head, Kevin turned away and almost ran into Zoey.

A red vampyre stood between Z and Stevie Rae. The girl looked nervous. She was also unusually gorgeous, even for a vamp. She was a young woman of color, and her skin looked like the sun hadn't just kissed it but had made out with it. And she had the biggest, darkest eyes he'd ever seen.

"Hey, Kev, I want to introduce you and Stark—" Zoey paused, nodding at Other Stark, who was standing beside him, "to our newest red vampyre—Kacie. Kacie, this is my brother from the Other World, Kevin, and, um, Other Stark."

"Merry meet," said Kevin. "Your tattoos are interesting. I've never seen water and fire mixed like that before."

"'Cause Kacie has affinities for water and fire," said Stevie Rae.

"Wow, that's cool," said Kevin. "Merry meet, Kacie."

"Merry meet," Kacie said to Kevin, then she turned to Zoey. "You look like your brother."

"Actually, I'm older. He looks like me," Z said—sounding exactly like his sister—no matter what world they were in.

"Merry meet, Kacie," said Other Stark.

Kacie's eyes got huge. "Uh, hi. So, what do we call you? Blue Stark?"

Kevin crossed his arms and watched his sister. He knew it was going to be amusing having two Starks in one world, and even though it sucked that there were also two Neferets here, he couldn't help but be entertained.

His g-ma pushed into the middle of their little group and handed them slickers, saying, "Don't be silly. We'll call this Stark James, and our world's Stark will remain simply Stark. Don't you think that's an excellent idea, James?"

Kevin's amused gaze went from Zoey to Other Stark, who was looking helpless against G-ma's Wise Woman logic. But there was zip he could do about being called a first name he hadn't gone by since the day he'd been Marked—no one back-talked Sylvia Redbird in either world.

"Yeah, sure. That's fine with me. I mean, James is my name."

"James or Jimmy?" asked Kacie as her pretty face emerged from an oversized slicker, and she swept back her thick Beyoncé-blond hair.

"James. Never Jimmy," said the Other World's James Stark gruffly.

"No need to get huffy, *James*," Aphrodite said. "Ice Cream Shoes doesn't know the history of the Stark aversion to first names."

"Ice Cream Shoes?" asked James.

"It's my nickname. It's cooler sounding than Jimmy, but, still, I feel ya."

Kevin covered his laugh with a quick cough.

"Are we all here?" Stark joined them with Damien close behind. He tossed a bow and a quiver of arrows to his Other World twin before Grandma Redbird handed him his own slicker.

"All present and accounted for," Damien said.

"How's Jack doing?" Zoey asked.

Damien looked grim and shook his head as he pulled on his slicker. "Not well. He's curled up in bed with Duchess watching the extended director's cut of *Return of the King*."

"I'll go see to him," said Grandma Redbird, patting Damien's arm.

"Oh, G-ma," Kevin said. "In the outside pocket of my backpack over there, you'll find a copy of a poem. The other G-ma Redbird asked me to bring it to you. Apparently, it's from a really old journal written by the women in our family. She wanted to get your take on it. Would you read it and make any notes that come to mind?"

"Of course, u-we-tsi. I shall study it as soon as I check on Jack. Actually, I will take it with me to see him. His mind is sharp. He can help me with it."

"Thanks, G-ma." Kevin kissed her soft cheek.

"Okay, so, we're ready?" Zoey asked.

"Everyone's here," said Stark.

Z nodded at her Warrior and then turned to Darius. "Were you able to reach the Warrior on guard at the park?"

"No. His phone rang until it went to voicemail."

"That's bad," said Damien.

"This whole thing is bad," agreed Stark.

"Then let's get it over with. Stark, should we cut through the neighborhood, or walk down Utica until we get to Twenty-First and approach the park from the street side where we'll have a clear view of the grotto?"

"The clear view sounds good to me. You, Darius?"

Darius nodded. "If she's there, we'll know it soon enough."

"Agreed," Stark said. "Warriors, you lead. Be ready for anything. Remember, protect the priestesses."

Zoey lifted her hand, and everyone turned their attention to her. "Damien, Aphrodite, Kacie, and Stevie Rae—if either or both Neferets are there, I want you to circle up around me immediately. I'll call the elements and see if we can force one of the Neferets—or both—back into that grotto, or at least keep them away from us long enough for us to get back here and regroup."

"Lenobia is casting an evil-repelling spell around the House of Night right now," said Stevie Rae. "It won't keep something as awful as the Neferets out forever, but it'll definitely slow them down and buy us time."

Z looked at me. "Kev, has your Neferet become immortal?"

"Not as far as we can tell, but she has been messing with Old Magick," he said.

"Alright. The Neferets have Old Magick and Darkness on their side," Z said. "We have the elements and Nyx and Light with us. And remember what happens when you shine light into the dark."

"It runs away," said Kevin, putting his arm around his sister. "Let's go make it run."

18

Other Kevin

The ice changed to rain as the Warriors led their group down the sidewalk toward the Twenty-First Street intersection, which was less than a block away from the school. Kevin stayed in the rear, walking beside his sister. Stark was on the other side of her, with James behind them. Stevie Rae, Kacie, and Rephaim were to Kevin's right, and behind him Aphrodite walked between Darius and Damien. He was glad he couldn't see Aphrodite. It was hard to think when he looked at her.

"How'd you two get here? I didn't feel you using Old Magick," asked Z.

"Oh, that's 'cause we didn't use it. And FYI, you shouldn't use it either. Stark—er, I mean *James* and I just got two major warnings about Old Magick. The first was from Sgiach."

Stark peered around Zoey at Kevin. "He said you went through Skye. I really like that island."

"You knew they went through Skye?" Z said.

"Well, yeah. Didn't you recognize the cuts on his arm?"

"They were all bloody. I couldn't see much." Z turned her head and looked back at James. "It was Seoras, right?"

"Right." He nodded and didn't say anything else.

Kevin sighed. "Yeah, Sgiach totally wouldn't let me ask the sprites for help. And by the way, when she called Oak just to get some simple info about whether Neferet was over here or not, the sprite acted super bitchy."

"Really?" Zoey said. "That's weird. When I was on Skye with our Sgiach the sprites seemed fine."

"Well, maybe they used to be, *before* we started calling on them so much." Kevin cracked his knuckles, rubbed his hands together, and then shoved them into his pockets—glad G-ma had made them all wear slickers. "They've changed. Or at least Oak has. Especially since the stadium … and what happened there." He couldn't say any more, but Z reached out and squeezed his arm.

As if an echo from his memory, Aphrodite's voice drifted from behind him. "So, how'd you get here if you didn't use Old Magick?"

He didn't turn to look at her. He couldn't. "Stark's blood and my connection to spirit summoned the Black Bull, and he gave us a ride to Nyx's Realm. I called you." Kevin paused, cleared his throat, and corrected himself. "Sorry, I mean my world's version of you— the one who's dead. She led us through Nyx's Grove to the portal."

"Holy shit!" The words burst from Aphrodite.

"You saw her again!" Z said. "You okay?"

He nodded but didn't meet his sister's knowing gaze. "I'm good. Actually, it helped to see her. And she was the one who gave us the second warning about using Old Magick."

"She said it's addictive," James added from behind them.

"Yeah, I can understand that," said Z.

"So, I want to know more about Other Aphrodite's ghost," said Aphrodite. "And also, how are you getting back?"

"She gets pissed if you call her a ghost," said James. "Even though she said that it's all about love over there, she's still pretty bitchy."

Kevin did turn then so he could frown at James. "She's not bitchy. She's real. Don't be an ass because she called you out on your shit."

James put up his hands in surrender. "I didn't mean anything. I'm glad all I have to do is cut myself and drop some blood on the ground before you call her to take us back. Losing a day of life for every day we're here is bad enough. I don't want to get sliced up again."

"What?" snapped Zoey.

Kevin shrugged. "It was part of the price for traveling through Nyx's Realm. For every day we're here we lose one day of our lives. It's not that big of a deal when you have a lifespan of a couple hundred years or so."

"Huh," James snorted. "Right *now* it doesn't seem like a big deal. Wait 'till you only have a few days left and then talk to me about it."

"Other Bow Boy has a point," said Aphrodite.

"You need to go back ASAP," said Z.

Kevin hiked his shoulders and didn't say anything.

"And that's how you're getting back? She's guiding you again?" Aphrodite prodded.

Kevin nodded without looking at her. "Yeah. Once James gives a blood sacrifice, then I just need to call her, and I guess the magick door thingy will appear again, and she'll be there."

They'd come to the intersection of Twenty-First and Utica and carefully crossed the icy street. To their right, Utica Square looked eerie and dead with no lights on. Across the street from the posh outside groupings of stores and restaurants, St. John's Hospital was the only thing lit up—and that lighting seemed strange and pale, as they were clearly using generators that were having trouble keeping up with electrical demand.

Kevin was trying to think of something else he could say— something, anything, that might get Aphrodite to talk to him without making it obvious that he really, *really* wanted her to talk to him, when Zoey broke into his thoughts.

"So, how's the truce going over there in your world?"

"It's going, but it's crappy."

Behind them James snorted again. "Heavy on the crappy. There's a whole group of vampyres who still support Neferet and her war."

It was Z's turn to look behind in shock. "Seriously? Like they didn't learn how awful war was and how twisted Neferet is?"

"Seriously," James said. "We have a lot to deal with when we get back. Makes me wonder why the hell Neferet came over here. She talked to Loren Blake. He musta told her she still has a bunch of followers."

Kevin snorted in disgust. "Not to mention they're pretty easy to find on the internet."

Kacie spoke up, and her voice sounded utterly certain—like she'd just had a discussion with Neferet. "She came over here to learn how to become immortal."

"Exactly what I was thinking, Ice Cream Shoes," said Aphrodite.

Kevin craned his neck around to look at Kacie while Damien said, "Oh, something else about Kacie. She knows stuff. And it's stuff Aphrodite usually knows too."

Stevie Rae grinned proudly at Kacie. "Yup. We have another prophetess in the makin'."

"That could be helpful," said James. "Especially since we're short a prophetess in our world."

"No Ice Cream Shoes over there?" Aphrodite asked.

"Not that I know of," said James.

"Well, if Kacie and Aphrodite are right—and Aphrodite usually is," said Kevin as he brushed rain from his face, "it means we have to find our Neferet ASAP, *before* she gets any more powerful."

Zoey adjusted the hood of her slicker. "Well, here's one bright spot. I don't for one instant think our Neferet would help anyone become immortal—and especially not anyone who would then be her equal in power."

"I hope you're right about that, Z," said Stevie Rae.

Silently, Kevin seconded that thought.

"Look sharp. We're coming up on the park," Darius said.

Everyone stopped talking as they crossed Rockford Street at the east edge of the park, walked past the beginning of the greenery and the arched wooden bridge that covered a small, frozen stream, and then moved quickly across Woodward Park Drive, the road that led up to the top section of the park, and the parking lot there.

Then the rock wall began.

"I wish those damn lights were on," muttered Zoey.

And like she had conjured electricity, the streetlights flickered and came on to illuminate a terrible scene.

It was like someone had set off a bomb in the middle of the grotto. Boulders littered the expansive lawn that stretched between the man-made ridge and the sidewalk. There was no wall left, and only a remnant of the rock ceiling that used to enclose the grotto tomb.

There was nothing left of the grotto except for a hole in the ridge and a pool of water so dark it looked like frozen ink.

"Is that velvet?" Aphrodite asked.

Carefully, the Warriors moved their group closer and Kevin saw what Aphrodite's sharp, fashion-attuned eyes had already caught. There were five piles of clothing scattered around the broken tomb.

"I think they're capes," said Zoey.

"What are those white things with them?" Stevie Rae asked.

Damien went to one of the piles and squatted down before it. He stood and looked at the rest of them, and his face was colorless except for his bold sapphire tattoo. "Bones," he said. "They're human bones."

A chill crawled up Kevin's spine as he peered over Damien's shoulder.

Kacie stumbled to a halt beside one of the discarded cloaks and a scattered pile of bones. "Oh, shit! I think I'm gonna be sick."

Stevie Rae grabbed her arm and guided her away. "Come over here. I'll hold your hair for ya, but don't puke on the evidence."

As Kacie retched into the bushes, the Warriors spread out and looked for signs of anyone left alive.

"Hang on. I need to call Detective Marx," said Zoey. She stepped away and began to speak earnestly into her phone.

Kevin followed the debris trail around until he saw a puddle of something darker than water beside a cluster of fist-sized rocks. He knelt and touched it gently with his finger. "Z, I have blood over here. And it's not human. Sta—I mean James, can you come over here?"

James hurried to him, with Zoey, Stark, Aphrodite, and Darius close behind.

Kevin stared at his blood-tipped finger. "Can you tell if this is our Neferet's?"

"Why would he be able to—" Zoey began and then Kevin saw understanding in her expressive eyes. "Oh. You've, uh, tasted her blood."

James grunted, but didn't say anything as he crouched beside Kevin, dipped his finger into the slickness of congealing blood, and then licked it. He grimaced and wiped his finger on his jeans.

"Yeah, that's definitely Neferet's."

Kevin stared down at the blood. "Is there a trail of this? She's hurt, but unless there's a lot more blood, she's not hurt badly."

They spread out, searching the dark, wet ground as rain continued to spit at them. Suddenly, Aphrodite shouted.

"Hey, over here!"

Kevin, Zoey, and James were closest, so they reached her first. Aphrodite was standing inside a clump of azalea bushes that hugged the ridge. It was shadowy within the bushes and they provided cover, but Kevin could see that if he parted one of them it was easy to peek through and have a good view of the grotto.

"Something feels weird over here. Get Ice Cream Shoes. I need a second opinion," said Aphrodite. She had her hands out, palms down, like she was trying to feel heat rising from the earth.

"What are you doing?" Kevin asked her.

"Trying to figure something out." Then her head snapped up

and she took a step into the bushes and disappeared for an instant. "Ah, shit!"

Zoey didn't hesitate. She pushed through the bushes to join Aphrodite with Kevin close behind.

Aphrodite was pointing at the icy ribbon of a stream that hugged the ridge and pooled at the base of the clump of azaleas. "That's not a weird mirror," she said.

"No. It's a stream. What are you talking about?" asked Zoey.

"My vision. Remember when I said the only glimpse of Lynette I got was in what I thought was a mirror?"

Kevin and Z nodded.

"I recognize this. Z, what I saw in my vision happened right here. Lynette was here. Other Neferet was here, and so was our creepy, spidery Neferet."

"Ah, hell. Does that mean she's dead?" Z said.

"I honestly don't think so. I know we didn't do anything to change the vision—or at least if we did, we don't know what it was, but my gut tells me that Lynette isn't dead. At least not yet. Where's her body? And that's not her blood—it's Other Neferet's."

Zoey paced, though she could only walk a couple feet before she had to turn around again. "Okay, according to your vision, Lynette was here with Other Neferet. They broke our Neferet out. Let's say none of those piles of bones are Lynette—so, where is she now? And where is Other Neferet? And why the hell did you get *that* vision if it wasn't so that we could change it?"

Kacie gasped as she peeked through the azaleas. "Wow! Can anyone else feel that?"

"Ah, good. Ice Cream Shoes," Aphrodite brightened and pushed back through the bushes with Kevin and Z following. Intrigued, Kevin watched the young priestess hold her hands out, palms down, exactly where Aphrodite had been. "It's the residue of something, right?" Aphrodite said.

Kacie nodded. "Totally. It was only here for a second, but it was crazy powerful."

"Powerful enough to open a portal between worlds?" Aphrodite asked.

Kacie looked up at her. "This is Old Magick."

"Exactly what I thought." Aphrodite turned to Z, and Kevin was struck by how much more confident this world's version of his Aphrodite was. *My Aphrodite would have been strong enough to live if she'd had her confidence*, he thought. And then he realized what she was getting at.

"My Neferet called Old Magick to take her—and Lynette—back to our world," Kevin blurted.

"I wonder why? You think it was because she was hurt?" Zoey mused.

Aphrodite huffed. "Well, for whatever reason it seems to have saved Lynette's life—and that was the important part of my vision."

"Oh, shit! Do you think that means *your* Neferet went with them?" The thought made Kevin's stomach flip-flop.

Zoey's phone rang. She glanced at the screen and said, "It's Marx," before answering. "Yeah, we're still at the park." She paused and then said. "Yeah, yeah, I know where you mean." And paused again. By the time she spoke again, all of the color had drained out of her face and her voice was thick with dread. "That's horrible. Okay, I understand. See you soon."

As Zoey disconnected, Darius jogged up to them with Stark beside him—both looking grim.

"We found the body of the Warrior who had been on duty. His throat was ripped out and he'd been drained of blood," said Darius.

"Shit, that's awful," said Kacie.

Zoey wiped more rain from her face. "One of the Neferets is still here—and I'm pretty sure it's ours. Detective Marx just got a call from the TPD. They're just down the street a few blocks. You know those apartments that face Twenty-First before you get to the river?"

Stark and Darius nodded.

Zoey swallowed before she continued, like she was trying not to throw up. "It's a slaughterhouse down there. There was one witness. She said *things* swarmed the complex. Awful things. They killed everyone. Maybe even took hostages with them. Marx can't be sure yet because the woman is completely hysterical."

"What does she mean by *things*?" asked Kevin.

"She means disgusting wormlike things with mouths full of teeth and no eyes," said Z.

"Fuck! That's what our Neferet's tendrils of Darkness looked like in my vision," said Aphrodite.

"Our Neferet's tendrils are fat and big—like supersized water moccasins." As Kevin spoke he watched Aphrodite, and not just because he was obsessed. He'd noticed that she looked more water-logged than the rest of them and kinda wonky. Then she flipped back her hair with a shaking hand.

Stark was saying, "Neferet wouldn't go anywhere without those tendrils, and after being entombed for a year they'd definitely be ravenous enough to eat an apartment complex full of people."

"She might be weaker than we think though," said Z. "Otherwise, Neferet would be with them. She calls them her children." She shuddered in disgust.

"Our Neferet is still here, but I'd bet this season's Louboutin boots that Other Neferet and Lynette are not. I'd also bet breaking cray Neferet out of her tomb didn't go anything like your Neferet planned," said Aphrodite.

The prophetess was trying to sound normal, but Aphrodite was clutching her hands together to keep them from trembling. As she spoke, she looked up at Kevin. The rain washing down her face had turned pink with tears. And then all he saw were the whites of her eyes as they rolled back, and she collapsed. Kevin surged forward and caught her before she hit the ground.

19

Aphrodite

Coming back to herself after a vision was always horrible, and this time was definitely no exception. Aphrodite had the mother of all migraines. Her eyes burned and watered uncontrollably, and, as per usual, she felt dizzy and confused—which made sense. She'd just experienced someone's death with them, and it was almost always a really violent, really awful death. This time violent and awful were understatements.

"I don't know why I can't—just once—have a nice vision. Like one where the good guy or girl wins? Or even a sweet, easy death in someone's sleep. I don't mean to be a complainer. It's just—" Aphrodite had to stop speaking and press the cool, damp washcloth someone had put across her eyes.

"It's just that it's a lot. I hear you and I totally get it. And I'm really glad you're back. You had me worried."

Z's voice was comforting. She was always there when Aphrodite woke from a vision and, along with Darius, she'd become her lifeline back to the real world.

"Where am I?"

"In your room."

"Shit!" Aphrodite grimaced and took a few deep breaths to combat the pounding pain in her head. "Fuck me, ouch! Remind me not to cuss emphatically until I'm better. Wait? Did Darius carry me all the way back here?"

"I did not, my beauty." Darius's deep, familiar voice was more balm to her ragged nerves. "I did not even catch you when you fell. Kevin beat me to it."

"Aww," Aphrodite said. "That's sweet. Kev? Are you here?"

"No, he's still at Woodward Park. Darius, Kacie, Stevie Rae, and I are here with you."

"Who carried me back here?"

"Marx brought all of us here in his truck," said Stevie Rae. "So, you can't ever complain again about big trucks only bein' extensions of inadequate men's penises."

"Sure I can, because ninety-nine percent of the time it's true," said Aphrodite. "When did Marx get to the park?"

"Right after you collapsed. He'd come from the crime scene at the apartments down the street. That monstrous truck of his pays zero attention to ice, so he gave us a ride here." Z's voice sounded like she was in the kitchenette, and Aphrodite desperately hoped she was putting together a cocktail that would knock her out—or at least knock out her headache. "Everyone else is still at Woodward Park, helping the TPD secure the crime scene and put up tarps. The ice has turned to rain, which is busily washing away any evidence that might be left."

"Doesn't matter," said Aphrodite. "They're gone."

"They?" Zoey asked.

Aphrodite nodded and then paused to grit her teeth against the pain.

From the kitchenette Z said, "Hang on. Don't say anything more. I'm brewing you some lavender CBD tea with a heavy dose of honey."

"Lavender and CBD?" Stevie Rae asked.

"It's medicinal and super relaxing—and also anti-inflammatory," said Zoey. "Grandma told me about it."

"You should get her some CBD bath salts to soak in," Kacie spoke up from over by Aphrodite's fireplace. "They help with aches and pains."

"Good idea, Ice Cream Shoes," said Aphrodite.

"Um, also, I have another idea," said Kacie hesitantly. "Or, I *had* one. At the park."

"Go ahead," Stevie Rae encouraged. "You can tell us. Don't worry 'bout getting everthin' right or soundin' perfect. Just speak your truth. You're part of our circle. We'll listen to you."

Kacie swallowed audibly. "Other Neferet and that woman with her—"

"Other Lynette," Stevie Rae said.

"Right. Other Lynette—she and Other Neferet didn't go back to their world because anyone was hurt. They went back because they were scared. Really, *really* scared."

"How do you know that?" Zoey asked, her voice getting closer to Aphrodite. While Kacie answered, Zoey helped Aphrodite guide the mug of tea to her lips and didn't let go until Aphrodite's hands stopped shaking and she could hold it herself.

"This is gonna sound crazy," said Kacie.

"Crazier than me passing out with a vision and bleeding from my eyes?" said Aphrodite between sips of tea.

"I'm not sure. But, here goes—I picked up leftover emotions while I was standing there—right there where we felt the Old Magick residue. I'm pretty sure it was because of the ice and rain."

"Explain that," said Zoey.

"I'll try. I was thinking about Old Magick and wondering what the hell went down at the park, and I was soaked with rain and standing in ice water—and all of a sudden, I felt terrified. It wasn't my fear. And I don't think it was the human woman's fear either. I don't think a human's fear would have been strong enough for me to pick up on, and I'm not saying that because I'm being all 'we're better than them,' or anything stupid like that. But Other Neferet is a powerful High Priestess, and I think that's why I sensed what she felt. Her fear was so strong, water carried it to me."

"That's bad. Really bad," said Zoey. "Other Neferet *is* powerful—so powerful that the fall from the press box at TU didn't kill her. So powerful that she managed to cross over to this world and release our Neferet from a tomb sealed by an immortal. It's hard to imagine what could terrify her like that."

"Batshit Neferet is that terrifying. I saw her in my vision," said Aphrodite. She blindly leaned forward and Zoey was there, taking the mug from her.

"More?" Zoey asked.

"Maybe in a little while, if I don't fall asleep first. It's times like this that I almost wish I was still into mixing Xanax and booze. But anyway, Other Neferet and Other Lynette aren't here anymore. That's for sure. And after what Ice Cream Shoes just said, we know it's because Other Neferet was so damn afraid that she ran the hell away. Also for sure is the fact that our Neferet—let's just call her Batshit to save confusion—is going to follow them if she hasn't already."

"You saw all three of them over there in your vision?" Z asked.

"Yeah, but more than that. In the vision, I was Other Neferet and I was with her friend, Other Lynette."

Zoey scoffed. "Friend? Don't you mean minion?"

"Actually, no. Something's going on with Other Neferet. I couldn't tell a lot of things from the vision because, as usual, all hell was breaking loose and it was chaotic, but two of the things I know for sure are that she's not in this world anymore, and that she cares about that Lynette. Like, they're for-real friends."

"Okay, okay, go back," Zoey said. "Describe the vision and we'll figure it out from there."

"Well, it was weird," said Aphrodite. "I mean, they all are. But this one especially. Apparently, I was out for a while."

"Yes, my beauty. As Zoey said, you were away from us longer than usual this time," said Darius as he gently lifted her feet before sitting on the couch with her. He rested her feet on his lap and began to firmly knead her arches.

"Ohmygoddess. That is wonderful. Don't stop," she said.

"Never," said Darius with a smile in his voice.

"If you didn't wear those crazy stilettos all the time, your feet wouldn't hurt so much," said Z, sounding way too smug.

"I wasn't wearing stilettos at the park. I was wearing flats."

It sounded like Ice Cream Shoes actually snorted but she said nothing because Z beat her to it.

"Wedges aren't flats, but go ahead. What did you see?"

"A bunch of things really fast, which is why I'm confused about being out for so long. The vision was short and violent."

"Go ahead. We're listening," prompted Darius as he continued to rub her feet.

The foot massage and the lavender tea worked perfectly together, and Aphrodite sank back into the down pillows as she held the cool, damp washcloth to her bleeding eyes.

"OK, I'm pretty sure we were at the other House of Night, out there by the east wall and the messed-up old oak tree, only the tree wasn't messed up, which confused me."

"That tree isn't messed up on the school grounds at the other House of Night." Z's voice came from beside her and Aphrodite decided that she must be sitting in one of the plush chairs facing the couch she reclined on.

"Then I'm sure the vision took place in the Other World. Everything was happening super fast, and Neferet was in a strange place—and I don't mean physically."

"She'd gone totally crazy, like our Neferet?" Stevie Rae asked.

"No. That's the weird thing. Okay, I was only inside her body for a few seconds. I knew she was not in this world. I knew Lynette was with her and that she cares about Lynette—that was easy because I saw Lynette, and Neferet's feelings for her were super clear. It was her feelings for Other Kalona and Batshit that were confusing."

"What?!" Aphrodite could tell that Zoey had stood and was pacing behind the couch. "Other Kalona was there?"

"Yeah. So was Batshit Neferet. I think we might have been there too, but it was really hard to tell because it was like Neferet was inside a fishbowl—something that made her sight confusing. She was totally focused on what was going on between Other Kalona and Batshit Neferet. Kalona was battling Batshit. He was hurt but holding her off—matching her, blow-for-blow, and it seemed like he was keeping her from getting inside the school grounds.

"Then something happened that really freaked Other Neferet out. I couldn't tell for sure what it was—there was too much noise and panic. All I know is that Other Neferet believed that she was losing. Lynette tried to talk to her—it was like the two of them were isolated in the eye of a hurricane—a really noisy hurricane. But Other Neferet rejected what Lynette was saying. She decided to retreat." Aphrodite paused, turning the washcloth over and pressing the cool side against her closed eyes. "It felt like that choice was key because as soon as Other Neferet yelled at Lynette to get the hell out of there, Batshit Neferet, who is super, *super* gross looking—like a mixture between a spider and a praying mantis and a human. She's just—" Aphrodite shuddered before continuing. "Nasty—seriously nasty. Anyway, Batshit Neferet got around Kalona and took off after Other Neferet. Actually, she took off after Lynette. It was weird, though, because the scene went from being filled with vampyres and tendrils of Darkness and Other Kalona fighting his ass off to a tunnel-vision view of Other Lynette and Other Neferet being completely isolated."

"You must explain that," said Darius.

"I don't know how real that part was. Sometimes I see things that are more metaphor than truth in my visions—which is one reason I hate poetry so much. I get enough confusion already in my prophecies and do not want to deal with any more bullshit symbolism and whatnot. But in the vision, when Other Neferet made the decision to run, everything changed. Other Kalona was gone—everyone literally disappeared except for the two Neferets and Lynette."

Zoey asked. "What color were Kalona's wings?"

"White—silver-white. They were really pretty. And he didn't have a shirt on."

"Of course he didn't," Z said. "But his white wings mean that he didn't fall, and he's definitely on our side. So, keep going. Everyone disappears, then what?"

"Batshit goes after them. Other Neferet was running. Lynette was with her but was a lot slower. Batshit's tendrils caught Lynette pretty easily. They covered her while she screamed and screamed. Neferet turned and it was like she froze. I could feel what was happening inside her, and everything just went numb with shock and pain and loss, then while she stood there reeling from Lynette's death, Batshit cut her in half. That was not symbolic. Batshit had a long, white, staff thingy with like, short swords at either end. She chopped her in half with it. And as Other Neferet's vision went black, Batshit Neferet's tendrils of Darkness multiplied and spread all over, covering everything and everyone. As Neferet was dying, I could smell blood and gore and I heard lots and lots of people screaming—including us. I heard all of us dying. It was the worst vision I've ever had, and it only lasted a few seconds." With a shaking hand, she pressed the washcloth against her eyes.

"So, basically, everything went to hell when Other Kalona was overwhelmed and Other Neferet takes off," Z said.

Aphrodite shrugged. "I think so."

"Wait, you're not sayin' Other Neferet was fightin' *against* Batshit Neferet, are you?" Stevie Rae said.

"It really seemed that way," said Aphrodite.

"That's bizarre," Zoey said. "I met Other Neferet. She's as

coldhearted and egotistical as our Neferet. She ordered the death of any High Priestess who stood against her. She would've had her Red Army slaughter an entire stadium full of innocent people. *She had Lenobia and Travis and all their horses killed.*" Z sounded incredulous and more than a little scared. "I don't understand how she could ever fight *with* us."

Ice Cream Shoes's voice sounded a lot older than her sixteen years. "She was also so terrified of Batshit Neferet that her fear stayed in this world even after she retreated to hers."

"I don't think the question right now is whether or not Other Neferet might be an ally," said Darius. "The question is, how are we getting to the Other World, and who is going with us?"

"And how are we gonna find Rephaim's daddy from another world?" said Stevie Rae.

"Well, however we do all that, we need to keep in mind that if Other Kalona can't handle Batshit, and Other Neferet is our ally but she runs, the whole world goes to shit—and that includes any of us good guys who are there too," said Kacie.

"I swear the key is Other Lynette," said Aphrodite. "In both visions, when she dies everything goes wrong."

"Great. We gotta keep a middle-aged human alive," said Stevie Rae. "Not that I have anything against middle-aged humans, but they're sure fragile."

"Ah, hell," muttered Zoey.

Silently, Aphrodite agreed with her.

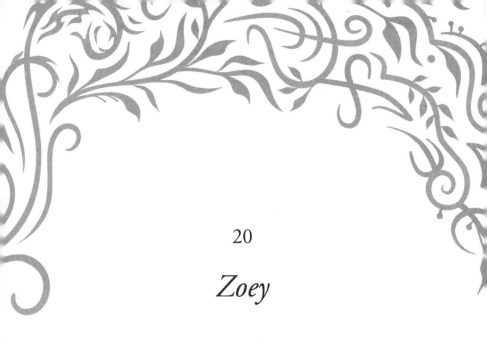

20

Zoey

The slickers could only do so much, and the Warriors who returned to school were all completely soaked. Intermittent ice had turned to rain—and then rain had turned to a thunderstorm—a winter thunderstorm.

Stark took the towel I offered him. "If a tornado happens, I'm going to talk to you seriously about moving to a different House of Night."

"You don't mean that." I tossed another towel to James and my brother, who looked equally drowned.

"He might not mean it, but I do," said James. "Isn't there a House of Night in the Bahamas?"

"Dude, you'd fry like bacon," said Kev.

"Nah," James said, sounding a lot more like my Stark as he teased with Kevin. "Not me. You two, sure. Blue vamps are just *uncomfortable* in the sun. Well, I'd rather be uncomfortable from sun than from freezing rain turned pounding rain turned goddess-only-knows-what-next."

Kevin actually laughed for a moment before changing back into the somber, unsmiling kid he'd been since Other Aphrodite had died. "Hey, how's Aphrodite doing?" he asked.

"She'll be fine," I said. "But her vision sucked. And we need to talk about it. ASAP. But first, did Marx have any news?"

Damien took my last towel and answered as he dried himself. "The medical examiner identified the bones we found as human and female. But I doubt they're going to be able to tell much more about them." He met my gaze solemnly. "The tendrils of Darkness hit their mouths so hard that their jaws were shattered and their teeth scattered everywhere."

My stomach rolled. "What about those capes?"

Damien shrugged. "They're nothing special. Probably bought at the ren faire in Muskogee. It'll take a while for Marx to track down the vendors and see if any of them remember selling five velvet capes in the colors of the elements to human females. The only other clothing items found were five pairs of Ugg boots, and you know how common those things are."

"There was nothing to identify them in the capes?" I asked.

Kevin shook his head. "Absolutely nothing. Whoever planned this made sure that identifying the five women would be almost impossible."

"This is our Neferet's doing," said James. "It reads like something she'd instigate, and we know she is the one who released your Neferet."

I nodded, still thinking about how insane it was to even consider any Neferet being our ally, especially one who sacrificed five women to break a monster out of jail—however she managed to do that.

"What about the apartment building?" I asked.

"Last count Marx said thirty-seven people were dead. They're still trying to figure out who wasn't home and who is missing, presumed dead," said Stark.

"As well as which body part belongs to which person," said Kevin.

"Does he have any leads on where Batshit might be?" I asked.

"Batshit?" Stark said, his lip curling up into the beginnings of a smile.

"Oh, yeah, that's what we're calling our Neferet. Aphrodite thought it'd be less confusing that way," I said.

"And accurate," added Stark. "No, he says that with the electricity out, the street cameras weren't working."

"What about the security cameras at the apartment building?"

"They were fake," Stark said with a scowl. "Cheap-ass landlord just got himself into some major shit for trying to pinch pennies. If the system had been for real, it would've had backup batteries and still been recording. We could've at least seen from what direction they came and went."

"And whether Batshit was waiting outside for them," I said. "Though Aphrodite's vision made it clear that Other Neferet, Other Lynette, *and* Batshit are all going to end up in your world. Sorry, Kev."

"I'd bet my favorite bow tie that Batshit is still in this world though" said Damien.

"Because of the slaughter at the apartment?" I asked.

"The apartment slaughter is indicative of why she's still here. She's been trapped in that tomb for a year. She and those loathsome tendrils have to be ravenous."

I nodded. "Yeah, that's why they're so much littler than they were before."

"She knows this world—especially this city," Damien continued. "She'll be here, feeding, for as long as it takes for her to regain all of her strength. Then she'll follow Other Neferet to Kevin's world. They may even be allies and have it all planned out."

"I would normally agree with you," I told Damien, "but Aphrodite's vision and some insight by Kacie is pointing to the two Neferets *not* being allies."

"Kacie?" James asked, still towel drying his hair that looked so identical to my Stark's adorable scruffy blondish mess that I had to look away as I answered him.

"Ice Cream Shoes," I said.

"Oh, yeah. She's an interesting vampyre," said James.

"I believe she is a young prophetess in the making," said Damien.

"I do too," I said. "Hey, where's Rephaim? We're gonna need his input on Aphrodite's vision."

"He'll be along soon," said Stark. "He stayed to help TPD with the rest of the tarps."

James put the towel around his shoulders and asked, "The wet and the cold don't seem to bother Rephaim at all, so he's definitely not human. What is he?"

"A raven," Damien said with a grin.

James's brow furrowed.

"It's a long story," I said. "And just part of what we need to talk about. Okay, Damien and Stark, do you two think you can find some dry clothes for Kevin and James and show them to a couple of the dorm rooms?" I looked from my Other World brother to my Warrior's twin. "Are the dorms okay? I think there's one professor's room that's empty if you'd rather stay there."

Kevin spoke right up. "Nah, I'm cool with the dorm. As long as the curtains are blackout."

Damien grimaced as he wrung out the bottom of his soaked sweater. "We have special dorm rooms for red vamps and fledglings—in case something happens like the ice storm and they're stuck here and can't get back to the depot tunnels," he explained. "The windows to those dorm rooms are totally blacked out *and* they have thick velvet curtains. That's where Jack and I are staying right now. I'll show you to an empty room."

"Thanks!" Kev said.

James hesitated, looking abashed. "Oh, um, that's fine with me, but I don't want to make Jack—that's his name, right?"

Damien nodded. "You are correct."

"I don't want to make Jack nervous or give him a PTSD setback." James picked nervously at the damp towel in his hands, but he kept speaking, his attention focused on Damien. "Back home we've been dealing with the aftermath of our Red Army having their humanity restored, and it's been tough for them. So, I understand that seeing someone from his old world might not be good for your partner."

"Thank you for acknowledging that," said Damien sincerely.

Stark said, "That's a good point. The professors' quarters are in the same building as the infirmary, and James really should get those bandages on his arm changed. They're soaking wet. So, Kev can go with Damien to the dorm and James can come with us."

"Sounds good to me. Jack already knows me, so I shouldn't upset him, right?" Kevin asked Damien.

"Jack really isn't that fragile. I think it was just a shock to see James so suddenly earlier. I'm sure he'll be fine with you, Kev." Damien looked Kevin up and down. "You're too big and muscular to wear anything Jack and I have, but I have a very comfy bathrobe you can borrow while we give your clothes a quick wash and a dry."

"Okay," said my brother. "I'll follow you."

"And James will come with us," I said. "Right now, the TPD is searching for clues about where Batshit might be hiding, so, let's take a couple hours to dry off, change, and grab something to eat—then we'll meet in the Council Chamber. I'll let Stevie Rae, Aphrodite, and Kacie know."

"And G-ma," said Kevin.

"Right—and Grandma. No way am I forgetting her," I said.

"Is it wrong that I hope she brings cookies?" Kevin asked.

I shook my head and smiled at him. "Cookies are never wrong—especially Grandma's lavender chocolate chip cookies."

(

It was all kinds of weird walking to the section of the House of Night that held the professors' quarters with Stark on one side of me and James on the other. Fledglings passed us in the hallway, gawking openly at the two Starks, and I realized that I needed to make a school-wide announcement to explain the Other Stark. As we dashed outside through the pouring rain, I was trying to decide if it would be better to tell the students James was Stark's relative or tell them the truth and take the chance that a precocious fledgling might try to open the door between worlds "for fun."

I decided that I definitely needed help making that decision and tabled it for the moment.

Stark and I showed James to the empty professor's room down the hall from the one we shared and promised to bring him some dry clothes.

James opened the door as we turned to leave. "Hey, Stark," he paused before he went inside his room. "Why didn't you come with Zoey when she crossed over? You're her Warrior. There was a battle going on. She needed protecting."

Stark cocked his head and James mirrored his expression. Then Stark's lip curved up in his cocky smile, and I knew what he was going to say before he answered.

"I didn't go because Z wouldn't let me. She knew I'd put her mission at risk because I'd be too easily recognizable."

James pursed his lips. "There's no way I'd let my High Priestess do something so dangerous without me," he said, sounding so much like my Stark once had that I laughed.

"That could be why you're *not* an Oathbound Warrior to a High Priestess," I said. "You need to realize that a Warrior doesn't boss his priestess around."

Stark added. "Yeah, he honors and protects her. Sometimes that means he has to trust that she can take care of herself." His arm slid around my shoulders. "This High Priestess can call on five elements. Plus, she had Rephaim and her brother with her. She was in good hands."

"And she didn't need to be rescued," I said.

James snorted.

"You really should go to the infirmary and have that bandage changed," said Stark.

"I will," James said and disappeared inside the room.

"He has a lot to learn," Stark said as we headed to our room.

"Please. He's exactly like you used to be," I said.

Stark kissed the top of my head. "Which is why I know he has a lot to learn. We're really going to the Other World?"

"Sadly, yes. Only I don't know how the hell we're going to get there." We'd come to our room, and instead of going in, I paused outside. "Hey, I'm going to Nyx's Temple. I need to do some serious praying before we meet and go over Aphrodite's vision and what we have to do because of it."

"How can I help?"

I smiled up at him, very, *very* glad I was with the mature Stark who had learned to respect me and to control his jealousy. "Would you send a group text to Aphrodite, Stevie Rae, Kacie, and Grandma letting them know we're meeting in the Council Room in two hours?"

"Absolutely. Say hi to Nyx for me."

I kissed him soundly and said, "Always."

(

Nyx's Temple always soothed my soul and brought my stress level down about 150 percent. Not that the Goddess appeared and told me what to do. That really wasn't Nyx's style. But what she did give me was peace of mind so that I could think clearly and, hopefully, be able to make smart decisions.

I loved the scent of the temple's lavender and vanilla candles—especially because I knew that they were Nyx's favorite. I sat cross-legged before the table laden with offerings to the Goddess, as well as the beautiful golden onyx statue of her that was lit from within, giving the stone life as well as warmth. An open flame that came from a recess in the floor perpetually burned before the table, but there was plenty of room for me to sit between it and the statue.

I closed my eyes and breathed in the scent of the Goddess, as well as the serenity of her temple. It took me longer than usual to ground and calm myself, which wasn't too surprising. Neferet had escaped. Other Neferet had fled, and after Aphrodite's vision, I couldn't even be thankful for that. We needed Other Kalona and another trip to the Other World. Then there was Kevin—in pain and forced to be around Aphrodite. And James ...

So, yeah, it took me a while to still my mind, but when I finally did, I was able to talk to my Goddess. I'd always spoken to Nyx like she was a friend. I'd had enough of religions where the god was some untouchable being who sat on high in judgment of everyone. When I first swore into the service of Nyx, I'd decided not to do what I'd watched my mother do every Sunday morning and Wednesday evening for years as she herded my siblings and me to church with our pain-in-the-ass step-loser. As she put on her carefully conservative clothes, she'd also dressed in an act—one where she bowed to a god whose followers demanded she reject everything joyous and fun about her personality so she could fit in with a group of women who were so concerned with what people thought of them that they had lost the ability to think for themselves.

No, I wanted nothing to do with that god.

When I talked to Nyx, Goddess of Night, it was like speaking to a good friend who was wiser and more loving than even Grandma Redbird—which took some doing.

"Hi, Nyx. So, crazy stuff is going down again. It's super bad that Neferet broke out of her tomb. I'm sure you already know this, but apparently, she has lost every bit of whatever had been left of her mind. I don't know how we're going to beat her. Again. I would definitely appreciate your help, even if it's just to coax Other Kalona to give us a hand. I'm not sure how this Other World stuff works, but I figure you might have an in with the version of you that's over there." I sighed and picked at the hem of my jeans.

"Speaking of that Other World, I could also use some help

figuring out how to get there again. I've been warned over and over about using Old Magick, so I'm gonna avoid that because I definitely do *not* want to end up like Batshit Neferet.

"And then there's Other Stark, who we're calling James because having two Starks is just too confusing, as well as my brother from that world—who you already know. Kev is super sad about Other Aphrodite. I know you helped him with his immediate grief, but he's still struggling. If there's anything I can do to help him, I'd be grateful if you would give me a hint." I sighed.

"James needs help too, but I have a feeling I can't do much about that. Stark—the one who's my Warrior—had a bunch of growing up to do, which we did together. But I won't be there to grow up with James. I would really appreciate it if you would help James get a clue, hopefully without things being too, too terrible for him." I paused and sighed. "Although knowing the stubbornness of the Starks, that might be impossible. So, I'll just say that I hope he learns fast and leave it at that." I grinned up at Nyx's statue. "And thank you for my friends and for the power you have given me. I'll try to do my best to not mess up. Basically, I want to be a High Priestess you are proud of. Blessed be, Nyx."

I breathed out a long sigh, and with it, the last bits of tension unknotted between my shoulder blades. I knew as soon as I left this temple sanctuary and rejoined the world, the stress would start again—and my shoulders would burn again—but for now, for a few precious moments, I felt completely at peace in the presence of my Goddess.

And then that peace was shattered by a familiar voice. "Oh, hey, I didn't know you'd be in here."

I didn't need to turn. I'd recognize the voice anywhere—and the words he'd spoken told me which body the voice belonged to.

"Hi, James."

He walked to the Goddess's table and took a long match from the ornate holder, struck it, lit a violet tea light and then put it at the base of Nyx's feet. He looked down at me and crossed then uncrossed his arms as he shifted from foot to foot like he might bolt.

"Um, I really didn't mean to interrupt. Should I leave?"

I stifled a sigh, but silently told Nyx, *You know I love you, but sometimes your answers are really annoying.* To James, I said, "No, that's okay. You're not interrupting. I was done talking with Nyx."

He sat beside me on the stone floor, which always felt comfortably warm from the eternal flame.

"You talk with Nyx?"

I brushed back my hair and studied him. "Yep. Don't you?"

"I pray. Or just sit in her temple and hope she knows I'm here."

"She knows you're here." As I spoke the words, I felt the truth in them.

"Good. Then she also knows how sorry I am," he said softly.

"About?" And then I realized how intrusive that question was and quickly added, "Never mind. That was rude of me. Not my business what you apologize to Nyx about."

He ran his hand through his hair and looked so much like my Warrior that it made my stomach flutter.

James sighed heavily. "No, that's okay. It's not like you don't already know. I'm really sorry that I supported Neferet."

"What do you wish you would've done?"

He answered immediately. "Stood up against her. Spoken out."

"Then you would've had to join the Resistance and hide from her, or she would've killed you. Either way, you wouldn't have been where you were that day at the stadium. The only reason you were able to stop the Red Army from following her command to kill all those humans was because the soldiers trusted you. They listened to you. No one else could've done what you did. And because of that, you gave Kevin and me the time we needed to get the sprites involved."

He met my gaze. "You sound just like your brother. I try to tell myself all of that, but I still feel like I let Nyx down by being on Neferet's side for so long."

I remembered that he'd even been Neferet's lover, and felt a weird stir of jealousy, which I quickly squashed like the stupid, hypocritical bug it was. Instead, I drew a deep breath and let my gaze turn upward to the Goddess. Then I spoke the words that drifted through my mind like the scent of lavender and vanilla perfuming the air around us.

"When you stood up and spoke out, you did exactly what we needed you to do when we needed you to do it. You honored the Goddess. You didn't let her down. You didn't let your House of Night down. Stop beating yourself up for not doing something sooner."

I could feel him staring at me, so I turned my attention from the statue of Nyx to him. Tears welled in his familiar brown eyes and his nose started to turn pink. My heart squeezed, and I reached out and took his hand. "Hey, it's okay. You can forgive yourself and move on. It's what our Goddess wants you to do."

"For real?" He wiped at a tear that escaped down his cheek.

"Absolutely, for real," I assured him.

And then, before I could say anything else, he leaned forward and kissed me. It was the strangest thing that had ever happened to me—and for the past year and a half my life had been totally filled with strange. It was physically like kissing my Warrior. His lips were the same. The arms that came around me were the same. But his touch was hesitant, not strong and sure and familiar. I'd kissed him once before in his world, but that had been fast and impulsive.

This was a real kiss.

I didn't return it, but I also didn't pull away. It was the most neutral kiss of my life. Not unpleasant. Just not right.

James eventually stopped and sat back. He stared at me through tear-glossed eyes.

"I'm sorry," he blurted.

"Don't be. I'm not mad at you. But, James," I took his hand in mine again, holding it gently. "I am not what you need to fix your conscience."

He pulled his hand from mine. "I didn't kiss you because I want you to fix my conscience."

"Then why did you kiss me?"

"Because I feel connected to you! There's something about you that makes me want to be close to you."

As carefully as I could I said, "James, that's because there *is* something between you and Zoey. Or rather, there could've been something between you and Zoey if Neferet hadn't killed her—but that Zoey isn't me. She's dead. What you feel for me is more an echo of what you could have felt for her than real attraction."

He attempted the signature cocky James Stark smile and said, "I dunno, Z, you're really hot. I'm pretty sure I'm actually attracted to you."

I wanted to roll my eyes at him and conk him on his thick head, but I figured that would be counterproductive. Instead, I said, "You're mistaking physical attraction for something a lot deeper, and that something is what I have with Stark."

"It's hard to understand."

I nodded and laughed softly. "I know, right? Here, maybe this will help. Think about Kevin. You know he and the Aphrodite from your world were in love."

"Yeah. I just saw her in Nyx's Realm. They're still in love."

"Right. And you've seen *this* Aphrodite. Are they the same people?"

"No. I mean, they're similar, but our Aphrodite didn't have friends like this one does, and she's obviously with that big Warrior."

"Darius," I said.

"Yeah, him. And in this world, she is different—more confident. She's nice to Kev and all, but she's not—" his words broke off as he got it. "Oh. She's a completely different person and that person is not in love with *him*."

"Yeah, and while she feels *something* for him because in another world they were lovers and together—"

He finished before I could. "In this world their relationship isn't the same because even though they're versions of the same people, *they aren't actually the same.*"

"Now you're getting it." I squeezed his hand. "In the presence of Nyx, I want to tell you what I wish for you. I wish that you will find your love—someone who makes your heart fill with joy just by looking at her—someone who you don't just want to be your best for, but who you *are* your best for. Someone who makes you laugh—a lot. Someone you'll grow old with and share a long, happy life with. And that someone is not me. Not in this world. Not in this lifetime."

He stared into my eyes as tears tracked down his face. "I don't know why this makes me so emotional. It's not like me at all."

"It should make you emotional. This is insanely difficult—not to mention we have a bunch of terrifying end-of-the-world stuff going on around us. But, James, what we don't have going on is a secret love affair. That's not us."

"What you're saying makes sense to my mind. I just need it to make sense to my heart." Then, carefully, he lifted my hand and pressed it to his lips before saying, "You're a wise High Priestess. I'm glad I came to this world and got to know you."

I smiled at him and suddenly felt a lot lighter. "Me too."

"If you don't mind, I'd like to stay here and talk with Nyx for a little while," he said.

"I don't mind at all. And you know what, James Stark? In *any* world you'll always be one of the good guys."

21

Other Stark

James didn't leave Nyx's Temple until he felt completely calm. He'd really not known Zoey was going to be there—not that he would've avoided the temple had he known. He totally would've gone in but been prepared to face her. Talking with her there had changed everything. She'd looked so young, but sounded mature and wise, and he'd felt so drawn to her that it had made him dizzy with desire.

He'd had lovers—lots of them, actually. He and Neferet had been lovers, though James didn't like to think about that. Having sex with Neferet had been hot and rough. There had been nothing intimate about it. It'd been like she had an itch that anyone could scratch—and that anyone had, temporarily, been him. In spite of her preternatural beauty, James had been relieved when Neferet had turned her attention to other vampyres.

But that one kiss with Zoey in the press box at TU in the midst of insanity and chaos had shaken his world. So, he'd tried again—desperately seeking a repeat, and this world's Stark could go to hell and be ready to move out of his way.

It hadn't been the same, and not just because Zoey hadn't

done much participating. That *thing* he'd felt at the stadium wasn't entirely gone. His stomach still flipped around when he saw her, but there had been no electricity—no gut-deep zap that made him want to pull her into his arms and crush her body against his and tell her Warrior to get lost.

It was confusing.

Sitting on the floor of Nyx's Temple before her offering table, James decided that maybe he didn't need to figure out the whys and what-ifs. Maybe he just needed to accept that this girl he'd traveled to a different world to find wasn't meant to be with him—and as soon as that thought came to James's mind, he suddenly felt better—freer—calmer and not as desperate and filled with nerves as he'd been since the day not so long ago that he'd taken a stand against Neferet.

James stood and touched the base of Nyx's statue. "You know I'm sorry. I've said it over and over again. I've shown you in my actions too. I guess now Zoey is right. I need to learn to forgive myself and let go—of my anger and disappointment and also of that fantasy I've been building up in my mind about Zoey. I think I'm ready. Maybe that's why I had to come all the way over here—to learn to forgive and to let go. I'm going to do it. I promise. Blessed be, my Goddess. Blessed be."

Feeling better, James left Nyx's Temple and sprinted to the rear entrance of the school. He ducked his head against what was now cold, constant rain and rushed inside where he had to put on the brakes and lunge to the side to stop from knocking some kid over.

"Holy shitballs! Watch yourself. And back the hell off—you're like a wet cat getting rain everywhere. Jesus, my hair!"

James backed against the closed door, wiping rain and hair from his eyes to see a very disgruntled vampyre glaring at him and brushing drops of rain from her clothes with one hand and patting her hair with the other. It took him a second to recognize her because she had her mass of hair pulled back in a spectacularly long ponytail—and he got sidetracked by her short, black biker's boots, her skin-hugging black leggings, and her oversized black sweatshirt that proclaimed WILD FEMINIST in bold white letters across her large, perky boobs.

"Hey, genius. My eyes are up here."

James lifted his gaze to meet her big, dark eyes and blinked in surprise. "Ice Cream Shoes?"

"You don't have to call me that, *James*. I mean, you can if you want, but it's really more of a this-world joke than a your-world thing."

"Sorry, Kacie. I was distracted."

"I know. By my large, gorgeous breasts."

"Well, maybe. Partially. But it's raining pretty hard, and I got it in my eyes—not to mention my hair was totally messing with my vision. I did almost run over you because I couldn't see."

She pursed her lips and studied him closely which, for some reason, made him want to fidget. "I'm not sure whether I should be insulted or glad you're not a boob creeper-stalker."

"I'm definitely not a boob creeper-stalker. Though I do appreciate breasts." He closed his mouth then to keep anything else stupid from coming out.

She let out one *Ha!* of amusement and shook her head slightly. "Good to know. I suppose you're going to be in the big Council Meeting in half an hour?"

"I suppose I am, since I came from another world to be here," he said. "Will you be there?"

"Yep. I'm the fire and water stand-in until Shaunee and Shaylin get here. Do you have a Shaunee and Shaylin in your world?"

He was surprised by the question, and then equally surprised that he couldn't answer it. "Uh, I don't actually know. I doubt if we have a Shaylin. She's a red vampyre, right?"

"Like me—yep."

"Well, I don't think we have any female red vamps yet."

Kacie nodded. "Yeah, that's what I heard. And it's a damn shame. Your red fledglings and vamps need a High Priestess of their own. What about Shaunee? Any beautiful women of color who have fire affinities in your Tulsa?"

He shrugged. "Shaunee might be a fledgling. I know she's not a High Priestess because Neferet got rid of all of them who wouldn't step down. I'd know if she had been one of those."

"Your world sounds like it sucks for women."

"I'm afraid my world sucks for more than just women, but I want to change that," he said.

"Good to hear. What are you doing right now?"

"Nothing much. I guess I was going to go back to my room and wait for thirty minutes to pass."

"Boring," she said. "Come with me. I'm going to the dining hall to get something to eat before the meeting. The *professors'* dining hall. You know what that means, right?" She watched him expectantly and when he just moved his shoulders and looked confused she sighed dramatically. "James, it means the food is fucking epic. Come on."

She started walking down the wide hall, and when he just stood there staring, she glanced back at him. "Unless you prefer sitting in your room and moping over Zoey. Your choice."

What the hell is wrong with me? She's super hot, and I'm starving.

He hurried to catch up with her. "I'm not moping over anyone."

She glanced at him and snorted. "Not now, you're not."

They wound their way through the large school. It was weird. It was basically laid out like his House of Night, but this one was somehow lighter—brighter—*happier.*

As if she were reading his mind, Kacie said, "So? Is this like your House of Night?"

Instead of answering right away he asked a question of his own. "Your affinities are for water and fire, right? Can you also read minds?"

"No. You don't need to panic about that, James. Anyone would be curious about the differences between two mirror worlds—if there are any. Oh, and besides an affinity for water and fire, I also sometimes know stuff."

"Stuff?"

She twirled the end of her ponytail. "Yeah. You know. Like at the park. The affinity is new—like my tattoos. I don't have it all figured out yet. So, what about your House of Night?"

"This one is nicer." After he said the words he realized how true they were.

"You mean your HoN is crappy and rundown?"

"No, I mean it's gloomy compared to this one." He paused as a fledgling and a human teenager walked past them. The fledgling waved at Kacie and then gave him a confused look. The human just kept talking like it was completely normal for a human kid to be friends with a fledgling *and* be hanging out at a House of Night.

"Stop gawking at the kid," Kacie told him. "I'm assuming humans and fledglings don't mix in your world?"

"No. Some of the Resistance members were human, and the vamp Resistance helped to get humans out of the battle area, but they definitely don't hang out at the House of Night."

"That's probably one of the reasons your place is gloomy. When you go back, you should change that. Z and her High Priestesses have been working really hard to desegregate the US. I don't think anyone believed it would work—or even thought it was a good idea at first. But they were wrong. It's true that education and familiarity fight racism. Once human kids hang around for a while, they get that we're all basically more similar than different." She snorted again and added, "Their parents are a different story, but old people tend to be a pain in the ass like that." Kacie stopped at a gleaming wooden door that had a golden sign that read Professors' Dining Hall. She pushed it open, and he followed her to a small booth.

A fledgling who was wearing a uniform with Nyx's golden chariot pulling a trail of shining silver stars over her breast pocket, which identified her as a fifth former, or junior, came to take their order, but she just stood there staring at James.

"Alison, close your mouth," Kacie said.

"Sorry!" The fledgling blushed bright red. "He just, uh, looks like—"

"Yeah, we know. I'm sure Zoey is gonna explain that pretty soon, but until she does, how about we *don't* make James feel like a hideous beast. 'Kay?"

"Okay. Yeah. Sure."

"Great! I'll take two Caesar salads—no croutons—extra dressing on the side, and one of those black bean veggie burritos. Oh, and that Moroccan mint ice tea you guys only have up here. What do you want?" Kacie said to James.

I want to get to know you better, popped into his mind and he had to mentally shake himself before he answered. "I'll just take a burger and some fries. And a beer. Please."

"Add a green salad to that because he ordered nothing that's healthy—and a carafe of blood." Kacie glanced at him. "Warm or cold?"

"Um, warm."

"Warm. And we have a Council Meeting in thirty, so, we gotta hurry."

"I'll get it right out," the fledgling hurried away, but not before shooting James a couple looks over her shoulder.

"Sorry about the gawking. I should've thought about that before bringing you up here."

"It's fine. I can't blame her."

"No," Kacie said. "It's rude. But I don't blame her either. I'll have to remind Stevie Rae to remind Zoey to make some kinda announcement about you."

The fledgling was back with their drinks and the carafe of blood, and James thanked her, which only made her stare more at him.

"Here," Kacie said after the fledgling left. "Drink the blood before the beer."

"Are you always this bossy?" he asked as he did what she told him to do.

"Are you always this compliant?" she shot back.

He laughed and almost choked on the blood. "You know, you look too young to be a High Priestess, but you definitely act like one."

"Yeah, well, my internal age has never accurately been reflected by how I look."

James laughed. "Really, *Ice Cream Shoes*?"

Kacie didn't crack a smile—not even a small one. "That nickname is about fashion—not about me being a kid. It would be stupid of you to underestimate me—especially right after you admitted that I act like a High Priestess. Thank you, by the way, for that compliment. I'm not one. Yet. But I will be. Soon." She paused as Alison returned to place two huge salads in front of her and gave a smaller one to James. "Thanks," she told the fledgling before she started squeezing lemons and adding extra dressing.

"Do you always eat this much salad?" James asked as he picked at his assortment of field greens.

"Yep. I was a vegetarian before I was Marked. I'm still kinda uncomfortable with the whole blood-drinking thing, even though it does taste ridiculously good."

He smiled at her. "You're not what you seem."

"Once you get to know me, you won't say that. The truth is I'm pretty much exactly what I seem. I don't like lies. I don't like to pretend to be anything but who I am." She took a big bite of her salad and then spoke around it. "Oh, and I also don't like school. Thankfully that was cut short by my dying and then coming back as—*wha-bam!*—a fully Changed red vamp. So now the classes I take are mostly just spellwork and such. You know, with other newly Changed vamps, which is cool." She chewed for a while as she watched him, and then added, "But you seem really sad to be a Warrior, and I think that's for real and not just *what you seem*. Don't let it make you sad."

"It?" he asked.

"Zoey. Even though it doesn't seem like she and Stark play stupid jealousy games, you gotta know that whatever might be going on between you and Z, they're seriously *together*. As in forever. She's not your girl over here."

Her words surprised him, but the more James talked with Kacie, the more he realized that she didn't need to read minds—she knew her own well enough that she was a good observer of others. "I know that, and there's absolutely nothing going on between Zoey and me." Then he tried to lighten the mood by saying, "Apparently, it makes me douchey to say that Z is anyone's girl except her own."

"Of course it does," Kacie said, waving her fork for emphasis. "I'm speaking metaphorically."

The rest of their food came, and they ate silently, though James didn't think it was an awkward silence. Kacie was easy to be around—even though he had a hard time predicting what she might say next. He looked up from dunking his fry in ketchup to see her watching him.

"What?"

She shrugged. "I was just thinking that you look like a guy who hasn't had fun in a long time."

He wasn't sure why that bothered him so much, but it did—so his response was more abrupt than he intended.

"Yeah, war is a real buzzkill."

But his tone didn't put her off at all. "I heard about that. How you were on the wrong side—then you figured it out, blah, blah."

He stared at her. "Blah, blah?"

"Yeah. You're on the *right* side now, and still—zero fun. So, blah, blah with all that self-indulgent angst." She reached over and snagged one of his fries. "I'm not trying to be mean. I'm just being real with you and telling you what I see. Let me know if I'm wrong."

James took a bite of his burger and chewed while he thought about his answer. Finally, he decided to be real too. "I was just talking to Nyx about that. Well, not about me having fun, exactly."

"But about you forgiving yourself and moving on?"

"Actually, yes. Exactly that."

"How's it going for you?"

"From what you're telling me, not very well," he said—though he did smile at her.

She grinned back for a second before shoving the fry in her mouth and saying, "You can start by not giving a shit about what other people think of you. Just be you. Fuck 'em if they don't like it or if they want to keep judging you for past mistakes."

"Is that what you do?"

"Me? Hell no. I'm a sucker for peer pressure. I *would* jump off a bridge if everyone else did." Then she snatched another one of his fries and added, "JK."

They laughed together and, as Kacie continued to steal his fries, James Stark forgot that people were staring at him.

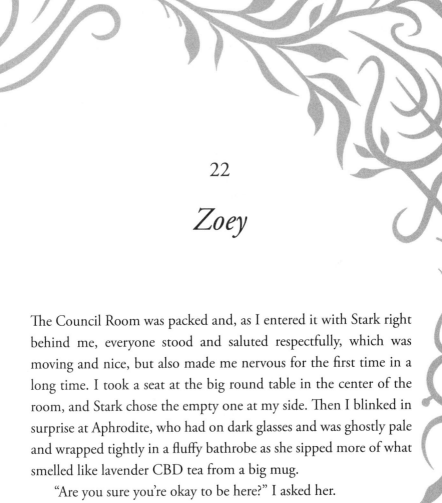

22

Zoey

The Council Room was packed and, as I entered it with Stark right behind me, everyone stood and saluted respectfully, which was moving and nice, but also made me nervous for the first time in a long time. I took a seat at the big round table in the center of the room, and Stark chose the empty one at my side. Then I blinked in surprise at Aphrodite, who had on dark glasses and was ghostly pale and wrapped tightly in a fluffy bathrobe as she sipped more of what smelled like lavender CBD tea from a big mug.

"Are you sure you're okay to be here?" I asked her.

"No, and I'd much rather sleep off my vision hangover, but I *need* to be here. I'll sleep after."

As always, Darius was at her side. I saw him send her a worried look, but I had to agree with Aphrodite. We did need her. We needed all the help we could get.

Stevie Rae was sitting on Aphrodite's other side, with a still-damp Rephaim next to her. Then Damien and Kevin were seated beside each other, with James and Kacie in the next seats. Lenobia was beside Kacie, then came Grandma—whose lavender chocolate chip cookies were piled in the middle of the table—and then me.

"I just got off the phone with Detective Marx," I began. "The rain is not helping. The TPD homicide unit has been working hard, but any trail or tracks left by the tendrils of Darkness have washed away. Basically, they could be anywhere in midtown."

"And wherever they are is where we'll find Neferet," said Stark.

I nodded. "Darius, Marx would like the help of the Sons of Erebus Warriors in searching for Neferet—who we'll call Batshit— not just to save confusion when we're talking about the Other World Neferet, but also because it's accurate."

"As soon as we're done here, I'll organize the Warriors and we'll start a search grid," said Darius.

Damien raised a finger, calling our attention to him. "Be sure you check her old penthouse suite at the Mayo. It's been under renovation for the past year, but she might be looking for somewhere familiar to hide."

"Good idea," I said.

Lenobia spoke up. "It would be wise to search the tunnels and then close off the downtown entrances and the newer additions from the depot. It's like a maze down there, and the last thing we need is for her to start kidnapping people and taking them underground to feed."

"Another good idea," I agreed.

"Got it," said Darius.

"Everyone needs to keep in mind that as soon as she's recovered all her strength, Batshit is going to be heading to Kev's world," said Aphrodite. "My vision was clear about only a few things—but the fact that she joins Other Neferet over there is one."

"Another is that your daddy in that Other World is gonna be at the showdown," added Stevie Rae to Rephaim.

"This seems a good time for us to go over the prophetic poem u-we-tsi was kind enough to bring from his world to ours. Might I read it aloud, Zoeybird?"

"Absolutely, Grandma," I said.

Grandma Redbird stood, strong and sure. She wore her age like a badge of honor, and I hoped that I would someday grow into a woman who was as wise and compassionate.

Grandma passed around copies of the prophecy and then cleared her throat and read from a paper she held before her.

> *"Ancient one sleeping, waiting to arise,*
> *When the dead joins with fire and water red*
> *Son who is not—his word is key; the raven will devise*
> *He shall hear the call from his sacrificial bed.*
>
> *By the blood of she who is neither foe nor friend he is free.*
> *Behold a terrible sacrifice to come—a beautiful sight,*
> *Ruled by love they shall be.*
> *The future will not kneel to her dark might.*
>
> *Kalona's return is not bittersweet*
> *As he will be welcomed with love and heat."*

No one spoke at first as we all studied the poem. Then Grandma said, "Before we talk about particulars, I wanted to let you know that I shared this with the Wise Woman Council, and we are all in agreement—this Kalona did not Fall as did ours. There is no negative reference to him at all like there was in our world's prophecy. Coupled with the fact that there are no Raven Mockers in that world, and that Kevin has told me that my ancestral journal in his world only mentioned a being called Silver Wings—and we know our Kalona's wings turned black when he was ejected from Nyx's Realm—it is our belief that there you are dealing with a version of Kalona who did not turn to Darkness."

"But for some reason, he retreated from the world and is sleeping, waiting to arise," said Rephaim.

"We need to hope that the reason he's sleepin' is good and not 'cause he did somethin' horrific and is basically hidin'," said Stevie Rae.

Kevin folded his hands in front of him on the table, which I knew was his way to keep from cracking his knuckles nervously. "Well, even though we don't know why he left the world and Nyx, I don't think we have much choice. We have to wake him up." Kevin looked at me. "Where was he entombed in your world?"

"Here," I said. "At the House of Night. He was buried under that big oak by the east wall."

"At least he'll be easy to find," said James. He glanced at Kacie and continued. "And I think Ice Cream Shoes is going to have to take a trip to my world."

Kacie shrugged nonchalantly. "I'm cool with it. I like to travel."

Grandma nodded. "I agree, though Kacie is only part of the equation. She definitely could meet the *fire and water red* reference, though she is, most happily, not dead."

Kacie grinned at Grandma. "Yeah, I'm glad about that part too, but the truth is, I was dead not too long ago. Maybe that whole line is about me."

"That seems logical, dear," said Grandma.

"Well, the next two lines are obviously about Rephaim," said Stevie Rae. "And that's good 'cause even though Other Kalona isn't his daddy, they still might have a connection. I mean, you and Kev aren't *actually* brother and sister in this world, but y'all are close like you are."

Rephaim added, "I will pray to Father about this. Sometimes he speaks to me through my dreams. Perhaps he can give me insight on what to say to this other version of himself."

Aphrodite lifted her sunglasses and rubbed her bloodshot eyes before saying, "Okay, guys, I'm gonna say this, and I wish I didn't have to, but something about the *she who is neither foe nor friend* line keeps messing with my mind. We need to consider that it might be referring to Other Neferet."

"Oh, hell no!" blurted James.

"Calm it down right meow, Other Bow Boy," said Aphrodite. "None of us like it. None of us would trust her. But read it again and tell me if you have a better answer to plug in there."

I reluctantly added, "Plus, we have the fact that in Aphrodite's vision it seemed Other Neferet could've been on our side."

"Well, if we have to count on Neferet to help us raise Kalona, we'd better come up with plan B," said Kevin.

I leaned forward. "Your Neferet isn't stupid, right James?"

He shook his head. "She's mean and selfish, but she's also cunning. No, I would never describe her as stupid."

"Maybe it's as simple as this," I said. "Neferet broke Batshit out and then was not prepared for the insanity she witnessed. We all know what Batshit is capable of, but your Neferet wasn't here to experience any of it. And she's smart. One good look at that amount of crazy would be all it took for me to understand that there is no way in hell that creature was going to help anyone but herself—*especially* not another version of herself who wanted to figure out how to be more powerful."

"So, she used Old Magick to skedaddle," said Kacie. "It does make sense that she might be freaked enough to help raise Kalona, if that also means stopping Batshit. 'Cause, seriously, your Neferet has to have a target painted on her back."

"Ice Cream Shoes is right," said Aphrodite. "Batshit does not share power, and we know she's heading to the Other World. No way is there going to be room for two of her over there."

James rubbed a hand through his hair. "Aphrodite, you really couldn't tell from your vision whether Neferet is helping Batshit or fighting her in that final showdown?"

Aphrodite answered, "The only part of the vision I got to see was just before your Neferet's death. Kalona was hurt but holding off Batshit. Something happened that I couldn't see, but it freaked Other Neferet the hell out so bad that, even though it seemed

Lynette was arguing with her about it, Neferet took off, taking Lynette with her. Batshit went after Lynette and killed her. *Then* she killed Neferet."

"And you didn't see any of us there?" Stark asked.

Aphrodite shrugged and then grimaced and pressed two fingers to her temple. "Yes and no. I couldn't tell whether we were there or not until Other Neferet was dying, and then I heard what I thought was us being killed. I can't tell you exactly which of us were there for sure because Other Neferet died too fast."

"I can tell you who was there," said Kacie.

"Go ahead," I said. I was increasingly impressed by her confidence and by her ability to speak up about her intuition. Too many young women silence that part of them. It was refreshing to meet someone who didn't have that problem.

"Your circle's there," Kacie said simply. "That would be Stevie Rae, Damien, me as either air or water, and then Kevin as the last element 'cause, like you, he has an affinity for all five. Oh, and also, I figure Rephaim will be there too, 'cause he has to talk to Kalona, and Darius to protect Aphrodite in case any of us need a second chance." She took a breath and frowned before continuing. "Not sure if that would help me or not." Kacie looked across the table at Aphrodite. "Can you give third chances?"

"You better hope so, Ice Cream Shoes. I have a feeling that smart mind of yours and your equally smart mouth are going to get you into trouble."

Kacie nodded. "That's what I figure too."

"Don't worry," Damien said with a reassuring smile. "Z's circle is always really powerful. You'll be safest if you stick with her."

I was staring at Damien as puzzle pieces fell into place.

"Holy shit!" I blurted.

Aphrodite and Stevie Rae sat straight up and gawked at me.

"You cussed," Aphrodite said.

"For reals," Stevie Rae said.

"I also just figured out how we're getting to the Other World," I said. "Thanks to Ice Cream Shoes and Damien."

"Seriously?" Stark asked. "How?"

"*Not* Old Magick," said Kevin.

"Not Old Magick," I agreed, my voice filled with the excitement that was rushing through my body. "My circle and I are getting there by using our own Goddess-given powers. We're going to call on the elements and have them open a portal between worlds, and then we're going to walk right through it."

"Zoey!" Lenobia clapped victoriously. "You're absolutely right. With the power your circle wields, it's logical that will work."

"You're welcome," said Kacie, winking at Damien.

There was a knock on the Council Room door and it cracked, allowing one of the senior fledglings to peek her head inside the room and say, "I'm really sorry to interrupt, but Detective Marx is downstairs. He says he's ready to begin the search with the Sons of Erebus Warriors."

I nodded. "Thank you, Astrid. Please tell him we're ending our Council Meeting right now. Stark, Darius, and I will be down to see him in a moment."

Darius stood. "With your leave, I will gather the Warriors and bring them to the foyer."

"You have it," I said. "But be sure everyone is clear. If you find Batshit, *you do not engage with her.* We have no immortal help right now. I'm not going to risk our Warriors."

"Understood." Darius saluted and left the room.

"Batshit isn't going to wait long," Aphrodite said. "I don't believe the Warriors will find her before she leaves this world."

"Whether they do or not, we need to get to the Other World fast," I said. "And raise Other Kalona so that we're ready and waiting for her."

"By fast, what do you mean?" Stark asked me.

"I mean as soon as I write the spell that will compel the elements to open the portal. And I'm a pretty fast writer," I said.

Stark turned in his chair so that he faced me. "This time I believe I need to come with you."

I smiled and nodded. "Oh, hell yes. We'll need as many Warriors as we can get over there—especially the kind whose arrows can't miss."

"Zoeybird, exactly who all will accompany you on this journey?" Grandma said. "I ask so that I may prepare protection for them, and to call the Great Earth Mother's blessing down on each of you."

"Well, unless anyone has a problem with it—I say Kacie's list sounds good to me."

Around the table everyone nodded, except Lenobia. I met her gaze and said formally, "Do you have a different idea, Professor Lenobia? You cannot come because you will be acting High Priestess in my place."

Lenobia drew a deep breath and said, "I would ask that Darius remain here. He is our Swordmaster, and with our Neferet free, even if she is only here for a short time, we need his strength and wisdom to protect our fledglings and priestesses."

"That makes sense to me," I said.

My gaze went to Aphrodite. She was frowning, but I saw her eyes cut to Kevin and then return to me. She sighed. "He's going to be pissed, but I'll talk to him."

"Okay, this meeting is over. If you need me, I'll be in the media center writing a spell," I said.

Lenobia and Damien filed out quickly, followed by Stevie Rae and Rephaim. Stevie Rae touched my shoulder on her way past me and said, "You need some help with the spell, Z?"

"Absolutely," I said.

"Want me to bring brown pop or blood to the media room?"

"Both," I said. "And Doritos."

"Um, should I get Damien, too?" she asked.

"No, let him be with Jack. This is going to be hard on them."

"'Kay. See you soon."

James and Kacie were still sitting beside each other. Their heads were tilted together, and they seemed to be talking easily. *James and Ice Cream Shoes …?* And this time I didn't feel even a twinge of inappropriate jealousy.

"Hey, James," Stark said.

When James kept talking to Kacie and didn't seem to hear him, Aphrodite loudly cleared her throat. Kacie and James looked at her, and she pointed at Stark.

"James, I thought you might like to come with us to meet with Marx and check out the Sons of Erebus—since you're a general in your world and all."

"Oh, yeah. I would," James said. He stood and then paused and turned back to Kacie. "Would you like to meet me in the Professors' Dining Hall afterward for a drink?"

Kacie didn't exactly smile, but her pretty face lit up with pleasure. "Yes, I definitely would."

"Great. See ya."

Stark and I shared a *look.* I winked, and he smiled. Then the two vampyres, identical except for the color of their Marks and the weight of their souls, left the room together.

Aphrodite fluttered her fingers at Kacie to get her attention. "Hey, Ice Cream Shoes, you know he's stuck on Z, right?"

Kacie lowered her voice dramatically and cut her eyes at Kevin. "Hey, Aphrodite, you know he's stuck on *you,* right?" Then she stood, saluted me, and left the room.

"That kid is kinda a pain in the ass," Aphrodite said. "I like her."

"Me too," I said.

"She definitely has spunk," said Grandma. "Zoeybird, I shall go. I believe I would like to make protective charms to carry with you."

"That would be really great, G-ma," said Kevin.

"Oh, u-we-tsi, it is always such a joy to see you." Grandma kissed Kevin on the forehead before she smiled at me and left the room.

Then I realized it was just Aphrodite, Kevin, and me, and I stood so quickly that I almost knocked over my chair.

"I better get to the media center and start on that spell," I said. I studied Aphrodite. "And you need to sleep. We'll be leaving soon, and you're definitely not a hundred percent."

"I'll sleep, but first, I need to talk with your brother. So don't forget to close the door on your way out."

My gaze found Kevin, who was watching Aphrodite with a mixture of fear and fascination.

I couldn't help them. I knew that from my own struggle with James. They would have to find their own way to acceptance, but as I left I sent a silent prayer to Nyx.

Please, Nyx, help Kevin's heart to heal and let Aphrodite be wise and kind.

And then I closed the door behind me on the way out.

23

Other Kevin

Kevin almost had to stop himself from shouting at his sister, *No, don't go!* It was stupid. He knew that, but being alone with Aphrodite made his palms sweat and his stomach hurt.

Clearly reading his terrified expression, Aphrodite raised one perfect blond brow at him. "Oh, for shit's sake, I'm not going to bite you."

His nerves made him go for levity instead of a wiser choice. "Unless I want you to?"

"No, Kev. Not even if you want me to. I'm not into pain." She paused and then added, "Well, not anymore anyway." Aphrodite patted the chair beside her. "Would you mind coming over here? My eyes hurt and my vision is still wonky and when I have a vision, I'm—"

"Tired and just generally feel like crap." He finished for her as he got up and walked around the round conference table to take a seat beside her.

"You helped your Aphrodite through visions, too?"

"Yeah," he said.

"That's nice of you."

He raised his hands and then let them fall in a *whatever* gesture. "It was just part of being in love with a Prophetess of Nyx. And I didn't mind. At all." Kev tried to smile at her, but it came out more like a grimace. "Plus, it made me feel useful. She was gorgeous and talented and really special—and I'm just me."

Aphrodite took off her dark glasses and studied him with her bloodshot but somehow still unsettlingly beautiful eyes. "By *just me* do you mean just the youngest red vampyre in your world and the only vamp of either color who has an affinity for all five elements?"

"Um, yeah."

"Always remember that a talented Prophetess of Nyx chose you as the love of her life. Don't underestimate yourself. That denigrates her choice."

He nodded but couldn't find the right words to respond.

"Goddess, you're young," she said softly. "And that's not a bad thing. Don't think I'm patronizing you or calling you a child or some stupid shit like that. I just hate that this happened to you before you were even eighteen. You should be getting in trouble for flirting with fledglings, not trying to heal a broken heart."

"War tends to make you grow up … Even if I hadn't loved Aphrodite, I still wouldn't be all carefree."

"If you hadn't loved Aphrodite, the red fledglings and vampyres in your world would still be lacking their humanity and your civilization would be on fire—metaphorically and literally."

"No, I believe she would have—"

Aphrodite's raised hand silenced him. "This is something I know better than you. I'm a version of her—just like she was a version of me. To be better, I needed help, just like she did. If Darius and Zoey and the rest of the Nerd Herd hadn't come along, I probably would still be lost in my own ego. You did good, Kev, even if it feels bad right now."

He looked down at his hands, not sure what to say.

"Thanks for catching me. Darius said you didn't even let me hit the ground."

He looked up at her. "I recognized a vision coming on and I was closer than Darius. It was no big deal."

"It was a big deal to me. Thank you."

"You're welcome."

"So, how are you?"

He shrugged. "Trying to deal. Just taking it day by day. It helped to see her, even though I couldn't touch her."

Aphrodite leaned forward, obviously intrigued. "Oh, that's right! You saw your Aphrodite in Nyx's Realm. Wait—you couldn't touch her?"

"No. She was just spirit, and since I'm flesh, we couldn't touch, even though she looked totally solid. It was weird."

"Sounds like it. How is she doing there?"

"Good. Really good. The same, but different." Kevin wiped his palms on his jeans and relaxed a little. Even though it was weird to be talking to Aphrodite about Aphrodite, it was also a relief. Everyone, even Z, tiptoed around him—which made him feel even more broken than he already was. "She was more of herself there."

"What do you mean?"

"Okay, don't freak."

"Saying that is making me freak. Just tell me," she said.

"She looked different—more relaxed. Her hair was different." He paused and smiled—and then, without even thinking about it, he reached out and brushed his fingers over a long strand of her thick blond hair that had fallen across her shoulder. "I didn't know you straightened that."

She snorted. "Of course I straighten my hair. This kind of perfection does not come without work. Wait—*she's not straightening her hair?* Is she in a version of hell?"

Kevin surprised himself by laughing. "No! And you should try letting your hair go sometime. It was adorable and curly and kinda frizzy."

"You blaspheme, but you're in mourning, so I'll let it go. What else was different about her?"

"She was wearing a cute long skirt with a lot of lace and a simple tee tied up." He grinned and added, "And she didn't have on any makeup or shoes."

Aphrodite clutched her pearls dramatically. "And you're sure she's not in hell?"

"Positive. You want to know the absolute truth?"

All teasing went out of her voice. "I always want you to tell me the absolute truth."

"It was like she was who she would've been without carrying around the weight of what her crappy parents did to her."

Aphrodite looked down and nodded.

"Hey, I didn't mean to hurt your feelings."

"You didn't. It's just that I understand what you're saying all too well. It's good to know that there is a place and a time where my past won't have the power to hurt me anymore."

Kevin slowly covered her hand with his. "There's more. You get to take love with you when you die. You get to remember everything and everyone, but something happens and the loss and grief and feeling like you miss someone so much that it might kill you goes away and leaves you with love—always love."

She covered their joined hands with her other one. "I wish I could help take away some of that hurt for you."

He met her gaze. "I thought you could. I was wrong. You're great, but you're not her. You're stronger and wiser. I love her exactly as she was, but if she'd been more like you, she would have been able to survive the loss of so much of her humanity like you did."

"Hey, I'm still learning and growing. I've been her—the difference was that I learned to let people in and to rely on my friends.

228

I want you to remember that. Let people in. Let your friends help you. *Any* world is too damn difficult to survive on your own." She lifted her hand and touched his cheek gently. "Love again. She wants you to. I know it because even though it breaks my heart to think about it, if I died I would want Darius to find happiness again. The only thing worse than losing him would be knowing that he was living a miserable, lonely, loveless life."

For just a moment, Kevin closed his eyes and rested his cheek against her warm, soft, familiar touch.

"There's someone in your world who will help you forget the pain that losing love has caused you, and when you do that you'll be able to remember the joy it brought you." She took her hand from his cheek. "Promise me you'll try."

He opened his eyes. "I promise. I'm just not sure how to do it."

"The awesome thing about love is that as long as you're open to it, not only will *it* find *you*, but it will also teach you things you never even thought you needed to know. Trust me. I'm an expert on unexpectedly being taught things by the people I love."

"Thanks for talking to me like this. I needed it," Kevin said.

"So did I. This attraction thing doesn't just go one way, you know. I see why your Aphrodite fell for you. Were our situations and our worlds different, I would show you just how attractive you are to me."

Their gaze met and held, and Kevin had to force himself not to lean forward and kiss her.

Aphrodite grinned. "Good choice. Like you said—I'm not her and being with me wouldn't fix that break in your heart. But come here. I would like to hug you, if that's okay with you."

Instead of answering, he pulled Aphrodite into his arms and held her for a long, long time. Before they let each other go, she whispered, "Always remember that you and I are friends."

"I'll remember," he whispered back—and when he left the Council Room, the break in Kevin's heart began to heal.

(

Neferet

The electricity returned not long after her delightful, loyal tendrils returned with her dinner—two young, semiattractive men who might have been considered handsome before they'd been possessed by her children and walked zombielike through the icy rain to the midtown villa she was borrowing from dead girls. She'd commanded her tendrils to leave the men's bodies just before she began to feed from them, as it was rather incestuous to drain the blood from someone possessed by her children. The young men made an annoying amount of noise and fuss for the few moments they were aware before she ripped out their throats and drained them of blood.

Delicately, Neferet used the corner of a thick bath sheet to wipe the blood from herself as she left the scarlet bathroom suite. "Children, drag these corpses to the backyard and eat them. Do remember to finish your meal completely and then hide the remains, and by that, I mean bones only, in the shrubbery. And we insist you lick up the blood in the bathroom as well. We cannot abide a mess."

Then she stretched her elongated limbs before going to the master closet and choosing a long, red silk slip dress to wear. It wasn't as formfitting as she wished it was; she'd become too thin for it to hug her skin tightly, and instead of brushing the top of her feet it came only to her knees, but when Neferet stood before the mirror, she admired herself. Her limbs were long and bone white. Taut flesh stretched beautifully, *powerfully*, over lean muscle. Her hands slid down the silk, caressing her ribs where they jutted out from her chest like armor. Her breasts were small, but firm, and her nipples pressed sensuously against the slick fabric. Her neck had lengthened—not like a swan—like a magnificent praying mantis. Neferet turned and peered over her shoulder, sweeping the thick fall of silver-streaked auburn hair aside so she could appreciate the strength of her sinewy back. No, she wasn't as she used to be, and her appearance should reflect that.

Neferet was not vampyre nor human. She was a dark goddess and as such, she no longer felt the need to conform to any world's standard of beauty. She felt good—so very good. Neferet did not allow herself to think of the months and months she'd spent in that dank burrow with only her children and the dark as companions. It would not do to think of such unpleasantness. Instead, she went from room to room in the villa, lighting every candle she could find. She eschewed electric lights as too harsh. They were not as flattering to the long, graceful lines of her new body—and she was discovering that her eyes were sensitive to light, which only made sense after what she had so recently been through. All that darkness. All that hunger. All that—

"No! We shall not think of it. We shall act instead to be quite certain no one ever imprisons us again." She clapped her hands. "Children! Come to us!"

From all around her, the faithful tendrils of darkness slithered from the shadows. They were still smaller than they were before they were entombed with her. She knew why. They had fed her while she had been trapped. Briefly, Neferet wondered what would have happened had they remained entombed for uncounted years. Would they all have become dried husks—mummified—unable to die, but also unable to live?

Neferet shuddered and closed that door in her mind.

"Darlings. How are you feeling?"

The tendrils swarmed her, crawling up her legs, wrapping around her waist, dangling from her arms and neck like living strands of serpentine jewels. Once again, they felt warm and pulsed with energy.

"Ah, that pleases us." Neferet stroked them. "Now, will you soon be strong enough to travel?"

Their wriggling became even more excited, and she understood them perfectly.

"Do not become too eager. We are going to a world we know little of—except that there is a lesser version of us there who has control of someone who is our property." Just the thought of Lynette being subservient to anyone else angered Neferet so badly that she had completely forgotten that she had already killed *her* Lynette. What mattered to Neferet was the fact that someone else had claimed something that belonged to her—and *that* would never do.

"No. It will not do," Neferet said. "But it will also not do for us to enter a world ignorant and unprepared. We need information and cannot ask *him* for it. We cannot go to *him* weak and needy." Neferet stroked the tendrils that slithered over her body. "Where shall we get the information we desire?"

When the answer came to Neferet, she laughed aloud at the simplicity of it. "Of course! The usurper called on their power—so shall we. They are probably still near, lurking like the little spies they have always been. We just need something to pique their curiosity so that they will appear to us." Her smile was reptilian. "We know what those meddling sprites would like—something they have not tasted for uncounted years. And we know where to find one."

Neferet hurried from the villa. She paused on the doorstep. It was still the deep of the cold, rainy night, but cold and rain weren't enough for her purposes. She imagined stretching up into the low-hanging clouds to agitate them. It felt good to use her power. Neferet was still enough vampyre that she could reach the elements, but now she called to them with something darker than what a High Priestess would invoke. As in all things, there was a balance between Dark and Light. Neferet remembered her priestess training that, more than one hundred years before, had taught her to join with the elements and manipulate them, though now she wielded the power of immortality granted to her through Darkness and death. So, she awakened rain with the wrath of storm clouds and the violence of thunder and lightning.

The trickle of rain changed to a downpour and fell in thick cords of water from the black sky. Thunder rumbled and lightning sliced the clouds.

"Now, my darlings, come to us. Cover us with the deep of your black, endless shadows. Do not let prying eyes—neither human nor vampyre—see us."

Her tendrils, still recovering from their year of famine, rushed to her. They swarmed her body, blanketing her in shadow and familiar darkness.

Neferet smiled.

"Let us hunt, my darlings."

24

Neferet

It wasn't difficult to find a Sons of Erebus Warrior—not even in the downpour Neferet had instigated. They prowled the waterlogged streets of Midtown Tulsa like lackeys of the Tulsa Police Department. While humans patrolled in the protection of their police cruisers, Warriors remained in the elements—heads bowed against the onslaught of rain and cold.

Neferet watched a small group of Warriors from behind a cluster of tree-sized crepe myrtles that slumbered the winter away. She murmured to her children, "Were we in charge, we would not subject our Warriors to such humiliation. Why do they do the bidding of those lesser than them? Oh, we know. It is because a lesser High Priestess rules. Let us follow them, children, and await our opportunity."

Silently, Neferet glided after the Warriors. Because they were on foot, they were able to trudge up and down alleyways and peer into windows. Neferet thought it was rather amusing. What did they expect to find? That she would be watching television and awaiting them in a living room? Did they really expect she would be easily captured?

The thought almost made her laugh aloud.

Finally, one of the larger groups of Warriors—Neferet counted ten of them—made their way to the intersection of Peoria and Cherry Street, where they cut across the street to head west, toward Maple Park, which gave her a brilliant idea.

"Go ahead, my darlings," she told several of her children. "Enter Grumpy's Garden, the little store there, across the street from that wretched McDonald's. Hide among the outdoor chimeneas. As the Warriors pass, create a distraction. We shall do the rest."

A clump of tendrils fell from her body and became one with the rain and night. Neferet followed more slowly, keeping to the shadows and avoiding the garish light of the fast-food establishment. She and her horde crept around the rear of Grumpy's Garden—the little outdoor novelty store and nursery that perfumed that section of Cherry Street with piñon and incense, cutting through the yards that framed it to find the perfect spot near the privacy fence that was the store's property line. There, Neferet waited.

The Warriors trooped past and as they did one of the chimeneas fell over, breaking against the cement lot with a sound that was more jarring than the thunder rolling intermediately overhead.

The line of Warriors turned—instantly on guard.

"Check it out!" their leader commanded.

Seven of the ten Warriors rushed to the chained gate across the lot from where Neferet was concealed. The other three Sons of Erebus Warriors stood stoically peering through the rain and waiting to be sure no one escaped.

It was laughably easy. Neferet emerged from the shadows and wrapped her arms around their leader from behind. With strength magnified by her dark powers, she pulled him from the sidewalk and back into the darkness with her while her tendrils covered his mouth.

Neferet didn't pause. She carried the Warrior swiftly through the storm to the villa. In the distance, between crashes of thunder, she could hear the Sons of Erebus calling for him.

"Odin!" they shouted impotently. "Odin! Where are you?"

"Odin. One of the old gods. How utterly appropriate." She purred the words into his ear.

The Warrior struggled to break loose. He was strong—a big, muscular vampyre in his prime. But he was no match for what Neferet and her children had become.

When they reached the villa, Neferet detoured to the backyard and the expansive grounds that were so tastefully maintained. There, she placed him on a wrought iron chair that belonged to small bistro table near the frozen koi pond. Her children tethered his wrists and ankles to the chair, as well as covered his mouth. Quickly, she went inside the villa. Neferet knew exactly what she sought and went directly to the sickeningly sweet Sevres urn that she had glimpsed in a niche just outside the garish downstairs sitting room. She tossed the blue and gold lid aside so that it shattered against the wood floor and carried the urn outside with her. Then she stood before the Warrior, smiling.

"Dear Odin, we recognize you. Were we not lovers several years ago?"

His eyes were wide and stared at her—and Neferet was not distressed to see terror reflected in them.

"Oh, we almost forgot. You cannot speak. That's a shame, really. It would be lovely to reminisce. Tell us, do you find that we are much changed? You may nod or shake your head."

Slowly, Odin nodded. Twice.

"So nice of you to notice, because indeed we have changed. We shall tell you a secret." She glided closer to him and ignored the fact that he flinched away from her, pressing his back into the cold iron of the chair. "Your death is very important. It is going to provide information for us. Soon we will rule not just one world, but two, and *you* will have had a hand in that." She was going to kiss him, but as she drew closer the revulsion in his eyes made Neferet angry. Instead, she reached out and cupped his face in her hands while her spidery fingers caressed his skin. As he shivered with disgust, Neferet lifted one sharp fingernail and slashed it down across his throat, severing his jugular vein.

Odin's body jerked spasmodically as Neferet held the urn to his neck to catch the spurting blood.

"Keep him still, children!" she commanded.

The dark tendrils wrapped around him until his weakening body stopped moving as his lifeblood pumped into the urn.

It was over quickly, which pleased Neferet. She was in a hurry and, though she appreciated the concealing storm, she was beginning to tire of being drenched. She needed to feed and take a hot bath—and bring up another bottle of that lovely red she'd found a case of in the wine cellar.

"So, we shall hurry, my darlings. Take the Warrior's body into the hedges. As with the two humans, strip the meat from his bones. Feast, sweet children. Then pile his bones with the others. We will have need of them soon. But for now, begone. Feed. Then wait for our call."

Her children swarmed over the Warrior's body, carrying it into the shadows as they fed. Neferet was pleased that the thunder and the downpour drowned the noise of it. She detested messy eaters. Then Neferet moved to stand beneath the nearby pergola where she was sheltered from the rain. There, she flung back her matted hair and smoothed her soaked silk dress—and hesitated, scenting the air around her.

"She called them!" Neferet smiled, not entirely put out that the vampyre who carried her name and her old visage in another world also so obviously communed frequently with Old Magick. "We shall remember this when we are in that world. We will not underestimate her."

Neferet placed the urn at her feet and dipped her hand within, catching the warm, scarlet liquid in her palm. As she spoke her voice echoed with power into the night. Neferet flung the Warrior's blood in a circle around her.

"Sprites of olde, we summon you.
Come to feast, if our will you agree to do."

The night was suddenly alight with glowing elementals. Neferet observed them silently. Most of them were water sprites. They caught the drops of blood before they hit the ground and then frolicked in the falling rain and splashed in the semifrozen water feature. A few air sprites hovered around the pergola after they, too, snatched the scarlet drops and stuffed them in their wide mouths.

Neferet said nothing. She dipped her hand in the urn again and flicked more blood into the air.

A large sprite materialized from the gnarled branches of the dormant wisteria that covered the pergola. Her skin was the color of bark. Her hair was maidenhair fern, which spread down her otherwise naked body. Her eyes were enormous and black as the shadows that surrounded them. The other elementals moved aside for her as she caught the new drops of blood in her fanged mouth, licked her lips, and then smiled at Neferet.

> *"The Warrior's blood is a treat*
> *and a lovely way for us to meet.*
> *I see you, Neferet, Goddess of all things Dark.*
> *Your entombment changed you—left its mark."*

"Yes, well, it was certainly inconvenient, though it taught us well. To whom do we speak, noble sprite?"

> *"Dark Goddess, you may call me Oak.*
> *Why is it me you did invoke?"*

Neferet dipped her head slightly in a respectful greeting, which Oak mirrored. Then Neferet said,

> *"We have need of information fair,*
> *So, to the sprites we call—earth, water, fire, and air."*

*"Just words—that is all you seek?
My curiosity indeed you do pique."*

"Excellent," Neferet said. Then she continued in the singsong cadence of Old Magick:

*"We wish to rule two worlds, not one.
We need information for that to be done."*

Oak nodded in understanding, a slight smile curved the edges of her mouth before she answered.

*"Ah, I know which world you do mean.
From me, information fair you may glean.
What payment do you offer, Goddess Dark,
For information with which you shall make your mark?"*

Neferet gestured to the urn.

*"How long has it been since you've had warm Warrior's
blood on which to dine?
Give us information we seek, and it shall be yours and
no longer mine."*

*"I accept your payment for information fair.
After I drink my fill, my knowledge with you I shall
share and share …"*

Neferet nodded and stepped back and the sprite descended on the urn, lifting it and draining the blood in several long gulps. It dribbled from her mouth and down her chin and neck to mix with the rain as the lesser sprites darted in, catching the drops and lapping them up eagerly. After Oak was done gorging on the Warrior's blood she wiped her bloody mouth with the back of her hand and bared her teeth in a feral smile at Neferet.

"Ask me what information you seek
now that I am paid, I am willing to speak."

Neferet began questioning the sprite, who was a font of knowledge. To Neferet's delight, Oak even knew specifics about the Other World's House of Night. The dark goddess had her children drag an iron chair into the pergola and fetch her a bottle of wine as well, so that she was comfortable as Oak talked and talked and talked.

(

From the water feature, one very small sprite did not frolic with the others. She swam in the freezing water, pretending to enjoy worrying the sleeping koi, but instead, wee Denise listened and learned …

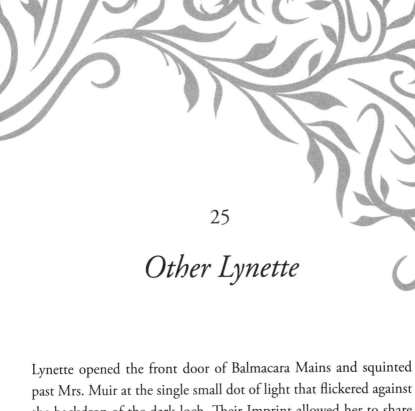

25

Other Lynette

Lynette opened the front door of Balmacara Mains and squinted past Mrs. Muir at the single small dot of light that flickered against the backdrop of the dark loch. Their Imprint allowed her to share Neferet's emotions, and Lynette had been awash in her conflict and anxiety since they'd returned to Scotland the day before. "How long has she been out there?"

Mrs. Muir made a clucking sound deep in her throat then said, "Och, Herself hasnae moved for hours. It's a foul, dreich day. She must be drookit."

"If that means soaking wet, then I agree with you." Lynette sighed. "I'm going to try to get her to come inside."

"What is it I can do ta help ye?"

"Put out a carafe of her favorite red wine and slice up some of your fresh bread with that delicious strawberry jam of yours. Have Noreen build a nice fire, and then make yourselves scarce. Our lady is highly upset. What I have to say to her she won't want anyone overhearing."

"I'll see to it." Mrs. Muir touched her arm gently. "If anyone can pull Herself from this funk, 'tis you."

Lynette patted the old woman's hand. "Thank you. I'll try my best."

Mrs. Muir began to turn away and then stopped. "She doesnea have to be Goddess to hae us care for her. We've seen her magick—aye, we ken her power. To us, she will always be Herself."

"Thank you, Mrs. Muir. My lady appreciates your fidelity."

Mrs. Muir bobbed a curtsy before heading to the kitchen.

Lynette went to Neferet's suite and retrieved a warm plaid wrap and then grabbed a down coat from her own room. She put on the wellies waiting near the door, lit another lantern, and then made her way carefully across the dark, rocky beach. The constant, dreary rain had stopped, but the wind had picked up so that the remaining damp seemed to penetrate into her bones. Lynette liked Scotland—but that didn't mean she liked the weather.

"Hello, dearest." Neferet didn't turn as she spoke, but continued to stare out at the loch and the black outline of the Isle of Skye.

Lynette wrapped the plaid around Neferet's shoulders. "I hate that you're out here in the cold and wet."

"It doesn't bother me, but thank you." Neferet glanced at her. "I know you're worried—just as you know I am conflicted."

"Will you please talk about it with me? I can help—if for nothing else than to just be a sounding board. And you know how good I am at troubleshooting. Give me a chance. I don't think there's anything we can't figure out together."

Neferet turned to face her. "I forget that I am not in this alone. It has been so very long since I had anyone who truly cared for me." She paused and shook her head sadly. "Do you want the truth?"

"Always."

"You are the first person I've had a real relationship with since my mother died when I was a teenager, just before I was Marked. I have not trusted anyone in that long. Forgive me for shutting you out."

"My lady, please come inside. Let's talk about it."

Neferet nodded. "Yes, you're right, dearest Lynette. But first, wait here a moment with me as I leave this offering for our wee

Denise. My thoughts have turned to her often since we've been back. I—I believe I let her down. She gave her life for a quest in which I was unsuccessful."

"Through no fault of your own!" Lynette insisted. "My lady, you did not know the extent of that creature's madness. You couldn't have."

"But that is the problem. I *should* have known. I should have stopped and considered what would have happen to me should I have been entombed alive in darkness. I understand her madness. It would have been mine too. But I allowed the desire for power to blind me—and that cost wee Denise's life as well as those five foolish young women."

"Those five weren't much of a loss."

"Do not do that, dearest. Do not become so hard that killing no longer bothers you. Your ability to empathize with humans is part of what I love about you—part of what I need from you."

Lynette hung her head. "I know. I'm sorry."

Neferet hugged her briefly and then said, "Now, I got this lovely blue ribbon from Mrs. Muir, who said it was Denise's favorite color." From the depths of the pocket in the long, plaid skirt she wore, Neferet brought out a few dried lavender sprigs that were tied together with a slender velvet ribbon the color of sapphires.

"It's fitting that she loved blue and is now a water sprite," said Lynette.

"It certainly is. Would you like to place it on the water for her?"

Lynette shook her head. "Wee Denise would much rather it came from you."

Neferet walked the few feet to the edge of the sleepy loch. "Wee Denise, this is to remind you that your Neferet has not—and will never—forget you." She bent and put the lavender and ribbon on the surface of the dark water, then she and Lynette watched it drift away, but before it went out of sight it shot up in a little geyser of water that morphed into a sprite that flickered many shades of blue and gray and yellow as it cavorted across the surface toward them.

When the little creature reached the shore, it flew up and hovered before Neferet and Lynette.

The sprite was the size of a woman's fist. Its blue body was like a dragonfly's, with a girl's torso, and around its neck was the velvet ribbon as well as a delicate chain that held an occluded sapphire set in diamonds—the gift Neferet had given Denise before she'd sacrificed herself as payment to the sprites for opening the portal to the Other World.

"Wee Denise! I am pleased you heard my call," said Neferet, smiling for the first time since they'd left the horror that they had released at the other Woodward Park.

"My lady! Och, I only have a moment to blether. I must warn ye of she who is thee."

"The Neferet from the Other World?" Lynette asked.

"Aye, the monster. Oak is with her. She plans to come after ye. Beware, my lady! She willnae stop until ye and yur handmaid are dead."

A terrible chill filled Lynette's blood. "How soon? Is she coming here now?"

"I dinnae ken when—but soon! Soon!" The little sprite stopped speaking and her oversized eyes grew wide. *"I must off! I fear what will happen if Oak catches me! Beware, my lady! Beware!"* And wee Denise disappeared with a wet plop.

Neferet's brow furrowed and she stared out at the water grimly before she lifted her chin and her expression cleared. "Come, dearest. We must talk. And we will need those news stories you brought with us from the Other World."

"Yes, my lady."

Quickly and silently, they went back to the manor house. Lynette tried not to be paranoid, but she had a terrible crawly feeling along the back of her neck like she was being watched.

Mrs. Muir had done exactly as had been requested, and after Lynette and Neferet changed into warm bathrobes they took their places before the fireplace—though neither touched the wine. Lynette put the file that held the copy of the stories about the immortal Neferet on the coffee table and then waited for her to speak.

With no preamble, she began. "Dearest, when I faced the Monstress I knew immediately that I had made a mistake by counting on her to show me the path to immortality. That creature would never help me or anyone who was not her servant—and even then, *help* would only be offered if it benefited her."

Lynette nodded, but remained silent, though that was exactly what she had feared after reading the events that had led up to that Neferet's entombment.

"When I looked at her—at what she had become—I glimpsed, for just a moment—my future."

Lynette held her breath as nausea overwhelmed her.

Neferet met her gaze. "I will not allow that to happen to me."

Lynette's breath released in a sigh. "Oh, my lady, I am so glad."

"I can feel the seduction of it, the pull of it. Being in control means that no one will ever have the opportunity to hurt me or anyone I love—and what better control than to become a goddess?" Neferet sighed. "But witnessing what that creature has become shook me to my core and made me realize that I cannot allow myself to be such a whore to power that I sell my soul to achieve it. I have power. I have wealth. And, with you, I now have a family. I believe that might be enough for me to find not immorality—not dominance over all—but, perhaps, contentment in this lifetime, which is something I have not known since I was an un-Marked girl in Chicago dreaming of the kindness of a husband and a family of my own."

Lynette leaned forward eagerly. "I have an idea! While you were out today, I did some research, and I think you might like it."

"Tell me, dearest."

"First, I have to ask you a crass question."

Neferet's dark brows lifted. "I am intrigued. Ask."

"How rich are you?"

The vampyre's full lips tilted up. "Very. I do not believe neither you nor I, even with our rather extravagant tastes, could spend close to all of what I have in several lifetimes. My money is very good at growing. I invest wisely."

"And no one can touch that money?"

"No one except me."

"Good. My idea is for you to buy an island—something in the Mediterranean that harkens back to ancient times."

Neferet sat up straighter. "Capri was our capital before Pompeii exploded."

Lynette nodded enthusiastically. "That's what I found as I researched. My lady, there are many beautiful islands in the Mediterranean—*developed* islands. If you bought one, you could rule there—not as a goddess, but as a queen. We could populate it with artists, musicians, storytellers, dancers, and artisans. It would be a haven for lovely things. And everyone on your isle would be willing, loving subjects of its queen."

Neferet said nothing for a moment and then, very softly, said, "But would anyone come?"

Lynette lifted the little silver bell that called Mrs. Muir, and the stout woman huffed into the sitting room. She curtsied stiffly, but her smile was warm. "Yes, my lady?"

"Mrs. Muir, if Herself bought an island and built on it a villa—no, better—a castle, would you consider coming there with her? You would, of course, run the household and have a staff befitting your station, which would be that of a loyal and trusted subject of a queen—*our* Queen Neferet. The castle and island realm would be filled with artists, musicians, and such talent—and all would be under the patronage of Herself. Would you come, Mrs. Muir? Would you serve Queen Neferet?"

"Och aya, it would be a bonnie dream come true." She curtsied deeply to Neferet.

Neferet stood and took Mrs. Muir's hands, helping her up. "Thank you, dear Mrs. Muir."

"Och, well, ye didnae think I would let someone else cook for ye, did ye?"

"No, of course not, Mrs. Muir."

"Weel, good 'en. Will there be anythin' else this night?"

"Not tonight, rest well until tomorrow," Neferet said.

Mrs. Muir bobbed her head and went from the room on feet that seemed lighter.

"Lynette, dearest, pour us some wine and let us discuss this very promising idea of yours."

As she poured, Lynette said, "I narrowed it down to five islands. I thought we would visit each of them—if you agree, of course. After you make the choice, I will manage everything. None of the islands are perfectly ready for what we need, so it may take a year or so for all to be in order, but I can use the construction time to recruit talent. Oh, my lady! You and I will have such a wonderful future." She smiled at Neferet. "I should start calling you *Your Majesty*."

"Your island dream sounds delightful," said Neferet.

Lynette's smile dimmed. "Why do I sense a *but*?"

"Because wee Denise's information changes everything."

Lynette wanted to shout, *We'll be on an island! We won't be with a House of Night!* Then the image of that monster—that obscene version of her Neferet—flashed across Lynette's memory and she knew it would not matter. That creature would find them—find *her*—anywhere in any world. Lynette stared at Neferet and she realized what her decision had to be.

"You're going to try to kill her."

"If we are to ever find peace, I must," said Neferet.

"But she's immortal. She can't be killed and, apparently, entombing her isn't permanent either."

"Then we need to enlist the aid of an immortal," said Neferet.

"The High Priestess in that world had an immortal. That's how she sealed their Neferet in that grotto."

"Ah, but that is one reason I asked you to bring these." Neferet tapped one long nail on the folder. "If I remember correctly, that immortal was a creature created by the Monstress. Perhaps that is why she was able to break the seal—because it was not powerful enough."

"Where do we find a powerful immortal of our own?" Lynette asked.

"Where is the interview with Zoey Redbird and that human detective? The one that was a tribute to the fallen winged immortal named Kalona, brother to Erebus."

"Oh, I know the one you're talking about." Lynette thumbed through the sheets of copied articles. "Zoey and the detective told his story."

"And they explained why Neferet was able to kill an immortal. I remember that part well. Kalona gave away a piece of his immortality to that world's Stark." Neferet sipped her wine and then said sarcastically. "Knowing *this* Stark, I would say that Kalona made a bad trade. Anyway, I am quite certain that the Stark in our world has never been brought back from the dead by an immortal."

"So, you think our world's Kalona would be fully immortal."

"I do, and if the version of him in that alternative world was willing to fight against their Neferet, then once awakened or called forth—or however it is done—he should be willing to fight again."

"Ah, here's the story." Lynette pulled out several pages covered with a lengthy and what she considered a rather maudlin interview.

"Good, I didn't finish reading it. Does it say how they called their Kalona?"

Lynette read through the questions and answers quickly until she found the section toward the end. "Here it is. Oh. Oh, no."

"What?"

"Their Kalona was called forth from the earth by a prophecy fulfilled. Zoey is only specific about one aspect of it." She looked up and met Neferet's emerald gaze. "He was entombed in the earth at the House of Night in Tulsa, and the prophecy was one guarded by Cherokee Wise Women, one of whom is Zoey Redbird's grandmother, Sylvia Redbird."

"How interesting. It seems no matter the world, the destiny of the winged immortal is tied to the House of Night." Neferet drummed her fingers on the arm of her plush chair. "What we need is our world's version of the prophecy that will awaken Kalona."

"But it's guarded by Sylvia Redbird. I don't think she's going to give you that information."

"No, she definitely won't, but I know who will." Neferet stood abruptly. "Dearest, wrap yourself in something against the cold and bring that tray of lovely fresh bread and jam. Let us go see if wee Denise will come to us again."

Lynette stood, but touched Neferet's arm gently. "My lady, I do not think you should call wee Denise specifically. She mentioned she was afraid of Oak. We don't understand the sprite's hierarchy. We have no idea how miserable Oak could make Denise's new life. She could even harm her."

Neferet patted her hand. "Your words are wise, as usual. I shall simply call to the sprites as if I have no preference in who answers."

They hurried outside. It had stopped raining, but the stars were still obscured by low-hanging clouds and mist rolled off the dark loch. At the edge of the water, Neferet took the tray of bread and jam from Lynette and held it before her, projecting her voice powerfully out across the loch.

> "Sprites of earth, air, water, and fire
> there is a small task of you that I desire.
> I ask you with payment fair
> to answer a question with wisdom and care."

Nothing happened for long enough that Lynette began to get worried, and then from the loch, a dozen or so water sprites lifted. One was larger than the others, about the size of a toddler. She was decidedly mermaid-like, with an opalescent tail and the torso of a buxom woman. Her hair was made of long ropes of seaweed and her abnormally large eyes were bluish gray—the color of the loch in daylight. She moved across the surface of the water in a strange mixture of hovering and swimming until she bobbed just a few feet from Neferet.

> *"I hear your call, she who is no longer High Priestess,*
> *and have permission to answer you in place of my mistress."*

The sprite swam closer to shore, sniffing the air.

> *"'Tis a payment small, this is true*
> *for such there is little I shall do."*

Neferet sounded utterly unconcerned.

> *"I merely have one request, and it is small.*
> *I require the prophecy on how to call*
> *An immortal named Kalona, whom I would find.*
> *I need this help of the simplest kind*
> *In exchange for treats sweet and fair,*
> *I ask for only a little wisdom and care."*

As the sprite hesitated, Neferet added nonchalantly as she began to turn away,

> *"Perhaps I should wait for Oak to return.*
> *I did not realize other sprites have so much yet to learn."*

The water sprite's response was immediate.

> *"I accept your payment well and true,*
> *And can easily accomplish this small task for you!"*

"How lovely. Thank you." Neferet turned and placed the tray on the loch. Instantly, it was pulled under the waves.

"Listen well,
for such a small price
I shall not tell and tell and tell."

Lynette sat on the cold, wet rocks and quickly untucked the iPad she held wrapped within her cloak. As the sprite recited the prophetic poem, Lynette's fingers danced across the keyboard.

"Ancient one sleeping, waiting to arise
When the dead joins with fire and water red
Son who is not—his word is key; the raven will devise
He shall hear the call from his sacrificial bed.

By the blood of she who is neither foe nor friend he is free.
Behold a terrible sacrifice to come—a beautiful sight,
Ruled by love they shall be.
The future will not kneel to her dark might.

Kalona's return is not bittersweet
As he will be welcomed with love and heat."

At the conclusion of the prophecy, the water sprite shot up into the air and then did a beautiful swan dive into the loch with the smaller sprites trailing her.

"Did you get all of that, dearest?"

Lynette finished the last line and then breathed a sigh of relief and nodded. "I've never been so grateful for my typing skills."

"Well done!"

"Psst! My lady!" Wee Denise hovered in front of Neferet.

"Sweet wee Denise! Are you well?" Neferet asked.

"No time to talk—no time to tell.
Just know, 'by the blood of she who is neither foe nor
friend his is free'
Refers only to thee, thee, thee!"

Then she dove into the loch and disappeared with the others.

Shock and dread shot through Lynette. "Oh, god! That means that you—"

"Not here, dearest. Inside." Neferet took her hand and helped Lynette to her feet and they made their way quickly back to Balmacara Mains.

Once inside, Neferet said nothing until they were once more before the fireplace with two full goblets of red wine. Then she lifted hers to Lynette and said, "We have no choice. We must return to our Tulsa House of Night."

"But, my lady! They'll arrest you for the murder of Loren Blake *and* for what they've been calling war crimes against vampyres as well as humans."

Neferet smiled. "No, they will not. Wee Denise has given us a great gift, and now we have something very powerful with which to bargain our freedom. Dearest, they need my help even more desperately than we need theirs. If they do not know it now, they will—very, very soon." She paused, sipping the rich red wine. "Remember, Zoey's brother is a red vampyre in our world, but he has been to her world—the world where the Monstress waged her own, very personal war against everyone. He will be well aware of how dangerous she is. And not only that, I will readily agree to leave the country after she is defeated. I will give my oath not to trouble any House of Night again. Perhaps, dearest, we will establish a new type of House of Night—one that is not shackled to a spineless, archaic High Council. Our island will be a haven for wondrous things. It would not be surprising if the best and brightest vampyres were drawn to it."

"I believe that too, my lady, but I'm frightened that they will be so blinded by the past that they will not be able to see that you have returned only to help them destroy the Monstress, and they will try to harm you."

"Do not be frightened, dearest. You know I am not without power. I will protect us. Always. Now, pour some more wine and contact a discrete private jet service. We need to get to Tulsa as soon as possible. And call a feeder. Suddenly, I am ravenous."

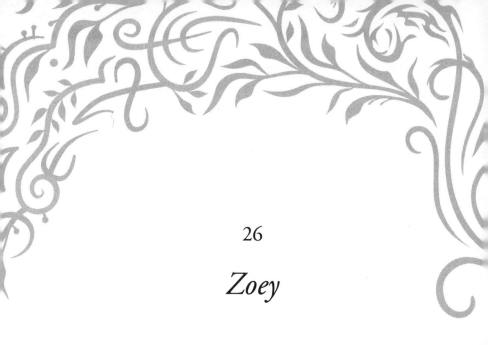

26

Zoey

I had just finished the notes for the spell that I 90 percent believed would open the portal to the Other World, and Stevie Rae and I were still in the media room relaxing and sharing a big bag of heavily buttered popcorn.

"So, when are we gonna circle and go to the Other World? I know it'll be crazy dangerous and all, but I am lookin' forward to seeing Anastasia and Dragon again. Plus, it is nice that Rephaim gets to be a boy all the time over there."

"Well, I know I said we need to get there fast, but I also know that for the spell to work we need a superstrong circle, and while I like Ice Cream Shoes, she's a lot less experienced than Shaunee and Shaylin. So, I want to give it a day and wait for them. I messaged them. Let's hope Shaylin's incel problem is settled and the stupid weather breaks and the airport opens—or I won't have a choice. We'll have to go without them."

"I do think Ice Cream Shoes would do fine if we can't wait. She's inexperienced, but powerful. Plus, she has that whole weird prophetess vibe going on."

"And she fulfills part of that prophetic poem about other Kalona, so she'll have to go with us either way," I said.

"Hey, speaking of Ice Cream Shoes, do ya really think there may be a *thing* startin' between them?" Stevie Rae asked around a giant mouthful of buttery goodness.

"*Them* meaning her and James?"

Stevie Rae nodded, and her short curls bounced around her face. "Yeah, James."

"Well, he did ask her to have a drink with him. You know Kacie better than I do, but she doesn't come off as a girl who'd accept a date with a guy she wasn't at least potentially interested in."

"Oh, Z, I can tell you this for sure—Ice Cream Shoes doesn't believe in wastin' her time. She woulda told him *no* quicker than a skunk will spray you if he's pissed."

"And that's quick?"

"Yup."

"Good. I'm glad. I mean, I don't know if there's any future for them since they're from different worlds and all, but I want James to be happy, which he cannot be if he thinks he's in love with a ghost."

"Or you," Stevie Rae added.

"Definitely."

"And you're not even a little jelly? I mean, Z, it'd be totally normal if you were. He is *Stark*."

"Oh, I felt some twinges of jealousy, but I got them under control fast. I can be selfish, but being all pee-pantsy about another version of my lover and Oathbound Warrior finding happiness without me is next-level selfish jelly. Not to mention super immature. The truth is that I see enough of Stark within James to honestly want him to be happy."

"It's gotta be weird, though."

"Epically weird," I agreed.

"Um, excuse me, High Priestess."

Stevie Rae and I looked up to see a fledgling, hand fisted over her heart, bowing respectfully to me. She was wearing the golden wings of Erebus embroidered on her school sweater, which signified that she's a fourth former. When she looked up, I recognized her immediately because of the name she'd chosen when she'd been Marked.

"Oh, hi, Snow." Snow—as in Jon Snow, not Snow White—was her hero. "What is it?"

"There's a Skype call for you in your office. It's from Queen Sgiach."

"Thank you." I was on my feet in an instant and Stevie Rae and I headed quickly for the door. Since Sgiach's Guardian and longtime lover had been killed the year before, my friend had been in deep mourning, and I knew if she was calling, it was super important.

"Why do I have a bad feeling about this?" Stevie Rae said as we hurried to my office.

"Batshit's free. Since that happened I've had a bad feeling about almost everything," I said.

Stevie Rae curled up in one of the comfy chairs facing me as I sat at my cool desk made of something called zebrawood with glass legs that were really reclaimed windows from an old industrial building that had been gutted for condos in Tulsa's growing Pearl District. The Skype call was still live, and I smiled at the image of my friend sitting on her carved marble throne in her magnificent castle with a laptop balanced on her lap.

"Your Majesty! It's great to see your face." I was relieved to notice that the dark circles under her eyes had lightened.

She smiled. "There is no need for such formality between us, my young friend."

"But I like calling you that. It reminds me how lucky I am to have a queen who is my friend."

"Very well, then I shall appreciate the title and enjoy that you call me by it. I wish this call were just to catch up. Sadly, it is not. I got your message that Neferet was broken from her tomb by her mirror version from the Other World."

I nodded. "We've started calling them *Batshit*—our Neferet—and *Other Neferet* for the other one. It's less confusing."

"And accurate if I'm reading the sprites correctly."

I sat up straighter. "What's going on with them?"

"They have changed. Though perhaps it happened slowly over the past year, and I missed the signs because I have been in mourning," she said.

"Hey, you loved Seoras for *five hundred years*. Taking a year off to be sad about his death isn't unreasonable."

She sighed and ran her hand through her long hair, which I noticed was now all silver-gray with no hint of her copper blaze. "Not unreasonable, perhaps, but irresponsible, though I am not sure what I could have done had I noticed before now."

"Noticed what?"

"They've become uncommunicative. Oak, the sprite who tends to be in a leadership position, is frequently absent, and when I am able to speak with her, she is strangely defensive and not forthcoming with information."

"I know Oak! She's the sprite who comes to Kevin, my vampyre brother from the Other World, most. And she was at the stadium in his world when we had the showdown with Other Neferet. Oak is the sprite who bargained for the other elementals and accepted Aphrodite's humanity, and life, in payment for returning the humanity to their red vampyres."

"So, she has been busy."

"Very," I said.

"Well, I summoned her after I got your message about Nef—I mean Batshit. As you might remember, I do not command the sprites and I rarely invoke Old Magick. My affinity is for this isle— not the fey."

I nodded. "I remember. It's like the Isle of Skye is a dam and you have control over how much water is allowed out of it."

"The analogy isn't bad, but it's more like I have my fingers perpetually plugging leaks—and several get past me—but the flood is prevented. So, I asked Oak if she had any knowledge about her escape, and the sprite instantly became defensive. Her answers, all in rhymes, were garbled—confusing. Around her, the other sprites were clearly agitated. I was only able to ascertain that a vampyre from another world—Other Neferet—instigated the release. It was clear that Oak played a part in it, but beyond giving me the general sense that she'd been the vehicle through which Other Neferet entered your world, I couldn't get more out of her."

"What we found supports what you're saying. We felt the residue of Old Magick at Woodward Park, but it wasn't around the tomb. It seemed to be the leftover power that it took for Other Neferet and a human traveling with her to return to the Other World."

"Your Neferet is going to follow her. That was the only other information I could piece together from Oak."

"Is Oak going to open the portal for her?" I asked.

"I did not get that impression, but I did get a notion of something that was more disturbing. Oak feels sympathetic to the Neferets. I think that's why she resisted giving me information. This is highly unusual, Zoey. Sprites *do not* take sides in the affairs of mortals. Sometimes they will do tasks for them, as you have seen, but always for a price."

I added, "And the price gets higher with each task."

"Not always higher, but their payment usually must amuse or intrigue the sprites—and they have been alive since the worlds were formed and then populated with gods. They aren't easy to amuse, especially after they've been called a few times. The biggest danger with using Old Magick is the side effect that I've already warned you about. Unless the Goddess has gifted you with the ability to wield it—Old Magick *always* changes its user."

A sudden thought came to me. "Is that change always negative? And, don't worry, I'm not asking for myself. I've already felt what you're talking about and I know for sure in my case, the change would be bad, which also means if my brother kept using it, the change would be bad for him too, since we're super alike. I'm just wondering …" I didn't want to say it aloud because it sounded crazy inside my head, but Other Neferet had been using Old Magick, and she'd also fled Batshit and was hanging out with a human who she actually seemed to care about. Could she possibly be—

Sgiach interrupted my musing. "As the nature of Old Magick is neither positive nor negative, my *guess* is that it could, indeed, affect its user in a positive manner. But there is no predicting it."

"Interesting," I said. "So, did Oak give you any idea of when Batshit is going over there? Right now, we're pretty sure she's hiding in Midtown somewhere, eating people. Well, she's for sure eating people. It's where she's hiding that we're not a hundred percent about."

"No. Oak only came to me because I am Queen of Skye, but I could not command her further. I believe that Batshit is gaining strength and as soon as she feels powerful enough, she will follow that other Neferet to her world."

"Did Oak give you any idea about why Batshit is so eager to go to that world? I mean, I'd expect her to attack us here first."

"I could read some of Oak's emotions as I asked her questions about your Neferet, and I got residual feelings of jealousy, greed, and madness. Your nickname for her is accurate. Personally, I believe a creature with her power and her incessant need to be worshipped can never be happy, let alone content, but as with almost all living creatures, she will continually quest for those things. I've watched it happen to human rulers for centuries. They have no true reason for conquering country after country except to stroke their egos and try to assuage the emptiness inside themselves."

"So basically, Batshit is a spoiled child with the power of a goddess."

"Who desires to conquer worlds to fill the void within herself. Yes."

"Ah, hell," I said. "Any clue how to stop her?"

Sgiach steepled her fingers. "I can tell you what won't kill her— Old Magick. Do not count on it. Do not invoke it. Something has altered Oak's allegiance, and you can no longer depend upon her neutrality."

"And the sprites all follow her?"

"If not all, I would say most."

"Okay, so, we need an immortal to fight an immortal."

Sgiach nodded. "And one not tainted by Old Magick."

"My grandma thinks that's Other Kalona," I said.

"Your grandmother is a Wise Woman—in all aspects of the title. I would take her sage advice."

"If I mix her advice and yours together, I'll be on the right track. Oh, and I think I figured out how to open the portal between worlds without using Old Magick."

She leaned forward. "How will you do it, High Priestess?"

I grinned at her use of my title. "With the elements. Any advice about that?"

"Yes. Remember that the only earthly power stronger than elemental power is love. Use those two mighty things together, and I do not believe you can fail."

I snorted. "Well, I'm sure I could figure out a way to mess it up, but that's why I have the Nerd Herd. They'll help keep me straight." Across the desk from me, Stevie Rae nodded so hard her blond curls looked like they were springs.

"I wish you well, my friend. And when you return to this world victorious, I would like you to visit me. I find that I grow weary of being alone. Perhaps it is time I reopened my isle to Warriors once more."

I felt a thrill of excitement. "That would be amazing! Yes, for sure I'll come see you."

"Bring your Guardian. I miss young Stark."

"I will. How about Aphrodite and Darius?" I asked.

Sgiach pursed her lips and then allowed them to lift in a smile. "The prophetess's candor is welcome on my isle—as is her courageous Warrior. Any of your friends will be allowed entrance."

Stevie Rae gasped in pleasure. "I can speak for the Nerd Herd. They'll *all* want to come."

"And that is?" Queen Sgiach asked as her smile widened.

"I'm Stevie Rae," she stood and poked her head around the side of the computer. "Real nice to meet you, Your Majesty."

"You are the one bonded to earth, are you not?"

"I am!"

"Zoey has spoken highly of you. I shall look forward to our future visit. Blessed be, my friend."

"Blessed be, Your Majesty," Stevie Rae and I said together.

The connection ended, and the screen went dark.

"Ohmygood*ness*, Rephaim is gonna be happier than a buzzard on a meat wagon when I tell him about this!"

"Girlfriend, that is a very gross analogy—and especially disturbing when I think about Rephaim in raven form."

"Point taken," she said. "But still—ohmygood*ness*, the Isle of Skye! The Great Taker of Heads! I cannot wait."

"Me either. So, let's hurry up and get the Neferets taken care of so that we can go to Skye. We'll be due a vacay."

"Serious understatement," she said.

And I agreed.

(

The Warriors returned from patrolling with the TPD not long before dawn. It was still raining heavily with thunder calling and lightning answering across the gray sky. Stark and I were just heading to bed when Darius knocked on our door.

He looked completely waterlogged. I was brewing some bedtime tea and offered him a warm mug, which he accepted gratefully and stood sipping in front of our fireplace.

"The news is not good. The rain has washed away everything. There isn't even enough blood trail left for us to scent. Then, around the intersection of Cherry Street and Peoria, Odin, one of our Warriors, was snatched from a whole group that were searching Grumpy's Garden."

"Wait, what?" I said. "Snatched? You mean like kidnapped? By Batshit?"

Darius ran a hand across his face. He looked unusually haggard, like he hadn't slept in weeks. "Yes, and he's dead now. He Imprinted with another Warrior. You know his mate, Stephan, don't you?"

Stark had stood and joined Darius at the fireplace. "I do! Very well. He's a promising bowman. And Odin was a fine Warrior."

I shuffled numbly to the nearest chair. I had to sit down. "He's dead? For sure?"

Darius nodded. "No doubt about it. Stephan felt it." Darius shook his head sadly. "Odin was brave to the end, which Stephan said was quick."

I felt super sick. When I first came to the House of Night, I'd Imprinted with Loren Blake, a predatory professor who had taken advantage of my idiotic naivete and also taken my virginity. In return, we'd Imprinted, so when Neferet cut his head off, I'd felt every bit of it.

"What does Stephan need? How can we help him?" I asked.

"You can figure out a way to do away with Neferet—both of them—for good. She did this. Stephan was bonded so intimately with Odin that he is certain our Neferet did it. His throat was slit, and his blood was drained."

"Did Stephan get any images of where Odin was killed?" Stark asked.

"He said Odin was outside. That's all he got. I—I think it was too painful for him to recall more."

"I know it was. Goddess, I'm so, so sorry! I'll speak with Stephan before we leave for the Other World tomorrow and I'll have the priestesses in the temple light candles and burn sweetgrass in honor of Odin."

"Tomorrow?" Stark and Darius said together.

I nodded grimly. "With what Sgiach told me today, we don't have time to wait. She's certain that Batshit is going to go to the Other World soon. We need to beat her there and raise Other Kalona—and get ready for a fight that will shape the future of both of our worlds."

Darius put the mug of tea down and saluted me formally. "High Priestess, I must remain here to lead the Sons of Erebus. It pains me more than I can put to words that I cannot go with my prophetess to protect her in the Other World; therefore, I formally request that you allow me to ask your brother to swear to be our Aphrodite's Warrior—if only for the time that she is in his world."

What Darius asked didn't shock me. A lesser vampyre would've let jealousy and his own feelings get in the way of his duty, but Darius was not a lesser vampyre.

"You have my permission as well as my gratitude. Kevin will watch over her. I know he will."

"As do I. Now, unless you have more duties for me, I ask to leave and go to Aphrodite."

"Go. Rest," I said.

Stark grasped his forearm. "My friend, I will also watch over Aphrodite—no matter how annoying she becomes."

Darius's lips twitched. "Thank you. I know how difficult that will be for you."

I walked Darius to the door where I hugged him tightly. "Nyx and I thank you for your loyalty and your integrity."

There were tears in his eyes when Darius hugged me back, nodded, and then silently left our chamber.

"We leave tomorrow? Really?" Stark said.

"Really. We don't have time to wait for Shaunee and Shaylin. I'm going to believe Kacie is ready. I promise you, James Stark, we are going to figure out a way to end Neferet. I do not give a damn if she's immortal. Our Kalona was immortal too, and he died."

"I know we can do it," Stark said. "I believe in us—I believe in you." Then he took me into his arms and held me for a very long time.

27

Zoey

At sunset the next night, Lenobia, Darius, and everyone who was traveling to the Other World with us—Stark, Damien, Rephaim, Stevie Rae, Aphrodite, and Kacie—as well as James and Kevin, gathered around me in the foyer of the school. There was an air of nervousness, but also of quiet excitement. Aphrodite and Darius were holding hands and the Warrior looked pale and intense. I addressed Lenobia first.

"Lenobia, I formally name you High Priestess of the Tulsa House of Night in my absence."

Lenobia saluted me. "Thank you, Zoey. I will take good care of the school and our people."

"I have no doubt about that."

"All the professors and the sixth former fledglings are assembling in the drama room. As soon as you have crossed through the portal, and Kevin and James have entered Nyx's Realm, we will begin casting protective spells all around the walls of the school. As you requested yesterday, we have opened our doors to the neighborhood, and humans are beginning to fill the dorms. We will probably need to expand the temporary accommodations to cots in the Field House, as we did the last time the House of Night was a sanctuary."

"I don't think it'll be long before Neferet goes to the Other World, but do whatever you need to do to keep people safe until then." I met Darius's gaze. "Darius, how has Marx decided to handle evacuating humans?"

"He wisely decided not to make a public announcement as Neferet could also hear it and turn her attention to the House of Night. Instead, under his direction, the TPD has been going house to house in Midtown, beginning with those closest to Woodward Park, warning people and giving them the option of seeking the safety of our campus. I will take a group of Warriors and join him shortly."

"Sounds good. Just remember, don't engage with Batshit if you find her. Just have everyone withdraw—quietly and quickly. Isolate her and make it difficult for her to feed. She won't want to use her energy fighting you or hunting, so it'll encourage her to leave this world for the other."

"We will remember, and I will make certain Marx and the TPD fully understand as well."

"Zoey?" Rephaim lifted his hand.

I nodded for him to speak.

"Father answered me. He came to my dreams today while I was in raven form." Rephaim smiled. "The news is good. He reminded me that at his core he is a Warrior, sworn to fight Darkness—in any realm—in any world. So, if the Wise Women are correct, in Kevin's world that version of my father never Fell from Nyx's Realm and was entombed for a selfless reason, he should be willing to join our battle against Batshit, as she is definitely on the side of Darkness."

A little of the tension between my shoulder blades released. "That's really good to know, Rephaim. Thank you."

Grandma hurried into the foyer and my friends parted so that she could make her way to my side. "U-we-tsi-a-ge-ya, before you leave may I gift your tribe with the things I made for them?"

"Of course!" I said.

She began walking among us. "Warriors and priestesses, I have made each of you a bracelet of power. My Wise Woman friends and I smudged them and prayed over them, asking that the Great Earth Mother invest them with protection medicine." As she came to my side and handed me my bracelet, I felt power radiating from the turquoise and amethyst stones. I put it on and it warmed against my wrist. "May these stones protect you—no matter which world you find yourselves in. May they bring you strength and clarity when you need it most," Grandma said.

Grandma stopped in front of Kevin and gave him a bracelet that looked similar to mine, only his turquoise was greener and mine was more robin's-egg blue. "Take care of yourself, u-we-tsi. And remember, love is always present, but you must open yourself to accept it, or it might pass you by."

My brother hugged her tightly. "I'll remember, G-ma."

She went from him to Darius and Aphrodite, handing Darius a bracelet first. "Wise, loyal Warrior, my Zoeybird tells me you will remain here to fulfill your duty by protecting this school. I have made your power bracelet an exact replica of your prophetess's and had a Tsalagi brave imbue it with courage as he strung the aquamarine beads beside the turquoise. Do not worry. I have dreamed that you and your prophetess will be reunited in this world."

Darius wiped tears from his cheeks as he bowed to Grandma and slid the bracelet on his wrist. Then Grandma gave him Aphrodite's matching strand, and he placed it on her wrist, kissing her hand.

Impulsively, Aphrodite hugged Grandma. "Thank you, Grandma Redbird. We needed that."

Grandma patted her cheek. "My Kevin will look after you, though the truth is, you can easily take care of yourself."

Kevin stepped up beside them and went to one knee, looking up at Aphrodite.

"Prophetess of Nyx and beloved friend of my sister. I swear to you and to your Oathbound Warrior, Darius, that I will stand in for him while we are in my world. I will honor your bond while I serve and protect the Goddess Nyx by serving and protecting you. Do you accept my oath?"

Aphrodite didn't hesitate. "I do."

Kevin stood and turned to Darius. "I give you my word I will protect Aphrodite with my life."

"I will hold you to that oath, Kevin Redbird."

They clasped forearms, and then Kevin returned to my side.

"Okay," I said, pulling everyone's attention to me. "Let's go outside to the east wall and the tree that we already know is filled with earth power. Remember, our intention is to maintain the balance of two worlds by defeating Darkness in one world that is threatening to overwhelm Light in two. We walk in Light. We honor the elements. And we also honor the strongest force in the universe, love—always love. Are you ready?"

My group solemnly murmured their agreement.

"Let's go take our places. Aphrodite, did you and Kacie decide whether you would stand for fire or water?"

My prophetess friend nodded. "We did. I'll be fire and she'll be water."

"Good. Stark and Rephaim—you'll need to be inside the circle." I met my brother's gaze. "Will you go before or after us?"

"I'll wait until you're safely gone and then call Aphrodite's spirit to guide James and me over. We'll meet you at the east wall in my world."

"That's the plan," I said a little nervously.

"It's a good plan," he assured me.

Jack rushed up and threw his arms around Damien and kissed him intimately. Then he stepped out of his lover's embrace and smiled bravely. "I didn't want you to go over there—to my old world—worrying about me. I'll be here, waiting with love, always love, for you to return. So, you go kick Darkness's ass for me too!"

"Sweetheart," Damien touched Jack's cheeks gently. "Thank

you. I needed that. And don't forget that this isn't goodbye. It's only à bientôt."

"I won't forget. Ever."

"Come on, child," said Grandma, taking Jack's hand. "Perhaps you would like to help me string turquoise light catchers to hang in the trees surrounding the school as a boost to the protection spells the professors are casting."

Jack's eyes brightened, and he nodded enthusiastically. "I would. I really, really would!"

Grandma led him away after blowing me a kiss. I had never appreciated her more than I did at that moment.

"You okay?" I asked Damien.

He wiped his eyes and nodded. "I am now that I know Jack is good and that Grandma will be with him."

I led my House of Night tribe across the foyer and through the school toward the rear doors. All the way there, fledglings began to appear until they lined the hall like a living tunnel. As we passed them, they saluted us and called well wishes.

"Blessed be!"

"You're our heroes!"

"Merry meet, merry part, and merry meet again!"

"We believe in you!"

The red fledglings were especially vocal as Stevie Rae passed. "You can do it, High Priestess Stevie Rae! Tell earth to kick Batshit's butt!"

With tears in her eyes, Stevie Rae met my gaze. "Looks like the name has stuck."

"It's accurate," I said.

"We're pulling for you, Prophetess!" they cheered as Aphrodite walked by, with Darius at her side. "You can do it, Aphrodite! Nothing can stop you!"

"May the Goddess bless you and keep you safe, Damien!" Echoed around us and I saw my friend's face take on that stubborn look he got when he was presented with a problem he was set on solving.

"Go, Ice Cream Shoes, go!" I was happily surprised to see the entire swim team, in their warm-ups, clapping and cheering for Kacie, whose grin was like a blazing star.

And over and over until my eyes were also filled with tears I heard: "May the Goddess bless you, High Priestess Zoey!"

"You can do it, Zoey!"

"High Priestess Zoey is awesomesauce!"

I hadn't asked them to—truthfully, I hadn't even thought about it, but the fledglings followed us out to the rear grounds and made a huge circle around the tree by the east wall. There they went silent, but even though they said nothing, I felt their positive energy and their belief bolster me and chase away my nerves.

I didn't have to direct my circle. They took their places quickly, holding their candles and looking somber. Kevin and James stopped outside the circle. My brother hugged me.

"See ya soon in my world."

I gave him one last squeeze. "See ya soon. Be safe, 'kay?"

"I'll do my best," he said as we broke apart.

I waved at James, and he nodded and smiled at me. Then he went to the westernmost point of the circle where Kacie stood, holding her blue water candle expectantly. I couldn't hear what they were saying, but her smile said more than words anyway. And then she surprised me by tiptoeing and kissing James softly. Even from where I was standing, I could see the cocky grin that was so similar to Stark's lift the edge of his lips—which meant he liked it—a lot.

Stark was by my side as I walked into the circle. "You good?" he asked, throwing a look at James.

"I'm great," I assured him. "Which you already know because you can feel what I feel, but thanks for asking."

"Always," he said. "Where do you want Rephaim and me?"

Rephaim left Stevie Rae's northern earth position and joined us in the center of the circle.

"I think you should stay here in the spirit position. I'm going to call the elements and cast the circle—and then try to get them to open the portal, there at the tree."

"Tree?" Rephaim asked, throwing a look at the mound of splintered trunk that had sprouted a few saplings this past year, but looked mostly dead right now.

I nodded. "It's a source of power. I know it doesn't look like it, but it's been cleansed and healed—and it already has new growth shooting up from it. I think it's perfect for what we need."

"Whatever you say, Z," said Rephaim.

"We'll be ready. Just let us know what you need," said Stark.

"Be ready to run through the portal. I have zero clue how long it'll stay open." I raised my voice so that my circle could hear. "This casting is going to be unusual. I'm going to focus on the power of each element, so you'll probably notice a difference when your element responds—or let's hope you notice a difference. Then I'll cast a spell that is meant to have the elements literally use their power to tear an opening between our two worlds. I don't know how long that'll hold, and I expect some chaos. But be ready to go through the portal *fast*. Okay?"

They nodded and murmured their assent.

I gazed around at the watching fledglings and realized that all the House of Night cats had joined them. I grinned at my fat orange tabby, Nala, who sat and groomed herself beside Skylar, whose size made Nala look miniature. I pitched my voice even louder so the fledglings could hear.

"Intent is key to a successful spell. I ask every fledgling here to join my circle in intention. We go to the Other World to keep the balance of Light and Darkness in check—and we do so with love, always love."

I felt their concentration and their support as I approached Damien in the east and used his match to light his yellow candle. I called air with words I had never before used.

"Air! I call the strength of tornados to our circle tonight!

Come, mighty wind, we have need of you!" I touched the match to Damien's candle and was amazed that it remained lit as I found myself standing in the middle of a whirling funnel that lifted my hair and battered against my clothing. Damien's smile was fierce.

"We're going to do this," he said over the roar of wind.

And suddenly, I had no doubt that he was right. I walked quickly clockwise to where Aphrodite stood clutching the red fire candle. I lit the match she offered me and said, "Fire! I call a forest blaze to our circle—wild and unstoppable! Come, great flame, we have need of you!"

I didn't have to touch the match to the candle. It was like Aphrodite was holding a flamethrower as fire shot from the wick to rise up above our heads.

"Are you okay?" I asked Aphrodite quickly.

"Never better! Go, Z. Let's get this thing done." Gripping the candle with both hands and standing with her feet planted and her hair lifting around her, she looked like Wonder Woman.

I jogged to Kacie and her blue candle. Her cheeks were bright pink, but she looked focused and determined. I lit the match and invoked her element.

"Water! I call tidal waves and typhoons and the rage of white-water rapids! Come, fierce flood, we have need of you!"

The force of a whirlpool swirled around my legs and battered against my body and the flame on the water candle burned bright blue.

"Hell, yes!" Kacie shouted, fist-pumping.

I shared a quick grin with her before I sprinted to Stevie Rae. She held her green candle up and nodded encouragingly at me.

"Earth! I call the force of a quake—a power that can reduce even the tallest, strongest buildings to dust! Come, indomitable earth! We have need of you!"

As the green candle lit, the ground around us vibrated, shaking with so much power that I had to plant my feet wide so that I didn't fall.

"That's right, earth! Show 'em!" Stevie Rae said.

I turned and, stumbling a little, rushed back to the center of my circle where Stark and Rephaim stood, eyes wide.

Stark handed me my purple spirit candle and said, "Look, Z! Look!"

I followed his gaze to see that the glowing thread that held our circle together looked like a living rainbow as it held each of the four colors of the elements.

"All right! Get ready!" I yelled over the ferocious elements that were building and building around my four friends. Rephaim gave me a match, which I lit and as I touched it to the wick I said, "Spirit! I call the infinite might of joy and love! Come, strength of courage and unbreakable will! We have need of you tonight!"

I'd never felt anything like the electric emotions that poured into and through me. I felt as if I could do anything as I whirled around and faced north where Stevie Rae stood on quaking ground in front of the giant oak that had once been a splintered, blackened mess, but was now a place of rebirth, alive with new growth. I stopped in front of Stevie Rae and motioned for my circle to face north. Then, with Stark and Rephaim beside me, I lifted my arms and held my purple candle over my head and cast the spell as I imagined that the tree was the door to my brother's world.

My voice was magnified by the incredible power of the five elements and it blasted the night.

> "Spirit, earth, water, fire, air—I do call.
> We seek the power of storm winds tonight.
> Fire, I need your fierceness—flames thick and tall.
> Air, mix with fire, strong and well—join our fight!
>
> Water, bring flood and fury unstoppable.
> Earth, you know our need is urgent and true—
> Wash all away with power nautical.
> Quake and shake, then we bid this world adieu!

Elements true, filled with power and might
I focus your immensity here—now.
We quit our world for another tonight,
Intent to banish Darkness we do vow.

Four joined by five—love shall open that door
We leave this world through spirit's mighty roar!"

Then I hurled my candle at the broken base of the tree. It hit the bark and shattered. Purple fire spread like a giant cobweb and it took the shape of a door! Against the closed door, air howled—fire blazed—water geysered—and earth shook the tree so violently that the door flew open and exposed a spinning vortex of stars.

"Let's go!" I shouted and ran forward, past Stevie Rae. Stark was only a step behind me, and after him, my circle followed. As we all entered the doorway, the rainbow of colors that had held our circle together whirled around us, creating a protective shield that was as beautiful as it was powerful. The last thing I heard was my House of Night break out in a joyous victory cheer. Then I was swallowed by cold and disoriented by flashes of light and color and I heard nothing at all, but I ducked my head down and continued to blindly run forward, falling into what felt like oblivion.

It seemed like entirely too long before my feet hit solid ground. I tucked and rolled and then laid on my back, trying to catch my breath. I was dizzy, and my eyes were watering so badly that I couldn't see.

"Zoey? Zoey! Oh, Goddess! It is you! Stevie Rae! Rephaim!" The voice was familiar, but my brain was having a tough time registering more than that. I felt someone smooth the hair back from my face. "Zoey, can you hear me?"

I blinked over and over, and finally managed to make my hand lift to rub at my eyes. The next time I blinked, a face slowly came into focus.

"Anastasia!" I thought I shouted her name, but my voice was a whisper as I struggled to sit.

"Hey, I've got you. You made it. You're here. Just breathe. The disorientation will pass."

I closed my eyes and nodded—took several slow, long breaths in and out, in and out. When I opened my eyes again, the earth wasn't spinning, and I could see. I sat, barely needing Anastasia's help now.

"My circle?" I sounded more normal as I tried to look around Anastasia.

She moved as Stark crawled on his hands and knees to me and pulled me into his arms. "You did it!" he said. "Look! We're all here."

He was right. Everyone was pale and they were still on the ground. I could see Dragon sprinting to us from the direction of the field house, followed by several other vampyres and my grandma from this world. I looked at Anastasia and said, "Kevin and James—I mean, your Stark—should be here soon too."

"It must be bad," said Anastasia.

I nodded, still shaky, but my voice was strong and a lot calmer than I felt. "The worst. Your Neferet is here—and mine is on her way."

Dragon skidded to a halt in time to hear me.

His mate looked up at him. "Gather all the generals. Call every priestess in the area. We need to get ready."

28

Other Kevin

The power of Zoey's spell still reverberated around Kevin in the cheers from the gathered fledglings when Travis, Lenobia's human Consort, whistled so loud and sharp that it quickly silenced the kids.

"High Priestess Lenobia needs you now!" Travis shouted across the school grounds. "Frightened humans are gathering in the Field House. While she, the professors, and the senior fledglings are setting the protective spells around the perimeter, you're needed to make up cots, ready the movie screen in the auditorium, and start popping a lot of bags of popcorn. Let's try to make our neighbors feel at home and do everything we can to lessen their fear."

Kevin was impressed by how quickly the fledglings responded. Setting off in small groups, some headed inside to the auditorium and kitchen, and others walked briskly along the sidewalk that led to the Field House.

Travis saluted Kevin, who returned his salute with a wave.

"I should've made time to see Lenobia and Travis—and the horses," said James. "I miss them in our world."

"Yeah, me too," said Kevin. "Maybe next trip."

James snorted. "Not really interested in doing this again."

"Really? That's not what kissing Ice Cream Shoes says."

James's gaze snapped to Kevin. "I, uh, didn't plan on liking her."

"But you do, right?"

"It's new. I don't really know her that well yet. She's actually pretty great. I just, um—"

Kevin put his hand on James's shoulder. "Dude, it's a yes or no question."

"Oh. Then yes. I do like her. A lot."

"Thought so. Better leave your world-hopping options open then. Come on. Time to return to ours."

"Where are you doing it?"

"Right here's good with me. You?"

James shrugged. "You're in charge of this part. I'm just glad I only have to cut myself once to get there."

"Yeah, I don't blame you. Want me to cut you this time, or you going to do it yourself?" Kevin asked as they walked to the oak and the place where the power was most concentrated at the House of Night.

"I'll do it. No problem."

Kevin stopped in front of the strange-looking tree and cracked his knuckles. "It's weird as hell that there's literally nothing left from Z's circle. Did you see what happened to their candles? Did they carry them into the portal with them?"

"Zoey's exploded all over the tree." James and Kevin studied the perfectly normal-looking bark. "But nothing's there now. And I think each candle blew up as they entered the portal, but I couldn't be sure because there was so much light."

Kevin nodded. "Yeah, I still have spots in my vision. It was pretty incredible."

"She's powerful," James said.

"Yeah—and her circle is amazing. I've never seen anything like that strand of light that tied them together."

"Now that I think about it, seeing that—getting closure with your sister—*and* meeting Kacie was all worth having my arm sliced up."

Kevin grinned. "See, dude! Your attitude is already better."

"Didn't know I had an attitude problem," said James.

"You were the only one who didn't." Kevin cracked his knuckles again. "Shit. I'm not sure how I'm supposed to do this."

"Well," he pulled a small knife from his pocket and flicked it open. "I'm gonna cut myself, and then I think you should take a page from your sister's playbook. Just invoke spirit and have love call Aphrodite. She did say she'd be listening for you."

"You're right! I'm ready when you are."

Stark drew a deep breath and then cut a long, thin line up his forearm. As it bled freely, he allowed it to drip against the exposed roots of the tree. Then he looked at Kevin and nodded.

"Okay. Here goes." Kevin faced the messed-up but oddly cool-looking tree. He cleared his throat, ran a hand through his hair, and invoked: "Spirit, I have need of you. Please come to me."

Immediately Kevin sensed the distinct swirling presence of spirit. It was like being at an incredible concert and hearing that one amazing song—the one that means something so special that it causes the hairs along your arms to lift and your soul to swell with pleasure.

That's what invoking spirit was like for Kevin.

Kevin's voice was strong and joyous. "Spirit! Thank you for answering my call. Now, please go to my love, Aphrodite, who is in Nyx's Realm, and tell her I'm ready to come home. She's waiting for me, so she should be easy to find."

Kevin felt spirit flow from him and go out seeking ... seeking ... seeking. And suddenly, the tree began to glow softly with a green light that reminded him of moss and trees and fields with sprouting alfalfa. It shimmered, then the tip of an enormous horn, black as fertile earth, materialized and touched the tree. Like a sheer curtain being drawn aside, Aphrodite was revealed. She was standing on the other side of the door smiling at him.

"Hi there, Kev."

"Hi there, Aphrodite."

Her gaze went to James. "You going back too?" she asked him.

"Yup."

"Well, okay then. Come on."

Kevin and James shared a look and then Kev said, "Um, how?"

She laughed and the green glow sparkled around her. "Just step through the veil, handsome. It's easy once it's parted. And stop looking up. There is no heaven in the clouds. Realms exist side by side—it's just that not many people can see them."

"Oh. Well, okay then," Kevin said. He glanced at James.

"After you," James said quickly.

Kevin cracked his knuckles and strode forward—and walked right through the door and directly into Nyx's Grove.

"It worked!" he said.

"Of course it worked." Aphrodite laughed. "I told you I'd come when you called."

"Oh, I believed that. I just didn't think it'd be that easy. It was a lot harder to get here the first time."

Stark appeared at Kevin's side and the glowing door disappeared immediately. "Yeah, you're telling me," he said.

"You're bleeding again," Aphrodite told him.

James wiped the cut on his jeans and shrugged. "Well, yeah, but not as bad as last time."

She started walking and Kevin and James fell into step beside her. "I'm kinda surprised that you're going back to your world."

"To be honest, so am I," James said.

"Why didn't you stay?" she asked.

"Because I realized I could never be happy chasing a ghost or loving someone else's girl." Then he hastily added. "And I don't mean that in a douchebag sort of a way."

"I get you," Aphrodite said. "What about you?" she asked Kevin. "How was it to see the other me?"

278

"Interesting," he said. "She's coming to our world. Should be there right now. Darius couldn't go with her, so I swore to be her Warrior and protector over there."

"That was nice of you." She cocked her head to the side and looked at him. "I'm not picking up any big surge of heartache *or* romantic longings from you. The two of you didn't hook up?"

"No! And I'm not comfortable talking about it with you. Sheesh, Aphrodite."

She grinned. "Oh, come on! *I'm dead.* And no longer capable of being jealous. Apparently, I can still be curious though."

"Or nosy," James muttered.

"I heard that, Bow Boy." She returned her attention to Kevin. "I just want to be sure you're okay."

"I'm okay. I'm not going to *hook up* with Aphrodite. I realize that's not what I want."

"What do you want?"

"You," he said.

Her smile faded. "I'm sorry."

"Yeah, me too. But it's getting better. It's helped to see you again."

"I'm really glad about that."

They didn't speak for a little while as they made their way through the verdant grove that was only a tiny portion of Nyx's Realm. This time Kevin noticed birds perching in the boughs of the emerald-leafed trees that were so brilliantly colorful that they looked like crystals glittering under spotlights. Butterflies drifted with the breeze, which was scented with oranges, and fat yellow-and-black bees buzzed lazily.

"Wow, I didn't see all this before." He stared around him. "This place is amazing."

"Oh, Kev, someday you'll see more of it, and it'll take your breath away," said Aphrodite.

"Do ghosts breathe?" asked James.

"We aren't ghosts, Bow Boy. We're spirits. Now hush and let

the grown-ups talk." She turned to Kevin as she led them around a cluster of silver-and-white marble boulders that glistened like moonstone and diamonds. "So, what's up with Neferet?"

"Our Neferet broke her out of the grotto and then she retreated back to our world, but not before letting the *super*-crazy Neferet know that there is another world. So, now the super-crazy one—that everyone is calling Batshit—is headed to our world too."

"Batshit. I like it. It suits her. Oh, that's why Zoey's Aphrodite is coming to your world. I assume she's with Zoey?"

"Yeah, and her circle and some other help."

"Good. You'll do fine."

They'd come to the edge of the grove, and when they stepped out of it, they were on a small patch of ground that led to a cliff—that led to nothing.

Aphrodite walked to the edge of the cliff with Kevin and James following more slowly behind.

"How do you know I'll do fine?" Kevin asked.

"Oh, that's easy. Because you have the most powerful force in the universe on your side—love. And you'll be surrounded by your friends who also are on the side of love and Light. Kev, Darkness may seem unbeatable, but think about it. People who have given themselves over to Darkness to gain power have actually *lost* anything that is actually powerful, like honor and courage and truth. The bad guys may win some battles—may defeat some of us—but they won't win the war. They have no substance. They fight for no one but their own selfish desires. How could that ever be stronger than the power of love?"

"When she puts it that way, it does make sense," said James.

"You're right," said Kevin. He turned to Aphrodite. Today she was wearing a pair of jeans that were baggy and decorated with embroidered flowers that kept blooming over and over again. Her top was a tank that showed her tanned shoulders. Her hair was wild and wavy and free—and her feet were bare. "You're the most beautiful thing I've ever seen."

Her lips turned up and her blue eyes shone. "Thank you. I love your face too."

"Hey, uh, how do we get home from here?" James was peering over the edge into unending blackness.

"You just have to 'Dorothy' and step off the edge," she said.

"Dorothy?" James asked.

Kevin laughed. "Dorothy! Like in *The Wizard of Oz*."

"Exactly."

James frowned. "We click our heels together?"

Aphrodite sighed. "Oh, Bow Boy, your attitude is better, but you still have a lot to learn. And FYI—Ice Cream Shoes can help you if you let her."

James's body jerked in shock. "How do you know about Kacie?"

"Us *ghosts*—we know things," she teased. "So, Kev, do you know how to Dorothy?"

"It's not about the shoes. It's about wanting to go home for real," he said.

"Your brain was half the reason I fell in love with you," she grinned.

"What was the other half?" he asked.

"That gorgeous chest and those muscly arms—of course. Now, you have to go. And you can't come back this way again."

Kevin felt his stomach clench. "Wait, why not?"

Her hand started to lift as if she would touch his cheek, but it dropped to her side instead. Her voice was kind but firm. "Because it's not good for you. You're alive, Kevin. *Live.* Someday, after a life filled with love and adventures, I'll see you again. But not for a long time. Remember that part."

He bowed his head, struggling with his emotions.

"Hey," she said softly. "Also, remember that love will be here, waiting for you, just like I waited for your call today. Do something for me?"

He lifted his head, wiped away his tears, and nodded. "Anything."

"Open yourself to the flame of love. Let it burn away your sadness so that only the memory of happiness is left. And, someday, we'll meet again."

"Will we?"

"Of course. Love always finds a way," she said. "Now go, and take my love and my blessing with you. Merry meet, merry part, and we *will* merry meet again."

Aphrodite backed quickly into the grove and disappeared.

Feeling old, Kevin turned to face the cliff. James was beside him and he bumped him with his arm.

"You okay?"

Kevin nodded. "I think I will be. You know how to do this?"

"Well, if I get the analogy right, we just have to think of home and really want to be there."

"You got it right," Kevin said.

James met his gaze. "Can you do that?"

"Yes. There are people at home waiting for me—counting on me to return." As Kevin spoke he realized that he did want to go home—he did want to live. "Aphrodite was right. I do have a life I need to live." He moved to the very edge. "Let's go home."

Kevin Redbird and James Stark jumped.

Time had no meaning. Kevin couldn't tell if a minute or a month had passed before his feet landed against solid ground. He didn't even fall. It was like he'd just stepped off the side of a curb. Feeling disoriented, Kevin opened his eyes to see his g-ma standing before him at the big tree near the east wall. He felt James land beside him and heard him mutter, "Wow, that was easy."

But his focus was on his g-ma. She opened her arms. Kevin stepped into her embrace and let her love round off the last sharp edges of his grief, leaving just the bittersweet ache of missing Aphrodite, which would remain with him for the rest of his life.

29

Neferet

At dusk, as she awoke from a deep sleep, Neferet called her children to her and began the final preparations for their journey to the Other World.

"Go, quickly. Feed. We do not care who you kill, just be certain they are not our neighbors. We will not have what we plan inconveniently interrupted by the banal TPD. Hurry, now, my darlings. There is no time to waste. We have things to do and worlds to cross."

While the tendrils of Darkness hunted, Neferet bathed and dressed carefully. She chose a lovely gown from one of the closets in the expansive villa. It was simple a Grecian-style dress that left one shoulder bare and was made of a cream-colored fabric that draped alluringly—almost hiding the fact that she was emaciated. She left her auburn hair loose so that it fell almost to her narrow waist. In the bathroom suite attached to her bedroom, Neferet found large diamond stud earrings that she placed in her lobes, but she could not abide the other gaudy jewelry. She did spend quite a bit of time tending to her makeup, lining her eyes heavily and choosing a deep red with which to stain her lips.

In the kitchen, she grimaced as she drained the last three liters of blood she found in the refrigerator.

"We do loathe cold blood." She shuddered. Neferet dabbed her mouth and then headed out to the rear grounds of the villa.

The evening was frigid, but it had stopped raining. Neferet considered prodding the low-hanging clouds so that she left Tulsa in a misery of another ice storm, but then decided not to waste her energy.

"Also, we do not know how long we shall be in that Other World. It may only take a few days to dispatch our impostor, reclaim our Lynette, and establish dominion over that Tulsa House of Night—then we shall return here to mete justice out upon Zoey Redbird and her friends before we take up the rule of two worlds." Neferet spoke to herself as she gathered what was left of the three humans she'd murdered. She'd directed her children to pick the bones clean, and they had done an excellent job of stripping them of tendon and meat—so much so that they reminded Neferet of driftwood. She placed three piles of bones in a triangle in the area under the pergola beside the partially frozen koi pond and fountain.

Then she searched the villa until she found a bottle of expensive brandy, a fat red candle that smelled of cinnamon, and three white pillar candles, which she placed before each mound of elegant bones. She sat on a wrought iron chair, sipping brandy from a crystal snifter as she stared at her reflection in the frozen water and thought how attractive she looked with her cheekbones and collarbones so very prominent, when her tendrils of Darkness returned.

"Ah, darlings! We are so pleased that you are recovering from our unfortunate fast." She drank the last of the brandy and then threw the snifter against the ice so that it shattered and rained diamond shards across the mirrored surface. Then she stroked the leathery serpents while they wound around her legs and slithered up her body. "You are gaining your size back! We are so pleased by that. Now, children, rest yourselves, but remain vigilant. This is the last step before we leave this Tulsa for the other and embark upon our quest to reign over two worlds."

The tendrils slithered away to rest watchfully, twined in living nests in the thickest of the shadows surrounding their mistress. Then Neferet shook back her hair, smoothed her dress, and began lighting the three white candles she'd placed before the piles of ivory bones.

When the candles were lit, she took the bottle of brandy and poured it over all that remained of two humans and a Son of Erebus Warrior and then, holding the red candle, she stood in the middle of the triangle of bones and faced south—the direction of the element fire.

Neferet lifted the candle and struck a long, wooden match, invoking. "Come, fire! We are the Goddess of Darkness, Neferet. With bone and power, we invoke you!" She touched the match to the flame, which lit immediately, burning high and hot. She walked to the first pile of brandy-soaked bones and began her summoning.

> *"I revere the old ways—deep magick that listens,*
> *watches from shadows of night.*
> *Fire, aid me as I burn these offerings, ancient sacrifice—*
> *to honor and delight."*

Neferet touched the lit wick of the red candle to the first pile of bones, and with a *whoosh* they were engulfed in a deep, blood-colored flame. She moved counterclockwise to the second mound of offerings.

> *"As in the days of Daeva, Rusalka, and Abyzou—*
> *I embrace chaos and encourage spite.*
> *I am Goddess! No longer shackled by Nyx and her*
> *command to walk only in the Light."*

She lit the second mound of human offerings, and the oily red flame leaped high, licking the top of the pergola. Neferet stood before the final pile of bones.

"Free from trite confines—the mores of goodness and
what modern mortals call right.
I summon thee, mighty beast who breathes death
and is clothed in magnificent white!"

Neferet threw the candle against the last of the bones—those that had belonged to the Son of Erebus Warrior. Red wax exploded against ivory as the flame consumed all that was left of Odin. Neferet strode to the center of the fiery pyramid. Surrounded by fire and the scent of boiling marrow, she waited.

She did not have to wait long.

From the deepest of the shadows, her children began to writhe with excitement, they glided to her, weaving through the flames to pool around her feet, and then from the dark that rested beneath the shadows—that was always there, waiting and watching—twin horns of slick white appeared, an impossible width apart, followed by the massive head and shoulders of the incarnation of evil—the White Bull.

He filled the grounds of the villa. His enormous cloven hooves cut into the winter grass and splintered the shrubbery, breaking apart the carefully laid stone paths and knocking over statuary.

Ah, my heartless one. It pleases me that you have escaped your tomb.

"It was but a temporary inconvenience," she said, breathing deeply of the foulness that was his breath. "Let us not speak of it again."

As you wish. He moved closer, and the ground shook each time his hooves cleaved the earth. The White Bull came to the first pile of flaming bones and inhaled deeply. *This pleases me. It has been years uncounted since the last human bones were burnt in offering to me.*

"Scent them again, my lord." Neferet pitched her voice to a seductive purr.

The hulking bull inhaled again, and his bottomless eyes widened. *Vampyre! Specifically, a Son of Erebus Warrior. You honor me, my heartless one.*

"That was our intent, my lord." She made a sweeping gesture, which took in the sizzling bones.

The bull dipped his head and in three bites devoured the burning piles, cracking and chewing the bones as liquid marrow leaked from his mouth and sprayed the ground. When he had consumed the last of the ivory offerings, he returned his attention to Neferet.

And now, what is it you wish of me? I admit, I am amenable as I had forgotten how delectable burnt offerings can be.

"We have only one simple request of you, my lord, and know that these offerings are not payment for our request. They are true offerings, meant to delight and flatter you, mighty bull."

His laughter brought to mind midnight mausoleums and the specters that haunt them. *You intrigue me. What is it you desire?*

"Open the veil between worlds for us, my lord. Our desire is to travel to the other Tulsa, where a lesser, weaker version of us set vampyres against humans—and then did not have the strength to finish the fight."

And what would you do there?

"Kill the impostor, of course, and finish what she started. Then we would return here to supplant Zoey Redbird and the followers of Nyx forever."

He moved closer to her and his tongue licked her bare shoulder, leaving a trail of blood and saliva in its wake. Neferet shivered with pleasure.

The bull's deep voice made the bare trees shake and ice fall from their nude branches. *And how will you pay me for such a thing? Will you finally agree to be my Consort and travel the worlds with me, stoking chaos?*

Neferet glided closer to him to caress one of his huge, opalescent horns. It was so cold that it burned her hands, but she did not mind. She welcomed the pain as a reminder of what it is like to be subjugated to a male—*any* male.

"No, my lord. Not yet. We have far too much to accomplish first."

Then what payment do you propose?

"Why, your favorite, of course. We shall amuse and surprise you."

He turned his head so that he could look into her eyes. *How so?*

"Have you ever, in all of your eons of existence, observed what happens when a dark goddess rules two worlds?"

I have not.

"Imagine it for a moment, my lord. Think of the wars we shall start—and finish. Think of the evil we will loose—evil that Light has dominated for ages uncounted. It will be like nothing you've witnessed. And it will all be in your name. We will fly pennants with your image. We will burn offerings to you in hecatomb, as in the ancient days, only ours will not be mere cattle. You will feast on human marrow and the bones of Sons of Erebus Warriors until you have had your fill. My lord, it will be glorious."

Once again you surprise me, my heartless one. I am also intrigued. Mount me. I shall, indeed, agree to your payment and take you through the veil to the Other World as you wish.

Neferet pulsed with victory. The White Bull knelt and offered her his knee so that she could mount him. She leaned forward, pressing her body against his and murmured, "Take us to the Tulsa depot in that world. The sprites tell me it is there we shall find the beginnings of our army."

His laughter shook the tiled roof of the villa. *Sly, heartless one. It was wise of you to summon the sprites. They have long been isolated and ignored.*

"When we reign, they shall be set free. Come, children! It is time to depart this world—but only temporarily." She motioned, and the tendrils of Darkness flowed up the flanks of the bull to wrap themselves around her and hang from his massive body.

Then the bull leaped up and into the moonless night sky, and Neferet was engulfed in darkness so thick that she could not breathe, but she did not panic. She held tighter to the frigid coat of the bull, wrapping her spidery arms around his massive neck as she reminded herself, *We are Goddess … We are Goddess … We are Goddess …* Until finally, the darkness gave way to the cold light of streetlamps, and the bull stopped beside the railroad tracks on the lower level of Tulsa's depot.

Neferet slid off his back and gazed around her, wrinkling her nose in disgust.

"It is as the sprite said. This depot is in disrepair."

I am quite sure you will set it to right quickly. As he spoke he nuzzled her, leaving a slug trail of wet on her bare shoulder as he licked off the blood his caress had earlier caused.

She laughed and stepped smoothly away from him. "Oh, my lord. You mistake us. We care not how our army is housed. We only care that they are loyal and effective."

I look forward to observing your future but know that what you plan will shift the balance of Light and Darkness, so unless the Black Bull of Light deigns to leave his lofty perch and become involved, I cannot aid you.

His words relieved her. She did not want the meddling bull appearing and acting as her savior. Right now, she only owed him amusement, and that was the last payment she ever intended to owe him. A goddess should be beholden to no one.

She curtsied deeply to him. "We understand, my lord. And we thank you for carrying us across the veil."

And how do you intend to return when your quest for dominance here is complete?

She shrugged. "That will depend on whether we amuse you or not, won't it?"

He chuckled. *Indeed. Before I depart I have a gift for you.* The enormous bull lowered his head and struck one of his horns against the iron rail that used to be part of a thriving railroad track but was now in the same disrepair as the depot building. The rail shattered with a deafening clang. He blew on it, turning it blue and then white with cold, and then it splintered, leaving a long iron spear double-tipped with curved, pointed blades that were the slick, death-like white of the bull's horns. *For you, my heartless one. A weapon with two blades to symbolize the two worlds you intend to rule.*

Neferet bent and lifted the weapon. It was icy to touch, but surprisingly light and perfectly balanced. Then she curtsied low again to the bull. "My lord! You honor us with such a gift. Thank you."

Do not thank me, my heartless one. Amuse me …

When she rose from her curtsy, the bull was gone. Her smile was fierce and feral. She twirled the spear, admiring how the street-light glinted off the deadly tips. "Oh, children, we are very pleased with this. Imagine how delightful it will be to skewer the impostor."

Her children wriggled around her, reflecting her pleasure.

"But first, let us begin to gather our army. Once Tulsa is ours, we will expand from here and we shall order our soldiers to scour the world for that lesser one than us and our Lynette. One thing at a time, children. One thing and then the next."

As she spoke to her children, Neferet moved to a rusted steel grate that was the exact duplicate of the one that had been used to guard the basement of the depot in her world before it had been renovated by Zoey Redbird and the traitors who followed her. She struck her new weapon against it and was delighted when the rusty iron shattered. The tendrils of Darkness descended into the basement before her, sweeping aside what remained of the grate. Neferet followed, frowning with distaste at the rubble and filth that littered the basement. She was quite certain she smelled feces and vomit.

"This will not do. Not at all," she muttered, and her children mirrored her annoyance by slithering restlessly around her feet. "No matter, children," Neferet said. "It is only temporary. Soon we shall rest comfortably in our suite at the House of Night. We do so hope the impostor has adequate taste." She shook herself. "Be ready, my dears. And show yourselves. The vampyres here understand one thing—power."

Neferet took position in the middle of the basement. She lifted the double-pointed spear and brought one end of it down, hard, on the broken cement floor. It collided with a thunderous clang that would've deafened a lesser being.

She raised the lance again—and again struck the floor with it. She repeated the action a third time and as she did she called, "Vampyres, come to us!" Then Neferet waited.

It wasn't long before they poured up from the hole in the far end of the basement that led to the extensive tunnel system below. They had weapons drawn and looked ready for a fight. The soldiers were led by a tall, thin vampyre who was completely familiar to Neferet.

"Ah, Dallas, we are pleased that our information was correct, and you and your soldiers are here."

His eyes went huge as he staggered to a halt several yards from her. Behind him was a group of mean-looking soldiers—all with blue Marks. They milled together by the tunnel entrance, staring at her.

"Neferet?"

"Yes and no."

"What are you?"

"I am of another world. I am your goddess. And we have much to do."

"I—I don't understand," he paused and then added, "Goddess."

"Oh, we think you do, *General* Dallas." She watched his expression change at the title. "How would you and your soldiers like to fight for us—a Goddess of Darkness—who will rule two worlds and subjugate all who stand against us? We know you have had a small taste of power—and then that taste was stolen from you and you have been denied more—relegated to this pathetic cleanup detail to ready these tunnels for vampyres too weak to live. We are offering you more—an entire feast of power and the freedom to partake of it as much as you desire."

Dallas's smile was a baring of teeth. He approached her and

dropped to his knees. "Goddess, I would like that very much."

"Excellent. Now, let us talk weapons, and we do not mean archaic swords and knives. We mean modern weapons of war our less powerful but progressive namesake stashed in the basement of the House of Night."

Dallas's face lit. "Finally! A goddess willing to do what it takes to win!" He bowed deeply to her and then continued. "They're still in the basement. Neferet didn't get a chance to use them before she was run out of town."

She skittered closer and was impressed when her new general didn't flinch back. Her long fingers reached out and stroked his cheek. His bright, mean eyes met hers and the immortal easily read his soul. *This one desires accolades and power more than sex or even blood. His need for violence is his addiction.* "Tell me, General Dallas, could you and your soldiers reach the basement undetected to coordinate an attack with us?"

He shivered with pleasure. "Yes, Goddess. But what will we be attacking?"

"The House of Night, of course. And from there, first one world and then the next."

"I will do as you command, my powerful Goddess of Darkness." Dallas bowed deeply to her and all of the vampyres behind him dropped to their knees as well. Neferet was pleased to note a female fledgling or two with the soldiers. *Excellent. It is past time I raised my own brand of Dark Priestesses ...*

"Now, listen closely, we have no time to waste. The faster we take the House of Night—the sooner the world will be ours. Here is what we command you do ..."

30

Other Kevin

Anastasia lifted her hand, and the Council Room went silent. "So, our consensus is we are going to have to find this world's Neferet so that we can fulfill the prophetic poem and raise Kalona?"

Zoey nodded. "Sadly, I really do think so. I mean, we've been going around and around about it for a couple hours now, and no one has come up with any viable alternatives to this Neferet. No one else fits the line."

Grandma Redbird added, "I have to agree as well. '*By the blood of she who is neither foe nor friend he is free*,' is quite specific. From what Zoey and our friends from the Other World have described, it seems that our Neferet is in as much danger as we are—and because of that she might ally herself with our cause. If only temporarily."

"It makes sense," said James. He'd surprised everyone when he'd announced at the beginning of the Council Meeting several hours before that they should call him by his first name—and not just while Stark was visiting from the Other World. Apparently, James had had quite an epiphany over the past couple days—Kevin was impressed with the change already noticeable in him. "Kacie and Aphrodite both felt the residue of her fear, and as those of us from this world know all too well—Neferet is not accustomed to being afraid."

Sitting beside James, Kacie spoke up. "Yeah, and remember, it wasn't normal fear. It was terror—a deep, visceral reaction to something—our guess is Batshit."

"Good point, Ice Cream Shoes," said Aphrodite. "All of us who came from the Other World saw what Neferet had turned into before we entombed her. Back then she was frightening. Now she has to be doubly awful."

"The first thing she did was eat an apartment buildin' full of people," said Stevie Rae.

"She was a monster when we entombed her." Damien looked grim. "And teetering on the edge of madness. It's logical that her captivity pushed her over into insanity. We cannot emphasize too much that she is utterly unpredictable and entirely dangerous. From what we know about her, none of us would find it shocking that she is set on destroying the other version of herself."

"Yeah," said Zoey. "There's no way our Neferet would help yours. Use her, *maybe*, but it's more likely that she'd see her as a threat and kill her."

Anastasia breathed out a long sigh. "Well, one thing we know about our Neferet is that she is far from stupid, and her self-preservation instincts are highly developed. Perhaps she will see the wisdom in allying with us temporarily."

Dragon snorted. "Whether she does or not, once she is found, she will be brought back here. Nowhere in that prophecy does it say her blood has to be given willingly."

"It doesn't even say she has to be alive," said James darkly.

Grandma Redbird stood. "I know I am only a guest here, and not a vampyre who has lived hundreds of years, but I am compelled to remind all of us that we follow Light, and the Great Earth Mother in her many forms—Nyx, specifically. Aphrodite's unique Marks and her gift of giving second chances remind us that we all have the ability to grow and change."

"Thank you, Sylvia," said Anastasia. "Your reminder is appreciated. James and Kevin, as it is almost dawn and you have already traveled from one world to another today, I would like you to rest and be prepared to take the jet to Scotland tomorrow at dusk. We need you to follow Neferet's trail and find her—quickly. Is there anyone you'd like to join you on your quest?"

Kacie raised her hand and Anastasia nodded for her to speak.

"I'd like to go with them. I don't know this world, but I know *things*, and I think those things could help us track Neferet. Plus, fire and water are good allies." She turned from Anastasia to Zoey. "That is, if my High Priestess doesn't mind."

Zoey smiled at her. "I think it's a great idea. Kevin and James, remember that Kacie has shown an aptitude as a prophetess, so if she gets a *feeling—*"

Kevin grinned at his sister. "We pay attention. For sure."

"Excellent. So, this meeting is adjourned. Stevie Rae, Kacie, Stark—as red vampyres I am aware that you would be more comfortable sleeping below ground, but though I dispatched a large group of our soldiers to begin cleaning and repairing it, our depot is in abysmal condition. Would you prefer rooms in the dormitories or the professors' quarters? Both have blackout windows and, sadly, after our recent events, there is plenty of room in either. It is entirely up to you."

Kevin gestured, "Um, Anastasia?"

"Yes, Kevin."

"I think Aphrodite should stay in my, well, *Aphrodite's* suite." He turned to look at the prophetess from another world who was so much like his lost love. "It's really your room—just over here."

"That's sweet, Kev," Aphrodite said. "But isn't that your room now?"

He shrugged. "Kinda, but I haven't made it my own. And I

know my Aphrodite would like it if you were there. Plus, all her clothes are still in the closet."

Aphrodite sat up straighter. "And her shoes too?"

"Every one of them."

"Sold!" she said. Then hastily added with a nod to Anastasia, "If the High Priestess doesn't mind."

"I think that sounds quite nice," said Anastasia.

"I'll bunk in the dorm," said Kevin. "I like it there anyway."

"Rephaim and I like the dorm too," said Stevie Rae, taking her mate's hand as he nodded.

"The dorm's all I know," said Kacie.

"The dorm is always nostalgic to me," said Damien. "Makes me feel like a fledgling again."

"Stark and I will take the professors' quarters near Aphrodite, if that's okay," said Z.

"Absolutely," said Anastasia. "Now, you should get something to eat and then rest well. Zoey, I would ask that you and your people, except for Kacie, of course, who will be on her way to Scotland, aid me tomorrow in casting protective spells around the walls of the school. Thanks to our Neferet, we have a tragic shortage of High Priestesses."

"We'd be more than happy to help," said Zoey.

"Okay, then," Anastasia said as she stood. "Please remember to make yourselves at home. Consider this campus yours. I believe it will seem rather dour and empty after what Kevin has described of your House of Night, but we are in the process of changing that."

"Thank you for your hospitality," said Zoey.

Everyone filed out and headed to the professors' dining hall, and Kevin hurried to catch up with Aphrodite.

"Hey, uh, while you eat, I'm gonna grab some of my stuff from the room and move it to the dorm," he said.

She stopped and faced him. "This is really nice of you."

"Well, I know that one of the things you and my girl have in common is a definite disdain for 'roughing it,'" he air-quoted.

"To say the least," muttered James as he walked by with Kacie, who covered her laugh with a cough.

Aphrodite narrowed her eyes and glared after them. "Different world—same pain-in-the-ass Bow Boy."

"Huh?" said Stark as he passed by with Z.

"Oh, nothing. Z, save me a spot. I'll be there in a sec," Aphrodite said.

"No, go ahead. You don't have to come with me to the room." Kevin put his hands in his jeans pockets. "And you'll be able to find it easily. It's the same one you have in your world."

"That's a massive coincidence," she said.

"Yeah, well, wait 'til you see it. I think you'll like the décor."

Aphrodite laughed, "*And* the shoes, no doubt."

"No doubt," Kevin agreed. He was glad that it had stopped being painful to talk to Aphrodite and, weirdly enough, he felt like he had his Aphrodite to thank for that.

"Okay, well, how about I save you a spot in the dining room? Want me to order anything for you?"

"Nah, I'm not sure what I want, but I'll see you soon."

Impulsively, Aphrodite stepped forward and hugged him. "You're a really good guy, Kevin Redbird. I know why your girl fell for you."

He felt his cheeks get hot, but no tears threatened, and it was easy for him to hug her and then let her go without feeling like his heart was shattering into little pieces. Then she swept her hair back and twitched after Zoey, calling, "Hey! Slow down. You know how I feel about jogging!"

Kevin took his time making his way to the room he'd shared with Aphrodite. As he collected his things, he realized that he wasn't going to move back in after Zoey and her group returned to their world. The room was more of a ghost than Aphrodite, and it haunted him with a sadness that wasn't good for him—not if he wanted to move forward with his life, and at the edge of Nyx's Realm, Kevin had decided that he *did* want to move forward.

Everything important to him fit into a duffel bag, and he slung it over his shoulder as he headed out of the arched doorway to follow the sidewalk along the rear of the school that led to the dorms. As he passed the tall marble statue of Nyx, he automatically glanced at the goddess. Someone was standing before the statue. At the moment Kevin looked, she struck a match to light the tea light she'd placed at the goddess's feet. Flame exploded from the match with a *whooshing* sound that Kevin heard from the sidewalk.

The fledgling made a little squeaking noise and dropped the match, but as she tried to stomp on it, the thing refused to extinguish. Kevin left the sidewalk and jogged to her as he took a bottle of water from his duffel bag and unscrewed the lid.

"Oh, shit! Shit! Shit! Shit!" she was saying when he hurried up to her.

"It's okay, I got it." He poured the water on the flaming match and it finally extinguished.

"That was crazy as hell. I—I don't know what happened," she said. Then she really looked at him and her confused expression cleared. "Oh, hey! It's you."

He blinked in surprise. "Hi, Shaunee. Good to see you again." Kevin made a show of looking around the statue. "No twin in sight?" he teased.

Instead of the grin he'd been hoping for, Shaunee's shoulders slumped. "No. No twin."

"Hey, I'm sorry," he said quickly. "I was just kidding around. I didn't mean anything."

She sighed. "It's okay."

"Are *you* okay?"

He watched her begin to say yeah and brush him off, and then her expression changed, and he saw tears fill her beautiful brown eyes. She shook her head. "No. Not really."

He gestured at the bench. "Wanta talk about it?" When she hesitated he added, "My grandma, Sylvia Redbird, you've seen her around, right?"

She nodded. "Hard to miss a human hanging out at a House of Night, so yeah. I've seen her."

"She says I'm a good listener. And I don't really have anywhere to be—at least not until dawn in sixty-three minutes."

"It's weird that you red vamps always know when sunrise and sunset are, but I do like a boy who quotes his grandma. So, yeah. I think I do wanta talk."

They went to the bench and sat, and Kevin offered her a drink from the half-empty water bottle, which she took with a smile of thanks. He hadn't made up that G-ma thought he was a good listener, and Kev knew that a big part of listening was really *hearing* what was being said, which took patience. Kevin clasped his hands in his lap and waited patiently for Shaunee to speak.

It didn't take long. She sipped the water again and said, "So, you do remember Erin, my twin, right?"

He thought about the last time he'd seen Erin and the show she'd put on with Dallas at the dorm with a vodka luge and wet T-shirt contest. "Uh, yeah. She's pretty hard to forget."

Shaunee glanced at him sharply. "Don't look like that. Most of that slutty Barbie thing she does is an act. She's insecure and thinks the only way people will like her is if she's a party girl. Under all of that, she's really funny and smart."

"Okay, sorry. You're right. I don't know her, and it's not my business to judge her. So, what's up?"

"I'm not sure. You remember last time we talked I said I was trying to get her to understand that we can still be besties, even if we're not together all the time and we don't agree about everything?"

He nodded.

"The last couple days she's been disappearing. A lot. It shouldn't be weird because she's really into Dallas."

Kevin snorted.

"What?"

"Okay, him I do know. He's a douchebag. Seriously."

She sighed and nodded. "I know. I didn't say anything when they first hooked up because she never stays with one guy long. 'Love 'em and leave 'em—unless they're millionaires' is her motto. Or it was. But not since Dallas. I wouldn't worry about it, well, except that I agree with you that he's a total bag of balls, but she's stopped talking to me. And that is Weird with a capital *W*."

"Aren't you two roommates?"

"Yep. But she's been sleeping with Dallas. So, tonight when she didn't answer my texts I went to his room and the guy who lives next door said that he's staying at the depot, which means that's where Erin is too." She shifted on the bench so she faced him. "That depot is *nasty*. I mean, seriously and totally disgusting." Then her eyes widened, and she pressed a hand over her mouth before saying, "Shit! Of course, you know that because you used to live there. Sorry. I didn't mean to—"

"It's okay," he assured her quickly. "And you're right. The tunnels *are* totally disgusting. Are you sure she's staying there? I can't imagine any girl doing that."

"That's exactly what I've been thinking. And, no, I don't know for sure that she's there, but she's definitely not here—and neither is Dallas. I'm worried about her, but I can't tell whether that's stupid or not."

"I don't think it's ever stupid to be worried about a friend."

She met his gaze. "But?"

He shrugged. "But maybe she has fallen for Dallas. People do weird things for love."

Shaunee snorted. "Or lust."

"True. Could she have Imprinted with him? That'd explain why she wants to be with him, even in those nasty tunnels."

Shaunee's look brightened. "That would make sense. And she wouldn't want to tell me 'cause she knows I'd be pissed. Dallas is an ass. She can do *way* better."

"And she knows how you feel about him?"

"Uh, yeah. Of course. We're *twins*. We usually tell each other everything."

"So, maybe it's as simple as the fact that she knows you don't like her new boyfriend, and she's avoiding you because of it," he said.

Shaunee's smile lit up the night. "And if you're right, then I'll use this to show her that we *can* be different and still be friends. Kevin, you're not just a good listener, you're a good figure-it-outer too."

"Thanks. Glad I could help you talk it through. Hey, uh, have you eaten yet? I was going to go to the dorm and put my stuff there, but I really should eat something before sunrise."

Shaunee's bright, intelligent gaze trapped him. "I thought you were living in Aphrodite's suite."

"I was, but recently I've realized that's not helping me move forward." He shrugged and smiled. "So, it's time for a change."

"You're moving into the dorm?"

He nodded. "Yup."

"Kev, I do believe I'd like to go to dinner with you."

"Really?"

"If you're planning on being around me much, you'll learn real quick that I do not say things I don't mean."

"Good." He met her gaze. "Because I like being around you."

"Good," she said. "Now, would you stand by while I try to light another match? I already asked Nyx to keep an eye on Erin, and I'd like to finish the prayer with that tea light I poured in spell class especially to invoke the Goddess's aid."

"Sure!" Kevin said. They walked back to the statue. "I have an idea. This time when you light the match think about controlling the flame. Focus on the fact that you need just a little heat—just a little light—and not a blaze."

She raised her brows. "That's right! I forgot that you have an affinity for all five elements."

"Shaunee, if that flame listens to you, then you have an affinity for one of them as well."

She blinked in shock. "Oh, shit! Seriously?"

"Seriously. Give it a try."

Her hand shook a little, but she closed her eyes and exhaled. Kevin watched her face relax and her shoulders loosen.

"Just a little flame this time. We're only lighting a candle, not a bonfire—for goddess's sake." Shaunee didn't have to strike the match against the rough side of the box. It burst into a happy little flame that danced around on the end of the piece of wood. Her gaze flew to his. "Did you see that?"

He grinned. "I did! Now, think about that little flame lighting your candle."

"Okay, little firefly. How about we do a small burn, baby burn?" Shaunee began reaching toward the tea light that still waited at the foot of Nyx, and she was several inches away from it when the flame jumped from the match to the wick, where it continued to burn cheerily.

"You did it!" he said.

She turned to him, grinning and pressing her hand against her chest like her heart might beat out of it. "Holy shit! Kev, do I have a fire affinity?"

"Yes, Shaunee, you absolutely do."

"Ohmygoddess, yes!" She threw her arms around him as she laughed happily. "I have a fire affinity!" Then she stepped back quickly. "Sorry. I just—"

"There's nothing to apologize for. I'm glad I was here to see that." He met her gaze, thinking, *And I'm* really *glad you hugged me.*

"Huh," she said, looking extremely pleased with herself. "I need tacos. And ice cream."

"After you, fire girl." Kevin made a sweeping, gallant gesture.

"I also like a boy with manners," she said as she walked past him, giving him a sexy smile over her shoulder.

"That's two likes so far. Let's see how many more I can rack up at dinner."

"Watch yourself," she said as he retrieved his duffel bag and caught up to her.

"Not when I have someone as beautiful as you to watch," he said.

She laughed—a full-throated, joyous sound that was completely infectious. And Kevin decided right then that he was going to work at making her laugh more often.

31

Zoey

The professors' quarters were interesting. Kevin had told me that Aphrodite's suite had been remodeled—by Aphrodite, of course—and as we'd said goodnight to our Aphrodite I'd peeked into her room and gotten a glimpse of velvet and lots of fancy throw pillows. But the room Stark and I shared was more of a reflection of the rest of this House of Night. Everything in it worked—the fireplace was easy to light. There was a love seat and two chairs in front of it—a kitchenette that included coffee and such—a bedroom with clean linens and a bathroom stocked with necessities, but it lacked personality.

"It's like their Neferet musta said to make the professors' quarters livable, but not like home," Stark said as he and I sipped coffee and ate fried egg sandwiches at sunset.

"That's how the whole school seems to me," I said. "I mean, there's nothing technically wrong with it, but it lacks color, personality, and something else."

"Happiness," he added. "That's what it lacks. Not that it's surprising that it does. They've been under Neferet's iron thumb *and* at war."

I nodded. "Yeah, you're right. It's a black-and-white copy of our House of Night."

"I hope that changes when all of this is over," Stark said.

"I think it will. Anastasia is a really awesome High Priestess."

Stark smiled. "It's so crazy to see her and Dragon again. Good crazy, but still."

"Yeah, it takes some getting used to. But I think under their leadership, happiness will come back to this Tulsa and this House of Night."

He reached over and wiped what must have been egg off my lip with his napkin. "I think you're probably right."

"Ooooh, I love it when you tell me I'm right," I grinned at him.

"Well, I—"

Three really loud knocks sounded against the door followed by a muffled curse.

I sighed. "It's Aphrodite. Come on in!" I shouted.

Aphrodite opened the door rubbing her fist. "It's far too early for me to be so physical. I need coffee to go."

"Knocking on a door isn't physical," I said. "And I think I saw travel mugs in one of the cabinets. Help yourself."

"Don't you have coffee in that overdone suite of yours?" Stark asked.

Aphrodite frowned at him as she walked past us and started rummaging through the cabinets. "Yes, but I make crappy coffee. Z's is always better."

"I swear I do nothing special to it," I said.

"Don't believe you," she said over her shoulder as she filled a tall to-go mug. "By the way, it is super weird to be in that other Aphrodite's room."

"How so?" I asked, honestly interested in her response. My Other World twin was dead. This Neferet had killed her shortly after she'd been Marked, so there really wasn't anything of her left at this school, but I was still curious about how much like, or unlike, me she'd been, which also made me curious about Aphrodite's take on her doppelgänger.

"Well, she did have a nice selection of frozen organic fruit and protein powder, so I could make my smoothie. And her clothes are pretty much my style."

I checked out the slim-fit Burberry jeans, vintage Rolling Stones T-shirt, leather jacket, and knee-high black suede boots. "So, is that outfit yours or hers?"

"Jeans and jacket are hers. Tee and boots are mine. As one would expect, she had no flat boots."

I looked at the wedges she was wearing. "Uh, Aphrodite, wedges aren't flats. Seriously."

"Like I've said before, we'll agree to disagree on that," she said, sipping her coffee before she added more sugar. "But these must be her fat jeans. Girlfriend was *skinny*. I couldn't get most of her jeans over my butt." Her blue eyes narrowed at Stark. "And do *not* say anything, Bow Boy."

He was laughing but held up his hands in surrender. "Not a chance."

"Now that I think about it, I do recall her seeming kinda frail, almost like an unfinished version of you."

She nodded. "I get that. About every third thing in her room was me, something I'd buy or wear or eat or drink, but the rest was just slightly off. It's really weird. She had a lot of pills stuffed in her bathroom, like enough Xanax to drop an elephant. And the fridge was well stocked in champagne and everything to make an excellent dry martini."

I told her the simple truth. "She was you without friends."

Aphrodite shocked me by coming over to where I was sitting at the little counter and hugging me. "Thanks for not letting me fade away like her."

Her unexpected affection had my throat closing, so all I could do was hug her back and nod.

She was, of course, the first to recover. She tossed her hair back and said, "We better get down there and see Kev and Other Stark off."

"He wants to be called James now," Stark said as we headed to the door.

"Whatever," Aphrodite said.

We made our way quickly and directly to the foyer of the school. Even though it was just after sunset, the school should have been buzzing with fledgling activity, but this House of Night was strangely quiet. We saw a few fledglings heading to their dining hall. They stared at us but didn't whisper and gossip like our kids would've done.

"It's depressing here," said Aphrodite. "I seriously never thought I'd say this, but letting humans mix with our fledglings has really brightened up our House of Night. I mean, most teenagers are a pain in the ass—fledgling or otherwise—but they're less idiotic when they expand their horizons and are around different types of people."

"Aren't you still a teenager?" Stark asked.

"Don't be a smartass. I've always been older than my years. Z, you need to tell your brother to work on making this place less gloomy."

"Well, I don't think they're going to be mixing with humans for a good long while. Gotta end that pesky little thing called the vampyre/human war first," I said.

She waved that away. "Mere details. That'll be done for good once we get rid of the Neferets."

We entered the main school building from the rear and went to the foyer where a young male vampyre directed us to Anastasia's office. High Priestess Anastasia sat behind a large antique walnut desk. The room was lit by fat vanilla pillar candles that made it smell wonderful. Stevie Rae and Kacie were sitting in the comfy leather chairs in front of the desk. James and Rephaim were standing beside them. I would've liked to have gawked at the gorgeous artist renditions of Nyx on Anastasia's walls, but my attention was pulled from them when everyone looked expectantly at me and then, seeing who wasn't with me, James muttered, "Where the hell is your brother?"

"Merry meet, High Priestess," I said first, fisting my hand over my heart and greeting her respectfully before I added, "I thought Kevin would already be here."

"Hey there, Z," Stevie Rae said. "We thought he was havin' breakfast with you and Stark."

I opened my mouth to say that I hadn't seen him when the door opened and in rushed Kevin followed by this world's version of Shaunee. I had to stop myself from grinning and hugging her, especially as she was still a fledgling, which made her look a lot younger than eighteen.

Kevin fisted his hand quickly over his heart. "Merry meet, High Priestess Anastasia." As Anastasia greeted him in return, he glanced at me and grinned.

"Kevin, why have you brought this fledgling here?" Anastasia asked, though not unkindly.

"This is Shaunee," Kevin said.

"Aren't you a second-year student?" Anastasia asked.

Shaunee looked nervous, but she fisted her hand over her heart and bowed to Anastasia before saying, "I'm a third year, High Priestess."

"Merry meet, Shaunee. Before this awful war began, I prided myself on knowing all of the fledglings. I plan on being able to say that I know you all again very soon." Anastasia's gaze went to Kevin. "And why did you bring this young fledgling to my office?" she asked again.

Kevin smiled and with a jolt I realized that he looked truly happy. "You should tell her," he said to Shaunee.

Shaunee cleared her throat and then, in a clear voice that was beginning to hold some of the power that her mirror in our world possessed she said, "Kevin helped me discover something that he said you would want to know. I have an affinity for fire."

Anastasia's eyes widened in surprise, and then her face lit with a smile as well. "What a lovely blessing Nyx has bestowed upon you—and so unusual in a fledgling. Kevin was correct. This is welcome news today."

I wanted to cheer and congratulate Shaunee, and one glance at Stevie Rae said she did too, but she only made a small fist pump and mouthed *yes!*

Anastasia was saying, "Shaunee, who is your mentor?"

"It was Lenobia," she said softly.

"Oh. Well, then. I shall mentor you myself. Lenobia and I were fast friends. Next week you and I will discuss your classes and be sure that you get plenty of training in rituals and circle-casting. You'll need to—"

She was interrupted by a massive commotion in the hallway outside her office, and the door burst inward to reveal Other Neferet standing in the middle of a nest of writhing, hissing tendrils of Darkness. Beside her was a middle-aged woman I instantly recognized as Lynette. Sons of Erebus Warriors were closing in around her. Their weapons were drawn, and they looked grim.

Neferet was utterly serene. "Hello, Anastasia."

Both of the Starks moved as one, pushing Kacie and me behind them. Rephaim and Kevin joined them as Stevie Rae, Aphrodite, and Shaunee sprinted behind the wall of Warriors they'd created.

"*Anastasia!*" Dragon's roar came from behind Neferet.

Neferet didn't so much as glance at him, but instead spoke in a perfectly reasonable, calm tone. "Oh, relax, Dragon. Your mate is completely unharmed—unlike my Lynette and I would be if my children weren't here to protect us. Anastasia, I must tell you that under your leadership, my House of Night has certainly become unwelcoming."

Anastasia stood. "*My* House of Night is welcoming—to friends. You are not a friend."

Her full lips turned up. "Well, perhaps not, but you will be very glad to receive the information I bring." Her emerald eyes found me. "I see that you already realize you are in danger—the little busybody from that Other World has arrived before me."

Dragon filled the doorway behind Neferet. I could see Damien in the group of Warriors that had taken position beside him. He was holding a fencing saber, which he wielded with deadly accuracy.

I couldn't keep my mouth shut another second.

"What the hell do you want, Neferet?"

She looked at me directly and said, "Why, oddly enough, the same thing you want. I want to kill the Neferet from your world before she kills all of us, and to do so, you need to call forth this world's winged immortal named Kalona, which I happen to know you cannot do without me. So, why don't you all stop this boringly predictable posturing, put down your toylike weapons, offer my handmaid and me a seat and refreshments—and let's talk."

32

Zoey

What followed was utterly bizarre. When no one moved or said anything, Neferet sighed dramatically.

"Lynette, dearest, please give the prophecy to Anastasia." Lynette began to walk forward, but Neferet's hand on her shoulder halted her. "First, I will need to know that none of the testosterone-filled Warriors standing between us and the High Priestess will harm my handmaid."

"They will not," said Anastasia.

I could feel tension radiating off the two Starks, Kevin, and Rephaim—Neferet must have as well because she continued to maintain a grip on Lynette's shoulder, saying, "Warriors, will you allow my handmaid to pass to the High Priestess?"

The four of them nodded.

"Go ahead, dearest."

Lynette moved from Neferet's side, and the tendrils of Darkness parted just enough to let her pass. She didn't look at any of the Warriors, but kept her gaze on Anastasia, going directly to her and handing her a piece of paper. I could see that it had what looked like a poem printed on it. Lynette turned and hurried back to Neferet's side.

Anastasia quickly read the paper. "Where did you get this?"

"Although it isn't important, there is no reason you should not know. Old Magick sprites gave it to me. They said it is an ancient prophetic poem that tells how to raise a winged immortal. One of the sprites, let us call her a *friend* of mine, was very helpful and translated one line in particular for me." She quoted, "'*By the blood of she who is neither foe nor friend he is free.*' Describes me perfectly, does it not?"

"Actually, no. You're definitely a foe," said Aphrodite.

"I thought you were dead," Neferet said.

"Same," Aphrodite shot back.

Neferet stared at her, taking in her red-and-blue tattoo. Then her gaze went to the two Starks and then me. She laughed softly. "I see! Several of you are from that mirror world. If I had more time and no life, I might find this interesting." Neferet paused and shrugged a shoulder. "No, that's a lie. I would never find any of you interesting. But what *is* interesting is the fact that I come to you today offering you a truce. We have a common enemy, which does not make us friends, but it can make us temporary allies. I have one piece of the puzzle that will call forth the winged immortal. I assume the rest of you can find the other pieces. But I am not going to stand here like a castle under siege. Are you willing to be allies, or shall I show myself out, disappear into Europe somewhere, and leave you to deal with that monster by yourselves?"

I walked around Anastasia's desk. One glance at the paper was all it took. "It's the prophetic poem," I said.

"The same one we have?" Aphrodite asked.

"Yep," I said.

Anastasia and I shared a look. I nodded slightly.

"We will talk," Anastasia said.

"Excellent," Neferet said. "But let us move to the Council Room. I can hardly bear the change in my office's décor."

"Dragon," Anastasia called. "The Warriors and you will lead the way to the Council Room. Keep the fledglings well back. Neferet will follow, and we will bring up the rear."

"So ridiculously dramatic," Neferet muttered.

Lynette touched her arm gently. "Be strong, my lady. It will all be worth it."

"Thank you for the reminder, dearest."

I watched their exchange with interest. I'd seen our Neferet fake affection. She used to be good at it. She'd even fooled me for a while. This Neferet appeared to actually care for Lynette, which could be an act. But what really struck me was the ease with which Lynette responded to her. She looked at her with genuine affection, and she seemed relaxed and confident in her presence.

Could this Neferet really have formed a true friendship? With a human! And if she had, would that change her?

As Anastasia had commanded, Dragon and his Warriors led the way, clearing the halls and keeping Neferet under close watch. Neferet and Lynette followed with the nest of fat tendrils that seethed around them, creating a living barrier between the two women and the Warriors. Then the Starks, Kevin, and Rephaim left the room, with Anastasia, Stevie Rae, Kacie, Shaunee, and me bringing up the rear.

I grabbed Shaunee's wrist as we came to the doorway. "Don't come with us. We don't know what's going to happen, and you might not be safe."

She looked at me and I had a moment of déjà vu when she said, "That's why you need fire to come with you, 'cause it can burn, baby, burn!"

I couldn't argue with that. I nodded gratefully, and we all trooped down the hall to the Conference Room. When we arrived, Dragon and a dozen linebacker-sized Warriors were already in the room. Neferet stopped just outside.

"This is absurd. We simply cannot all fit in there." She turned and looked between the two Starks to find Anastasia. "If I wanted to hurt anyone here, I would not wait until I was in that room to do so. I give you my word that I have no violent intentions."

"What is your word worth?" I asked.

She narrowed her green eyes as she turned her gaze to me. "You are no less annoying than you were the last time we met. If you won't accept my word, accept logic. No matter how many Warriors you pack into that room, my children could devour them, and I would get free. More logic—you know your Neferet better than I, and I believe she is completely mad and a danger to us all. Don't you?"

I answered truthfully. "I do."

"Then let us do away with this boring show of force and get to work on how to stop her."

"Dragon, the Warriors can wait outside the Conference Room," said Anastasia.

As they trooped out, Neferet said, "Would one of you be a dear and bring me a lovely bottle of the red from my private collection and a carafe of blood—with two glasses."

The Warriors looked to Anastasia, who nodded slightly.

Neferet smiled silkily, and she and Lynette entered the room. She glided past Dragon and then Damien, where she paused briefly. "You must be from Zoey's world too."

"I am," Damien said, still holding his saber.

"You seem less morose than your version in this world was. Huh. Odd how small things can change us, is it not?"

"You expect us to believe you've changed?" James said as he took a seat beside Kacie.

Neferet's eyes sparkled with amusement as she and Lynette took their seats—with her tendrils filling the space around the two of them. "Ah, *you* I recognize. You're *my* Stark. You look as deliciously uptight as usual. Still following every tiny little rule possible?"

"I was never *your* anything," James snapped.

Aphrodite whispered to me, "Does their Neferet have a sense of humor?"

"Who knows?" I whispered back. "All I know for sure is, right now, she doesn't seem as crazy as ours."

As we were taking our seats, Grandma rushed into the room.

"Merry meet, High Priestess Anastasia," she said, fisting her hand over her heart, though her eyes were on Neferet.

"Ah, good. Please join us, Sylvia."

"Why is a human here?" Neferet asked.

"Why is *that* human here?" James countered with, pointing at Lynette.

Neferet waved James away dismissively with a flick of her well-manicured nails and said, "Because she is *my* human. Who is she?"

Stevie Rae went to Grandma's defense before I could. "She's *our* human, so back off, or we'll be on you faster than a dog on a bone."

"And she knows more about the prophecy than any vampyre," I said. "She and her people have kept record of it for all these years. Her name is Redbird. You can call her that."

"Redbird ..." Neferet turned to Lynette. "Dearest, why is that familiar?"

"It's Zoey's last name."

"Oh, I see." She looked at Grandma, who sat across the circle from her, beside me. "Which world are you from?"

"This one."

"And this prophecy, it is Native American?"

"It is," said G-ma.

"Well, then, what other pieces of the puzzle do you have? I fulfill the line about neither friend nor foe. My guess is Zoey and her little band of morons—"

Lynette touched her arm gently. "My lady, we talked about this before we arrived, remember?"

Neferet sighed and patted Lynette's hand. "Thank you, dearest. You are correct as usual. There is no need for rudeness." She turned back to Grandma. "As I was saying, Zoey and her little band of travelers must have some idea to whom the rest of the poem refers."

The wine and blood came then, and Lynette poured Neferet equal parts wine and blood before filling her own goblet with wine. I watched them touch their glasses together and continued to be amazed at the ease and intimacy with which Lynette handled her. *I think they're actually friends!*

"High Priestess, do I have your permission to proceed?" Grandma asked.

"You do," Anastasia said.

Grandma stood. "We believe this prophecy refers to an immortal my people called Kalona of the Silver Wings—or just Silver Wings. It seems, from this poem and from other sources," she glanced at Rephaim, who nodded, "that he was Nyx's Warrior, perhaps even brother to Erebus, and he retreated from the world for a noble reason. In Zoey's world—"

"Yes, yes, yes," Neferet interrupted. "I read the articles. In Zoey's world Kalona was killed by that Neferet because he'd given a portion of his immortality to Stark." She looked from my Stark to James and her lips twitched up. "Which means Stark got the better deal. Our supposition is that if we call *our* Kalona forth and raise him from whatever is imprisoning him, that he will be grateful and help us destroy your world's Neferet."

"We call her Batshit. It saves confusion," said Stevie Rae.

"Batshit—accurate, but too vulgar. I call her the Monstress, as she is truly twisted and unimaginably monstrous," said Neferet. "And I know all of this. What I do not know is who fulfills the rest of the prophecy."

Kacie lifted her hand. "I fulfill the fire and water red part."

"Interesting," Neferet said. "Not one, but *two* female red vampyres. And why do you fulfill that line?"

"I was dead—pretty recently, actually. And when I resurrected I was fully Changed *and* gifted with affinities for fire and water."

"That *is* fascinating," said Lynette.

Rephaim spoke up. "I fulfill the other part. In our world, I am Kalona's son."

"Does he have no son in this world?" Neferet asked.

"No," said Rephaim.

"So, with me you now have all the requirements you need to call forth the winged immortal and secure his aid in defeating the Monstress." She sipped her wine before continuing. "Though I think we should all be prepared if he refuses. I have some experience in freeing immortals. They tend to show their gratitude in odd ways—like trying to kill you and your friends."

Grandma Redbird lifted her hand. "I can address that. Kalona of the Silver Wings was a Warrior of Nyx. He battled Darkness. This Other Neferet, the Monstress, is definitely in league with Darkness. So, it is his duty to battle her."

I couldn't help but add, "And those of us who follow Nyx and are on the side of Light believe in doing our duty."

"Yes, we've already established what tedious little rule followers you are," said Neferet. "Do any of you know where we must be to call forth Kalona?"

"We all know," I said. "It's the same place he came from in my world. Out there in the rear grounds at that big oak by the east wall. You know—right by where you killed this world's version of me."

"You carry a grudge. I can appreciate that, but perhaps you should set aside your personal grievances until after we've saved both of our worlds," said Neferet.

Dragon was standing behind Anastasia's chair and he stepped up. "Which brings up another point. If you believe a temporary alliance with you exonerates you from your many crimes, you are mistaken."

Neferet let out a long-suffering sigh. "Of course, you would feel the need to threaten me, even when the danger we face is so much worse. Let me remind you, Swordmaster, until modern times vampyres had always been allowed to kill humans who threaten them. That is what I did. Loren Blake was a traitor who conspired against this House of Night—consider it an execution that I carried out before you could."

James shook his head, and I thought he looked like he was going to be sick. "You're responsible for the deaths of other vampyres—noble, blame-free vampyres."

"Like my sister," said Kevin.

"And our wonderful Lenobia," added Anastasia.

Neferet ignored everyone except Anastasia. "That was war. I was on one side—a side, you should note, that General Stark was on as well—and those vampyres, or fledglings, were our enemies. It was that simple. But I care little for your uninspired exoneration or your pedantic laws. Do you really think I came here without being completely sure that my children, my handmaid, and I could leave when we wished to? If you do not accept my aid, that is exactly what I shall do—leave. I will disappear, and you will have to face that creature I mistakenly allowed to be free, and, I assure you, she is no longer vampyre and is certainly not goddess, but she is more dangerous than you can imagine. I have the ability to hide from her and live a long and pleasant life. Can all of you say the same thing? Or shall we agree to work together to destroy her?"

When Dragon and James began to shout a response, Anastasia lifted her hand, silencing them. She met Neferet's gaze steadily and asked, "And after we destroy her, then what? Do you think you will return to this House of Night as its High Priestess?"

Neferet laughed gaily. "Oh, no, no, no. I have formally renounced my title as High Priestess. My future has changed, and for the better. When the Monstress is destroyed, I will leave Oklahoma and this country. I intend to establish a place of my own where things of beauty are revered, and I am benevolent mistress of all I survey." She sipped from her goblet. "So, shall I stay or go?"

"You will stay and fight with us to defeat the monster you loosed," said Anastasia firmly.

Just as firmly, I added, "And *then* you'll go."

33

Zoey

"Are you ready to do this?" Damien asked me as we began to take our places around the big oak at the east wall.

I wasn't, of course, but I definitely couldn't say that. So, instead, I tried to sound strong and sure of myself, hoping that the real feelings would follow. "Yeah, and remember, it's not going to be like last time. This time we're raising a different version of Kalona and we're doing it on purpose."

I couldn't help but remember last time—it seemed like ages ago but had really only been about a year and a half. Back in our world, I'd planned to introduce the House of Night to a new kind of vampyre, the red vamps, and also to hopefully prove that Neferet was an enemy. That plan had gone horribly wrong when Neferet had appeared with a newly resurrected Stark, who definitely hadn't had a good handle on his humanity yet. She'd ordered him to shoot Stevie Rae so that her blood flowed around the tree and completed our world's prophecy, allowing a fallen and decidedly evil Kalona and his Raven Mocker children to rise and, as Stevie Rae would say, open up a whole can of whoop-ass on Tulsa.

"Today will be different." Stark was there beside me. He put his arm around me and murmured, "Different me—different Kalona—different Neferet. Remember that and don't be freaked out."

I nodded and stepped fully into his arms, just for a moment, to absorb some of his strength and confidence in me.

"Excuse me, Zoey."

Reluctantly, I moved out of Stark's embrace to face Anastasia. The High Priestess looked somber, but her voice was calm and confident. "I have all of the fledglings confined to their dorms, so they will be out of harm's way. Your grandmother is with the girls in their dorm, helping to keep them calm. Dragon has ordered half of the Sons of Erebus Warriors to stand guard at the dorms, and the others will be here, outside the circle."

I followed her gaze to a group of armed Warriors taking position around the rear grounds.

Just as I was thinking that I wished there were more of them, Dragon joined us, saying, "I still cannot reach Dallas and the soldiers you ordered to clean out the depot tunnels."

"Dallas is alive over here?" Stark asked.

Kevin and Shaunee were walking past us, and he paused to answer Stark. "Yeah, but he's not a very good guy."

Stark snorted. "Same Dallas—different world. Looks like it's a good thing he's not here. Plus, he might distract Stevie Rae."

"What's up with that?" Kev asked.

"Once upon a time, before Dallas chose to be a turd, he and Stevie Rae were together," I explained.

Stevie Rae joined us, with Rephaim beside her. "Did I hear y'all say Dallas's name?"

"Yeah," I said. "He's alive in this world."

"And a douchebag," said Kevin.

"Same Dallas—different world," Stevie Rae echoed Stark and me.

"Where is he?" Rephaim asked, glaring around at the Warriors.

"Not here," Dragon said. "He and a group of soldiers Anastasia was admonishing are cleaning out the depot. They are also not answering my phone calls."

"Hey, Shaunee said something about Erin being with Dallas, and she's MIA too," said Kevin.

Anastasia sighed. "I thought one of the professors told me she just saw him over by the Field House. Well, no matter. Dragon, when this is over and we've raised Kalona, please find Dallas and his compatriots and explain to them that if they do not want to follow my leadership then they will no longer be welcome at this House of Night—and I will inform the Vampyre High Council that they are rogue."

The hairs on the back of my neck started to prickle. "Why are they in trouble?"

"They still support Neferet and her war," said Dragon grimly.

I'd opened my mouth to say that my gut was telling me we needed to keep an eye on them, when Neferet breezed up with Lynette at her side.

"It seems they have excellent taste," Neferet said. "Though I assure you, I have had no contact with them. Dallas and his ilk are even more tedious than this House of Night. They are fit for nothing except to be soldiers of war, and I have had my fill of war."

"So, basically, you just stir the shit pot and then leave others to clean it up," said Kevin.

"A disgusting way to put it, though not entirely inaccurate." Neferet shrugged. "Young vampyre, before you judge me you should understand that the world I grew up in was divided into two types of people—those with power, and those who were controlled by the people with power. I decided one hundred years before you were born never to be in the latter group again. Vilify me if you must, *after* we defeat the true villain here."

"Who you set free," Kevin said.

Neferet looked from Kevin to the rest of us. "You do realize I did nothing extraordinary to free her, don't you? I fed her. That's it.

Sprites could have been summoned to do the same thing. Actually, pouring fresh blood into that grotto would have probably allowed her to feed enough to break free. I do understand it was a mistake to loose her, but had I not done it, *someone* would have. You think I don't know about the humans who began worshiping her? So, keep your blame to yourselves. It helps nothing."

She had a point, though I was reluctant to agree with her. Instead, I changed the subject. "Anastasia, I'm ready to begin. Are you?"

"Yes, Zoey."

"Let's get nearer the circle and I'll go over what we're going to do. Do you have the music ready?"

Anastasia nodded and lifted a small remote. "All I have to do is press this and it will begin."

I know it seemed a little weird to have music and such when what we were doing was so serious, but I'd decided that we needed to mimic what had been done to raise our Kalona, which had begun as a cleansing ritual for the school. Traditionally, the High Priestess who called the elements and cast the circle would enter it dancing joyously to music as the vampyre who was playing the part of her Consort would speak the lines of a poem that was reflective of the ritual.

The poem wasn't a necessity, and neither was the music, so I'd done away with one and kept the other, hoping it would help us set our intention and concentrate. There would be no one playing my Consort because Neferet was going to be within the circle taking his place.

I remembered clearly the night Kalona had broken free. Erik had played the Consort role. It had been his blood that was shed before all hell broke loose and Stark, newly resurrected and completely not himself, had been ordered by Neferet to shoot Stevie Rae. *Her* blood had been the sacrifice that had risen Kalona.

The irony wasn't lost on me that tonight it would be a different Neferet whose blood would awaken an immortal—as she was going to have to take Stevie Rae's place.

I was standing in the middle of what would be our circle, before the giant oak that looked exactly as ours had before Kalona had burst out of the ground beneath it. I swallowed and licked my lips. My hands were fisted at my side to keep them from shaking with nerves. "Okay, here's what's going to happen. At first, it'll be kinda like a regular cleansing ritual. Anastasia will start the music, and I'll dance to the center of our circle. Try to let the music relax you as you use it to focus. Our intention is to raise an immortal to battle Darkness alongside our Light."

"Do you not think you should change your clothes?" Neferet asked, looking me up and down. She was wearing a gorgeous cashmere dress that hugged her curves and left her arms bare. It was the exact color of her eyes. I was wearing jeans and my current fav peasant top from Free People.

I shook my head. "No, Neferet, I don't. The elements don't care what I'm wearing. Nyx doesn't care what I'm wearing. You do know that all that extra stuff is just for show, don't you?"

Lynette chimed in: "Looking your best is always important."

"Neferet, don't you want your human to wait inside the dorm with my grandma? She'd be safer there," I said.

"Lynette stays with me. Always," Neferet said.

Anastasia said, "Then she'll need to be quiet and remain outside the circle."

"Will you keep her safe?" Neferet asked.

"Of course," said Anastasia.

Panic flashed across Lynette's face, but Neferet patted her shoulder gently. "It will be fine, dearest. Remain with Anastasia. She and I have our differences, but she is a High Priestess who keeps her word. You will be safe."

"So, to continue," I drew their attention back to me. "I'll come in with the music. As in a regular ritual, I'll call the elements. As always, Damien is air. Shaunee," I paused and nodded at her, "are you sure you're okay to represent fire?"

"Absolutely," she said without any hesitation. "I can do it."

"All right. That's good because we need a superstrong circle. So, that means Kacie will be water and Stevie Rae earth, of course. And I'll invoke spirit." I met my brother's gaze. "Kev, I'd like you to be inside the circle with me, and I want you to move to each element with me too. It can't hurt to have double the affinities."

"I'll have your back," he said.

"Rephaim," I continued. "You'll need to be inside the circle too. When I cut Neferet, her blood will drip on the base of the tree. When it does that, I'll need you to call Kalona. Then, hopefully, he'll bust up out of the tree like he did in our world. Our circle will still be intact in case he's, um, disoriented." I had a flash of memory about the first time I'd seen our Kalona and how mesmerizing he'd been, literally causing fledglings and vampyres to fall to their knees and worship him. I was counting on the fact that that was only a thing with bad Kalona, but just in case, I planned to be safely inside a very strong circle with the elements invoked and ready to persuade him not to be an immortal douchebag—if necessary.

I also had an alternative plan that Stark and I had discussed. I met his gaze. He touched the bow he'd slung across his shoulder and nodded just enough for me to see.

"So, questions?"

"I do not think this is going to be pleasant for me," said Neferet.

Aphrodite snorted. "Ya think? And that's not a question. I have one you should've asked, though. What are we going to do with Neferet's disgusting snake things?"

Lynette's response was immediate. "They aren't disgusting. Nor are they snakes. They're affectionate and a lot more loyal than most people!"

"Regardless," I said. "Aphrodite has a point. They can't come inside our circle."

"Children, conceal yourselves so as not to offend these simpletons and remain with our Lynette."

"Whatever." Aphrodite rolled her eyes. "Z, where do you want me?"

"Last time you were able to cross the circle barrier when we needed you," I said. "This time I think you should be inside it with us."

"Will do," she said.

"And we'll be outside the circle?" James asked.

I nodded. "You and Stark keep your bows ready, but don't draw them, and position yourself around the circle with Dragon. Remember to look protective and not menacing. This Kalona is supposed to be good, and we don't want to seem threatening and be mistaken for forces of Darkness."

Anastasia clasped her hands in front of her and said, "Then why the show of force at all? Perhaps we should have our Warriors back off."

"You know, that's not a bad idea," I agreed. "Dragon, please have the Sons of Erebus move away and not draw any weapons."

He didn't look happy, but he nodded and went to the circle of watching Warriors and relayed the order. They dispersed, finding shadowy spots near the school where they silently waited and watched.

"Okay, take your places and let's do this," I said.

My circle was a well-oiled machine. Shaunee fit right in, and even though she was still a fledgling and didn't actually know any of us—except Kevin—she seemed at ease and more excited than nervous.

I, on the other hand, was just nervous. I took my place outside the circle and nodded to Anastasia, who started the music.

I easily recognized the hauntingly beautiful tune of Loreena McKennitt's "The Mummers' Dance," which was especially perfect because it was just the orchestral version, which allowed all of us to focus on the beat of the drums and the pulse of the music.

As always, as soon as I began to move with the tempo, my nerves slipped away. As I swayed and twirled to the music, I felt myself enter the presence of our Goddess and I was filled with confidence and intention. I danced a full pass around the outside circumference of the circle and loved that my people were swaying with me. When I danced into the circle, I could see that Aphrodite and

Kevin, Rephaim, and even Neferet were twirling with the music as well, and for a moment I saw real joy on Neferet's face—something I'd never before witnessed. I glanced outside the circle to see Lynette standing beside Anastasia. Both women were also swaying to the music and Lynette was grinning happily at Neferet.

Let her be different, I sent an unexpected prayer to Nyx. *Let this Neferet actually know love and happiness and forgiveness.*

I moved to take my place before Damien with Kevin by my side and the music faded away, leaving only its memory pulsing through our veins. Then I began my invocation—starting, as always, with air and my friend Damien.

"Wind, you are as dear to me and familiar as the breath of life. Tonight, I need your strength to cleanse anything stagnant from us. I ask that you come to me, wind!" As I spoke the invocation that was traditional for a ritual cleansing, Kevin touched the match Damien gave him to his yellow candle. It lit instantly as the first element of our circle rushed to us, lifting our hair and circling precociously around Damien.

From there Kev and I moved deosil to Shaunee, who grinned at my brother before eagerly lifting her red candle.

"Fire, you warm and cleanse. Tonight, we need your cleansing power to burn Darkness from us. Come to me, fire!"

Kevin didn't have to light the match. Shaunee's candle burst into a bright, beautiful flame.

She sucked in a breath, and her gaze met mine. "It's incredible!" she said.

"Yes, it is," I said.

"And so are you," Kevin added before moving clockwise to Kacie and her blue candle.

I shot a look at him and was glad to see a happy smile on his face. *Shaunee and Kevin, huh? I like it. I like it a lot!*

We paused before Kacie. "Water, we go to you dirty and rise from you clean. Tonight I ask that you wash us free of any Darkness that might want to cling to us. Come to me, water!" Kev lit the match Kacie had ready and touched it to her candle, and we were rewarded with the scent of spring rains.

We moved quickly to the northernmost point of the circle where Stevie Rae stood with her back to the huge oak. She lifted her green candle and we shared a smile before I invoked her faithful element.

"Earth, you shelter us and feed us. Tonight, I ask that you also strengthen us and help us stand against any Darkness that might try to come against us. Come to me, earth!" When Kevin lit the green candle, birdsong whistled around us and I smelled the sweet scent of jasmine.

We moved to the center of the circle where Rephaim, Aphrodite, and Neferet waited. They formed a little minicircle around us as I lifted my purple spirit candle and said, "Spirit, you are what makes us human. You are always with us—from beginning to end and beyond. Tonight, I ask that you fill all within this circle with Light and allow no Darkness to penetrate. Come to me, spirit!" When my brother lit my candle, I felt the wonderful inrush of hope and happiness and love that spirit brought with it. With new confidence, I carefully placed my pillar candle on the ground and then looked around my circle.

Stretching along the circumference was a glowing silver rope that bound us together. It was thick and bright and undeniably strong, imbued with the five elements.

"I have never seen anything like that," said Neferet, sounding honestly in awe.

I turned to her. "Let's go to the tree."

She nodded and swept back her thick auburn hair with a trembling hand.

With Neferet beside me and Kevin, Aphrodite, and Rephaim following, we walked to Stevie Rae, who stood directly in front of the thick old oak. Once there, Neferet turned to face me so that her back was to the tree as well.

"Rephaim, I'm going to cut Neferet's hand and after it's bled onto the ground, that's when you call Kalona."

"I understand," he said.

"You can do it, Rephaim!" said Stevie Rae.

I faced Neferet. I didn't have to say anything. She had been a High Priestess for considerably longer than I'd been alive. This definitely wasn't her first ritual, though I did wonder briefly how it felt for her to be in the center of what was obviously a circle infused with power granted by a goddess she'd forsaken.

Mentally, I shook myself. *Focus—this is far from over.*

Aphrodite handed me a ceremonial dagger that was razor sharp. I pressed it against the meaty part of Neferet's hand, just below her thumb as I had to Erik's hand that night so long ago. The blade sliced her skin easily, welling with scarlet. Neferet didn't flinch or grimace, she only held her arm out and turned her hand over, palm down, so that blood began to drip on the thick roots of the tree that were exposed through the sparse winter grass.

After it had dripped for several minutes so that there were dark stains spattering the roots, I nodded to Rephaim. He, too, faced the tree and spoke in a deep, strong voice that filled our circle.

"Kalona of the Silver Wings, I call to you! I am Rephaim— son from another world—though my love for you is strong in any world. We have need of you, Warrior of Light! Come forth!"

We waited. And waited. And waited.

Surreptitiously, I moved to the side as Neferet's blood continued to drip onto the oak's roots.

"Try again," I told Rephaim.

He nodded, cleared his throat, and repeated, "Kalona of the Silver Wings, I call to you! I am Rephaim—son from another world—though my love for you is strong in any world. We have need of you, Warrior of Light! Come forth!"

Still we waited. Still there was no answer.

I moved another step farther away from Neferet and told

Rephaim. "Something is going to happen in just a second. When it does I want you to call him again, only this time use words from the prophecy. Do you remember them?"

"I do."

"Well enough to change some of them to reflect the fact that you're calling him now, and it's not just an old, stale poem?"

His face brightened. "I do, Z. I memorized it well."

"Good. Get ready."

"What's going—" Neferet began, but I turned and met Stark's gaze outside the glowing circle and nodded.

Quick as a striking viper, Stark lifted an arrow, drew, and as he fired he said, "I aim for the true mark, the one who is neither foe nor friend, and by her blood he shall be free!"

Stark's arrow caught Neferet in the chest, exactly where his arrow—in another world and another time—had caught Stevie Rae. Neferet dropped to the ground, clutching the quill that decorated her chest as blood gushed from her body and covered the ground. I knew it wasn't fatal—just as Stevie Rae's injury hadn't been—but Neferet had no way of knowing that. Neither did Lynette. Her scream was heartbreaking. I glanced outside the circle to see that Anastasia had her arms around the woman who clutched her own chest as she shrieked in agony.

Goddess! They're Imprinted!

Then my attention had to snap back to Neferet. I went to my knees beside her and shifted her body so that she was laying on her side, bleeding heavily into the ground.

Her emerald eyes were glassy with shock. "What have you done?"

"Exactly what was done before," I said. "It's not fatal. He's taken your blood, not your life. I give you my word." Then I looked up at Rephaim who was staring at me in shock. "Do it! Call Kalona now!"

His face was pale, but when he spoke his voice blasted around us.

"Ancient one sleeping, it is time to arise,
The dead have joined with fire and water red
I am son who is not—my raven call I did devise
Hear me—hear my call—rise from your sacrificial bed!

By this blood of she—neither friend nor foe—you are free
Behold her terrible sacrifice—it is a bittersweet sight,
Ruled by Light we do wish to be
No one will kneel to Darkness tonight!

Kalona, your return shall be sweet
We welcome you with love and heat!"

The massive oak's branches began to sway in its own wind. I grabbed Neferet's shoulders and was ready to drag her out of the way should Kalona explode out of it like he had in our world.

But everything was different that night.

Instead of the tree bursting apart, it bloomed. At the first massive fork it began opening—gently, with no violence or horrors. And from that opening wings appeared—so silver-white that they matched the glowing thread that bound our circle. They spread and beat against the wind, and Kalona lifted from within the heart of the tree.

34

Other Neferet

Neferet could not believe that annoying child had conspired with Other World Stark to shoot her! She could tell that the little bitch had spoken the truth about the injury though. The wound was deep and painful, but it had missed anything vital and it would heal. She was trying to send Lynette comfort. Her screams were heartbreaking because her dearest had no way of knowing she wasn't mortally wounded, but then Rephaim used the prophecy to call to Kalona—and the tree opened to allow the immortal to fly free.

For a moment Neferet forgot the pain of her wound and the anguish of Lynette, and all that filled her senses was Kalona.

He was truly magnificent. His smooth skin was gilded with statuesque perfection. His hair was long and black and loose around his shoulders like ancient Warriors used to wear theirs. Neferet wasn't fond of men. The truth was she had little use for them outside of sex, feeding, or protection, but even she was moved by his preternatural beauty. She'd never seen eyes like his—perfect amber orbs that blazed with joy as he soared in a circle over the tree and shouted, "Freedom! At last!"

He's going to fly away before we can even ask for his help and this will all be for naught, she thought wearily as blood loss made her dizzy. Then he glanced down, and she watched his expression shift from wonder and joy to surprise—and he dove to land in the middle of their circle. As he touched ground, there was a powerful sizzle, and the silver ribbon that had held the circle together swirled up, making the beautiful spiral design that was often associated with the Goddess, before it rushed to Kalona, straight into his wings. They glowed white-hot for a moment before the light disappeared.

"Who should I thank for awakening—" Kalona began, but his gaze found Neferet, crumpled and bleeding across Zoey's lap, and he rushed to her, his wings tucked neatly against his broad, bare back.

"No shirt in either world," she heard Zoey mutter, and would've liked to have asked her to expound on that comment, but the immortal was suddenly there, crouching beside her.

"Priestess, is it your blood that awakened me and completed the prophecy?"

Neferet tried to say, *Yes, and you required entirely too much of it,* but her voice wouldn't obey her.

The annoying child answered for her. "This is Neferet. She fulfilled the neither friend nor foe bleeding part of the prophecy."

Kalona looked from her wound to Zoey. "I thought it was interesting phrasing when my mother created the prophecy. I shall have to discuss exactly how it was fulfilled when I have more time, but for now, I give you my thanks."

With one quick motion he pulled the arrow from Neferet's chest. She did find her voice then, and Lynette echoed her shriek of pain. Then he covered the bleeding wound with his hand, bowed his head, and whispered, "None should be harmed to free me, as I slept of my own will and wish no one ill."

Neferet's chest felt as if it was on fire and she gasped as pain assaulted her, but it lasted only for a few beats of her frantic heart. Then there was no pain, no fire, only warmth as her strength returned to her. She blinked tears of agony from her eyes and looked down at herself. There was a jagged hole in her dress, but beneath it was the pink of newly healed flesh. She sat up, moving out of Zoey's arms, and hissed, "*Bitch!*" under her breath before she peered around Kalona and the rest of them to find Lynette. Anastasia had a tight grip on her, but she was still struggling to get free—to get to Neferet. Tears and grief ravaged her face.

"Dearest! I am well! All is well!"

Lynette froze and then her gaze met Neferet's and she collapsed into Anastasia's arms as her sobs changed to relief. Only then did Neferet look up at the immortal who now stood over her, wings already spread so that he could take to the sky. Shakily, Neferet struggled to her feet. Zoey was beside her and she had to fight the urge to slap her—hard. But right now, it was more important to keep the immortal from fleeing.

"Thank you, Kalona of the Silver Wings," Neferet said formally, fisting her hand over the jagged rip in her dress and bowing to him as her mind whirred, trying to think of something—anything—to say to keep him with them.

"It is the least I can do, Priestess. And I would not have anyone suffer for my awakening."

"Good!" Zoey said. "That's great to hear, because we all had a part in awakening you, and we really need your help."

Kalona gazed around the circle and the school grounds. "Much has changed over these many years. I wonder how long it has been." He seemed to speak more to himself than to them. "I do thank you for releasing me, but whatever payment you desire must wait, though I do give you my oath that I shall return to thank you properly and perform whatever task you wish, should it be in the service of the Goddess and Light." He spread his mighty wings, causing Kevin, Rephaim, and Aphrodite to move back so as not to be struck by them. "Now, I must go. I have too long been absent from my Goddess's side." His wings beat the air as they lifted him.

"Father!" Rephaim shouted, his arms wide and beseeching. "Wait! Please do not go! We need you."

The immortal drifted back to the ground, though he did not close his wings. "Child, I am not your father."

Rephaim hurried to stand in front of him, and bowed his head respectfully before saying, "Yes, I know. You are not my father in this world, but in another world, *my* world, you are—" He paused and then added, "Well, you were."

Kalona cocked his head to the side, studying Rephaim. "How can one be a father, and then not be a father?"

"Because my father—my Kalona—he died."

Kalona shook his head. His voice gentled. "You are mistaken, child. It is impossible for any being like me to die."

Stark dropped his bow before moving quickly to Rephaim's side to face Kalona. "No, it's not impossible. In our world, a mirror version of this one, our Kalona died because Nyx commanded that he give me a sliver of his immortality to heal me."

Kalona looked Stark up and down. "You must be very special to Nyx."

Stark closed the few feet between himself and Zoey and took her hand. "Actually, it's my High Priestess who is special to Nyx. I'm her Oathbound Warrior and Guardian—that's all."

Kalona's lips tilted up. "That is enough."

Zoey said, "When our Kalona gave Stark a sliver of his immortality, it left him vulnerable to our fallen High Priestess who'd become a powerful immortal Tsi Sgili."

Kalona's handsome face mirrored the disgust in his voice. "Tsi Sgili! They are demons."

"Yes, Fath—I mean, Kalona," Rephaim said. "That is why we need your help defeating her. The Tsi Sgili has come from our world to this one, and she threatens the balance of Light and Darkness in both of our worlds. Please stay. Please be our champion against Darkness."

Kalona's sigh was heartbreaking. He tilted his face up and said, "My only love, Nyx, Goddess of Night, be patient but a moment longer. Your Warrior has an earthly job to do before he may return home."

When an answer came it was on the wings of several pearl-breasted doves that flew from the oak. Neferet's soul lifted, and she felt hot and cold at once as Nyx's voice fluttered through the air. Filled with love, it drifted down to them and settled into their hearts.

My Consort, my love, my Kalona. I have waited lonely centuries for you. My arms ache with your absence, but greater than my ache is the world's need for your mighty onyx lance. Know that when your battle is over, my arms will be open and eager to hold you once more. Blessed be, my love—and may my favorite children blessed be as well.

Kalona bowed his head, and Neferet saw that he actually wiped away tears before he looked up and lifted his hand. A great black lance materialized, and the winged immortal grasped it.

Neferet was staring at the incredible weapon when she was distracted by Zoey, who was rubbing a turquoise bracelet around her right wrist as if it was causing her pain. Her gaze went from both Starks to the kids who still stood in their places of the circle. Each of them had a similar bracelet—and they, too, were either rubbing it or shaking their wrists.

"Tell me, where is this demon that I must defeat?" Kalona was saying.

Neferet lowered her voice and asked Zoey, "What is wrong with your wrists?"

Zoey looked at Stark and her gaze snapped around the circle as she noticed that her friends were being bothered by their bracelets.

"Ah, hell!" she said.

At that moment an explosion rocked the House of Night. Stone shrapnel fell among them as a section of the east wall shattered not far from where they stood.

"Lynette!" Neferet shouted, and her dearest tore herself from Anastasia, but before she reached Neferet, a piece of the rock wall smashed into her shoulder and she dropped hard to the ground.

"No!" Neferet ran to her and pulled Lynette into her arms. "Dearest! Answer me! Dearest!"

Lynette's eyes fluttered open. "I'm—I'm okay. It's just my arm." Her trembling hand reached up and touched Neferet's cheek. "Oh, my lady, I thought you were dead."

"It would take more than one of these children to kill me." She wiped away Lynette's tears.

Around them was chaos. No one could see through the smoking mess that had been the wide east wall. Dragon was shouting at the Sons of Erebus. Zoey had called her circle, in which Neferet and Lynette were roughly the center of, and she was hastily invoking the elements again as Anastasia and James ran inside the circle to join them. James and Stark had their bows up and ready with arrows nocked.

Then there was a series of popping sounds that utterly confused Neferet, and Dragon began shouting. "Sons of Erebus! Barricade the dorms! The rest of you, to me!"

"What is that? What's happening?" Lynette's voice shook with panic.

"It's gunfire," Stark said grimly. "Whoever it is has—"

Lynette screamed. Her eyes were huge with terror, and she was staring over Neferet's shoulder at the broken wall.

Neferet shifted around so that she could follow her gaze, and what she saw made her so physically ill that she had to swallow bile to keep from vomiting in fear. Climbing over the still-smoking rubble of the wall was the Monstress. Her elongated limbs made her look insectile, and hundreds of tendrils of Darkness slithered with her. Toxic and menacing, they bared their teeth and hissed as they swarmed into the school grounds.

"Tsi Sgili, abomination! Return to the Darkness that spawned you!" Kalona roared as he took flight. He hurled his onyx spear. Laughing, Neferet raised her own spear—an evil-looking thing that was the white of dead eyes, curved and pointed at both ends.

The Monstress easily parried the blow and laughed. "Ah, Kalona, my old lover. So very good to see you again."

Kalona hovered in the air above them, reached his hand out and his spear appeared in it instantly. "I have never been your lover, demon."

The Other's emaciated face looked skeletal as she pouted. "Oh, I do hate it when I get my worlds mixed up. But, no matter. Soon they shall both be ruled by me, and I need not keep them straight. Children, destroy everyone who stands against us!"

Her tendrils began attacking the Sons of Erebus Warriors, ripping huge pieces of flesh from them as they toyed with them cruelly.

"You have to help them," Lynette said.

Real fear filled Neferet. "Then who will protect us, dearest?"

"That doesn't matter right now. What matters right now is stopping that monster."

"We must get out of here!" Neferet insisted.

Lynette shook her head. "No, my lady. We must help them. It's the right thing to do."

"But we could be killed."

"You won't be killed," Zoey said. She'd returned to the center of the circle and invoked spirit. "Neferet, I give you my word that my circle and I will protect Lynette—and you."

Neferet pointed over Zoey's shoulder at the monster that used to wear her face. "You're not stronger than that thing! She'll kill us all."

Lynette touched Neferet's cheek. "Then we'll die knowing we did the right thing. But I believe in you, my lady—your strength and your power. She's just a bad version of you, but she's still like *you* somewhere inside all of that horror. You can defeat her. I know you can. I know you will."

"Stay within the circle," Neferet said as she stood. "Children! Show yourselves!" Around Neferet, hundreds of her tendrils suddenly materialized.

"Holy shit! When did they grow eyes?" Aphrodite asked.

Neferet looked down at her children. They had altered in

appearance. They were still snakelike, but the prophetess was correct. Instead of blind faces and fanged mouths, they blinked up at her with golden eyes and expressions of adoration. She crouched and they came to her, eager to be close. She caressed them and whispered, "You are my beauties—my own. Be brave, children. Be brave." Then she stood and pointed to the beleaguered Warriors. "Protect the Sons of Erebus. Kill those vile creatures who belong to the monster who wants to rule our world!"

The tendrils sped off, and Neferet stood frozen, watching them attack. Her children were vastly outnumbered, but they seemed stronger than the eyeless tendrils—and Neferet had no doubt they were. It had only been a few days since the Monstress had been released and they'd fed. It wasn't possible that either she or her tendrils were fully recovered from a year of starvation and imprisonment.

"That was a good thing you just did," said Aphrodite, looking surprised. "And Zoey was telling you the truth. You're with us now, and we don't abandon our own. You can count on the fact that we'll do everything in our power to protect Lynette and you."

Neferet began to say something sarcastic, but within the prophetess's surprised expression she saw something else—perhaps it was appreciation—perhaps it was almost acceptance, and it brought to mind the Aphrodite from her world. The one who had died that day to give the red vampyres their humanity. *She would have been my friend had I been able to let her close to me, as I have Lynette.* The thought so shocked Neferet that all she could do was nod and say, "I will stand with you and your circle against that."

Both women's gazes went to the Monstress, who had her back to what remained of the wall, battling Kalona. Neither appeared to be winning, and as they watched, the Monstress parried a blow and then, with the speed of a skittering spider, she struck and the tip of one side of her spear turned red with the immortal's blood.

"Can he defeat her?" Neferet asked.

"He has to," Aphrodite said grimly.

"Z!" Stark shouted. He and James were side by side, lethal mirror images who fired together—their arrows slicing through tendrils of Darkness that seethed around the battling Sons of Erebus Warriors, hitting only the children of the Monstress and allowing Neferet's tendrils to continue fighting beside the Warriors. "We're almost out of arrows! We have to get inside—regroup—rearm!"

Zoey ran to the center of the circle. "Okay, we need to move this circle to the school, but *do not* let go of your element! No matter what, do *not* break this circle!"

"We got you, Z!" Stevie Rae shouted. As one, the four who represented the elements moved together toward the center, so that their circle was smaller and easier to manage.

The *pop, pop, pop* of assault rifles invaded the grounds as vampyre soldiers poured out of the Field House. They began cutting through the Sons of Erebus Warriors—who were armed only with swords, knives, bows, and courage.

"Anastasia!" Zoey turned to the High Priestess. "Where can we find more weapons?"

Anastasia was staring at the Sons of Erebus as they scattered and took cover. Tears poured down her pale cheeks. "I—I don't know. The F-Field House is where we store the weapons."

"Nyx's Temple—the basement. Hurry!" said Neferet. She met Zoey's gaze. "I hid weapons down there as well as the basement beside the Field House. There are grenades, guns, and crossbows down there."

"Okay, you heard Neferet," Zoey said. "Move this circle to Nyx's Temple!"

Slowly, they all began walking across the grounds toward the distant temple. Neferet put her arm around Lynette's waist to help her stand, and then half carried, half dragged her with them.

"Anastasia!" Neferet shouted at the High Priestess, who was still frozen and almost outside the moving circle. "You have to move! Now!"

Anastasia turned and looked at her. She wiped a hand across her face and nodded weakly and then began walking toward her—and a bullet sliced through her leg.

The High Priestess screamed and went down.

"*NO!*" Dragon's roar was a clarion call of agony from across the school grounds.

"Earth! Shield us!" Stevie Rae shouted, and a green bubble formed around their circle just as several more bullets ricocheted from it.

"Help her!" Lynette said. "I can walk on my own."

Neferet rushed to Anastasia, and Rephaim met her there, along with Zoey and Aphrodite. Neferet pressed her hand over the bloody hole in the High Priestess's thigh.

"Someone give me something to make a tourniquet!" Neferet said as blood poured from Anastasia.

Zoey ripped the hem of her shirt and handed it to Neferet, and she quickly wound it around Anastasia's thigh, over the wound.

Without looking up Neferet ordered, "Now give me something to press over the hole!"

Rephaim handed his shirt to her. Neferet quickly folded it and pressed it against the wound as Anastasia moaned in pain. Neferet looked up at Rephaim. "Carry her!"

Neferet stood as Rephaim lifted Anastasia. She stared at the carnage spread across what used to be her school grounds. The Sons of Erebus Warriors were losing—that was obvious. They had taken cover and were still shooting arrows, and even though they outnumbered the attacking soldiers, their modern weapons more than made up for that.

Her tendrils were still fighting. They'd taken cover with the Sons of Erebus Warriors. They would dart out and strike at one of the Monstress's black, eyeless creatures, but they were vastly outnumbered by her nest of vipers, and it was only a matter of time before they, along with the Warriors they protected, were overrun.

Neferet's gaze went to Kalona and her insane counterpart. Still, they battled. Kalona had several wounds that bled freely down his body, but he didn't seem to be tiring. The Monstress was unwounded. Her smile was feral as she parried the immortal's blows over and over again.

He cannot defeat her—just as she cannot defeat him, Neferet thought. *But she will keep him busy while her army slaughters everyone. And then what? Then who will Kalona protect?* Neferet stared at the creature she'd almost become and saw nothing but a woman filled with power and madness, one who was completely devoid of happiness, friendship—and love—always love.

Neferet turned to meet Lynette's gaze. Her friend, her dearest one, smiled and nodded. "I believe you can do it." Her voice was strengthened by the bubble of earth power that protected them.

Beside her, Zoey said, "I believe you can do it too, and while you do, we'll keep Lynette safe."

Aphrodite turned to Neferet and met her gaze. "You're the only one who really knows how to stop her."

Bleeding in Rephaim's arms Anastasia said, "You *must* stop her, High Priestess."

Tears filled Neferet's eyes. "I have forsaken that title many times over."

Anastasia's reached out and grasped Neferet's blood-slicked hand. "But Nyx has never forsaken you—nor will she ever."

The truth of her words shivered through Neferet, and a dam broke within her, allowing the love of Nyx, her betrayed Goddess of Night, to pulse through her veins and fill her heart.

"Zoey, promise me that you will care for my Lynette, even should I not return."

"I give you my word that if you fall, I will take Lynette back to my world with me and give her a home at the House of Night," Zoey said solemnly.

"Oh, holy shit! I understand the vision now," blurted Aphrodite.

Neferet turned to her. "Will you tell me—truly—what your vision foresaw?"

"Yes, High Priestess, I will," said Aphrodite. "I saw Lynette fall—and with her fell two worlds. But now I get it. We're here to protect Lynette. It's not about Kalona. It's not about us or weapons or Warriors. It's about *you*. With your *friend* safe, you can take on Batshit."

Neferet nodded. "With my dearest safe, I take on another version of myself, a version that could've so easily been my fate, and hope that for the first time since the day I was Marked, good will triumph over evil in my life. It did that day because it made me a vampyre, but I did not see that then. I saw only what had been broken within me and my desperate need to never be broken again. I know better now."

Aphrodite fisted her hand over her heart and bowed to Neferet—and everyone in the circle, as well as the four who still held the circumference—did the same.

"If I survive this, I will be different," said Neferet.

"You already are," said Zoey.

Neferet squared her shoulders and smoothed her tattered dress. "Let me walk free of the circle."

Zoey smiled at her. "We don't have to let you. Those who are in the service of Nyx can enter and leave it whenever they want."

Neferet drew a deep breath. "Then the first step is to see if our Goddess has forgiven me and taken me back into her service." She turned her head and met Lynette's gaze one last time. "I love you, my dearest sister."

"I love you too. And I'm so, so proud of you."

Neferet walked free of the circle, feeling only a caress of warmth as she broke through the green barrier.

35

Other Neferet

Neferet started forward, moving to the place where the Monstress still battled Kalona. She glanced back over her shoulder to see Zoey and her friends—her *family*—surrounding Lynette protectively, keeping her safe within their shield of earth and power.

Neferet had always longed for that—the safety of a family. But she'd forever been on the outside looking in at others who had attained it. Even when she was the High Priestess here, she'd never felt as if she belonged.

So, she'd chosen power and control and even fear because she'd believed they would keep her safe. Neferet had never tried love. Until Lynette, she'd never let love in, and she realized then that unless you allow love in so that it can shine light on the loneliness and destroy the Darkness, love cannot exist.

Which brought her to what she must do.

Neferet felt very calm as she strode toward the monster that was the darkest version of herself. Bullets whizzed by her but they did not strike her. She knew deep within her newly awakened heart that Nyx had granted her a small bit of protection. The Goddess would allow her to do what she must. Neferet fervently hoped the Goddess would continue to accept her afterward, but she did not let herself dwell on that hope. She was not doing this for Nyx, though she was content that this would serve the Goddess.

Neferet was doing this for love.

Some of her tendrils began detaching from the Warriors, but Neferet lifted her hand and called across the green. "No, children, remain with the Warriors." Then she kept walking.

Her voice had caught the Monstress's attention, and like a praying mantis, her head swiveled, and her lips lifted to expose her teeth in the parody of a smile.

"Ah, good! We were hoping you would come to us of your own will!" she said as she continued to battle Kalona.

· "Kalona of the Silver Wings—step aside," commanded Neferet.

The immoral did so, though he backed off only a few feet, hovering above the wall and the creature who crouched before it with her bloody spear.

The Monstress stood as Neferet came to her and stopped—just out of reach of that spear.

"We would ask whether you've come to your senses and joined us, but you already answered that question when you ordered your children to continue to beleaguer ours. So, do you simply come to embrace your inevitable death?"

"Perhaps," Neferet said honestly. "But first, I'd like to ask you something."

"How interesting. Ask, weak, pathetic version of what you should be."

Neferet raised a brow. "You're right about that. I have allowed myself to be a pathetic version of what I was meant to be. I hope to rectify that now. Tell me, Emily Wheiler, did he brutalize you too, the night you were Marked? Did he leave you broken and bleeding—raped and wronged?"

The Monstress's emerald eyes narrowed. "Yes, our father did

leave us thus—and since then we have shunned all human weakness that allowed us to be used so."

Neferet felt a sick jolt of shock. "Our *father* raped and beat you? Not our betrothed, Arthur Simpton?"

Mirrored shock flashed across the creature's cadaverous face. "Arthur? That coward! No, he only abandoned us, as did our mother—leaving us to our father's vile lust."

Neferet took a step closer to her twisted, broken mirror image. She felt lightheaded with shock. "Did your mother not die along with your brother at his birth?"

"Yes, of course. That is what we said."

"No. You said she abandoned you like Arthur did." She took another step closer to her counterpart.

"It is the same thing!" The Monstress's elegant brows lifted and her emerald eyes glinted with spiteful humor. "Do you think you can destroy us? You, a weak *mortal* and unfinished version of us?"

"No, I do not," said Neferet. "You destroyed yourself long ago. I am only here to witness the end of it. You see, I know you, Emily. I know your pain and your sorrow—your loneliness and your disappointment. How you seek happiness or even mere content-ment—but how both always evade you. And now I know why."

The creature's laughter was poisonous. "Oh? Then why, foolish, unfinished one?"

"Because you lost your capacity for love, and without love and family and friends, life is only one day leading into another in an interminable repetition of nothingness that no amount of money or power can alleviate." Neferet took the last step to her and stared into eyes that were mirror images of her own. With so much compassion that her voice broke, she said, "I know how tired you are. I'm the *only* person who knows that. Do you not long for it all to simply end?"

The Monstress's two-pointed spear wavered and then lowered slightly. She stared at Neferet for a long moment before finally dropping the hand holding the spear so that it hung loosely at her side. So quietly that only Neferet could hear her she said, "*Yes.*"

"Then now it ends." Neferet closed the remainder of the space between them and grasped the center of the spear—her hands on either side of the creature's—and she struck, plunging one ivory horn tip into the her other self's chest so that it went all the way through her emaciated body with such force that it was driven into the wall behind her.

"Oh!" The Monstress's eyes went huge and round. Blood sprayed from her lips as her chest heaved. "You cannot kill us," she gasped. "We are immoral."

"I didn't. You murdered yourself more than a century ago. I only helped you complete the job today. Remember, you admitted you long for an end." Neferet felt only sadness as she watched the creature struggle for her last breaths. "I do not know what happens to you next, but I want you to know that I feel only sadness and pity for you. I'll pray to Nyx to have mercy on your soul."

The Monstress looked at Neferet, and her scarlet lips lifted in a final, vicious smile. "And I have only hatred for you!" With the last of her strength, her insectile arms reached out and seized Neferet by the shoulders and pulled her into a deadly embrace, impaling her on the other end of the spear.

Neferet felt only a tug and the warmth of her life's blood leaving her as she stared into the eyes that were so like hers until the light went out of them. She heard Lynette's scream of anguish, and felt her friend's heart break along with hers.

"No!" Kalona swooped down to gently pull Neferet from the spear and lay her on the bloody ground.

She looked up at him with his white wings gleaming and his handsome face crumbled in sadness and thought, *This is where angels came from.*

Neferet closed her eyes. *Forgive me, Nyx. I have been a very great fool.*

(

Zoey

"This is not going to end well for Neferet," Aphrodite whispered to me as we watched her approach Batshit.

"Yeah," I whispered back so that Lynette, who was crying softly as she stared across the grounds at the scene unfolding by the wall, didn't hear us. "But she knew that."

"She's sacrificing herself," Stark said.

James nodded in agreement. "It's hard to believe, but I agree with you."

I glanced at the two Starks. They were out of arrows. Everyone, even the traitorous soldiers and the tendrils from both Neferets had stopped fighting and were watching the two powerful women—one a vampyre, one a Tsi Sgili demon—meet.

While everyone's attention was focused elsewhere, I spoke urgently to my Warriors, "Stark, James, Rephaim—get to the temple. Go to the basement and grab as many weapons as you can, then get them to Dragon and his men. Now!"

Rephaim carefully put Anastasia on the grass, then the three young Warriors sprinted through the bubble of protection and raced to Nyx's Temple, disappearing inside—and I turned my attention back to the Neferets.

"I wish I knew what they were saying," said Aphrodite.

"My lady is confronting the Darkness within herself," said Lynette, wiping her eyes. "Her whole life has led to this moment. She is calm—serene even. And she is sure the Monstress will defeat herself."

"Like Stark did!" I blurted.

My circle had come in close so that we were just a few feet from each other. Still in the northerly position, Stevie Rae was standing in front of me. "What do you mean, Z?"

"To get into Nyx's Realm to save me, Stark had to face and

347

defeat himself. Only he didn't, really. He realized he had to love himself—even the bad parts—and accept who he really was. When he did that, the good in him defeated the bad."

"He killed himself. Sorta," said Stevie Rae.

"And that's what Neferet is doing," said Damien.

"Well, what she's trying to do," said Aphrodite.

"She *will* do it. She's stronger and better than you know," said Lynette firmly.

I looked at her. "I believe you."

Lynette smiled. "Thank you."

From the corner of my eye, I saw three figures, laden with weapons, running as they hugged shadows of the school, heading toward Dragon and his men.

Then Lynette screamed, and my gaze whipped back to the Neferets in time to see the good one be embraced by the monster—and impaled on the two-pointed spear.

Then everything happened really fast.

Lynette took off. Hugging her broken shoulder with one hand, she ran through the green barrier.

"Shit! I gotta get there too!" said Aphrodite, sprinting after her.

"Go to her! Help them!" said Anastasia from the ground.

"Well, hell," I said. "Guys, break the circle and come with me. We're gonna have to trust that our Warriors will keep the soldiers off us."

"Done, Z! Let's go!" said Stevie Rae.

We ran across the grass, racing toward the Neferets. We got there just behind Aphrodite and Lynette. Our dark Neferet hung from the wall like a macabre scarecrow, lifeless and covered in blood. Kalona had pulled this world's Neferet from the spear and placed her on the ground.

Lynette dropped to her knees beside Neferet as her beloved friend closed her eyes. She took Neferet's hand and held it to her own breast as she cried.

"My lady! Open your eyes! Don't leave me—please! You can't leave me!"

I watched Neferet's bloody chest rise one last time and then Aphrodite was there.

"Help her!" Lynette sobbed. "She's not dead. Our Imprint has not broken!"

"Don't worry. I'll help her." Aphrodite bent and rested her palm on Neferet's forehead, saying, "I grant you a second chance."

Instantly, Neferet's body began to writhe uncontrollably. Lynette fell backward, sobbing hysterically. I had zero clue what the hell was going on, so I grabbed the woman under her arms and dragged her away from Neferet's contorting body.

Neferet's tendrils rushed to Lynette. I stepped back as they surrounded her and crawled onto her lap while they made terrible keening noises.

I tried to find Batshit's tendrils of Darkness, but they had completely disappeared, leaving only ugly, dark stains on the brown grass.

I heard the *pop* of gunfire, and Kalona suddenly went airborne. He soared to the House of Night where soldiers and our Warriors had squared off against one another. Kalona landed between the two groups. Wings spread, he was as magnificent as he was terrifying. His deep voice boomed, *"ENOUGH! Put down your foolish weapons and witness the honorable death of a High Priestess!"* He faced the traitorous soldiers and brought his hands together in a mighty clap that battered them, causing them to drop their weapons and clasp their ears.

Dragon and the surviving Warriors were on them in an instant, kicking their rifles out of the way and forcing them to the ground.

"Ohmygood*ness*, Z! Look at Lynette!" Stevie Rae said.

I turned to see that Lynette was still sitting on the ground, sobbing, but instead of a nest of Neferet's children, on her lap was a large, long-haired orange-and-white cat. I gulped in shock. "Skylar?"

"Holy shit!"

Aphrodite's shout had me changing my focus to Neferet's body. In its place, a girl sat up and turned to blink at us in surprise.

She was young—probably barely sixteen—and she was wearing a simple white dress. Her green eyes were Neferet's, as was her thick, wavy auburn hair. But little else about her looked like the world-weary High Priestess who had just sacrificed herself for love. Her face was beautifully cherubic—and her forehead was newly Marked with a crescent moon in scarlet.

"My lady!" Lynette staggered to her, still holding the big cat. When they reached Neferet, the cat—who I swear was the absolute twin of Skylar, who had been our Neferet's familiar before she'd denounced Nyx—jumped out of Lynette's arms and began purring magnificently and rubbing against Neferet.

The girl smiled and stroked the cat. "Oh, hello!" she said in a pleasant voice that sounded so much like Neferet that it was shocking. "I know you! Your name is Skylar—and aren't you handsome!" She ran her hands through his fur as she looked up at Lynette. "I—I feel like I know you too, but I can't seem to remember your name. I'm s-sorry." Her full bottom lip quivered, and she looked like she was going to burst into tears.

Lynette fell to her knees and took the girl's hands in hers. "Oh, dearest, that's okay. My name is Lynette." She smoothed back the girl's hair and kissed her forehead softly. "I am your family."

"Who am I?"

"Emily," said Lynette. "But the truth is, you can be anyone you wish to be now."

"I—I wish to go home, but I don't know where that is," said Emily.

I went to them and crouched down, smiling at Emily. "You *are* home, Emily. You're at the House of Night."

Emily gasped and a tentative smile lifted her lips as she gingerly touched the crescent on her forehead. "You mean, I'm a vampyre? Like you?"

I grinned. "Well, you're a fledgling right now. But someday you'll be a vampyre—and I'll bet you'll be a wonderful one."

Above us, clouds began to form. They roiled and billowed and then parted to expose a full moon that I was sure hadn't been there when the night had started. On a fat moonbeam, Nyx appeared in full regalia. Her hair was silk brushing against the generous curve of her waist. She wore a headdress of stars so brilliant that it was difficult to look directly at. She rode the moonbeam down to us and stepped lightly off of it.

"Merry meet, Nyx!" I said. I was already crouching, but I went to my knees. All around me everyone, including the defeated soldiers, took to their knees and shouted, "Merry meet, Goddess!"

Kalona strode to her, dropping to his knees in front of her and bowing his head. "My Goddess, my love! Forgive me for being absent so very long."

Nyx bent and put one slender finger under his chin, lifting his face. It was hard to look at him too, as his love shined as brightly as Nyx's headdress.

"There is nothing to forgive. What you did for your brother was worthy of my Consort and his great capacity for love, and I thank you for it—though I do hope you never have to leave my side for so long again."

"It is my greatest wish to spend eternity beside you, Goddess."

Her smile was the full moon, brilliant and bewitching. "You should seal that oath with a kiss."

He stood so quickly his body blurred and he took her into his arms. As he kissed her passionately, his wings spread and then wrapped around her, shielding their love from our prying eyes.

Finally, cheeks bright with color, the Goddess moved from his embrace. "Merry meet, children," she said as she approached the Warriors, who followed Dragon's lead and bowed their heads reverently.

"Rise."

They did as commanded, and she smiled at the Sons of Erebus. "You have been faithful and true. Your Goddess appreciates your strength and courage."

"Thank you, Nyx," Dragon said.

Nyx turned her head to look across the ground to where Anastasia had somehow dragged herself to her knees. Her head was bowed, though she had to brace herself with her hands on the cold ground, as if she might fall over at any moment.

"Beloved High Priestess, know your Goddess loves and appreciates your wisdom and compassion as well."

Nyx raised her hand and flicked her wrist. Diamond stars from her headdress flew across the ground to engulf Anastasia, who gasped in surprise. When their brilliance faded the High Priestess lifted her head as she smiled beatifically while she straightened, her leg fully healed.

"Thank you, my wondrous Goddess!"

I heard Dragon sob softly in relief, and Nyx touched his head gently. "All will be well, Warrior. All will be well." Then she faced the soldiers that had fought against us. "You disappoint me. You grasp for power cruelly, selfishly." She held out her hand to Kalona, saying, "Your spear, my love."

Kalona gave it to her without hesitation. She struck it on the ground, and the soldiers cowered in fear as she commanded, "Begin anew!" Light flashed from where the spear touched the earth, temporarily blinding me, and when I blinked the spots from my eyes I saw that the entire group of Warriors had lost their vampyre Marks and youthened—and I don't mean turned into newly Marked teenagers. They were little boys, probably all about five years old, sitting in pools of clothes and blinking up at the Goddess with happy faces that were chubby with youth and innocence as they grinned.

Nyx turned in time to greet Anastasia as she hurried up and curtsied deeply to Nyx.

"High Priestess, these young ones will be the first of the humans to mix here at your House of Night. End the conflict with the community. Now. Raise these children to be kind, compassionate young men. Some of them will be Marked. Some will not. *All* of them will be important to mending what has been broken in this world.

Anastasia bowed her head. "Yes, Goddess."

Then Nyx approached us. "Rise, children."

We did as she commanded.

"I recognize you, Zoey Redbird. Your twin from this world and I talk often in my realm."

I bowed my head and then smiled. "Your twin in my world and I talk often as well."

She returned my smile. "I expect that your Nyx will be happy when you return." Her gaze took in the rest of my group, lighting on Kevin. "Ah, Kevin, it is lovely to see you again."

My brother blushed ferociously and bowed. "You too, my Goddess."

She walked to him and touched his chest gently, over his heart. "I am glad you have decided to allow this to heal."

Kevin had to clear his throat before he was able to speak, and still his voice sounded gravelly. "Me too."

The Goddess's gaze found Shaunee. She was staring in open wonder at Nyx. Nyx crooked a finger, gesturing for her to come to her, which Shaunee did instantly.

The young fledgling curtsied deeply. "Merry meet, Nyx."

"Merry meet, young fledgling. I approve of your taste in men."

I wanted to fist pump and say *YEA*, but didn't because it would've been totally inappropriate.

"But remember, you must be equally as wise in your taste in friends. Part of how we define ourselves is through those who we allow close to us. Be wise, Shaunee. Be strong. And know you cannot save everyone in your life." Then Nyx kissed Shaunee's forehead and an amazing adult vampyre tattoo made of sapphire flames bloomed across her face.

"Wow!" Kevin said. "That's incredible."

Shaunee's hand shook as she touched her forehead and happy tears washed her cheeks. "Thank you, Goddess."

Nyx turned to James, who was standing beside Kacie. They both bowed deeply. "I forgave you before you asked it of me, James Stark. Now my wish is that you forgive yourself and allow love to fill your life."

James was crying openly. "Yes, Nyx. I will."

Nyx smiled at Kacie. "Little Ice Cream Shoes."

Kacie dimpled. "Merry meet, Goddess!"

"I see your heart. Know if you decide that is truly your wish I shall allow it. I will add one thing to perhaps help you in your decision—this world does need a prophetess, and you are, indeed, a Prophetess of Nyx, along with your other gifts."

I felt a jolt of shock—though it was happy shock.

Nyx nodded at Aphrodite, who smiled as she curtsied. "Merry meet, Goddess."

"Merry meet, Aphrodite from another world. You were wise today. I understand why you have been gifted so greatly."

"Well, I tend to mess up, but—like my gift—I also get to try again and again, and I seem to, eventually, get things right."

That made the Goddess laugh, and the sound was so fantastical that it made the night shiver around us and the stars blaze in the dark sky above us.

"Stevie Rae—Rephaim, merry meet."

They bowed to the Goddess together, saying, "Merry meet, Nyx!"

Stevie Rae looked up, grinning. "You look just like our Nyx."

The Goddess returned her smile. "That is because we are all really one." She turned to Rephaim. "And as such I release you from your penance. Spend your long life together creating joy." She touched Rephaim's forehead and it blossomed into a fully formed adult vampyre's tattoo in scarlet—in the shape of a raven's wings spreading from the crescent.

"Oh, Goddess! Thank you!" Rephaim fell to his knees before her. With a happy cry, Stevie Rae dropped to his side, laughing and hugging him joyously.

I had to blink the tears from my eyes so I wouldn't miss what happened next.

With Kalona at her side, the Goddess walked to where Emily Wheiler still sat on the ground with Lynette. They both bowed their heads as she approached them.

"Children, your love for one another did not simply save you, it also saved two worlds. Know that you shall forever be family. Lynette, I task you with helping Emily, who finally found herself today, not to make the same mistakes again."

"I gladly and gratefully accept that task, Goddess."

"Good. Then you shall need this so that you will not leave her side too soon." Nyx kissed Lynette's upturned forehead and the sapphire tattoo of a fully Changed vampyre appeared in the shape of interlocking knots that created hearts.

"Oh!" Lynette breathed in awe, touching her forehead. She bowed, and in a voice filled with happy tears she said, "Thank you, my Goddess!"

"Young Emily, welcome back to my service. I look forward to what you shall do this time around with the new gifts you have been given."

Emily's voice was shaky, but she bowed her head and said, "Th-thank you, great Goddess. I will do my best to serve you."

Finally, she faced the body of our Neferet. The Goddess sighed sadly. She lifted her hand, and a form raised from Neferet's body. It had a vague outline of a person, and if I squinted hard, I saw the resemblance to Neferet, though even her spirit was twisted, deformed. "You chose vengeance when you could have chosen to heal. You chose cruelty when you could have chosen mercy. You chose hatred when you could have chosen love. Had you also chosen to remain mortal, you might have been redeemed, but you *chose* to become immortal, so I must judge you on scale with the gods. I judge you unredeemable."

Nyx raised both hands and drew a circle in the air. Within that circle I saw a terrible, unending blackness. "And now you will cease to exist. Begone!" At her command, Neferet's spirit was sucked into the blackness as it shrieked in anger one last time.

Nyx turned to us, and there were tears in her eyes. "Remember, my children, you are powerful. Your choices matter. *You matter.* It is my greatest wish that you choose love, always love. Until we meet again, may you blessed be."

Nyx, the Goddess of Night, stepped into Kalona's arms, and he lifted her into the sky, holding her tightly, lovingly, until they disappeared in a shower of diamond sparks.

EPILOGUE

Zoey

We spent what was left of that night helping Anastasia and her House of Night figure out where to put the several dozen soldiers who were now little boys, and who definitely needed dinner and then bedtime.

The school's fledglings helped a lot, but it was Grandma Redbird who swung into high gear and fixed everything—because even High Priestess Anastasia admitted to being out of her range of expertise when it came to human boys who were barely older than toddlers.

"Of course I will stay and help you set up a nursery," Grandma said, holding one chubby boy on her lap while another played with her long, silver hair. She sent a smile my way and said, "I find that in this world I am short at least one child, and they shall do my heart good."

Anastasia actually went to Grandma and kissed her soundly, which made them both laugh.

When the little boys were finally asleep, tucked into dorm rooms with fledglings nervously watching over them, I would have been happy to lead my circle in calling the elements and returning to our world—but we were just too damn tired. Instead, I sank into bed beside Stark and fell fast asleep in his arms.

The next day we met in the dining room just after the sun had set. We'd pulled together several tables and were just finishing breakfast when I stood. My circle went silent and gave me their full attention.

"I understand if you want to stay for a few days and help Anastasia," I said with no preamble. "Personally, even though I love being here with Kevin," I paused to grin at my brother, who returned my smile, "I'm eager to get home and let our people know they don't have to be afraid anymore. But because of what we've all just been through, I wanted you guys to vote on it, and I'll be fine either way. So, what do you want to do? Stay for a few days, or go home now? Stark?"

"Home," he said with no hesitation.

"Aphrodite?"

"Home to my Warrior."

"Rephaim?"

"That is up to my High Priestess," he deferred to Stevie Rae.

"Okay, Stevie Rae—what's your vote?"

"Home, definitely," she said firmly.

"Damien?"

"You know my vote, Z. Jack's there, stressing out while he waits for me."

"So, another home vote. Ice Cream Shoes?" I asked.

She was sitting beside James, who—along with my brother—had joined us for breakfast. Kacie cleared her throat and stood. "I don't get a vote because, with your permission, I would like to stay in this world—permanently. The red fledglings and vampyres over here have no red High Priestess. I want to be here for them." She looked down and smiled softly at James. "Among other things." His face flushed pink, but his smile blazed as he took her hand and kissed it. Then her attention returned to me. "Do I have your permission, High Priestess?"

"You do, but you don't actually need it. Nyx already gave it to you. And you're right—they need you here."

Stevie Rae wiped tears from her cheeks and said, "You're gonna make a great High Priestess."

"Thanks, mentor. I learned from the best. And I'll still cast the circle with you guys—I just won't go through the door with you."

"So, it's unanimous. We leave today for home," I said.

Everyone nodded, and I felt the stress between my shoulder blades release. I *really* wanted to go home. As we finished up and gathered our stuff, Anastasia came into the dining hall.

"We've decided to leave today—pretty much now," I told her.

"You know you are welcome to stay as long as you'd like," she said.

"Thank you, but we left our Tulsa terrified and wondering whether we're alive or dead—not to mention whether Batshit was going to show up and eat everyone."

Anastasia nodded. "I can see how you would need to get home and assuage fears. But I think it would be a happy thing if we remained in touch."

"What do you mean?" I asked, and my friends fell silent around me.

"Well, you had the elements open the veil between worlds— and you'll do that again in just a few minutes. Why not plan on visiting once or twice a year?"

"That would be cool!" said Kevin.

"Do you think it'd be okay? I mean, with the universe or whatnot?" I asked.

Damien spoke up. "I believe if it would cause a problem, Nyx would have forbidden it yesterday when she was here."

I grinned at my brother. "I believe he's right!"

"As usual," agreed Kevin.

"Wanta make a date?" I asked my brother.

"How about my birthday?"

"August second it is," I said.

"And don't forget a present."

We all laughed and talked animatedly as we meandered from the dining hall and made our way out to the rear grounds. The school had already begun to transform. Little boys ran down the halls with fledglings chasing them as they giggled delightedly.

Anastasia sighed and then whispered to me, "Are you quite sure you don't want to take some of them with you?"

I laughed. "No way! Nyx gave them to you! But I am leaving you with your first red vampyre High Priestess, who also happens to be a budding Prophetess of Nyx."

Anastasia's eyes widened. "Ice Cream Shoes? Well, that's lovely. She is most welcome here."

Kevin's phone bleeped with a text, and then he was at my shoulder. "Hey, Z, would you come with me for a sec?"

"I'll meet you guys out by the tree," I said, and then followed my brother toward the foyer. "What's up?"

"Don't be mad, 'kay?"

"Huh? What do you—" We turned to our left into the foyer and the guy who was standing there looking out the front window turned. The breath left my body as I staggered to a stop. "Heath?" His smile was unmistakable. "Heath!" I shouted and took off, running to him as my brother went out the back door, leaving us alone. Heath caught me as I sailed into his arms, hugging me as I clung to him while we laughed and cried together.

Finally, he let me go, but only enough so we could look into each other's face.

"Hey, Zo. Good to see ya."

"Good to see ya too, Heath."

He reached into his pocket and brought out a handful of balled up Kleenexes, sharing them with me as we wiped our faces, and I blew my nose.

"Thanks," I said. "Glad you remembered them."

"Zo, there's nothing about you that I'll ever forget."

I touched his damp cheek. "It's not *me* you're remembering though. You know that, right?"

He nodded. "Yeah, I do. Kev explained as much as he could to me. It's why you didn't come see me when you were here last time."

"I wanted to, but I didn't want to make you sad."

He bumped my nose with his finger in a gesture so Heath-like that I found it hard to breathe. "It doesn't make me sad to know that somewhere a version of you is still alive, Zo, 'cause you'll always be alive in this world—right here." He touched his chest over his heart.

I cleared my throat and asked, "Are you okay?"

"Better. I'm kicking ass at OU—totally starting quarterback. And, you'll be happy to hear that I'm watching my drinking and studying way harder than I ever thought I would. I'm a business major with an animal science minor. When I graduate I'm gonna open a kennel where we'll rescue dogs from shelters and train them to be service canines. It's gonna be cool!"

"Heath, that's an awesome idea. Your Zoey would love that."

"I know, right?"

"Do—um—you have someone?" I asked, my stomach clenching.

He nodded. "Yeah. She's smart and funny. You'd like her. How 'bout you?"

It was my turn to nod. "Yeah. Over in my world he and my Heath actually became friends, so I know you'd like him."

And as if on cue, from behind us I heard, "Heath! My man!" And suddenly Stark was there. Heath's taller than him, but Stark lifted him off his feet in the mother of all hugs before putting him down and pounding his back affectionately.

Heath looked at me—kinda shell-shocked. "Is this him?"

"Yep."

"Oh, crap. I forgot you don't know me." Stark stuck out his hand. "Hi, I'm Stark. And, damn, it's good to see you."

Heath took his hand. "Nice to meet you, Stark. You taking care of Zo in your world?"

"As much as she'll let me," Stark said.

"Dude I hear ya. She's, like, *super* stubborn."

"Right?" Stark said.

"And *she's* standing right here," I said, hands on my hips, loving every moment of being able to glare at my guys together again.

"Sorry!" they said together, and then they laughed.

"Hey, I didn't mean to interrupt, but the circle is ready—and Emily and Lynette have come to say goodbye," said Stark. He clapped Heath on the back. "Be well, okay?"

"I will. Make her happy, okay?"

Stark's answer was completely serious. "Always. I will always be there, and I will always try to fill her world with happiness."

A tear slid down Heath's cheek. "That's all I can ask."

"We'll wait as long as you need," Stark said. He squeezed my arm and then left Heath and me alone.

"I know," Heath said. "You're all Captain America or Wonder Woman or whatever—and you gotta go be a superhero somewhere else."

"That's cooler than the reality, but yeah, I gotta get my people back to our world."

"I'm really glad Kevin called me. I needed to be able to say bye to you," Heath said. He took my face between his hands gently and said, "Bye, Zo. I'll love you and miss you forever." Then he kissed me—long and sweetly and intimately—until I was dizzy.

I blinked up at him when he finally, reluctantly, let me go. "Bye, Heath. Over in my world, I'll miss you and love you forever too." I stepped into his arms and we held each other.

Finally, we parted. "I hope you live a really long, happy life," I told him.

"I'm gonna try. I'm gonna be the man my Zo believed in."

"I think you *are* the man we believed in." I kissed him softly and started walking away. Then I paused and looked back at him. He was standing there, watching me with those eyes that said he'd loved me since third grade. "She's waiting for you—just don't be in a hurry to get to her."

"Promise she'll be there for me?"

"Always." And then I made myself walk away, because if I didn't, I was afraid I'd never leave.

I wiped my face and blew my nose again, and then joined my circle. Grandma was there, beside Kevin. I went to my brother first and hugged him. "Thank you," I whispered. "Oh, and I'm glad you're with Shaunee. I think Aphrodite would approve."

Kevin smiled through tears and said, "I know she does."

Then I was in Grandma's arms. "I shall see you at your brother's birthday, u-we-tsi-a-ge-ya."

"You can count on it, Grandma," I said, kissing her soft cheek.

My friends—my family—had already taken their places, but as I joined them, Lynette and Emily were standing just outside the circle, with Skylar sitting beside Emily, leaning against her leg.

"I'll look forward to seeing you two again in a few months," I said, and as I spoke the words, I realized I was telling the truth. I was really looking forward to what the future would bring for them.

"Thank you," said Lynette. "You're a big part of the reason things turned out like this."

"Oh, I don't know. I think love is the reason things turned out like this," I said.

Emily looked at me through Neferet's beautiful, emerald eyes—and I saw curiosity and kindness there. "I like you," she said unexpectedly—and then she hugged me—which *really* surprised me.

But I gladly hugged her back and whispered the truth. "I like you too, Emily." Then I disentangled myself from her, wiped my eyes again, and said, "Okay, well, this circle isn't going to cast itself, and it takes a bunch of concentration and elemental power to open the door between worlds. So, I gotta go."

As I entered the circle, I heard Emily say, "I wish I could help you get back to your world an easier way."

There was a weird sizzling and popping sound, and I watched my friends' eyes go round with shock as everyone gasped. I whirled around to see that dozens of sprites had suddenly appeared to hover around Emily and Lynette. My friends dashed to me as we gawked.

The largest sprite, with a girl's torso and blue dragonfly-like body, flew down to hover at Emily's eye level. Around its neck was a blue velvet ribbon and a delicate chain that held an occluded sapphire set in diamonds. She grinned, showing a lot of sharp teeth, and then said,

Dear Emily! We shall always be here for thee!
We have waited so long for you—
For one who can wield us, faithful and true!
So, because you ask, back to their world they go—
Fast, not slow! Slow! Slow!

With the sound of a sigh, the portal between worlds opened in front of us with such force that it pushed us forward, but before we stepped from one world to another, Aphrodite said, "Oh, for shit's sake, you know what this means, don't you?"

Damien answered quicker than I could formulate my whirring thoughts. "Yes, it means Emily has been gifted with an affinity for Old Magick."

As we were sucked into the portal and then spit out back in our world, my voice echoed around us.

"*Ah, hellllllll!*"

THE END ... for now?

ACKNOWLEDGMENTS

As always, big love and thanks go to Kristin for being the best frontline editor in the universe. Mommy-baby!

We appreciate our Blackstone family so very much, most especially Courtney Vatis, Kathryn English, Anne Fonteneau, Jeff Yamaguchi, Lauren Maturo, Greg Boguslawski, Josie Woodbridge, and Josh Stanton.

Thank you to our personal publicist, Deb Shapiro, who keeps the wheels turning smoothly.

Thanks to our wonderful, hardworking agents, Ginger Clark and Steven Salpeter. We heart you.

A very special thank-you to our loyal House of Night fans who came with us on the Other World adventure. We heart you forever. Always remember—you are strong and unique and worthy of love, always love.

FAN Q&A

You have questions? P. C. & Kristin have answers for you!

Are you going to introduce a new world when this one ends, or is this the final goodbye to our beloved characters?
—CAROLINA ETTINGER

P. C.: As you can see by the conclusion of *Found*, I left a giant opening for another book/series, but at this time I'm going to focus on the TV series. In the future, though …

Did you ever imagine that the world you created would become as iconic and magnificent as it is in modern literary culture?
—JOSETTE PITMAN

P. C.: I did not. I simply began HoN as I begin everything I write—I create the book I most want to read. I'm honestly astonished when other people love my worlds, too.

K. C.: I was nineteen when we started writing the first book. Even though I'd watched my mom work a full-time job and write books for multiple publishers, I knew that this series would be enormously successful. Was I naive? For sure! But I was also super lucky.

How did it feel rewriting characters for the Other World / returning to characters who were alive in the Other World, but killed off in the original HoN series?

—**KATHRYN EMILY**

P. C.: Returning to the HoN was like coming home. I hadn't realized how much I'd missed Zoey and the gang until I began writing them again. I love that the Other World has given me an opportunity to revisit characters! It's nice to see a version of Heath happy and healthy and living his dream. And Jack! It was so great to return him to my beloved Damien.

What steps did you take, or what life choices would you say lead you to the success you have today? With that said, any advice for aspiring authors?

—**STINA FITRAKIS**

P. C.: Joining the USAF before I finished high school and going active duty five days after I graduated taught me very young the value of tenacity and hard work. I served six years active duty. In the military you do not give up when things get tough, and that's a lesson that has stayed with me ever since. During my USAF years I gained confidence, independence, and an excellent work ethic, which definitely helped me get published.

My advice for aspiring authors is twofold: (1) Treat the job of being an author as you would any other career. Educate yourself about how a manuscript becomes a book on the shelf of Barnes & Noble. Learn what agents and editors do and don't do. Take off the rose-colored glasses too many people view publishing through and be realistic about your chosen career. (2) Hone your writing skills.

Pay attention to everything you write—and that includes emails, tweets, and Insta posts. What you write represents you. Always.

K. C.: I've worked really hard on creating a great circle of people around me. For a long time, I felt like I had to minimize my successes or laugh off my passions because I was trying to fit in with the wrong people. Eventually I realized that I am in charge of who I let into my life. Taking the steps to cultivate personal and work relationships with kind, successful, motivated people has made such a difference in my life.

My advice to aspiring authors is to read (or listen to) as many books in as many genres as you can. Take note of what inspires you, how authors describe scenes and characters, what you love and what you loath. Every book is a class on writing.

I have followed the HoN series from the beginning, and there have been some life lessons I have taken away from the series. So my question is, what is the biggest thing you would like your readers to take away from the series?

—HEATHER MAY

P. C.: I want my readers, especially young women, to take away the knowledge that they can and should make mistakes, learn from them, and then do better without carrying around the baggage of judgment and hypocrisy under which the patriarchy likes to smother us. Double standards *should* be called out, barriers *should* be smashed. I also want the HoN stories to help my readers open themselves to others who are different from them—to know that what's important is the quality of a person's character and not the color of her or his skin, what goddess/god she/he does or does not worship, or her/his/their sexual orientation. Basically, I hope HoN has taught its readers to believe that the strongest force in the universe is love—always love, and to live their lives accordingly.

Out of all the characters in the series, who would YOU choose to be in your circle?

—BRANDALYN MARTIN

P. C.: Zoey! She has an affinity for all five elements and the blessing of a goddess.

K. C.: Shaunee! I love me a good fire spell.

When writing not just this series but any of your books, do you have any specific routines you follow, something that helps you focus or keep you motivated to write?

—MAUREEN GURNEY

P. C.: Well, if I had to, I could write anywhere, but I'm fortunate to have a lovely home office. I prefer to write on a treaddesk (yes, I walk and write). My desk holds specially chosen crystals, and I always light scented tealights. I'm a tea snob and I have lots of fabulous loose-leaf teas that I brew and drink while I'm writing, too. My dogs and cat hang out around me and I usually have some kind of orchestral music playing softly in the background.

K. C.: Listening to the mixes I create in the Relax Melodies app through my Bose noise-canceling headphones keeps me focused. Without my headphones, I just stare at my computer. They really put me in the zone.

My questions for both of you: Which character will always stay with you? How much of the locations and cultural factors were from Oklahoma when writing this series? And were there other places y'all pulled from?

—NATASHA VANNATTA

P. C.: The entire Nerd Herd will always be with me. After fifteen years of writing them, they are part of my life forever—and I couldn't be happier about it!

I've said many times that Tulsa is more than just a location in the HoN. Tulsa is a character. Shining a spotlight on the close-minded, hypocritical Bible Belt culture is a big part of why I wrote the HoN and set a society of Pagan, matriarchal vampyres deep in the middle of evangelical land. I'm happy to say that I've watched hordes of Oklahoma teens grow up to be inclusive of others unlike themselves and question the subjugation of the Bible Belt patriarchy. I hope HoN had something to do with that.

K. C.: Like P. C., the entire Nerd Herd will always stay with me. But if I had to choose just one character, it would definitely be Aphrodite. I love her story and her transformation.

If you could bring back a character from any books prior, who would it be and why?
—SARA ABRAHAM

P. C.: Jack! Which I did in writing the HoN Other World books. He is the personification of kindness and love.

What was your favorite part about writing the new book? Did you have a special place you went to for inspiration?
—LIZZY JOCCLEANN

P. C.: I loved writing this whole book so much, but the epilogue is my special favorite! It was fun to bring in Heath and give him and Zoey some closure. It was also awesome to show that Z will get to visit Other Kevin and he her. But my very favorite is the last part where we learn what affinity Nyx granted Emily/Other Neferet.

As for inspiration—I'm always inspired by Tulsa. For this book I returned to Woodward Park and then wandered around Cascia Hall (the school on which I base the Tulsa HoN) and reminded myself of my early HoN roots.

When writing, is it easier to have everything planned out from start to finish or have an idea form and just wing it as you go? Always been curious how professional writers think. When I have to do a paper for class I always have my topic and gather my support and then just wing it.

—**KAYLA DOKU DOKU WARD**

P. C.: This differs for each writer—there is no correct way to plan and then write a book. I approach it different ways, depending on whether I'm writing alone or with Kristin. If alone I do a lot of research and brainstorming. I make notes and do a rough outline that ends up looking more like a long synopsis. When I write with Kristin we research and brainstorm together then we write a general outline of the book. We divide the cast of characters (who writes the chapter depends on whose character is the focus) and then we outline each chapter for the entire book. Remember, for the HoN Kristin is/was my frontline editor. We don't actually cowrite the series. We are, however, cowriting a brand-new trilogy at this time called Sisters of Salem.

K. C.: For me, it's easier to have everything planned out from start to finish. I don't always write chronologically, so it's important to know what's happened before and after each scene that I write. I'm also much less stressed if I have a chapter-by-chapter outline. Then each day is already mapped out and I can skip the plotting step and just get busy writing.

How long does your research process take for the different places in the HoN series?

—**ALEXIS MAPLE**

P. C.: The HoN series is unique. A huge amount of the research happened before I even thought of the HoN because I lived in Tulsa. I was fortunate that when I began expanding the HoN world to Scotland and Italy I was able to travel to the Isle of Skye and the Scottish Highlands, where I lived on and off for about a year, as well as visit San Clemente Island outside Venice and Capri and Pompei. I was even able to research in New Orleans (for "Lenobia's Vow"), St. Louis ("Dragon's Oath"), and Chicago ("Neferet's Curse"). It's not really about time, but about travel.

If you could go back in time before ever writing the first House of Night novel, what advice would you give to your younger selves?
—ANDREA BUCHANAN

P. C.: I'd tell myself that I should try writing two books at the same time sooner than I actually did it. It makes my professional life a lot easier. I'd also tell myself to be wiser about "friends" who were wolves in sheep's clothing.

K. C.: Drop out of college. I'm still paying off loans for a degree I never completed.

Was it always your plan for Heath to die? I also want to point out that it was super clever to do the opposite meaning for the bulls ♥ I really hope they hold open auditions for the cast!
—HANNAH NICOLE

P. C.: No! I didn't know that was going to happen until Kalona did it! Often my characters do things I don't expect, and this time it was a massive shock. And yes, our producers do plan on holding open auditions!

If you and Kristin were to live in these books, what would your roles be? For example, would you want to be a professor, a High Priestess, someone on the side of evil, etc. Also, thank you so much for writing these books!! They have let me travel into a different world and are so amazing!!!

—MOIRA DAVIS

P. C.: If I could live in the HoN world I would want Lenobia's job! I'd be a High Priestess and Horse Mistress for sure.

K. C.: I'd for sure be on the side of evil. I don't know what I'd be doing, but I'd be doing it evilly.

To me, Loren Blake seemed like he had a story that was waiting to be told. As much as he gave in to Neferet, he had some humanity in him that stood out when Neferet killed him. Did you ever have any other plans with Loren's character?

—SARA WESTERKAMP

P. C.: Loren Blake was a predator in the original series and a weak, egotistical man in the Other World series. When he writes Skye with his blood as he was dying he didn't do it because there was a good guy lurking below his shallow surface. He did it because he wanted revenge.

Regarding the House of Night TV series, what is it like behind the scenes for you? What decisions do you have to make to transfer this book into a show? What's the process like? And, if you picked the actors for the show by the time you publish these questions, what helped you know they would portray the character the way you wanted them to?

—JESSICA MARIE

P. C.: Well, right now (early 2020) we're in the beginning stages. Kristin and I are highly involved in advising our wonderful screenwriter and also helping our producers compile analytics on our HoN fanbase. We'll continue to be highly involved in every aspect of the series with the blessing of our wonderful producers, Don Carmody and David Cormican at DCTV. They, too, want to get it right!

What's next in your guys' writings? Are you going to continue HoN or work on other series?
—**LACHELLE FRANKLIN**

K. C.: Other than the TV series, I'm taking a break from the HoN to work on my solo trilogy, the Key. The first book, *The Key to Fear*, releases October 2020, and I am so excited to introduce readers to a postpandemic world where touch is outlawed. I am also coauthoring Sisters of Salem with P. C. It's a witchy young adult trilogy that releases in 2021.

P. C.: As Kristin mentioned, we're coauthoring Sisters of Salem, which will begin releasing in 2021. I've also been working on two other solo projects for some time now—one adult and one YA—but I'm not at the announcement stage yet!

How did you come up with the background for the "mythology" of the vampyres?
—**KALEIGH HOOVEN**

P. C.: My dad, Dick Cast (a biology teacher), and I worked together on the idea of having vampirism be more physiological than magickal. Then I set about creating a matriarchal Pagan society for my vamps by mixing Wicca with Celtic shamanism. And the HoN was born!

So a few questions … you are or were an English teacher. Did you come up with the idea for the original HoN series so that your students would enjoy reading and assignments, and did you hope they would get hooked on the series like we all have? I love English as a subject and I would have been in heaven if my teacher had done so.

—STACY RENEA DEWBERRY

P. C.: I taught high school English for fifteen years and had published over a dozen adult books when I began writing the HoN. I chose to make the HoN YA because I was excited by the excellent storytelling that was beginning to happen in that genre. As an English teacher I read the same books my students were reading, which made me want to set up the HoN as an alternative high school. The fact that my students started reading and loving HoN was a wonderful bonus surprise.

With the TV series starting soon, which person in the books are both of you most excited to see come to life?

—JESSIE SCHRECENGOST

P. C.: I'm going to love seeing all of them come alive on-screen, but especially Zoey and Grandma Redbird.

K. C.: I am most excited to see Neferet come to life!

Are there any famous actors either of you dream of portraying certain characters?

—NICHOLE ARNOLD

P. C.: I've always seen Angelina Jolie as Neferet, Michelle Pfeiffer as Lenobia, and Dwayne Johnson as Kalona.

K. C.: I would love to see Joel Kinnaman as Dragon Langford. But, honestly, I would love to see Joel Kinnaman as anyone.

What are some of the main takeaways you want readers to get from the House of Night Other World series?
— **ELIZABETH AGUILAR**

P. C.: That even very small changes in your life can make an enormous difference in your world.

I love these books so much!!! Thank you for writing them!! For the characters who have Marks, how did you guys come up with what they looked like? Each person's mark is such a great representation of themselves and what has happened to them. How did you first come up with how the marks were going to be? Also, if there were marks that were to represent you guys, what would each of them look like and mean?
— **MOIRA DAVIS**

If you and Kristin were to have vampyre facial tattoos, what would they look like? What symbols, patterns, etc., would they contain?
— **MARTHA FARRALL**

P. C.: I do the writing, so I made up the tattoos. I came up with the idea as a nod to the ancient Pagan tradition of physically marking a woman as she entered the service of her goddess. I usually made them symbolize some aspect of the character's personality or affinity. Were I to have a Mark I'd want it to be Celtic knots with vines and animals woven within the design to symbolize my heritage as well as my affinity for the earth and her creatures.

K. C.: My facial tattoo would be a thick, black, Wolverine-style mask. No symbols or patterns, just *boom*—menacing mask tattoo.